HER
DAUGHTER'S
MOTHER

Daniela Petrova

HER DAUGHTER'S MOTHER

G. P. Putnam's Sons

NEW YORK

PUTNAM
— EST. 1838 —

G. P. Putnam's Sons
Publishers Since 1838
An imprint of Penguin Random House LLC
penguinrandomhouse.com

Library of Congress Cataloging-in-Publication Data

Names: Petrova, Daniela, author.
Title: Her daughter's mother / Daniela Petrova.
Description: New York : G. P. Putnam's Sons, [2019]
Identifiers: LCCN 2018052505| ISBN 9780525539971 (hardcover) |
ISBN 9780525539995 (epub)
Subjects: | GSAFD: Suspense fiction.
Classification: LCC PS3616.E872 H47 2019 | DDC 813/.6—dc23
LC record available at https://lccn.loc.gov/2018052505
p.   cm.

Printed in the United States of America
1   3   5   7   9   10   8   6   4   2

Book design by Francesca Belanger

3361408143071 1

To Ana and Ivan,
with love and gratitude

PROLOGUE

I watched her walk down the street. She had a fast, determined pace, knew where she was going. No hesitation, no window-shopping as she passed boutiques and gourmet grocery stores. Not even cute dogs or babies distracted her. A woman on a mission. A woman who didn't bother glancing back. A woman easy to follow.

I kept my distance just in case.

The sidewalks were busy without being packed. Traffic moved slowly up and down Broadway. She went into the Starbucks at the corner, holding the door for two women who were coming out. I lingered by the AT&T shop next door. It would be a long wait. The line for espresso drinks was huge, I could see through the window. I knew she'd get a latte. She always got a tall latte. I liked that about her. None of that fancy caramel-double-mocha-Frappuccino crap but not a plain Jane regular coffee, either. My kind of woman.

Dark, fierce clouds were moving in from the west, pushing over the city's rooftops and water towers. I could smell the rain in the air. A gust of wind swept up a plastic bag and it swirled past me, waist-high. I turned to watch it slap the windshield of a yellow cab before falling to the ground. Pieces of paper flew out of the overflowing trash bin at the corner. A storm was coming.

She walked out with a tall Starbucks cup in her hand and a resolute expression on her face, ready to conquer the world.

I liked her. I liked her a lot.

PART 1

IF
SHE ONLY
KNEW

1.

LANA

I looked at the half-dozen women sitting around the table. I loved these women. They were my family, the only friends I had left. But tonight I couldn't stand being among them. I wanted to get the hell out of the fluorescent-lit room in the basement of the West Side YMCA I came to religiously every other Friday.

We were members of a club nobody wants to join—the Barren Women's Club. We weren't called that, of course. Officially, it was a support group for couples struggling with infertility. But mostly it was only the women who came.

Today, it was just a few of us. You had to be really desperate to show up on Good Friday.

It was a particularly hard night for me, and the rich chili smell wafting through the room, courtesy of the skinny woman on the other side of the table who was wolfing spoonfuls of it from a paper cup, didn't help. We all came after work (except for Robin, who showed up in Jimmy Choos on her way to one glamorous event or another). But if you had to bring food to this windowless, pain-soaked room, couldn't you at least pick something less odorous? I usually had a bottle of water or juice. On the rare occasions I needed a boost, I'd pick up a latte at the Starbucks across the street.

We went around the table, sharing our stories and catching up with each other's progress. When my turn came, I took a deep breath and settled my gaze on Angie, a petite woman with a mane of brown hair and a big laugh, who was sitting across from me. Her warm fuzzy personality endeared her to you instantaneously, making you feel at once cozy and invigorated, like a good cup of coffee. The two of us had been coming here the longest—nearly four years. Our odds had been much better back then. She was thirty-nine now and I had just turned thirty-eight. Angie was my hero. She was single, trying on her own with donor sperm. On her latest IVF round last month, she'd finally gotten pregnant and was about to graduate from Group.

I quickly went over my long history of failures for those who were joining us for the first time tonight and explained that my partner, Tyler, and I had finally moved on to a donor egg cycle. It was a huge emotional and financial plunge, but we'd exhausted all other options. The whole point of using a young woman's eggs was that they would be better than my own. But my doctor had called me in the afternoon with the bad news that only two had fertilized. That meant we would have no embryos left to freeze and use in the future should this cycle fail.

"My transfer is on Monday," I said. "And I'm terrified. This is my last chance."

"Don't say that." Robin smiled at me from across the table, fiddling with the big rock on her finger. "You can always try again."

Next to her, Angie mimed a gun to her head.

I considered ignoring Robin—I was sure she meant well—and, on any other occasion, I would have. But I was not myself tonight. "You know, Robin," I said, trying to keep my voice even, "some of us can barely afford it *once*."

She flushed and looked away and I sat back, grimly satisfied at having shut her up.

❖

"Can you believe the bitch?" Angie said as soon as we walked out.

Bitter wind blew in our faces and we zipped up our jackets, dug our hands into the pockets. It was unusually cold. If it weren't for the daffodils, tulips, and azaleas blooming all over Manhattan, you'd think it was February, not April.

"To hell with Robin," I said as we headed to the subway. "All I can think of is my transfer on Monday."

Angie squeezed my shoulder. "I know, hon. Try not to worry too much."

That was why I loved Angie. She knew better than to say something stupid like, *Don't worry!* Because of course I would worry. I'd have to be made of stone not to worry after three miscarriages and eight IVFs.

Angie and I boarded the train at Lincoln Center and sat down across from a woman with a stroller. I waved to the toddler girl, who leaned over the bar to check us out. Her hair was braided and pulled up in a fluffy bun, fastened with a pink ribbon. "She's adorable," I said to her mother, before turning back to Angie.

"Why don't we go get a drink?" she said. "My doc told me a glass of wine doesn't hurt and can help you relax."

"I can't. Tyler's waiting for me. And I still have work to do."

The little girl was getting fussy, kicking her chunky legs. Her mother unbuckled her and sat her down on her lap. She had on a pink dress and matching shoes. I smiled, waved at her again. She stared at me with her big brown eyes before finally giving me a grin. My whole body seemed to relax, all the tension draining away.

"How's he dealing with the bad news?" Angie asked.

I frowned. "I haven't even told him yet."

Tyler hadn't been happy about spending the last of our savings on a donor egg cycle that cost more than half my annual salary. We did okay between the two of us—he as an associate philosophy professor at Columbia and I as an associate curator at the Met—or rather, we would have been doing okay if we weren't pouring it all into fertility treatments.

"He's been weird lately," I continued. "Going through the motions as if he doesn't care about the cycle. He's been irritable, too. We fight about the smallest, stupidest things."

"Men don't know how to deal with stress. Make him give you a massage tonight," Angie said with a wink. I shrugged, distracted by the little doll in a pink dress across from me. I put my hand in front of my face and mouthed, *Peekaboo*, as I pulled it away. She stared at me, then lifted her hand, imitating me. I turned to Angie. "Do you think her mother would let me hold her?"

"Are you crazy?"

"Don't you just want to hug her?"

"Yeah, but mothers usually don't hand their babies to strangers."

"It's not like I'd bolt with her at the next stop." I looked at the girl, then back at Angie. "On second thought . . ."

"You're a freak!"

"I just want to breathe in that sweet baby smell." Angie shook her head. "Who knows," I continued, "maybe it'll bring me good luck on Monday."

"Right."

"Why not? Women's cycles sync when they live together. Maybe motherhood's contagious, too." I gave Angie a nudge with my elbow. "Why do you think I've been hanging out with you so much since you got pregnant?"

"Freak," she said again, and hugged me good-bye before getting off at 86th Street. We didn't wish each other a happy Easter. Family holidays were hard on us, especially those that revolved around children.

I got off three stops later, at 110th Street. I loved living in Morningside Heights, near the Columbia campus. I'd come for graduate school and never left. The area pulsated with life. Students, faculty, visiting scholars from all over the world. You could overhear passionate conversations about gender politics, the rise of populism, or poetry on the streets, in the cafés, even in the grocery stores. The neighborhood was at once steeped in the past and forward-looking into the future. It was like its own island within the island of Manhattan.

The buckets of tulips lined up outside the corner store on 111th Street caught my eye. A bit of color might brighten my mood. It was important to stay positive, my fertility acupuncturist insisted. It hadn't helped me before but it couldn't hurt, I thought, and grabbed a bouquet of the orange ones. A Reiki woman I'd seen years ago had told me it was the color of the reproductive chakra.

Inside, I hesitated in front of the ice cream freezer. I'd been avoiding dairy and gluten for the past two months, since some believed it affected fertility. But a pint of Ben & Jerry's Mint Chocolate Cookie couldn't possibly make a difference.

I'd just pulled a tub out when my mother called. The woman had a sixth sense. I shouldn't have picked up and I certainly shouldn't have told her that I was buying ice cream.

"Oh, honey," she said, "all these sweets are ruining your figure." My mother had been worrying about my figure since I was five.

"Mom, I have my transfer on Monday and I'm really not in the mood—"

"I keep telling you, Lana. You need to stop stressing out. You won't get pregnant until you relax."

Of course, it was all my fault that I couldn't have a child. I loved my mother but she had a gift for making me feel like shit even when she meant well. She'd never said outright what a huge disappointment I was, but she'd made me feel it in more ways than I wished to remember. And this wasn't like failing at ballet or the piano or not being good enough to get into Harvard. Even the stupidest, least deserving people could make a baby. Often without trying to. I shook my head, wished her good night, and put my phone back in my purse.

Upstairs, I stood in front of the door for a moment before pulling out my keys. Something didn't feel right. On Group nights, I usually returned home to Tyler blasting his favorite punk bands—the Clash or the Pogues or Gogol Bordello—while preparing dinner. He'd meet me at the door, hand me a glass of wine, and sit me down at the kitchen table with a bowl of olives and a plate of crackers while he finished making the meal. Tall, with long limbs, he clumsily navigated our tiny kitchen, the wooden spoons looking like toys in his enormous hands. Watching him hum to himself as he sliced and chopped and stirred was my favorite part of those evenings. But tonight the apartment was eerily quiet. I unlocked the door and pushed it open.

Before I even walked in I saw Tyler's extra-large roller duffle bag standing in the corner by the coat rack, stuffed to the gills. The last time I'd seen it was eight years ago when he'd moved in.

❖

"I'm sorry but I can't take it anymore," Tyler said. I stood there, my hand clutching the tulips, the plastic bag with the ice cream cutting into the skin on my wrist. He was wearing the oxford shirt I'd given him for Christmas, the one I liked so much because it brought out the blue in his eyes. My gaze locked on an ink stain right above the pocket, where he usually kept a pen. The source of many ruined shirts.

"All that pain is killing us, Lana. We need to take a break."

"A break? But . . ." My throat was so dry, the words came out hoarse, rusty. "But our transfer is on Monday."

"I know." He looked down. "I'm sorry. I can't go through with it right now."

I stared at the ink mark on his shirt, my eyes cloudy with tears. My ears began buzzing.

"We need some distance," I heard him say as if from afar. "To figure things out."

My mind was racing. I thought of the texts he'd been getting lately at all hours of the day. Of how distracted, even cross he'd become over the past few months. "Is there another woman?"

"Christ, Lana! This is about you and me." He shook his head. "I'll move out for a month or two. Just to give us both some space."

Before I had a chance to respond, to tell him that I didn't need any goddamn space, he leaned over and hugged me, holding me tight the way he'd done after each miscarriage. At five seven, I was by no means petite but in his big arms, I felt like a dainty porcelain doll. If he squeezed any harder, I'd break.

Then, just as abruptly, he let go of me, took his duffle bag, and, without looking back, he left.

A cold breeze ruffled the curtains. The beeping of a truck backing up down the street, then quiet but for the distant noises of the city. Only when I heard the ice cream tub crash on the floor did I realize my hand had dropped the bag and flowers.

2.

LANA

It was nine a.m. on Monday and I was still in my pajamas. I should have gone to work but I'd already told my boss I was taking a sick day. Might as well stay home. I was an art curator. If I missed a day, the world wouldn't stop.

Slumped on the couch, I stared at the phone in my hand. Finally, I sighed and pressed the number on the screen. "Fertility clinic," a female voice answered.

My throat tightened. The words felt like lead on my tongue.

"Hello," the woman said, her voice rising. "Can you hear me?"

I opened my mouth to speak, but no sound came out.

"Hello?" she said again, waited, then hung up.

I threw the phone on the floor. What would I have told her anyway? My partner left me? He decided he no longer wanted a baby?

I wondered if anyone had ever canceled their transfer before. After all the hormones, the ludicrous amount of money, the shrink evaluation, the daily doctor visits, the endless pages to initial, the papers to sign, had anyone ever really called to say, *Never mind*?

The phone buzzed on the floor. I brushed the tears away with the back of my hand and got up to get it.

A text from Angie: *Good luck today! I'll be thinking of you. xo* ♥

"Is your husband at work, too?" the woman sitting next to me asked.

I looked up from the *Vanity Fair* I'd been leafing through. She had perfectly blow-dried hair, trendy highlights, and a flawless manicure that seemed out of place with the blue, giant-size hospital gown she was wearing. I scanned the clinic's pre-op waiting room. Furnished with pastel armchairs and sofas, it looked more like the reception area of a law firm than a hospital. About a dozen women were having their transfers today. All of them were sitting with their men except for the two of us.

I considered her question. A few days earlier I would have said, "My *partner* is at work," stressing *partner* just enough to give it an accusatory quality. For years, I'd passionately defended my right to have a family without the formality of a signature, without the sanction of the church and government. I would explain at length that marriage was an inherently patriarchal institution that subordinated women to men. That the term *wife* meant I was someone's property, whereas *partner* suggested equality. One thing I'd never considered was how easily a partnership could dissolve.

"He has a really busy day at the office," I lied. What was I to say? *I'm doing it alone?* Just the thought of it made my eyes well up. But what was I doing here then?

"Tell me about it," she said, leaning closer. "If it's not a meeting, it's an important conference call or a client."

I nodded and picked up my magazine, but she wouldn't let go. "This infertility business is so difficult on relationships. We women do all the hard work—the injections, the hormones, the surgery—and all the guys have to do is jerk off into a cup. How fair is that? Then they bitch that we're all moody and—imagine!—we don't want to have sex."

I felt a lump in my throat. Just a week ago I would have rejoiced guiltily at how lucky Tyler and I were not to have to deal with any of that. He'd always come with me to the doctor's appointments, even given me the injections, making all sorts of silly faces to make me laugh so that I'd relax. The hormones hadn't really affected me much, either, except for making me feel bloated. I'd certainly never lost my sex drive. If anything, Tyler had seemed less interested these past few months. I'd assumed it was the stress. That, like me, he was feeling jaded, depleted after our latest miscarriage. It had never occurred to me that he might be having an affair. That he might bail on me, leaving me alone and childless after nearly a decade together.

I'd thought about it all weekend, looking at it from every possible angle. He could deny it as much as he wanted, but I was sure he'd met another woman. There was no other plausible explanation. If he truly just wanted a break, he would have left before we'd started the donor egg cycle and wasted all that money—and with it our last chance to have a child.

"I'm sorry," I said, standing up. "I need to run to the ladies' room."

In the bathroom, I splashed my face with cold water and stared at myself in the mirror. *What am I doing here? I shouldn't be having this embryo transfer. Not without Tyler.*

"Oh, honey, I'm sure he'll be back," my mother had said when I'd called her crying on Saturday morning. She was a smart woman who'd managed to escape Communist Bulgaria back in the day, but when it came to men, she was utterly delusional. I didn't have it in me to point out that all three of her ex-husbands—my dad included—had left and never looked back.

I'd spent the rest of Easter weekend at home with the shades drawn, curled up on the couch with my red tabby, Plato, binge-watching shows on Netflix. It'd been a relief when Monday had finally rolled around. I'd showered, dressed, and come to the clinic as if nothing had changed. In many ways, it hadn't.

Tyler and I had already paid and filled out all the required forms at the start of the process. There was a specific clause somewhere in there that asked what should be done with our remaining embryos in the event that one or both of us should die. Maybe even in the case of us splitting up one day. I couldn't remember. There had been so many questions to answer, pages to initial, and consent forms to sign. But I was pretty sure there had been no mention of a separation in the midst of a cycle. Even lawyers wouldn't think of something so absurd.

Whatever the legal implications, could I really go ahead and have Tyler's baby without his knowledge?

I sighed and dried my face. I would go back inside, change out of the hospital gown, and go home. It was the right thing to do. I should have canceled over the phone this morning, spared myself the humiliation.

In the waiting room, I paused and took in the scene: throw pillows and side tables piled with magazines; the muted flat-screen TV on the wall, permanently tuned to NY1. The familiarity of it ran like a chill through my body. Only the faces of the men and women, waiting anxiously for the one procedure that could change their lives, were different each time.

A young couple huddled on the sofa in the back reading their iPads attracted my attention. Her feet in blue hospital socks rested against the coffee table, tapping nervously. He'd draped his free arm over her shoulders and was stroking her softly. I had a flashback of Tyler and me on that very couch. He'd always rubbed my back to calm my nerves before the transfer. With a stab, I realized there was probably some other woman he now—

"Lana?" I heard the nurse call out behind me.

I stood there gutted by the thought of Tyler, my Tyler, rubbing some other woman's shoulders. Kissing another woman, I could deal with. But that simple—if imaginary—act of intimacy was what drove home for me his betrayal.

"Lana Stone?" the nurse called out again.

I turned with sudden determination. To hell with Tyler. He could be married with a kid before the end of the year. But this was it for me. The two embryos waiting to be transferred into my womb were my last chance at motherhood. I would never again be able to save enough money on my own for a donor, and my crappy eggs were clearly past their expiration date. Tyler could walk away from me, but he shouldn't be the one deciding if I'd ever feel the kick of a baby, if I'd ever experience the pain and elation of birth.

It was *my* choice to make.

❖

In the taxi on the way home, I pulled up my egg donor's profile on my phone and stared at her photo. "Will you bring me luck?" I whispered.

The decision to use another woman's eggs hadn't been easy. Tyler and I must have browsed through hundreds of profiles. We'd joked that it was as if we were choosing a partner for a threesome. But to me, it had felt like we were picking out my replacement. After all, Tyler's sperm was to fertilize *her* egg. I would just carry the baby they had made, even if the work was done in a lab without them ever meeting.

If my child wasn't going to inherit my DNA, I wanted it to at least carry my people's genes. I longed for a connection, a common thread that would run through me, linking my baby to my mother, a gymnast who had defected from Communist Bulgaria during the Montreal Olympic Games. But there weren't any Bulgarian donors to be found. I'd almost given up on it, thinking of using a Russian or other Eastern European woman, when one of the agencies called me with the good news. A Bulgarian girl had just signed up.

Everyone thought I was foolish to go with a donor I knew nothing about just because of a shared heritage. "What if she's ugly?" friends asked. Then her file landed in my mailbox. If anything, Donor CN8635 was too beautiful. The baby wouldn't look anything like me. But she was undeniably Bulgarian in appearance and that was the whole point. She had the same wide Slavic cheekbones as my mother, the same slightly elongated eyes, inherited from the Bulgar tribes who'd made their way south of the Danube from Asia in the seventh century. But while my mother's eyes were brown, the donor's were dark green. In many ways, she looked more like my mother's daughter than I did. She even had her lithe, straight-backed gymnast's figure. I'd inherited my father's big-boned frame and had to work hard to stay in shape, spending hours on the elliptical each week.

Donor CN8635 was twenty-one, an Ivy League graduate. She was an only child and there was no history of cancer, heart disease, or depression in her family. I had a feeling I would have liked her if I'd met her in person. But the process was anonymous. There were couples who insisted on meeting their donors and looked for agencies and girls who were okay with that. I didn't understand it. Why complicate matters? Once the donor knows who you are, you can never be sure she won't change her mind one day and come looking for your child.

There are crazy people out there.

3.

KATYA

THEN
Seven months earlier

"I don't need a shrink," I said, first thing after I walked in and sat on the sofa. I literally said that. First words out of my mouth. What was wrong with me?

He nodded, picked up a legal pad and a pen from his desk, and sat on the armchair by the window across from me. I hadn't expected him to be that young. I took a sip of my latte—I'd stopped at Starbucks on the way here—and left the cup on the side table.

"I'm not depressed," I said. "And I'm certainly not crazy."

I waited for him to ask what, then, had brought me to the Counseling and Psychological Services Center. But he just sat there, waiting, staring at my face a bit too hard, as if he were worried his gaze might slip down my shirt without his knowing. I was tempted to tell him that I was used to guys checking out my breasts but didn't want to embarrass him. It was only our first session.

"I'm Bulgarian," I said instead. "Only crazy people go to the shrink in Bulgaria."

The hum of the city drifted in through the open window along with a cool breeze. The smell of rain and wet leaves. It had been hot and sticky when the semester started three weeks ago, but by mid-September the humidity was gone. The early autumn sky was an intense blue, smooth and solid like marble.

"Anyway, I thought I better check it out," I said. "The therapy thing, I mean. See what all the fuss is about. It's free, after all. I guess the university wants to make sure we all have someone to talk to."

I took another sip of coffee. Looked at him. He couldn't have been more than thirty. Handsome, in a dorky, earnest way. That puppy look, eager to please. I wondered if he blushed easily.

"My friend Zoe is in the hospital," I blurted. "In the ICU."

He leaned forward, locked me in his gaze. "What happened?"

I ran my hand through my hair and began picking the split ends, unsure how much I wanted to tell him.

Zoe was in my advanced econometrics course. We'd run into each other before—we were both econ majors—but had never really hung out much. Maybe because this was a tough class or because we were in the same dorm our senior year, we'd started studying together, comparing lecture notes and consulting on homework assignments. When she found out that in the four years I'd been at Columbia I'd barely set foot in Central Park, she took it upon herself to remedy that great injustice. Zoe was from New York. Brooklyn, really—as she loved to point out. Whatever. When you come from another country those distinctions don't matter.

Anyway, we went to the park together the other day. The weather had turned warm again and I loved it. After wandering the pathways for an hour, we sat on a bench by the pond with the model boats. I'm no fan of water: lakes, rivers, even small ponds like this one give me the shivers, but I wasn't going to tell Zoe about it. And in all fairness, it was pretty—the Fifth Avenue skyline, the birds chirping in the trees around us, the kids pushing their scooters.

I avoided looking at the water. But then two mothers pushing strollers stopped near the edge in front of us. There was a little boy with them, around five, who seemed fascinated by the boats. Zoe was telling me something about coming to the pond as a kid but I could barely hear her, my eyes trained on the boy, who sat down on the stone ridge that runs along the pond. He had on a pair of baggy jeans and a dark blue T-shirt with Superman on the front. His mother, chatting busily with her friend, was holding his denim jacket in her hand. The boy lay sprawled on his belly, leaning all the way over the stone. "This kid's gonna fall," I said, interrupting Zoe.

"His mother is right there," she said, but from what I could tell, his mother wasn't paying him any attention. I stood up and walked over to the two women, who stopped talking and looked at me, confused, suspicious.

"I'm sorry," I said, and pointed to the boy, "but I'm worried that he's going to fall over."

The taller woman put her hand on his shoulder. "He's okay, actually. We come here every day . . . But thank you." Her voice was calm but her strained smile seemed to say, *Mind your own business, weirdo.* I turned to her friend for support, but she, too, was looking at me as if I'd grown a second head. I kept standing there. The two of them exchanged glances and, without a word, gathered the boy up and moved farther down the pond. I shook my head and walked back to the bench.

Zoe had an amused smile on her face. "At least you didn't get into a fight this time."

She was referring to an incident the week before when we'd run into a couple about our age arguing on the sidewalk on Broadway right outside the subway entrance. The woman had tried to stomp off, but the guy grabbed her by the arm. I told him to leave her alone, which didn't go well. Both of them started shouting at me to mind my own business, the guy calling me a bitch. Zoe showed them the finger, hooked her arm around mine, and pulled me away.

The night of our park outing, I caught her puking in the bathroom. It was the third time that week. At the sight of her pale, vacant face, I snapped. She'd been nice to me and I wanted to help her. I really did. I told her that she was stupid to do that. That she ought to accept she's fat and move on. No point in torturing herself puking her guts out. If it were working, I could see how one could argue that it was worth it. But with all that purging, she was still overweight.

"You have two options," I told her. "Be fat and happy or be fat and miserable." I meant to be supportive, of course. But I could see how it might have come off the wrong way. Jesus. How could I have been so stupid?

I looked back at the shrink. "She tried to kill herself," I said. "She came to my room in the middle of the night. All freaked out, sobbing. I barely understood her when she told me that she'd taken an entire bottle of Advil."

He shook his head, a faint frown across his forehead. "That must have been horrible."

"They pumped her stomach and all. But she'll be okay, thank God."

"How about you? How do you feel?"

I leaned back on the couch and looked at the ceiling. There was a tiny stain, the shape of a man's profile, the nose barely jutting out like a Roman bust. I sighed and turned back to him. "I'm sad, I guess," I said, and watched him make a note of it. "Angry. Guilty."

He looked up from his pad. "Tell me more."

I didn't want to tell him more. I crossed my legs, listened to the student voices coming in through the open window. Guys shouting, throaty laughter. Girls shrieking in the distance.

"Luckily, she wasn't that smart about it," I said finally. "I mean, Advil? Everyone knows Advil will give you stomach ulcers before it kills you."

"Maybe it was a cry for help," he said. I shrugged, and he went on. "I'm sorry you're going through this. It must have been so scary to hear what she'd done."

She did it because of me, I wanted to tell him. "I'm only glad she's better," I mumbled.

The back of my T-shirt felt damp against my skin. I zipped up my hoodie and wrapped my arms tightly around my chest. The shrink was looking at me intently, his head slightly tilted, nodding as if weighing my words with each movement of his head.

"I'm afraid we are out of time," he finally said, and stood up.

I followed suit, feeling a bit frazzled at the abruptness. My hand shot forward but I pulled it back, uncertain. "I'm sorry. Do we shake hands? I don't know the protocol."

He smiled. "No need to. I'll see you next week." Then, "One more thing before you go. We don't use the word *crazy* in this office."

I stared at him. "Not even *I'm crazy busy?*"

He shook his head.

"How about *I'm crazy about you?*" I asked, batting my eyelashes.

Another shake.

"But that's crazy!" I laughed and picked up my empty coffee cup. "Thanks, Dr. Wozniak."

"Call me Josh," he said, and explained that he was a mental-health counselor, not a psychiatrist. Whatever. They were all shrinks, as far as I was concerned.

At the door, I turned. "Josh?"

He looked up from his notebook.

"Maybe I am a bit lonely," I said. "That's why I came . . . in case you're wondering."

He smiled again. "Perhaps we can start with that next time."

I nodded. Something told me that we wouldn't. A lot could happen in a week.

4.

LANA

I was at the office when the nurse called just before noon. My blood test from this morning had come back positive. I sat there, stunned, staring at the phone in my hand.

I was pregnant.

My first instinct was to call Tyler. It's funny how long it takes for our brains to adjust to new circumstances. Two weeks after he'd left, I still woke up in the morning with my body looking for his to curl against. I still unlocked the apartment door and listened for his voice calling out to me in greeting. I still reached for his favorite ancient grains granola in the store.

I called Angie instead. "Holy Toledo!" she shrieked, and I pulled the phone away from my ear. "We're going to be mothers together!"

An hour later, she was waiting for me at the museum's entrance with a Zabar's bag in her hand. With her cropped jean jacket and loose ponytail, she looked much younger than her age. As a freelance writer, Angie worked from home and made her own office hours. She often came over to join me on my lunch break, since her apartment was a short walk across Central Park.

The April sun was bright, the air crisp and clear. Visitors lounged on the front steps, sitting cross-legged or leaning back, resting on an elbow. Some had red paper bags with the Met's logo; others held selfie sticks. Pigeons ambled about, bobbing their heads, picking at crumbs. In six weeks, the weather would turn hot and sticky and everyone would be hiding indoors, blasting the AC. But for a few brief weeks in the spring and fall, New Yorkers—and tourists—got to enjoy being outdoors.

Angie and I made our way through the throngs of nannies pushing strollers and dog walkers with at least a half-dozen dogs fanned out in front of them. The road looping around the park was packed with bicyclists and runners, and we had to weave around them. Finally, we found a bench in the sun overlooking the Great Lawn and sat down.

"Are you going to tell Tyler?" Angie asked, as she unwrapped her sandwich.

I shrugged. "I'm taking it one day at a time, praying I make it through the first trimester. I'll worry about telling him once there's something to tell."

"Like after you give birth?"

"Anyway, why should I? He decided he didn't want the baby."

"He kinda didn't know there was a baby."

"Technically, he did." I opened the plastic box with the salad I'd picked up from the Met's staff cafeteria. "By the time he left, fertilization had happened and the cells were already multiplying like mad. Just because the action wasn't taking place in my womb doesn't mean that it wasn't happening."

Angie looked at me, her expertly plucked eyebrows arched high on her forehead. "Have you considered a career in law? Maybe politics?"

We laughed. It was so good to laugh after so many tears.

"But it will be *his* child," Angie said. "His flesh and blood. Doesn't he have the right to know?"

I took a bite of my salad. "Women have always had the option of keeping such news to themselves. I won't be the first." Truth be told, it hurt like hell not to share with Tyler what should have been joyous news. Which only made me that much angrier with him.

"But don't you *have to*? I mean legally. Can't he sue you or something?"

"Why is it that when it happens naturally, it's okay? But when a lab is involved, there are all these legal issues?"

A couple of pigeons pecked at half a bagel lying on the ground by the trash can on our left. A toddler who was passing with his mother ran toward them. I pulled out my phone and snapped a shot of the little boy and the birds as they flew away. I wasn't big on social media but loved capturing interesting moments and posting them on Instagram.

"By the way, I have a secret admirer," I said.

Angie lit up. "Oh, do tell."

"He 'likes' all of my photos and watches all of my stories."

Angie laughed. "You mean you've got a new *follower*." Her editors expected her to have a huge social media presence and she worked hard at it, spending hours curating her image. She had thousands of followers, most of whom she'd never met. But I still got excited when someone who didn't know me found my photos compelling enough to follow me.

"Is he cute?" Angie said.

"I don't know, his account's private."

She laughed even harder. "How do you know it's a *he* then?"

I showed her his profile on my screen: *Peter Bogdin.* Instead of a photo the circle had some sort of black-and-white graphic.

She raised her eyebrows mockingly and I waved her away. "I know. You can call yourself anything."

"Just keep posting and soon you'll have too many followers to notice who's liking what."

"I used to hate it that Tyler wasn't on social media," I said, "but now I'm grateful I don't have to deal with unfriending him." My phone rang in my hand. "Speak of the devil."

"Tyler?"

I stared at his name flashing on my screen, my stomach in a knot. He'd sent me a few e-mails over the past two weeks that I'd deleted without opening, but this was the first time he was calling. "What the hell does he want? He can't expect that we'll be friends now . . ." I paused as a new worry rose up my chest. "Could he have found out? About the pregnancy?"

Angie shook her head. "I doubt it."

He left a voice mail and I played it on speakerphone so that we could both listen: *Hey. It's me,* he began, and I felt a pang at hearing his voice.

I clasped my salad box as he continued. *Just checking in to make sure you're okay.*

"Why wouldn't I be okay?" I said, and dropped the phone back in my purse. "Oh, yeah, my partner of eight years dumped me for another woman at the worst possible time."

"I'm sorry, hon." Angie reached over and patted my shoulder. "You're a strong woman. You'll do just fine without him. You'll see."

As I got up to go back to the office, Angie stopped me. "Aren't you forgetting something?"

I looked at her questioningly.

"C'mon, let me see her." Angie extended her hand.

"Who?" I asked even though I knew. I'd refused to show even Angie the photo of my donor, saying that I didn't want to jinx myself. The truth was I'd been embarrassed about her looks. But now that I'd gotten pregnant I had no more excuses. I sighed and pulled the photo up on my phone.

Angie did a double take. "This is your egg donor? I sure hope you have a girl. Those looks would be wasted on a boy."

"This is why I didn't want to show it to you," I said, and waved good-bye.

Back in the office, I sat at my desk and looked at the photo again. "Thank you," I whispered.

The sun was streaming through the window and I got up to adjust the shades. It was getting late and I had a bunch of loan requests from museums all over the world to deal with. They seemed to have flooded my inbox all at once. I took one last look at the woman who had given me the gift of what I hoped was a healthy pregnancy before I put my phone away.

I'd already decided I would not be calling Tyler back.

5.

LANA

I was on my way home, sitting on the number 1 train, reading my book, when I saw her. I'd stopped at Barnes & Noble before getting on the subway and bought *What to Expect When You're Expecting*. I hadn't dared get it when I'd first found out I was pregnant a week ago. But my second blood test was good and the doctor had reassured me that everything was going according to plan. "With the egg of a twenty-one-year-old woman, you have nothing to worry about."

It was an unseasonably warm early-May day, the streets buzzing with the promise of summer, and I dreaded returning to the empty apartment. I blamed it on the weather, but the truth was I had nothing to go home to. I found cooking for myself depressing and it was still too light outside to turn on the TV and lose myself in the dramas of others. Which was why I'd ended up at the bookstore, killing some time.

The subway was nearly empty. I was sitting in a middle seat, engrossed in my reading. Shortly before my stop at 110th Street, I closed the book and put it in my bag. I was about to get up when my eyes landed on a girl in a hot-pink summer dress, leaning against the pole across from me, looking at her phone. My breath caught in my throat. I squeezed my eyes shut for a moment, convinced I was seeing things. But when I opened them, she was still there, the girl whose face I knew so well.

The train stopped, the conductor announced 110th Street, and the doors opened. People walked out, others walked in. I remained in my seat, my sweaty hands clutching my bag.

This was not supposed to happen. Not in New York, a city of more than eight million people. Sure, I'd run into friends before—at parties, on the street, in the park. Once, at a bodega in the Village, I'd even come across a guy from my high school in suburban Chicago. It was weird to see him outside the context of New Trier, but it was inconsequential. I never gave it much thought. But the beautiful girl leaning against the pole in a hot-pink dress, this girl was CN8635—my egg donor. The girl whose genes my baby would inherit.

I stared hard at the bag in my lap. What if she looked in my direction and our eyes met? She, of course, didn't know what the woman she'd donated to looked like. She didn't know my name. But what if she somehow sensed who I was? What if she felt some telepathic connection with the baby growing in my belly?

Her presence in the car was electrifying. I gripped my purse with my damp hands, stealing peeks at her. The way her hair fell down her shoulders in loose brown waves. The casual manner in which she held the phone in her palm, confidently swiping with her thumb.

A few stops later, at 168th Street, she got off, and without so much as a thought, I rose from my seat and rushed after her.

My stomach tingled with excitement mixed with apprehension as I followed her out of the subway and down the street, keeping a safe distance. I didn't ask myself what I was doing. I just kept walking, my eyes glued to the pink dress, making sure I wouldn't lose her. It would have been a lot easier if I'd had flats on. But, no, I'd decided this morning on three-inch navy pumps to go with my navy skirt and cream blouse.

When she stopped at the traffic light, waiting to cross Broadway, I hid behind a shish kebab food truck at the corner. People sauntered past me, talking loudly, laughing. I'd always liked the cheerful, relaxed vibe in Washington Heights. On a warm spring evening like tonight, everyone seemed to be out—families with kids, groups of teenagers, friends—shopping, hanging out, horsing around.

I followed the girl in pink along Broadway for a couple of blocks before she turned left onto a quiet side street lined with low-rise residential buildings with white-brick façades. If she were to look back now, I had no place to go, no group of people to hide behind. I slowed my pace, leaving a greater distance between us, then crossed to the other side of the street so that I could keep an eye on her more easily. I wondered if she lived around here. If she walked this route every day on her way to and from the subway.

It happened so fast, I barely registered it. I didn't see her trip or lurch forward. One moment she was walking, the next she was sprawled face-down on the sidewalk. I looked around. Except for a guy talking on his phone farther down the block, there was nobody in sight. Before I could give it another thought, I was running across the street toward her. "Are you okay?" I shouted as I approached. She was starting to move, to pull herself up onto all fours. "Miss, are you okay?" I hovered over her, unsure how to help.

She rolled over and sat with her back leaning against the building and looked up at me. "I felt a bit unsteady for a moment," she said, her voice feeble, dreamy. "Probably low blood sugar or something." She examined her scraped knee, a few drops of blood forming, shrugged, and started to get up. She was already on her feet when she rocked a bit and held on to me.

Her hand on my shoulder felt hot, burning my skin through the shirt. The baby growing inside me was her flesh and blood.

"I'm sorry," she said, and gave me an embarrassed smile. She spoke with my mother's accent. Of course, she would. "I was late for class today and had to skip lunch," she continued. "I just need to eat something. There is a coffee shop around the corner on Broadway."

She let go of my shoulder and took a wobbly step forward. I grabbed her arm. "Wait. I'll walk you there."

"Really? Oh, thank you." She smiled and we started walking slowly.

It felt wrong. I was not supposed to know my egg donor. I was not supposed to be talking to her. But it was also thrilling. The act of doing something forbidden and getting away with it. Like sneaking an extra scoop of ice cream behind Mom's back.

"So sweet of you to help me," she said, and eased onto my arm. Two friends on an evening stroll. "People say New Yorkers are rude. But I've been at Columbia for four years and everyone has been so nice and friendly." She looked at me. "I'm Bulgarian."

"My mother is from there." I knew it was a mistake before I'd finished saying it.

"Seriously?" She stopped, beaming, and hugged me. Just like that, she hugged me. As if I were a long-lost relative. "Do you speak Bulgarian?"

Malko," I said, using my thumb and index finger to identify how little I knew. I used to be fluent but hadn't spoken it since I was a kid.

"Most Americans I meet don't even know where Bulgaria is." She hesitated. "You aren't in a hurry, are you?" she asked tentatively. "There's a great Irish place just around the corner. We can grab a quick bite if you'd like."

"Actually, I was going to—"

"Oh no! Please tell me you don't have dinner plans." She peered at me expectantly, pleadingly, her face already getting some of its color back. "I'd so love to hear about your mother and how she got here. It must have been back during Communism, right? I've heard some crazy stories."

I stared at my pumps. What had I gotten myself into?

"I should have something more substantial than a bagel anyway," she went on. "It's just that . . . it's so lonely to eat a meal on your own. You know?"

She was remarkably candid and unguarded. I found it difficult sharing my hardships even with close friends, let alone admitting loneliness in front of strangers.

"Please." She looked at me with her radiant green eyes—commanding attention, demanding you follow her every whim, her every desire.

I thought about all the reasons I shouldn't. And yet. How could I turn down a chance to get to know my donor while she had no clue who I was? It didn't get better than that. Sure, it was wrong. But I hadn't sought her out. She had fallen into my lap. Almost literally.

I checked my watch, stalling.

What was the big deal? I would have dinner with her and then we'd go our separate ways, never to see each other again. No harm in that. I'd learn a bit more about her life, her family, and any health problems that she might not have owned up to on her donor form. If there was anything worrisome, it was better to find out about it in advance so that I could prepare.

"Sure. Why not?" I finally said, and followed her. I still couldn't believe it. I'd been worried about running into Tyler around campus. That would have made sense. But my donor?

She was nearly skipping now, all but dragging me along. It was flattering to see her excitement, even if it was on account of my mother being Bulgarian. A young, beautiful girl like her—she was even more beautiful in person—I was sure she had trouble shaking people off. And here she was, delighted to have me join her for dinner. I wondered what it must be like to go through life looking the way she did. Everyone scrambling to please you. Having any man you wished. I wondered if my child would have that same magnetism.

As we walked, I tried to come up with a story, an explanation of what I was doing in this neighborhood. It sounded like she'd been on her way home, but what about me? Maybe visiting a friend? And what if she asked for the street or the friend's building? Before I'd had time to land on a solid story, we'd arrived.

At the entrance, my donor stopped and extended her hand. "I'm Katya, by the way. Katya Dimitrova."

6.

TYLER

I hadn't intended to discuss my personal life with Rachel. As her thesis adviser, I saw her once a week to check in on her progress. It was one of those cold and wet November days, a gray mist lingering in the air after it had rained on and off since morning, that reminded me of growing up in Eugene. There was a lot I missed about it—the national parks and mountains, the rugged cliffs and beaches along the Oregon coastline—but not the winters.

Rachel was gathering her papers at the end of our meeting, getting ready to leave. The old heater in my office groaned and clanked as steam made its way up the pipes. I stared out at the fading light across campus, already lost in thought.

"Is everything okay?" Rachel said with that disarming earnestness she had about her. I met her big brown eyes and, as I tried to figure out how best to dismiss her concern, she leaned forward, resting her chin on her hand, elbow propped on the table, ready to listen. If it were any of my other PhD candidates, I would have shrugged it off and said something like, *Ah, you know, long night working on an article.* But when Rachel asked, it seemed like she truly cared. That I would actually be letting her down if I didn't tell her.

I hesitated. It had been a week since Lana's latest miscarriage and the doctor's words sounded in my head on a continuous loop: *I'm not finding the baby's heartbeat.* The pain was crushing, debilitating, but I had to be strong for Lana. She needed me to comfort and reassure her that it would be all right. Even if I didn't believe it.

I had nobody else to talk to about it. Most of my friends had families and either had moved to the suburbs or were caught up in kid stuff. My sister, Sam, lived in the city with her husband and two young daughters, but we had never been close. As she liked to point out, she had more of a relationship with Lana than with me. The few single buddies I had left weren't particularly helpful. Guys get weirded out about sharing emotional stuff. We'd grab a beer and they'd ask how I was doing and I'd say something like, "Ah you know, man, it's tough. Lana just had a miscarriage." And the guy would say, "I'm sorry, man. Hope she feels better soon," followed by a pat on the shoulder. End of story.

So when Rachel asked, it just poured out of me. All of it. The miscarriages, the IVFs, the whole goddamn infertility battle that had become our life for the past eight years. In turn, Rachel told me about her sick mother who had been living with MS for fifteen years. Rachel had watched her go from a vibrant supermom to a wilted woman in a wheelchair to a bedridden skeleton. I had an inkling of what she was going through. I'd seen my own mother wither in the grip of cancer before she'd died ten years ago.

"My friends don't understand," Rachel said, twiddling her right earring. "The worst thing to happen to most of them is not getting in to Harvard."

A cool breeze came in through the cracked window. The smell of wet earth and dead leaves.

Pain was defeating and exceedingly isolating at any age. It was what Rachel and I bonded over.

I began looking forward to my thesis meetings with her. We would spend hours in my office or in coffee shops around campus, discussing not only her doctorate and philosophy but also books, films, and music. A cynic might say that I wouldn't have hung out with Rachel if she weren't pretty. I would be lying if I said that I was blind to her looks, that I didn't notice her slim waist, her shiny hair, her velvety skin that looked as if it had been airbrushed. But even if I were single—which I wasn't—I knew better than to mess around with a student.

If anything, my friendship with Rachel was forcing me to face the fact that Lana and I had fallen into a rut. We were drowning in hurt and disappointments, our lives reduced to an endless quest for a baby. Something had to change if we had any chance of surviving as a couple. The only sure way to avoid more pain and resume normal life was to stop the fertility treatments. Or at least take a break from them.

"Are you saying we should give up on having children?" Lana said when I brought it up at dinner that evening.

"I'm saying let's forget about it for a week or two and go away for the winter break. Someplace warm. We can swim and lounge around in the sand all day, take sunset walks on the beach."

Lana hesitated, took a sip of her wine. I could see the temptation, the old spark in her eyes.

"We'll forget all about doctors and treatments," I went on. "Reconnect." I took her hand. "I miss our—"

She pulled her hand away, a hurt look on her face as if I'd suggested a visit to a torture chamber. "We can't."

She was right. It was a terrible time to be going on vacation, for both of us. She had a big show coming up. I had to prepare for my tenure review.

"A short trip will recharge our batteries," I pressed on. It might have been professional suicide but it was the right thing for *us*.

"Tyler, my clock is ticking, remember? It's bad enough I have to give up on having a child that would carry my genes." She sighed, took back my hand. "You understand, don't you?"

That was the first time she'd brought up the option of using donor eggs. I knew it was a big hit on her identity, on her pride as a woman.

I nodded, clasped my other hand over hers. Lana was a fighter. She didn't know how to stop and take a break. It was that determination— along with her curiosity and passion—that had first attracted me to her.

We'd met the old-fashioned way. Offline. In the real world. And I don't mean a bar in Manhattan. I mean hot-and-sweaty, foot-calluses real world; days of sore legs, sleeping on a thin pad on the ground, lungs laboring for oxygen, freezing temperatures on the morning of the ascent. We were a six-person group—four men and two women—who'd come from all over the world to climb Kilimanjaro. I was smitten by this strong, determined woman with almond-shaped brown eyes, who wouldn't take no for an answer. Lana was tougher than the rest of us. While we'd gone looking for an adventure, she was there for a cause—to raise money for the Lymphoma Research Foundation in memory of an aunt who had died earlier that year.

I watched her now as she took another sip of wine, set the glass back down, and stared at it, her jaw clenched. I wondered what was going on in her head. I wondered if she ever wondered about what was going on in mine.

7.

LANA

Coogan's was a typical Irish pub—dark and buzzing, the smell of beer thick. But it had outdoor seating right on Broadway that looked particularly appealing on a balmy May evening. Katya knew one of the bartenders—a tall young guy with a shaved head and densely tattooed arms. He managed to get us a tiny table in the corner that fit snugly against one of the wooden planters, bright with yellow and purple pansies. Most everyone seemed younger than me, but this was a casual unassuming crowd, nothing like the trendy kids in the Meatpacking District or the hipsters in Williamsburg.

Katya told me that they were mostly from the nearby Columbia University Medical Center. She, too, was a Columbia student—a college senior majoring in economics. That explained our chance encounter on the 1 train, a couple of stops from campus. If anything, I was surprised it hadn't happened earlier. Or maybe it had. For all I knew, we'd passed each other numerous times in the neighborhood. Only I hadn't known of her existence until about four months ago when we'd chosen her as our donor. Tyler, especially, must have walked by her on campus a million times. Luckily, econ majors weren't known for frequenting philosophy classes.

Katya ordered the cheeseburger and a glass of pinot noir. I got iced tea and the beer-battered fish and chips. Not exactly gluten-free, but fish counted as a healthy choice.

"Don't you want a drink?" Katya asked after the waitress left with our orders.

I shook my head. "So how do you like New York?"

"I love it. But listen, you have to try their pinot. I know it's an Irish pub but they have great wine. Let me order you a glass." And she started looking around to wave the waitress back.

"No, thanks, really. I'm fine."

"Trust me, it's good." The busboy brought the bread basket and Katya pulled out a piece. She took a bite, moaned with satisfaction, and proceeded to butter the rest of her slice. "I used to work weekends in a wine bar," she said. "I *know* wine."

I smiled. "Maybe next time." There wouldn't be a next time, of course. It was just an expression, what people said to be polite, but this girl was so forthright and personable, I hoped she wouldn't take it at face value. "It must be hard going to college so far from home. Do you miss your family, your friends?" I asked, hoping to change the topic.

"We Skype," she said, and pointed to the bread. "It's warm, try it." I took a slice even though I didn't plan to eat it. She leaned back against her chair, chewing. "I feel much better already." Then, "Would you like some olives? Let's get some." And she raised her hand to flag our waitress.

I was amazed to see how at home Katya felt in New York, how sure of herself. Unlike my mother, Katya had grown up in post-Communist Bulgaria. She'd studied English in school, watched MTV, CNN, and an endless list of American movies. She'd been on the Internet since she was a child, used Facebook and Instagram and Twitter. Coming to New York was hardly the cultural shock my mother had experienced.

"Are you going to miss New York?" I asked. She squinted at me, confused, so I added, "You said you're a senior, right? You must be graduating in a few weeks and going home."

"Oh, no, no, no." She wagged her finger like a metronome in front of her face. "I am *not* going back."

The olives arrived and she popped one into her mouth before continuing. "My dad died when I was a kid," she said, her voice taking on a somber tone. "My mother and I can't stand each other. This is home for me."

I smiled, remembering how excited I'd been to leave Chicago, first for Boston and then New York. And my mother and I were close. Maybe too close.

"So you plan to stay in New York?" I asked.

"This guy I've been hooking up with wants me to move in with him after graduation." She popped in another olive before continuing, "But he can be so possessive. Do you have a boyfriend?"

I shook my head.

"Oh," she said, and her eyes went big with surprise. Maybe she thought every woman over a certain age was either married or in a committed relationship. "We need to find you one, then. What about the cute guy over there?" She motioned toward a man dining on his own. Good-looking, fit, young. Way too young for me. I was flattered.

I shook my head and put my hand on her arm. "I'm pregnant," I blurted out.

"*Bozhe moi,*" Katya said, and raised her hands to her head, the way my mother does. "Why didn't you tell me? And here I am, pushing the pinot on you." She lowered her voice. "Do you know who the father is?"

I laughed. Her familiarity didn't offend me. It was endearing. "There haven't been that many men in my life and certainly never at the same time. We were together for eight years."

"What happened?"

I looked away, straightened my fork and knife. "He left me."

"Well, that's his loss. You don't need him."

"Exactly."

"Another woman, ah?" Katya said, furrowing her brow.

I pulled back. "How did you know?"

"Isn't that how relationships usually break up? Someone meets someone else?"

I sighed. "Or people get fed up with each other." I was thinking more about my mom and dad than my relationship with Tyler. But, if I were to be honest, I had to admit that one surely begets the other. "He didn't say that there was another woman, but . . . I think you're right."

Our dinner plates arrived and Katya bit into her burger. She ate like a guy, unafraid to show her appetite. "You have to make him pay for it," she said.

I took a French fry and then another. "It's not like that would make my situation better. And he's not a bad guy, really."

She stopped chewing and stared at me. "But he left you . . ."

"Nobody's perfect. I'm not. Frankly, I'd have left myself a long time ago."

I laughed but Katya was still looking at me like I was from another planet.

"So you'd let him go on with his life as if he's done nothing while you—"

"I can't possibly worry about him," I said. "I need to focus on myself and my baby now."

That's one good thing about getting older. You gain perspective. Things are no longer black-and-white. Life happens in the gray, unglamorous middle. Only in books and movies does the action take place in the extremes, where it's all or nothing and people die for love and principles. I didn't expect this young girl to understand.

"So tell me about the possessive boyfriend," I said.

"He's not my *boyfriend*." She made a face as if she'd tasted something spoiled and explained that they'd been hooking up since the fall semester, that's all. "He was pretty chill at first but then turned clingy on me." She rolled her eyes. "I tried to get rid of him a few times but he's got a temper. You don't want to mess with him."

I put my fork down. "Has he hit you?"

She laughed. "God, no," she said, then added: "Not really."

I knew what *not really* meant. "Is there someone on campus you can talk to about this? There must be a counseling center."

"You kidding? I'm Bulgarian. We don't believe in shrinks." She laughed. "Psychics and fortune-tellers—now that's another story."

"But it might—"

"It's not an issue, really. I told him the other day that I'd found myself a cheap room to rent in a friend's apartment and he was totally okay with it. We're cool now. He has his moments but he's so damn hot." She giggled. "Picture Tom Cruise. You know that blue-steel look?"

I stared at her. "How old is he?"

"In his thirties." I raised my eyebrows in surprise—and maybe even reproach—but she seemed to take it as a sign of disbelief because she added, "Okay, *late* thirties. But what does age matter?"

"It doesn't. But if he's violent, you need to—"

"Oh, no, he's not *violent*," Katya said, interrupting me. "I really don't want to talk about him." Then, perking up: "Hey, so tell me about your mother. How did she leave Bulgaria?"

I told her about the Montreal Olympics, how my mom had defected along with one Russian and four Romanian athletes. Seeing Katya's face light up with awe was moving. A sense of pride, even if it was on account of my mother, washed over me and I straightened in the chair, my voice turning stronger, more confident. I was touched by Katya's youthful curiosity and enthusiasm. She wanted to know everything: how long I'd lived in New York, how I'd fallen in love with art, what it was like to work at the Met. Before I knew it, I'd forgotten all my worries about Tyler and the pregnancy. I was just a regular woman enjoying dinner with a new friend at a cool sidewalk café in a part of town I rarely went to.

As we parted outside the restaurant, Katya hugged me like an old friend. "That was so much fun. We should do it again," she said, and pulled out her phone. "What's your number?"

My throat went dry, my thoughts blank.

"I'll call you right now," she added. "This way you'll have mine."

She was just being nice, I told myself as I walked back to the subway. People always take your number but they never call. It's just a formality. A polite ritual. I'd done it countless times, exchanging numbers with women I'd clicked with at parties and events, promising to stay in touch. But then life had taken over and I hadn't called, nor had they. I had nothing to worry about.

Still, I was pissed at myself. I'd rationalized having dinner with Katya as a way to learn more about her and her family's health history. Instead, she'd been the one asking the questions. And I'd happily obliged, seduced by her excitement, flattered by her interest in my life.

8.

LANA

"Have you worked things out with Tyler yet?" my mother asked in response to my cheerful "Good morning."

I'd called her on my way to the museum as I walked the few blocks down Fifth Avenue from the crosstown bus stop, phone in one hand, coffee cup in the other. I'd switched to decaf since the transfer, trying to trick my body into responding to the taste rather than the caffeine. With all that milk in Starbucks lattes, I couldn't tell the difference. Traffic was heavy, but there were hardly any people on the sidewalks except for the occasional runner or a dog walker on their way to or from the park. I'd debated for days if I should tell my mother about the pregnancy, and having finally decided to do it, I wanted to get it over with before starting my day. "Mom, Tyler and I are over. Finished. How many times do I have to—"

"But honey, didn't you tell me he said he wanted a *break*? That's not the same as a *breakup*, now is it?"

"What man in his right mind asks for a break in the middle of a $50K fertility treatment? If Tyler wanted to take some time off—which, by the way, never works, but assuming that's what he really wanted— wouldn't he have done it before we emptied out our bank account?" I caught myself shouting and looked around, making sure there wasn't anyone walking within earshot. "The only way this makes sense," I continued, lowering my voice, "is that he met someone else and bailed in a rush before he had a child on his hands."

My mother sighed on the other end, letting the silence build, thick and reproachful. As if I'd made Tyler leave me just to spite her.

"Don't worry, Mom," I finally said, resentful that she'd put me in the position of comforting *her* when it was I who'd been left. "I'm okay, I promise. I don't need a man to be happy." Not that my mother, who was on her fourth husband, would ever understand.

"Oh, honey." She sighed again. "I told you that you should marry Tyler while he was still smitten with you but, no, that was too old-fashioned for you."

Because marriage has worked so well for you, I wanted to scream at her. "Mom, I need to go. I just got to the museum and I'm late already."

"Hurry, then. You can't afford to lose your job now that—"

"Why would you think I'd lose my job?" She was really getting on my nerves this morning.

"I'm not saying that you will, honey. But you told me your boss wasn't happy with your being late all the time and with Tyler gone—"

"Yeah, when I would come in an hour late because of my appointments at the clinic. That's different." I never should have told her about it. But she was right. The head of the department had been on my case for months now and I couldn't afford to piss him off further.

"I'm sorry, honey. I just worry about you," my mother said before hanging up. I put the phone down feeling guilty to have worried her yet again. Thank God I hadn't told her I was pregnant.

I'd been back from lunch for an hour at least when my phone pinged with a text, then another one. I ignored it. I was finally getting some traction today, going over research and loan reports for an upcoming show.

To be living in New York and working at one of the finest museums in the world was a dream come true for a shy Midwestern girl who'd felt more at home among the paintings lining the halls of the Art Institute than among her classmates at school. As an associate curator in the Drawings and Prints Department, I was responsible for researching and publishing the collection, acquiring new works, organizing exhibitions, and administering loans with other museums. For the past year, I'd been working on a joint exhibit with the European Paintings Department that would showcase the work of the sixteenth-century Italian artist Parmigianino. It was scheduled to open in less than ten months and was a great opportunity for me to shine—and then, hopefully, to move up the ladder, drop *associate* from my title. My expertise was Italian prints, and Parmigianino was one of the first Italian painters to experiment with printmaking himself. This show was made for me, as Tyler had pointed out more than a year ago. "You'll become a curator before I make professor," he'd joked.

The problem was, as my mom had reminded me this morning, the head of the department and I didn't get along. He'd hired me eight years ago and at first he'd been my cheerleader. But that had changed as my fertility treatments had intensified. He wasn't wrong to complain. During IVF cycles, I would come in late after my morning visits to the clinic. Often I would call in sick. But what irked him the most was my missing dinners and fund-raising events. One of my responsibilities as an associate curator was to schmooze with donors, dealers, and collectors, or, as it was subtly stated in my job description, "to actively cultivate potential sponsors." And I couldn't do that from home.

I was doing my best to make up for the hours I missed, staying late at the office, even doing work at home on weekends. But he only seemed to notice my shortcomings and had in effect put me on notice a few months ago.

I was hoping to finish the research for a piece we wanted to include in the Parmigianino show—an exquisite drawing in brown ink with brown wash. It was the only surviving study for the complete composition of the altarpiece known as *The Vision of Saint Jerome*, painted for the church of San Salvatore in Lauro, in Rome. The painting was now at the National Gallery, and my colleague at the European Paintings Department was working on the loan for it while I secured the drawing from the British Museum so that we could exhibit them side by side. I was so absorbed in the report that when the phone rang, I nearly jumped. I remembered it pinging a few times earlier with texts. Worried it was urgent, I dug into my purse, pulling out my wallet, a packet of tissues, my bronzer—I could never find the damn phone when it was ringing—until I finally felt it in an inside pocket. In the rush to answer before the call went to voice mail, I barely noticed it was a 646 number.

"Hello?" I said, assuming it was one of the nurses from the clinic. They called from different 646 extensions.

"Hey, it's Katya!"

I nearly dropped the phone. While I'd worried that she might call, I hadn't expected to hear from her just two days after we'd met.

"Are you at work?"

"I am," I said hesitantly. "Why?"

"I was Rollerblading in the park and as I passed the museum I thought of you," she said. "All these years in New York, I've never been to the Met."

"Oh."

"So here I am!" she squeaked with delight. "In the lobby."

My legs felt weak. My stomach clenched.

"I sent you a few texts but when I didn't hear back," she continued, "I thought I'd call."

"Sorry, it's been busy around here and I haven't looked at my phone."

"I'm sure you have work to do," she went on, clearly sensing my hesitation, "but maybe you can point me in the right direction. Show me which galleries to see."

What could I do? I told her to wait for me by the information desk and grabbed the chain with my ID and keys. "I'll be right back," I told my boss's assistant and, motioning with my head toward his closed door, added, "in case he's looking for me."

Katya was standing by one of the flower arrangements in the lobby, dressed in colorful purple, green, and yellow leggings, a white tank top, and sneakers. She must have checked in her Rollerblades since she was empty-handed except for a small denim cross-body bag. Seeing me approach, she smiled widely and took a step forward. "This must be the biggest, most beautiful bouquet of flowers ever," she said, and gave me a hug. "What an amazing place. I can't believe this is your office."

I laughed. "Except that my work space and desk are just as crappy as any other office."

"Oh, really? Can I see it?" Noticing my reluctance, she added, "I don't mean now. At the end. After I'm done touring."

"Sure," I said, hoping she would forget about it. I took a folded map from the information desk and circled some of the highlights—the Egyptian wing, the Impressionists, the European paintings—as well as a few of my favorite places tucked away in dark corners, spared from the crowds. Like the Chinese garden, the rooms with eighteenth-century furniture in the American wing, the little fountain in the Lehman Collection downstairs.

"Hopefully, I'll find at least one of them," Katya said, looking at the map with an expression of doubt and confusion.

I felt guilty and told her to text me when she was done with the main galleries. I'd come meet her then and show her whatever she hadn't been able to find. "I usually go get coffee in the afternoon anyway."

She lit up. "Perfect. I'd actually love to join you for some coffee. I'll come pick you up. What department do you work in?"

❖

Katya texted me at ten to four and I went out to get her. It felt weird bringing her to my office. Even Angie hadn't seen where I worked. *This is worse than stalking*, I thought as I swiped my card to the department's entrance with Katya at my side. I hadn't just followed my donor; I'd inserted myself into her life. It was no excuse that *she* had made the next move and was the one keeping the "friendship" going. She had no idea who I was.

"At least you have a window," Katya said as we walked into my office.

"Not much of a view." It faced the wall of another wing of the museum, so close I could nearly touch it. "But I still get to hear the traffic on Fifth."

Katya laughed and came over to check it out. "Are these your parents?" she asked, looking at my framed photos on the windowsill above my desk.

"Long time ago," I said as she picked up the frame. "When I was a kid."

It was perhaps the first photo I'd ever taken, at least the first one I remembered. I was in second grade. It must have been at some point before Christmas because we'd gone to Marshall Field's, where we'd had lunch under the tree, then strolled along State Street, looking at the windows. It had snowed the day before and the street was picture-perfect with holiday displays and shoppers decked out in coats and furry hats. Despite the frigid temperature, we were in no hurry to go back home. My parents were already fighting at that time, but that day they were both in an exceptionally good mood. They'd alternated posing for photos, squatting next to me in front of window displays and pretending they didn't know I held my fingers as bunny ears over their heads. I don't recall how I came to ask if I could take a photo of them sitting on a bench in front of one of the stores, but I remember the surprised look they exchanged and then my dad saying, "Why not?" He focused the camera for me, told me to hold it still before pressing the button, and rushed to join my mother on the bench. I was so proud when a few days later my mom returned home with the developed film and pronounced my photo the best one of the bunch. Never mind that the horizon was somewhat tilted. My parents looked great and, most important, happy.

A year later, when my father left us and my mother dove into the photo albums with vengeance, tearing up every image of the two of them, I'd hidden this one in a box of old toys in the back of my closet.

"Your mother is beautiful," Katya said. "I can tell she was a gymnast. So graceful." I was used to people commenting on my mother's looks. When I was growing up, my girlfriends had been captivated by her beauty. But what good was it when it hadn't been enough to keep my dad around? As I'd watched one husband after another leave her, I'd sworn that when I grew up, I wouldn't let men break my heart.

Ha, right.

"Oh, wow, where is that?" Katya asked, picking up a photo that Tyler had taken of me on top of Kilimanjaro. There had been a picture of the two of us at the summit in that frame just a few weeks ago.

"Seriously?" Katya said after I told her where it was. "Are you a climber?"

"More of a hiker really." I took the photo from her. "*Was* anyway. A gazillion years ago."

"Not anymore?"

I shrugged. "No time."

"Don't you get vacations?"

"Sure, but . . ." How could I tell her that I'd used up my vacations on IVF procedures: a few days for the retrieval surgeries, a few days to mourn a failed cycle or a miscarriage, and it all piled up. To make up for it, Tyler and I would rent a house in the Catskills for a long weekend or visit friends in the Hamptons. But in the past couple of years, we hadn't even done that. "Let's go," I said, putting the frame back in its place. "I don't have much time."

I took her to the staff cafeteria, where we both ordered lattes (decaf for me). "You drink lattes, too?" Katya said. "I love lattes." I nodded, trying to ignore the fact that it was my second one of the day. She insisted on paying to thank me for the tour, which made me feel guilty for not spending more time with her in the galleries. We sat in the back by the vending machines and were talking about the art she'd seen, my work, what she wanted to do after graduation—or rather, I'd just asked her about it—when out of the blue, Katya looked at me and said, "Come dancing with me on Saturday."

I laughed. "God, no."

"You never know. Maybe you'll meet someone."

"I can't possibly think about guys right now."

"Why not?" she said, thrusting her arms out, palms up, with flair. There was a breathless energy about her, an excitability that was contagious.

I tried to picture myself talking to a stranger in a bar, but all I could see was Tyler sitting on the stool across from me on our first proper date after we'd returned from Kilimanjaro, cradling my knees with his and peering into my eyes as he prodded me to tell him stories about my childhood, school, my job.

"Oh, c'mon." Katya tilted her head like a little girl asking for a doll. "We'll go to Mehanata."

"Where?"

"The Bulgarian place on Ludlow. Tell me you've been there."

I shook my head, took a sip of coffee.

"Then we absolutely have to go," she said. "C'mon. What else are you going to do on a Saturday evening? Stay home and mope over the man who left you for another woman? I'm not saying that you should jump into another relationship. Just have some fun. Before the baby comes. It's Mother's Day weekend, after all."

She was right. For the first time in years, I didn't have to feel wretched on that particular holiday, avoiding social media and the endless images of mothers with their babies. If all went according to plan, I'd be celebrating next year, too. I was touched and flattered that Katya wanted to hang out with me, even if I didn't understand it. We barely even knew each other. But that was Katya for you. She'd hugged me the other day on the street just because I was Bulgarian.

"You're sweet but I can't," I said. I wasn't even tempted. Ten years ago I'd have leapt at the opportunity to go dancing at some trendy Bulgarian club downtown. I used to be the girl who had to try everything. Climb every mountain.

"I'm not going to take *no* for an answer," Katya said.

"I really don't feel like—"

"Do it for me, then. See, the girls in school don't like me much and I . . ." She leaned closer over the table and touched my arm. "Please! I don't want to go alone."

How could I say no? If it weren't for Katya, I wouldn't be pregnant right now. I owed her that much and more.

9.
KATYA

Josh looked good today, like he'd made an effort. I wondered if he had a date. He was wearing a black T-shirt under a gray jacket and black jeans. It was a much better look for him than slacks and a shirt, and I told him so. He didn't exactly blush but he was clearly caught off guard. "Thanks," he said, and scrambled to get his pen and pad. "So how are you feeling today?"

I shrugged. Rain fell steadily outside, drumming on the windowsill. It was only the beginning of October but the weather had already turned cold and gray. Josh's eighth-floor office at the counseling center overlooked the campus, and from where I sat, I could see Hamilton Hall's green copper rooftop and a snippet of the dome atop Low Library.

"I've started running again," I finally said. "I was on the cross-country team back in high school." I watched him make a note of it on his pad. Or so I assumed. For all I knew, he was doodling. "I love the punishing physicality of it, feeling light-headed and gasping for air. My mind goes blank. It's an awesome feeling."

Josh nodded. Not once or twice but continuously, like those bobble heads on car dashboards. "Sounds like you enjoy running."

It used to drive me crazy when he'd point out the obvious. But I'd been seeing him for a few weeks now, long enough to figure out that it was his way of nudging me to continue. He would take what I'd said and wrap it up into a neat short sentence with a bow on top, then hand it back to me.

"It helps me sleep better," I said. "Some nights, anyway."

"You have trouble sleeping?"

I looked at my wet shoes; the gray suede at the toes had turned nearly black. I'd been avoiding going there but it was too late now. I'd opened the can of worms. "Being busy helps," I said. "Loading up on classes and activities fills up the hours. But there is no escape during the night. The nightmares find me anywhere."

He shifted on his chair and leaned closer. "Tell me about your nightmares."

"Memory is a funny thing," I said. "You can't trick it by simply changing your address."

"Do you dream about something that happened? Back home?"

I looked up at the Roman profile stain on the ceiling. After all this time, it had become familiar, like a good friend I met up with once a week. *I should give him a name*, I thought before turning back to Josh. He was looking at me intently, expectantly. But I wasn't ready to talk about my nightmares. "Are you on Tinder?" I asked instead.

He cocked an eyebrow—a question mark and a reproach all at once.

I was not supposed to ask him personal questions. Any questions really. I couldn't even ask what he thought I should do when I was at a crossroads. He was there to help me figure it out myself, not to make decisions for me. That was what he'd told me anyway back when I'd started seeing him. He wasn't a coach, he'd said. He was a mental-health counselor. When I'd pointed out that "to counsel" means to advise, he'd said that he counseled on people's emotions, not actions.

"What I mean is, you know how Tinder works, right?" I said. "Or should I explain?"

He smiled. Shook his head like a father displeased with his naughty but clever daughter. "No need to."

I suppressed my I-got-you grin. Not that I'd doubted that he would be on Tinder. Weren't all guys?

"I don't mind Tinder," I said. "It's better than hooking up at the drunken campus parties. But you need to have thick skin. Guys can be such assholes online. God forbid you turn them down. This girl in my dorm, Courtney, was in tears the other night over some moron's insults.

Nobody likes rejection but that's the whole point of the app—if you can't take it, don't sign up. Instead, the guy went mental after she made it clear she wasn't interested. 'You fat cow,' he messaged her, 'I wasn't even into you but thought a fat girl like you should be an easy fuck.' Can you believe it?"

Josh watched me with narrowed eyes, seemingly unmoved. I knew what he was thinking: *What the hell does Tinder have to do with what we were talking about?* I returned the stare. So what if I was stalling? He could call me on it if he wanted to.

"When I want to get laid, I go to a bar," I said, and went on to tell Josh about the hot guy I'd met the other night. I didn't mention the fake ID and he didn't ask. That's the beauty of shrinks. They can't tell you what to do, but they can't judge you, either. Josh was pissing me off today for some reason, so I told him about my night in detail. I took my time describing how awesome the guy was. Gray-blue eyes. Straight dark hair swept to the side. Shirt unbuttoned. No white T-shirt showing under it. I never understood why most American guys do that. "It's such a turn-off," I told Josh. "I like to unbutton the guy's shirt, working my way down as I kiss his neck, my lips moving lower with each button, tracing his chest, his abs, all the way to his zipper."

I paused to let the image sink in before I added, "I couldn't do that with a T-shirt, could I?"

Poor Josh. He averted his gaze but couldn't hide his embarrassment. He was picturing me doing it to him. That had been the whole point.

I ran my tongue over my upper lip and went on with the story.

I'd known the guy was going to be hot in bed just by looking at his hands, the way he held them confidently on his thighs as he leaned forward talking to me. Strong, knowing hands. I liked older guys. The boys on campus were such kids. And the girls, having to get smashed to have sex. What was the point if you weren't going to remember it the next day? That was why I preferred to get away from campus and the neighborhood bars. I went out on my own. I didn't get the whole gaggle-of-girls thing. Pretending to have a grand time, barely listening to what your girlfriends are saying because you're scanning the place, hoping some guy will come talk to you.

Not me. I would walk in, take a seat at the bar, and pick my guy. One drink, two max, then we'd go to his place. No games, no pretense, and, most important, no strings.

Josh was looking at me intently, his head tilted. "You're not worried about going to a stranger's house?" he asked. "I mean—"

"Oh, I know what you mean. I'm a girl. That worry is ingrained in my bones. But I have bigger fears." I saw Josh open his mouth to ask about it, and I rushed to stop him. "Don't you worry. I carry Mace just in case."

He frowned, clearly unimpressed, but I ignored him. "Anyway, guys are so funny," I said. "The look on their faces when I tell them that if they want us to hook up again that's great, but I'm not going to waste my time on dinners."

Josh stirred on his chair. "You find dinners a waste of time?"

"I can eat dinner with friends. Or while I'm studying. Why pretend? Let's just get straight to the point."

"You don't want to spend time with—"

"God, no! I don't believe in the whole romance bullshit. Love is an elaborate excuse to have sex."

He chuckled. "How come?"

I shrugged. "Sexual desire is considered too base or something. Especially for a woman. But if you are in love, oh well, then you can—"

"What I mean is," he said, interrupting me, "how come you don't believe in romance?"

"It's like asking me how come I don't believe in illness. No, thanks. I don't want my heart broken."

"Falling in love means getting your heart broken?"

"There is no 'happily ever after.' I haven't seen it anyway. Have you?"

He scribbled in his pad, then looked up at me. "Tell me more."

I hated it when he did that. Sometimes, there just wasn't anything more to say. I told him so, but he gave me one of those eyebrows-raised looks as if to say: *This is not one of those times and I'm not that stupid, so go on and tell me more about it.*

I smiled. I liked men who didn't let me get away with shit. Josh got extra points for being subtle about it. And playful.

"Take my parents," I said. "My mother broke my father's heart. *Literally.* He died of a heart attack at thirty-eight. Thirty-eight. I was five. By the time I turned six, my mother had remarried and had another child with her new husband. You do the math," I said, the familiar anger rising up in my throat.

"I didn't know you have a half . . . sister or brother?"

I stared at Josh as it hit me that I'd let out more than I'd wanted to. *"Had,"* I said quietly. "Alex, my baby brother, died when he was three."

Josh bit his lip. "I'm sorry."

"The point is," I went on before he could ask more about Alex, "my mother had been cheating on my dad for months. I didn't know better back then. I thought it was my fault. My father's heart attack, I mean. I thought I'd upset him because I hadn't been good or something. I always got in trouble for breaking things, getting my shirt dirty, sneaking an extra cookie—you know, kid stuff. My mother made a point of telling him all the trouble I'd gotten into each day when he got home from work. He would laugh in response and pick me up and whisper in my ear not to worry, that I was Daddy's girl no matter what."

I put my face in my hands, my elbows pressing against my knees. "Sure, he had a heart condition," I continued after a while. "My mother told me all about it. But what a coincidence, right? He finds out his wife's cheating on him and, bam, his heart condition kicks in that very evening." Josh opened his mouth to ask a question, but I raised my hand to stop him. "Years later, my aunt told me that my father had actually caught them together that day."

I closed my eyes and leaned back against the couch. "So there you have it. And it's not just my parents. I see it all around me on campus. People hurting each other. It's endless. No, thank you. Not for me."

◈

I barely recognized him when he walked out, the hood of his jacket pulled low over his face. He headed across campus toward the Broadway exit, looking at his feet as he went around the puddles, keeping a brisk pace. The rain had stopped but strong cold winds whipped through the branches of the trees. I stepped out of the building's shadow. "Josh."

He stopped and turned. "Katya?" His expression went from surprise to excitement, but he quickly collected himself and put on a concerned face. "What are you doing here?"

"I need to talk to you."

He cocked his head. "Has anything happened since I saw you?" I'd been his second-to-last patient.

"Not exactly."

"What's the matter, then?"

I smiled and pulled up the collar of my jacket. "How about we grab a drink? It's really cold out here."

In the yellow glow of the campus lights, I could see the temptation that washed over his face. He shook his head but he couldn't hide the struggle. It came through in his voice when he finally said, "You know the rules." It was as if he were speaking to himself.

I batted my eyelashes exaggeratedly. "Please. Just this time."

He shook his head again. His lips were pursed with the effort. "If you need to talk," he said, "come in tomorrow during office hours."

"But this can't wait until tomorrow." I considered touching his arm but worried it was only going to scare him off. "I'm feeling like shit," I said. "We ended at the wrong place today. Our conversation only made me feel worse."

I saw the distress in his eyes and pressed on. "I haven't slept for days, Josh. I can't spend another night . . ." I let my voice trail off as I looked at him, teary-eyed.

He was nodding, thinking, the concern loud on his face.

I bit my lip. "I don't know what I might do . . ."

"In that case," he said, and held out his phone, "I'll call the emergency room."

"Oh, no, no." I pulled back. "I don't want to go anywhere. I want to talk to *you*."

"You leave me no choice." The phone lit up in his hand as he unlocked it and started punching in numbers. "I have to report any cases—"

"You don't understand!" My voice rose with alarm as I realized I'd taken this bluff too far. "I just meant . . . It's my last year and I'm starting to panic that I have to return to Bulgaria. The thought of facing my mother—"

"I'm sorry to hear that, Katya, but we can talk about it at length tomorrow in my office. Good night." And he walked off. Just like that, he walked off on me. The bastard.

I stood there, in the middle of the walkway, glaring at his back until he vanished around the corner. Students hurried past me on their way to the library or the dorms, huddled in jackets and hoodies. The wind blew my hair. My hands and ears felt raw with cold, but I was too pissed to care.

I was the wrong girl to turn down. Josh would pay for it. Sooner or later.

10.

LANA

NOW

We met at a tiny restaurant on the Lower East Side not far from the club. The place was loud and crowded and served weird paleo fare, including a bone marrow dish that Katya ordered. To my horror, it was served on the bone. She insisted that I try it, scooping up some of the slimy stuff in her spoon. I gagged just looking at it, which she found hysterical. Katya seemed to be in a great mood, prattling about Bulgarian food and music—the two things she apparently missed from home. But I felt uneasy. I picked through my roasted chicken over a bed of spinach, thinking: *What the hell am I doing?*

"Before we go," Katya said at the end of the meal, "let's come up with fake names and jobs."

"What?"

"Just in case someone decides to stalk us." She gave me a sideways look.

I gripped the table. Could she know who I was?

Katya must have seen my discomfort, because she laughed and said: "Don't worry. Nobody is going to stalk us. I'm just kidding. But don't you hate it when people ask you all the time what you do? It's like a part of greeting someone. *Hi, I'm So-and-So. What d'you do?*"

I shrugged. The only parties I'd been to in the last few years were with Tyler's or my colleagues, hardly ever any new faces to ask that question.

"Sure," I said. "I'll be Natalia, then. It's my mother's name, easy to remember. And I'll be a teacher."

"Boring." Katya looked at me, eyebrows pulling together. "Think of something absurd. That's the whole point. To rub in how stupid the damn question is. I love saying that I'm a gold digger."

"A gold digger? How's that a job?"

"Exactly. People totally freak out. Men eventually get it and start laughing. 'Funny one,' they say. Women tend to get angry with me. They feel threatened or something." Katya smiled at me. "That's why I like you. Maybe because you're Bulgarian—okay, your mother is—but I don't get that catty vibe from you."

I could see how women her age would hate her. Between her looks and her blunt manner, they must find her insufferable.

"So if I'm Irina, the gold digger," Katya said, playing with the pen she'd used to sign her credit card slip, "you're Natalia, the . . . ?"

I tried to think but my brain was still trying to catch up with the exercise.

"C'mon. The most absurd thing that pops into your head."

I looked out the window and my eyes focused on the tall glass-façade building punctuating the skyline to the west. "How about a window cleaner? You know, the ones who rappel outside skyscrapers?"

"Perfect," she said, and put the pen down. "You can add that you have a fear of heights. But you avoid looking down."

We laughed. I hadn't laughed like that in years.

❖

Walking around the Lower East Side with Katya made me feel as if I were the foreigner and she the local. I hadn't been to this part of town in a couple of years and had missed the transformation it had undergone. Trendy clubs, bars, and restaurants lined the small streets packed with young people. New residential buildings had sprouted everywhere, replacing the old walk-ups. I wondered if most people over thirty-five eventually stopped going out and retreated into their small worlds or if it was just me, caught in the whirlwind of infertility.

You wouldn't have known there was a club behind the red metal door if it weren't for the line of people waiting to enter. Inside, the action was spread over two floors. Upstairs, people danced to a Gypsy-punk band that Katya told me was Bulgarian. Downstairs, there was a DJ. The most popular attraction was the ice chamber where people donned what looked like Soviet uniforms to get smashed on vodka shots. Or maybe the outfits were Bulgarian. I'd only been to the country once. My mother had taken me there soon after the fall of Communism. The streets looked grim; the buildings, gravely dilapidated; the people, miserable. But in Sofia's pubs and bars, people drank and danced like they had not a worry in the world. I felt the same exuberant vibe in Mehanata. The only thing missing was the thick cloud of cigarette smoke.

Mehanata was clearly popular with the cool crowd. Unsure what anyone wore these days to clubs, I had put my jeans aside in favor of black slacks and a gray-blue sleeveless silk shirt. But next to all these girls decked out in short, sparkly dresses, I felt dull and ugly. I fought the urge to bolt. What was I thinking going clubbing with Katya? I didn't belong in this trendy place full of beautiful young people.

Katya managed to look glamorous in a plain red spaghetti-strap top and skinny jeans. It was something about the way she carried herself, the way she walked with her back straight, her eyes—green and sparkling—sweeping the room like she owned it. And she did. I watched the other girls give her dirty looks and, for the first time, appreciated my age. It was much easier to have fun when you weren't competing for the attention of men. My ego didn't take a hit when the young men who joined us ignored me, focusing entirely on Katya. I could pull back and watch, even laugh at, the mating game that unfolded, like an anthropologist witnessing the interactions of an exotic species.

From what I could tell, dancing these days consisted of jumping or endless grinding, hips locked onto hips. Just in case it wasn't sexual enough, there were three dance poles downstairs and women weren't shy about using them. The music blasted, so any meaningful conversation was out of the question. The swings at the bar upstairs—simple wooden planks hanging on ropes from the ceiling—were my favorite feature. Katya and I managed to claim one and she snapped a selfie of us. The swings apparently weren't the only creative design element in the place. According to Katya, the urinals in the men's room were made of red ceramic and looked like open mouths. The sink was a matching red statue of a naked woman bending down with the bowl sitting on top of her lower back so that you had to stand behind her to wash your hands. I wondered how Katya knew what was in the men's room but had no chance to ask her because a group of three guys approached us and asked what we would like to drink. I didn't see Katya alone again for the rest of the night.

We tried our fake names and jobs on two guys from New Jersey. They laughed heartily while Katya and I exchanged conspiratorial looks. "Are you sisters?" one of them asked. It was the greatest compliment I'd ever received. Before I could shake my head, Katya said, "Yes, of course," and winked at me. She went on to explain that I'd lost my accent because I'd been in the country five years longer than her.

I couldn't believe how much fun I was having with a girl who was seventeen years my junior. I barely knew her, but I felt an almost familial affection for her. The sister I'd always wanted. According to her records, Katya was also an only child. It occurred to me that it might be great to have her in our lives (I was already thinking in plural about my baby and me). I pictured pushing the stroller with Katya by my side, chatting while the baby slept.

While I'd been with Tyler, I hadn't wanted anyone encroaching on us. Having a donor who knew us felt threatening, a third wheel wedged into a perfect union. But things had changed. My baby and I would be a family of two. No uncles and aunts, no cousins. A grandmother all the way in Chicago. I would be a single mom without much of a support network other than Angie and a few of the other women from Group. Katya could be the cool auntie. Why not? I'd read somewhere of a woman who, years ago, had had a baby from a sperm donor. At twenty-two, her son decided to find his biological father. It turned out the guy had a wife but no children, and the two families became close, getting together regularly on holidays. I'd thought it was absurd when I'd first heard of it, but I was beginning to see the appeal.

Katya started dancing with an imposing dark-haired guy in a suit who looked like he'd come straight from the office. He couldn't quite move in time with the music, but that didn't seem to bother him, judging by the confident eyes he trained on Katya. I stayed at the bar, watching them, wondering how soon was too soon to make my escape. A tan young man with close-cropped hair and a lazy smile caught my attention and started making his way toward me. I suspected he was going to ask me about Katya, but he didn't seem interested in talking. He began dancing in front of me, his face only inches from mine. To my surprise I smiled back, my body responding to his charm before my brain could process it. He grabbed me by the waist and pulled me in. I put my glass of club soda on the bar, among the flickering candles, and hesitantly started moving my hips along with his. I hadn't danced in years and was amazed at how easily—eagerly, even—my body responded to the music's throbbing rhythm and his touch. The place was so packed, my back was rubbing against the bar as we danced. He was strong and taut and sure of himself. I couldn't even remember the last time I'd danced with someone other than Tyler. Why on earth was I thinking of Tyler right now?

I chased his image away and focused on the guy in front of me. His hand at the back of my waist kept moving lower until it rested on my ass. He pulled me closer and I felt his erection against my pelvis. Before I had time to be shocked, he leaned forward and started kissing me. His tongue felt warm and huge in my mouth and I arched my back with unexpected pleasure. Still holding my ass with one hand, he slid his fingers down my jeans into my panties with the other. The world around me vanished. All that existed was his tongue in my mouth and his hand in my underwear.

Slowly, as if through a fog, I became aware of the smell of burnt flesh. "Your hair!" a woman next to me screamed, and started patting my head with her hands. I jolted forward, shoving the guy off and pull-ing my hair away from the candle. Luckily, the woman had already killed the flame. I mumbled, "Thank you," without looking at her or the people around us. My cheeks were burning with embarrassment. I glanced at Katya in the middle of the dance floor, but she was busy kissing her partner and didn't seem to have seen anything. I pulled my hair over my shoulder and smoothed out the burnt ends.

"You okay?" my dance partner asked. I didn't bother answering.

What was I thinking? I was pregnant. I had no business going to a nightclub, dancing and kissing a stranger, let alone letting him prowl around in my panties. I should be home, relaxing, curled up on the couch with a book or watching a show. The baby growing inside me needed me in top shape.

"I have to go," I said, and started to make my way through the crowd toward Katya.

He grabbed me by the arm. "Where are you going, beautiful?"

I pulled away. When I looked back a few steps later, he was already dancing with another woman.

Katya and her partner had stopped kissing. He was strikingly hand-some from up close—angular face, olive skin, and caramel eyes that shone like a panther's in the pulsing light. The two of them made quite the couple, even if he was closer to my age than hers. Older men seemed to be her type. I tugged on her arm and she turned.

"I'm leaving," I shouted over the music.

"No, wait." She put her hand on my shoulder. "You can't leave now."

"I have to. Sorry."

"But the fun is just about to begin. Natalia and Irina have more hearts to break!"

"I have a feeling Irina can break enough on her own," I said, frus-tration rising in my chest. I had to get out of there and I didn't want to have to argue about it. She was clearly having plenty of fun with this guy. What was it to her if I went home?

I gave her a hug and rushed out before she could stop me.

◈

It was past midnight when I finally made it home. I had already taken a shower and was brushing my teeth when my phone beeped. I rinsed my mouth and looked at it. It was a text message from Katya—*Hey sis ;)*—along with our selfie on the swing. I stared at the two of us, side by side, thinking: *What if my child likes her more? Kids love the cool aunt.*

Except, in our case, Katya would be the cool mom. The real mom.

◈

Four hours later, I woke up with sharp cramps in my belly and my pajama bottoms sticky-wet with what I realized in horror was blood.

11.

TYLER

I told Rachel about Lana's quest for a Bulgarian donor. It was a cold mid-December day before the holidays. We were having our last meeting for the semester in what had become our preferred spot—the Hungarian Pastry Shop on Amsterdam. I was late, coming straight from a lecture, and had taken the few blocks at a quick pace. I wiped the sweat off my forehead and walked in. A Columbia institution among professors and students, the coffee shop was teeming with people reading books and newspapers, typing on laptops or writing in notebooks. That was why I liked the place. There was no music, no couches, no Wi-Fi. No healthy treats, only decadent pastries and desserts. Like my favorite syrup-drenched baklava.

I spotted Rachel at a table in the back, legs crossed, eyes fixed on the door, a cup of coffee in front of her. She looked pretty. More so than usual. Maybe it was the bright lipstick. Or the way she'd pulled her hair back, revealing the elegant line of her neck.

"Sorry, they wouldn't let me go," I said, and draped my coat on the back of my chair before sitting down.

Rachel laughed. "They adore you!" She'd been my TA in a couple of classes last year.

"It's my fault." I made a self-deprecating face. "You know I'm a sucker for questions."

I loved teaching. Some of my colleagues would rather focus on their own work, doing research, writing and publishing. Many of the assistant professors complained about being given lower-level intro classes. But I found those big Introduction to Philosophy lectures a thrill. Delving into questions like: *What is consciousness? Can machines think? How do you know you're not living in a matrix?* There was nothing more rewarding than seeing enthusiasm on my students' faces, especially those who'd never been exposed to philosophy, or even better—those who thought they didn't give a damn about it. Until I asked them, "If you had the option, would you choose immortality?" The debates following this particular question got so heated that I often had to forgo the rest of the material I'd prepared for the day. But if all that my students took away at the end of the semester was to question things, particularly things we took for granted, I was happy.

"Makes sense," Rachel said when I told her that Lana wanted a Bulgarian donor. "Our roots are important. They keep us grounded." I could tell she was thinking of her mom.

"The problem is," I told her, "there aren't any Bulgarian girls. We checked all the agencies—here in the area and in states as far away as California."

Rachel nodded thoughtfully. She took a sip of her coffee, leaving a bright red smear on the porcelain. "Wait," she said, and I shifted my eyes from her cup to her face. "Why don't you put up a flyer on campus? I remember seeing some as an undergrad at Princeton. You know, Ivy League genes are in high demand." She wrinkled her nose, and I laughed as she continued. "There must be a few Bulgarians among the foreign students here."

I nearly ran back home, pumped with excitement to tell Lana my brilliant idea. I knew better than to mention that it was Rachel's. I'd have to explain who Rachel was and answer why the hell I was sharing personal information with one of my grad students. And that was a fight I wasn't prepared to have.

What mattered was that Lana was crestfallen about not being able to find a Bulgarian donor and I had found a possible solution.

◈

On Group nights, Lana usually didn't come home until eight thirty, sometimes even nine. I used the time to answer student e-mails and catch up on my reading. Tonight, I couldn't concentrate, anxious to tell Lana about the flyer idea. I barely skimmed an article that pertained to my book on the metaphysics of coincidence before giving up on working altogether.

I made a chicken stew for dinner instead of one of the quick pasta dishes I threw together when it was my turn to cook. I even spoke to my sister, whom I'd owed a call for weeks. In the time Lana and I had been trying for a baby, Sam and her husband had managed to meet, get married, and have two beautiful girls. Lana adored them. Having children had always been a bit of an abstract proposition for me, but every time I watched Lana play with my nieces, I felt a crushing desire to make that happen for her. For us.

When I finally heard Lana's keys in the lock, I rushed to meet her at the door with a glass of wine. It had started to snow outside, and I brushed the flakes off her hair, took her wet coat. I'd keyed Buena Vista Social Club on the stereo and had even remembered to light some candles. *"Dos gardenias para ti,"* I sang along as I raised my empty hand pretending to be bestowing her flowers. That was, more or less, the extent of my Spanish.

She laughed. "What's the occasion?" she asked, and took a sip. I waited for her to kick her boots off before leading her to the living room.

"First things first. Sam invited us to dinner on Saturday. She doesn't want to hear how much work we both have."

"Great." Lana plopped herself on the couch and I sat beside her. "But that's not what prompted . . ." She made a sweeping gesture to the candles and wine and looked at me expectantly.

I couldn't hold it any longer. "I have an idea," I said, grinning like a little boy.

"Not another attempt to entice me into going on vacation, I hope." She raised her eyebrows, a smile tugging at the corners of her mouth.

"Better. About how to find a Bulgarian donor."

She straightened her back. "How?"

"There are no guarantees, but at least it might increase our chances."

She shifted on her seat, twisting toward me as I continued. "I was thinking, there have to be some Bulgarian students on campus. Maybe if we put up a bunch of flyers advertising that we're looking for—"

"No way," she said, shaking her head. Her smile faded. "We want an anonymous donor. Remember? We already discussed it."

"I know we did." I took a deep breath, trying not to let the frustration at her talking to me as if I were a moron get to me. "But since there are no Bulgarian girls at any of the agencies, I thought it might be a—"

"I'm sorry, Tyler, but I don't want some woman knocking on our door in five years, coming to mess with our child's head."

I wanted to scream that she was being paranoid. That it might actually be good to know the donor anyway, should our child face any medical problems one day. And, finally, that we should be making decisions together.

"Your call," I said instead, and stood up, too deflated to bother fighting about it.

❖

When Rachel asked about the flyer a few days after our conversation, I felt embarrassed to tell her that Lana had shot down the idea. How could I explain it? Lana had reacted as if I'd suggested something preposterous, like, *Let's go steal ourselves a baby*. I would have questioned my own judgment if it weren't for Rachel. That's the problem with sharing relationship stuff with a third person. It's no longer a fair game. In Rachel, I'd found an ally. Someone who proved me right every time Lana and I had a disagreement. Not because Rachel took my side, but because that was the only side she knew.

I told Rachel that I'd appreciate her help with making the flyer as I wasn't even sure what it should say. Three days later, on a bright but freezing afternoon just before the end of the semester, the two of us went around campus putting up pink, yellow, and purple flyers that read: *Loving couple seeking egg donor from Bulgaria*.

I didn't worry that Lana might see one of them. The chances of her walking on campus were close to nil. I felt bad about going behind her back. Of course I did. But I was doing it for her.

What's the worst that can happen? I thought as I pinned a pink sheet to the cafeteria bulletin board.

12.

LANA

The waiting room wasn't as crowded on a Sunday morning as it was during the week. Still, there were at least a half-dozen women ahead of me, their faces betraying anguish and struggle, particularly acute on Mother's Day. Fertility clinics didn't fully close on weekends and holidays. Patients doing IVF needed to be monitored closely, their hormone levels checked daily. They also needed regular ultrasounds to measure the size of the follicles and determine the best time to retrieve the eggs.

I checked in with the girl at reception and sat down to wait my turn with a copy of *People*. The fact that I was bleeding didn't constitute an emergency. If I'd miscarried there was nothing to be done about it. I'd been down this road too many times. I knew the drill.

I hadn't even opened the magazine before I was assaulted with the photos of three pregnant celebrities, two of them older than me. Having babies seemed to be the newest fad—from teenagers to women in their forties, everyone was flaunting their baby bumps. I didn't remember people obsessing over babies nearly as much in the nineties; or maybe babies hadn't been on my radar back then. I'd spent my late teens and early twenties terrified that I'd get pregnant. I hadn't even thought of my biological clock until Tyler and I had started trying for a baby and failed to get a positive on the pee stick for a whole year.

I picked up the *New Yorker* instead but ended up leafing through the pages, unable to concentrate enough to read even the cartoons.

It was over. I'd blown it.

It had to be the dancing last night. How could I have been so stupid? Dr. Williams had told me no exercise. Or at least nothing that got my heart rate over 140. I'd been so intoxicated at meeting my egg donor that I'd dropped everything else. I'd stalked the girl and then befriended her. And here I was, paying the price. Tears welled up in my eyes and I pulled a tissue out. I couldn't start crying, not in front of all these women. The clinic's waiting room was much bigger and plainer than the pre-op's. Hardly any guys came with their partners for regular checkups. If I saw a couple I could bet they were here for a consultation, pre- or postcycle.

I checked my phone. I'd texted Katya at four in the morning that I was bleeding and was terrified I'd miscarried. As irrational as it might seem, part of me thought that her good wishes might bring me luck since she was the genetic mother of the baby. When you're desperate, you'll believe in anything. During my long and grueling battle with infertility, I'd prayed to all sorts of gods and deities, tried numerous diets, done acupuncture, yoga, and meditation. I'd even worn orange for days in a row to stimulate the damn fertility chakra.

There was no word from Katya yet. Most likely, she was still asleep after a long night out. She'd sent me another text about twenty minutes after the selfie: *OMG. This guy has a jacuzzi on his rooftop terrace!* For all I knew, she was still in the Jacuzzi.

I shouldn't have followed her out of the subway. I shouldn't have continued to hang out with her. It was wrong and this was my punishment. I dabbed my eyes with the tissue. It hadn't been fair to her because she'd had no idea who I was. But maybe it wasn't too late to make it right. Maybe I still had a chance. And so, sitting in the clinic's waiting room, surrounded by a dozen or so women, I made one of those desperate pleas with God, promising that as long as my baby was okay, I would tell Katya the truth.

Finally, my turn came. My least favorite nurse, Kim, called me up. She never smiled, never greeted me, never asked how I was doing.

"Is Dr. Williams here?" I asked as I followed her down the corridor.

"Nope," she said without as much as a look in my direction. She opened the door to the examination room, pulled my file up on the computer screen, and squirted some gel onto the ultrasound wand. "You know what to do," she said, and shut the door behind her.

I undressed from the waist down. The bleeding appeared to have slowed, just a bit of spotting on the pad I'd put on before leaving for the clinic. I sat on the exam table and fit my feet into the stirrups, draping the sheet over my lap and legs. The room was cold, as usual, and I wrapped my arms around my chest to keep warm. Finally, there was a knock on the door, and one of the clinic's fellows, Dr. Bouchard, walked in, followed by Kim. He'd done my ultrasound on a couple of occasions during the monitoring stage of the cycle. A perfectly nice guy in his early thirties, if a bit formal.

"Hi, Lana," he said with a blank face. "How are you?"

I was disappointed at being seen by a fellow. Still, it was better than a resident or no doctor at all. With a shaky voice, I told him about the bleeding and cramping in the middle of the night. I didn't say anything about having gone dancing.

He slipped a pair of gloves on and sat on the little stool in front of me. "Let's see what's going on."

I held my breath and stared at the screen as he inserted the wand. Kim stood next to him waiting, her face portraying profound boredom.

Dr. Bouchard adjusted the wand a few times, pressing against my uterus. A dark blob the size of a plum appeared on the screen.

"It's looking good," he said.

I exhaled slowly.

"This is the sac." He pointed to the blob. "And we can even see the fetal pole." There was a little light dot to one side of the blob. "It's too early to see the heartbeat, but everything is looking good. Measuring right on schedule."

"Why am I bleeding, then?"

"You see that little black spot, to the right of the sac?" he said. "It's a little hemorrhage. It's called a subchorionic hemorrhage or hematoma. It happens sometimes. Most likely, it will either bleed out or be absorbed by your body. The good news is that it's small and it's not close to the fetus. You might have another bleed or two. But don't worry." He pulled the wand out and took off his gloves.

I sat up, my muscles still tight, my mind trying to process the news that I hadn't miscarried again.

He noted something in my chart and turned to me. "Don't you worry, everything looks good. Next week, we should be able to see the heartbeat." He stood up. "Go home and relax. Put your feet up and take it easy for the rest of the day." He walked out, followed by the nurse.

My legs were shaking when I got up. The aftereffects of a fear-induced adrenaline rush. I sat right back down and took a few slow, deliberate breaths. My baby was okay. I breathed in and out, allowing the thought to sink in. I hadn't miscarried.

I was too scared to rejoice. I wasn't out of the woods yet. But right now, at this very moment, it looked good. Relief spread through my body in warm waves.

❖

Back home, Plato greeted me at the door. He'd become needier since Tyler left. We'd gotten him from the ASPCA as a kitten, a few months before we'd decided to stop using birth control. He'd been our test baby, our first commitment as a couple. It was just Plato and me now. I scooped him up and held him close, his warmth soothing against my cheek. "Don't you worry, buddy," I said. "The doctor says everything's okay."

I fed him, then lay on the couch with my legs propped on a pillow, opened my MacBook Air, and googled *subchorionic hemorrhage*. The consensus seemed to be that only up to three percent of women who had this condition miscarried. But I'd been on the wrong side of the odds too many times to take comfort in it.

I closed the laptop and picked up my phone. It was past noon but there was still no text from Katya. I decided to call her and invite her to dinner. A loud, crowded restaurant was the last place I'd want to tell her the truth. I could make my pasta carbonara, and then—at the end of the meal—explain who I was. This way, she could yell at me or storm out, or both. Of course, I hoped that she'd hug me and tell me how happy she was to meet me. But I knew how unlikely that was. What if she didn't want to know the woman she'd donated her eggs to? What if she hadn't wanted to donate to a single mother? She'd signed up to help an infertile couple.

I dialed her number. As the phone rang, I thought that I couldn't worry about her reaction. I had to tell her—end of story. But Katya didn't pick up and I left a voice mail asking her to call me back. While I waited, I signed in to Fertile Thoughts—an online forum I'd been a member of for years. I'd posted regularly there before I'd joined the Upper West Side support group. These days, I only logged on when I had a problem. In the thread devoted to donor egg cycles, I wrote an update about my bleed scare. Within minutes, other members wrote back, reassuring me that everything would be okay. Some had had experience with SCH, as they referred to it; others simply wanted to send me their positive thoughts and vibes. It was comforting to connect with other women in the country—and around the world—who were going through the same thing.

I phoned Angie next. I didn't mention anything about Katya or going dancing the night before. If I was to come clean about what a fool I was, I'd better do it in person. Angie was on a deadline but, hearing about my bleeding, offered right away to come over. It took me a while to reassure her I didn't need any help. But as soon as I put the phone down, I felt strangely alone in the apartment. Even Plato was gone, sleeping somewhere out of sight. There was a stillness, a heavy fog that enshrouded me. The silence only magnified the loud chatter in my head.

I opened the piano—a Schiller upright my mother had given me when I'd moved to New York—and began playing a Bach sonata in an attempt to quiet my mind. My hands moved seamlessly, as if of their own accord. Playing was meditative for me. It was the only steady thread in my life. It felt like returning home, traveling back to my childhood when the days were sunnier, the jokes funnier, and mastering the skill to play a simple piece of music was intoxicating. Until my mother's ambitions had kicked in and spoiled it. I glanced reproachfully at her portrait among the photos on top of the piano and continued playing.

I was on the third movement when my phone rang on the bookshelf next to me. *Finally*, I thought, and reached for it. But it was Tyler's sister. I hesitated. Sam and I had always liked each other. So much so that Tyler often joked that if it weren't for me, they would hardly see each other. I picked up.

"I don't know what's going on between you and Tyler," Sam began, "but I hope that the two of us can still—"

"I sure hope so," I said, relieved she wasn't calling to advocate on his behalf. I wouldn't have expected it from her, but you never know. As my mother loved to say, *Blood doesn't turn into water.*

"I don't want to put you in an uncomfortable position," Sam continued, "and I don't want to meddle . . . Why don't we just say we don't mention my brother, okay?"

I laughed. "Thank you. That might be best."

"I've missed you. And so have the girls. They keep asking about Auntie Lana." Just picturing their adorable little faces made me smile. "You want to come over for lunch next Sunday?"

"Don't you have the book club in the morning?"

She sighed. "Not going this week. Steve's away and our babysitter can't make it."

"Why don't I look after them and you go? We can have lunch ready by the time you come back."

She hesitated. "I'm sure you have things to do."

"Don't be silly. You know I'd drop anything to spend time with those two angels."

After we ended the call, I resumed playing. The prospect of seeing Sam and the girls in a week loosened the tight knot in my belly.

Five minutes later, the phone rang again. I grabbed it, sure that this time it was Katya. Instead, Tyler's name flashed on the screen. The man I was supposed to grow old with. The man whose child I was carrying in my womb. I had tried to push him out of my mind, but it was proving harder than I'd thought. Especially on a day like this, when more than anything I craved snuggling in his arms, having him whisper in my ear that everything would be okay. I didn't have to believe it. I just needed to hear his soft reassuring voice that made all my fears go away.

The call went to voice mail after the fifth ring and I put the phone back on the shelf next to me, strangely disappointed. I needed more time to decide whether I wanted to speak with him.

He had left me. What more was there to say? Unless he'd somehow learned about the pregnancy. Only Angie and Katya knew so far. But I wouldn't be able to hide it much longer. If I was lucky and all went according to plan, I'd start showing soon. Tyler would find out one way or another. People talk. Someone would mention something: *I ran into Lana the other day. So happy to see her finally pregnant.* Would Tyler put two and two together? Could he force me to terminate the pregnancy when he finally found out?

The phone rang again and I snatched it off the shelf. Tyler. I was tempted. I didn't have to mention the pregnancy, the bleeding, or my fears about it. My finger hovered over the Talk button before I finally pressed it. "What do you want, Tyler?"

"Oh, hi . . . I didn't expect you to pick up," he said, sounding confused and uncertain.

The familiarity of his voice gutted me. I squeezed my eyes shut till it hurt. "What's up?"

"Just making sure you're okay."

I opened my eyes. "Why wouldn't I be okay?"

"I don't know . . . It's been nearly a month since we . . ."

"Since *you* left me, you mean?"

I could hear him swallow on the other end. "I just miss you and wanted to—"

"You don't expect me to comfort you, do you?"

"Even I know better than that," he said, deadpan, and I chuckled despite myself. Tyler was a brilliant scholar but he could be clueless about basic social norms and interactions. I used to love teasing him that he was the stereotypical philosophy professor, sauntering through life with his head in the clouds. "No," he continued. "I was just wondering how you're doing."

I almost fell for it. His soft, guttural intonation, his concern about how I was. As if he'd simply gone away for a few days, to a conference out of town, and was calling to say hi and check in on me. Then his packed duffle bag flashed in front of my eyes, his stony expression when he'd walked out on me.

"Believe it or not," I said, snapping out of my brief nostalgia, "I'm doing just fine. You can go ahead and enjoy your new life guilt-free." I hung up. *And your new girl*, I mentally added. There had to be a new girl. He wouldn't just leave like that. He was a good man. I'd never thought of him as the bachelor type, the guy who liked to keep his options open. If anything, Tyler was more into nesting than I ever was. He'd asked me to marry him three times despite knowing my feelings about marriage.

I'd replayed the scene of his departure on Good Friday over and over in my mind. There was so much I wished I had said to him that night. Questions I'd asked. But I'd been so unprepared, I'd frozen.

I still had a hard time believing he'd left me in the middle of our donor egg cycle. We'd had a good relationship. Maybe not perfect but good enough.

I buried my face in my hands, the pain of losing Tyler hitting me with full force all these weeks later.

Before I went to bed in the evening, I checked my phone again in case I hadn't heard it ring. It was 11:00 p.m. Still not a peep from Katya.

13.

TYLER

I was in the grocery store when she called. It was the second week of January; the neighborhood seemed deserted with most students gone for the break. Snow had started falling an hour ago, big fat flakes swirling in the halos of streetlamps and car lights. One of those mega storms that threatened to shut New York down at least once every winter. More than a foot of accumulation by morning, disruption of the subways, people unable to show up at work. Having lived in the city for more than ten years, I knew that most of these blizzards never fully materialized. Still, I decided to get some provisions on my way home from the university. Just to play it safe. I wasn't the only one. The tiny aisles of the store, which couldn't have been much bigger than our apartment, were packed with people, bundled up in puffer coats and hats. It was hard to pass through.

I was reaching for Plato's favorite Crave Salmon Paté when I felt the phone buzz in my pocket. I was tempted to ignore it, but it occurred to me that Lana might need me to buy her something and I sure didn't feel like going out again on a night like this. I didn't recognize the number, but I'd already gone through the trouble of unzipping my coat and pulling the phone out, so I answered it.

"Hi, my name is Katya and I'm calling about the donor ad," said a woman on the other end.

I nearly dropped the phone. It had been a month already and I'd given up hope of anyone responding.

"Oh, hi," I said, and looked around guiltily, scanning the place for familiar faces. "Hold on a moment, let me go someplace quiet." I abandoned my basket on the floor by some crates of oranges and headed straight for the door. "There, that's better. Can you hear me?" I said as I walked outside. Traffic was light on Broadway. People had heeded the advice not to drive into the city today.

"Yes, I hear you great." Her voice was clear. Youthful. Full of excitement. Her accent barely noticeable.

"So you're Bulgarian?"

"Yes, I am."

"And you're interested in becoming an egg donor?" I zipped up my coat, brushed the snow off my hair with my free hand.

She giggled. "That's why I'm calling."

"Wonderful. What did you say your name was?"

"Katya."

Pretty name, I thought as my eyes followed a white fluffy dog in a red coat and matching boots scampering past me, pulling hard on its leash. "Katya, why don't we meet in person and discuss the details? I'm sure you'd like to know about the money and what being an egg donor involves, et cetera."

"That would be great." She hesitated for a moment before continuing, "I'm quite curious—why exactly do you want a Bulgarian donor?"

I laughed, kicking some snow with my foot. "Yeah, well. The thing is, my partner's Bulgarian and would like the baby to have the same genes," I said, leaving out the fact that it was her mother actually who was Bulgarian.

Katya seemed to like that and said she was really excited about helping us out. We arranged to meet the next day at the Hungarian Pastry Shop. My suggestion. After all, that was where the idea to look for a donor on campus was born.

"I'll see you tomorrow, *Tyler*," she said, pronouncing my name slowly, with care, as if it were a new flavor of ice cream she was trying.

I put the phone in my pocket, feeling like a kid who'd just been told he's going to Disneyland. I was dying to call Lana and tell her the good news. But I knew she'd be pissed I'd gone behind her back, ignoring her wishes. I couldn't risk Lana turning down this girl. Who knew how long it would take to find another? Instead, I phoned Rachel, who was in St. Paul for the break.

"I got a call!" I nearly pumped my fist in excitement. "Her name's Katya and I'll meet her tomorrow."

"Great," Rachel said. "How are you going to tell Lana about it?" I'd eventually shared with her Lana's reaction to the flyer idea.

I shook the snow off my boots, kicking first one heel and then the other against the curb.

"I won't," I said, and with a smile on my face, I walked back into the store to collect my groceries.

14.

LANA

"It's been a week already."

"She could be studying for finals," Angie said.

We were walking down 86th Street after our prenatal yoga class. It was a warm Sunday with big puffy clouds moving fast across the sky. One of those rare moments in New York when nobody seemed to be rushing home. People lingered outside, neighbors chatting in front of building entrances, parents with kids talking to other parents in the middle of the sidewalk, their bulky double strollers blocking the way, friends having brunch in outdoor cafés, dog walkers waiting patiently while strangers leaned to pet their puppies. I should have been relaxed after the yoga; instead, I felt edgy and unsettled.

"I don't know. I'm starting to worry. What if something happened to her?"

"Don't be ridiculous. She's a college kid. Between studying and partying, she's got no time for you."

"I'd understand if I hadn't told her about my blood scare. Fine. But a quick note to make sure I'm okay would take her all of a minute."

"You never should have gone clubbing with her," Angie said. "What were you thinking?"

"Who said I *was* thinking?" I hadn't even told Angie about the candle incident.

"I still can't believe you ran into your donor. On the subway, of all places."

"She's a Columbia student, for Chrissake. I'm surprised it didn't happen earlier. We had no idea she was still in school, let alone in our neighborhood. All she wrote on her application forms was that she had a BA from an Ivy League university. I know it's a matter of a few months, and maybe she thought that by the time she got picked as a donor she would have already graduated, but still . . . she just seems like such a flake. I mean, she lies on her donor application; she shows up unannounced at work and expects me to take her around the Met; she calls only when it suits her." I stopped and looked at Angie. "I hope it's not genetic."

Angie put her hand on my shoulder. "Of course it's not. She's just a beautiful girl who's used to everyone dancing to her tune. Literally, in your case." She began laughing. Angie had a bubbly laugh—sweet and addictive like champagne.

"Very funny," I said, and resumed walking. She was right. What was I doing hanging out with some college kid? I had plenty of mature friends. Like Angie, who was also single and pregnant after a long battle with infertility and knew what I was going through. But I had to see Katya one more time. I didn't have to like her or hang out with her. I just had to tell her the truth. That was the deal I'd made with God and I had to get it done even if I had to go looking for her on campus. I couldn't tell Angie about it, though. She'd think I was foolish. Maybe I was.

"You sure you didn't make her up?" Angie said, the fizz fading out of her voice. "It sounds too good to be true. Even people who decide to meet their donors don't exactly go out eating or dancing together. I mean, you just met her and boom"—she snapped her fingers—"you're now best friends?"

"You jealous?"

"What if I am?"

Two mothers with strollers walked past us, seemingly returning from the park. Angie and I followed them with our eyes.

"Will we ever be so lucky?" I said.

"Just wait. I give us three months before we're sick of listening to each other babbling about diapers."

We laughed, the image so sweet I didn't want to let go, savoring it like the first bite into a luscious peach.

The ring of my phone pulled me back into reality. "Damn!" I said, looking at the screen.

"Is it her?"

I shook my head. "My mother. I've been avoiding her calls."

"What happened? I thought you two were close."

"She's been giving me shit about Tyler as if it was my fault that he left," I said, my jaw clenching at the memory of our last conversation. "Maybe she's right. I took him for granted, didn't I? Anyway," I said, rushing to change the topic. "How's it going with Funny Guy?"

Angie had met him online and had been calling him Funny Texter until they'd finally had a date in person last week. Since then, they'd seen each other a couple of times and she'd sounded quite taken with him. I was hoping she'd found the right one at last. Four years ago, her boyfriend at the time had told her that he didn't want kids after all, never mind that he'd led her on for two years. She'd gone straight to the fertility clinic and started trying on her own.

Angie frowned. "Funny Guy is no more. He's Gone Guy." She laughed but I could hear her disappointment. I stopped and stared at her. "He wasn't interested in starting a relationship with a pregnant woman," she said and shrugged mockingly as if to say, *Go figure.* "How about your *secret admirer*? Have you finally seen what he looks like?"

I had to laugh. "He abandoned me, too. First Tyler, then Katya, then Peter Bogdin."

◆

I stood in front of Sam's door trying to gather the courage to ring her bell. Sam was gracious and generous, with an easy warm smile. She liked to make fun of me for watching what I ate or worrying about how to dress. Clearly, she hadn't been criticized growing up the way I'd been. I often thought that Sam and I would have been friends even if she weren't Tyler's sister. If we had met, say, at work or yoga or someplace else. But could we keep up a friendship now that Tyler and I were no longer together? And what about the girls?

Chloe was four, two years older than Tessa, and when I finally rang the doorbell, they came running to the door. My heart melted just seeing them.

When Sam returned from book club, we were on the floor drawing. I was trying my best at an elephant. Chloe knelt next to me watching intently, while Tessa squirmed on my lap reaching for a crayon, then dropping it to get a new one. Sam joined us, twisting her legs in the lotus positon, and began telling me about the latest novel they were reading. She had Tyler's lopsided smile, his way of looking at you as if you were the most interesting person in the world. But unlike his calm, thoughtful demeanor, Sam was all breathless excitement. The girls interrupted her constantly, but it was my own thoughts that kept me today from following Sam's recap of the plot. As I inhaled Tessa's sweet baby smell, I couldn't help but think of the baby growing inside me. Sam had been a great support during all the treatments, cheering us along the way, giving her brother shit that he had it easy compared to what I was going through. I felt guilty for keeping my news from her. I would have to tell her soon or stop seeing her altogether. I couldn't imagine doing either.

"So when are you coming back?" Sam asked. "We miss you."

I'd started that book club nearly a decade ago with friends from my graduate program, and later on, when I'd met Sam and we'd clicked, I'd brought her on board. As my infertility treatments intensified over the years, I began missing meetings and eventually had to let go of the club. But now that Tyler and I were no longer together, Sam must have assumed that that part of my life was over. Was that why she'd brought it up?

"Hopefully soon," I said. My phone buzzed on the coffee table and Chloe shrieked, "Your phone!" Before I could stop her, she'd jumped to get it.

"It's okay," I said, waving my hand, but she picked it up and handed it to me.

"It could be important," she said, her face all serious, clearly imitating her father, who was a marketing executive and on call at all times.

"I doubt it," I said. "There are no weekend emergencies in the life of a curator." Sam and I exchanged a knowing smile. She was a librarian.

"Check it, check it," Chloe insisted, and to humor her, I did. A text from Angie. All it said was *OMG, have you seen this?* followed by a web link. I silenced the phone and put it in my pocket. I could read it later.

"Nothing important, sweetheart," I said, and leaned over to give her a kiss.

❖

Half an hour later, I emerged from the subway to a dark sky and gusts of wind. I could smell the rain coming—that damp earthy scent. I picked up my pace, hoping to make it home before the storm. I was wearing my new sandals—an impulse purchase meant to brighten a particularly drab day a few weeks ago—and didn't want to ruin them. Around me, people walked briskly, some already pulling their umbrellas out. Traffic crawled up and down Broadway, the usual Sunday late-afternoon rush. I was feeling crappy, my stomach queasy, my breasts swollen and sore, and was looking forward to a nap. There was nothing sweeter than an early-pregnancy nap.

I smiled *hello* at the used-books street vendor, who was putting away his folding tables. He shook his head in response and raised his eyes to the sky as if to say, *You can't fight Mother Nature.*

Just before I turned onto my street, I saw a flyer affixed to the lamppost at the corner. A regular letter-size white sheet of paper—some writing on top, a color photo below it. The lower left corner flapped loose in the wind as I neared it.

I recognized her face before the words on top—in block red letters—came into focus: *Missing Columbia Student.*

My stomach turned. My ears started buzzing. I stood there, staring at the flyer, as the rain came down, big fat raindrops smacking the side-walk, building up speed until it became a deluge and the windshield wipers of cars raged back and forth and my vision went black at the edges.

PART 2

THE
WRONG GIRL
TO TURN
DOWN

15.
KATYA

"Remember the guy I told you about? The one without the T-shirts? I've started hooking up with him pretty regularly."

Josh nodded, the suggestion of a smile making its way on his face. I knew he'd be happy to hear it. I was still feeling crappy for having hit on him the other week. We'd talked about it at length the next time. Therapist-patient boundaries, transference, father figure, and all that psychobabble. The truth was I felt so empty sometimes, so broken that I would get scared—like I-can't-breathe scared—and grasp for anything. Guys were my drug of choice. I craved that warm, fuzzy feeling of a man wrapping his body around mine. Of being wanted, desired. It was proof that I was not as damaged as I feared. But like any drug, the effects didn't last. I needed a new hit again and again. And, that day, after I'd opened up to Josh about my parents and gotten so dangerously close to telling him about Alex's death, I'd felt particularly vulnerable. I hadn't wanted just any guy. I'd wanted Josh to want me. Simple as that.

"His name's Damian," I said. "A hedge fund manager or something like that. He's crazy busy, which works perfect for me." Josh opened his mouth but I stopped him. "I know. No *crazy* in your office. Sorry. Anyway, Damian's great. Strong, passionate as hell, yet detached and quite unpredictable. It's almost like being with a new guy every time. He exhausts and distracts me. Still I can't sleep." I sighed. "If only I could quiet the chatter in my mind."

Josh wanted to know what I thought about when I couldn't sleep. Of course, he did.

"I don't know," I lied.

He raised an eyebrow.

I shrugged. "About how I fuck up everything, I guess. Like with Zoe, who—by the way—is no longer talking to me."

"We all make mistakes," he said, sounding a bit too patronizing, too impatient. "We all hurt people without meaning to."

I felt the anger rising up my throat. "You don't understand!" I blurted. "I've done some really awful things."

"Awful like what?"

I stared at my Roman friend on the ceiling to steady myself. Josh had nearly tricked me into telling him.

"Go ahead," he said. But the moment was gone. I was safe.

"You have no idea what it's like to live your life fearing that . . ." Tears stung my eyes. I dug my nails into the flesh of my wrist, a trick I'd learned as a kid.

"Fearing what?" he asked.

"I've never told anyone."

Josh waited. I dug in my nails harder.

"You won't think I'm pathetic, will you?"

"Of course not," he said, and held me in his gaze. I didn't exactly believe him, but at this point I couldn't care less what he thought of me.

"I fear that I'm marked," I finally said. "That everything I touch turns to ashes and I can't do anything to change that."

Josh tilted his head questioningly.

"I was supposed to start fresh in America. I was going to reinvent myself," I said, and released the tension on my wrist. "But it looks like I'm stuck with me, Katya the Horrible. It's like a bodysuit I can't wriggle out of. I fear that I'm . . ." I let the sentence hang unfinished and hid my face in my hands.

"You fear that . . ." he said, prompting me.

Barely audible, afraid that by saying it out loud I would make it true, I finally told him: "I fear that I'm unlovable."

I started sobbing, hard and breathless, like a child. As if years of tears had accumulated inside me, building into enormous waves that crashed against my chest.

16.

LANA

The department buzzed with activity. Seemingly all assistants and research fellows were in today, poring over books and photocopies of drawings in the front room or staring at computer screens, typing up description data or other information on the Museum System database, sifting through online journals and publications, conducting research. My assistant, Caitlin, was at the desk right outside my office, working on the lending history reports for a couple of new acquisitions. A third-year PhD student at NYU's Institute of Fine Arts, she came in four times a week. She was smart, pretty, and ambitious; a bit too pushy for my taste, but that made for a good assistant.

I was sitting at my desk with the shades half drawn. The light felt too bright today, too distracting, even offensive. I was supposed to be working on my presentation for the upcoming Visiting Committee meeting but had a hard time focusing. The purpose of these quarterly meetings was to update patrons on our work, upcoming shows, and new acquisitions. The next one was coming up in a week and our department, along with European Paintings, was to jointly introduce the Parmigianino show to a group of supporting trustees. I spread out my notes and started working on the outline. An hour later, all I had was a blank page but for the title, *Parmigianino's Drawings*. How could I possibly concentrate when my mind was flooded with questions and worries about Katya?

I'd returned home in quite a state last night. After taking a hot, numbing shower, I'd finally looked at my phone, remembering it buzzing in my purse as I'd walked home in the rain. Angie had left me two voice mails and four more texts following the one I'd seen while at Sam's. The last one read: *Where the hell are you?* She'd forwarded me the *Columbia Daily Spectator*'s missing-student article, which linked to a PDF of the notice I'd seen on Broadway and to a Facebook page, Finding Katya, that had been created. There was no additional information except that her photo was also shared on social media under the hashtag #FindingKatya.

Anxious to find out more, I abandoned Parmigianino's outline and googled Katya's name. There was nothing new. I grabbed my phone and before I could change my mind, punched Tyler's number. He picked up on the third ring. "Hi there. Good to hear from—"

"Is it true?" I interrupted him. I had no patience for pleasantries today. It was bad enough I was calling him.

"What?"

"About our donor."

"What donor?"

"Christ, Tyler." I took a deep breath. "Our egg donor. Remember?"

"Yeah?"

"She's missing."

"What do you mean *missing*? From the agency's database?"

It occurred to me that Tyler, of course, didn't even know Katya was still a student, let alone at his university. I sighed. It was time he found out. "Just google 'missing Columbia student,' then call me back. Okay?" I said, and hung up.

A shaft of light streamed through the window below the shades and pooled on my desk. Children's voices drifted in from outside, playful shrieks and laughter, punctuating the hum of traffic on Fifth Avenue. Many student groups came to the museum in spring.

I pulled my chair forward and clicked on the *Spectator*'s link to the missing-student notice.

MISSING COLUMBIA STUDENT

The Department of Public Safety has been notified that
Columbia University student **Katya Dimitrova**
has not been in contact with family and friends for several days.
Ms. Dimitrova is 21 yrs/5'9"/115 lbs/green eyes/brown hair.
There is a coordinated effort to locate Ms. Dimitrova.
If you know her whereabouts or have any information
that will be helpful in locating her,
please call immediately **Public Safety at 212-854-5555**
or the **26 Pct. Detective Squad at 212-678-1351.**

As I read through it once more, I wondered what *several* days meant. Two? Five? The last I'd heard from Katya was on Saturday night, more than a week ago. Could she have been gone since then? A sinking feeling made its way into my stomach. I'd been bitching about her disappearing on me, calling her a flake, when I should have been worrying about her.

"Should I have done something?" I'd asked Angie when I'd finally called her back last night. "Gone to the police?"

"You barely knew her," she'd said. "What were you going to report her for? Not getting back to you? If I ran to the police every time an editor ghosted me, they'd lock me up just so I'd stop bothering them."

Angie had been right, of course. But still. I couldn't help feeling guilty about it. I'd abandoned her in the club with some stranger.

My cell buzzed on my desk and I snatched it up anxiously.

"Just read the *Spectator* article," Tyler said. "It's her, all right."

"Didn't you get any information from the university? A briefing or something? I was hoping you'd have an update."

"Haven't looked at my e-mail today but I'll check."

It was just like Tyler to ignore his e-mail for hours. He'd never bothered joining Facebook or any other social media and would often leave his phone at home when he went out for the day. I used to joke with him about it, finding it endearing or infuriating depending on the situation. But now that we weren't together, I couldn't even get upset with him.

"Do you think something bad happened to her?" I asked.

"I'm sure she's fine. She couldn't deal with the finals and took off. Or something like that." He spoke with such conviction that I already felt some of the weight lifting, my shoulders relaxing. I'd always envied Tyler's optimism, his ability to trust that things would work out. It had kindled my courage and faith through endless disappointments and heartbreaks. With a pang, I realized how much I missed it. I began crying. Out of nowhere. Loud embarrassing sobs.

"Are you okay? Do you want me to come over?"

"No." I snapped out of it. Damn pregnancy hormones. I'd been so weepy lately, I cried at the smallest provocation, even watching comedies. It was like having PMS on steroids.

"Are you sure? You seem distressed." He sounded genuinely concerned, which upset me even more.

"Since when do you care?" I said, wiping my tears with my sleeve.

"That's not fair."

"You wouldn't have left me for another woman if—"

"For God's sake, Lana! I didn't leave you for another woman. Let me come see you and we can talk—"

"I don't want to talk about it, Tyler. I only called you because I was worried sick about our donor."

"Why? I mean, of course, hopefully nothing happened to her. But no need to get worked up about it." He cleared his throat. "It's not like we know her. Besides, I'm sure she just got overwhelmed with the stress of finals. Like that other girl who went missing for a week. Remember? A few years ago?"

I'd forgotten all about it. We were in the midst of our first in vitro at the time and after the initial celebration of a positive result, the doctor had explained that my hormone levels were low and he was worried it could be a chemical pregnancy. We had to wait two more days to test again and make sure the numbers doubled. But they hadn't. Nor had they gone down as they should have if it were just a chemical pregnancy. So then the doctors tossed in another scary term—ectopic pregnancy, which meant that the embryo had taken hold not in the uterus but in one of the fallopian tubes. After numerous blood tests and sonograms to confirm it, I'd had an injection to terminate the pregnancy before it ruptured my tube and put my life in danger.

I'd spent those two weeks in a daze. I'd only found out that there'd been a missing student after she'd turned up. I remembered Tyler complaining about how stupid and immature she'd been to have everyone worried, wasting the police's time and resources.

"No need to panic," he continued, "just because some girl you don't really know wants a fresh start."

He was making a huge assumption—two, actually—and I certainly didn't want him to find out how wrong he was about me not knowing Katya, so I let it go. "Can you get more info?"

He sighed. "How?" I could tell he was growing impatient with me.

"I don't know. You're a professor there. The police must be keeping the administration in the loop. Ask around. I'm sure people are talking."

"Lana, I cannot get involved in this," he said sharply.

I pulled the phone away from my ear as if it had zapped me. What was I doing? If I pushed him too hard, he might get suspicious. If he hadn't already.

"What I mean is," he continued in a softer voice, "in light of the connection you and I have to her, we can't ask questions about her. It might be seen as stalking—"

"I know. I know," I said, and laughed nervously. "My outsized curiosity again."

Tyler and I had a running joke about it. He claimed it was one of the things he'd loved about me from the start. "That's what makes one a philosopher," he'd told me. "Asking questions. People think it's about the answers, but you can't have answers without questions."

"You and your outsized curiosity," he repeated fondly. The familiarity of his teasing felt like an embrace.

I didn't just miss Tyler. I missed *us*, I thought as I put the phone down. The playful dynamic we'd had, the feeling of togetherness, of being part of a team.

◆

By the afternoon, the *New York Post* Metro section had picked up Katya's story with the additional information that she was a foreign student from Bulgaria. "*To miss her finals just short of graduation makes no sense,*" a classmate of hers was quoted saying. But, again, there was nothing indicating *when* she'd gone missing. The thought that I could be the one to have seen her last that night at the club kept nagging me.

On the way back from work, I decided to skip the crosstown bus and walk through Central Park before getting on the subway. It was a breezy day and I hoped the fresh air would help clear my mind, ease my fears. We were barely a month away from the summer solstice and the sun didn't set until past eight. Now that I was newly single, my evenings had grown longer, leaving me with a lot of free time. And that was the last thing I needed right now. When you're waiting to get past a certain hurdle—like the three-month mark in pregnancy—time slows to a snail's pace. Each morning I woke up excited to mark one more day on the calendar and each evening I dreaded the long night ahead, terrified that I would wake up again in a pool of blood. I was still spotting a bit but my ultrasound wasn't until Wednesday. One day and two nights more to go before I'd have some news of how things were going.

The Great Lawn was crawling with people having picnics, throwing balls, or chasing Frisbees; a team of students was playing baseball in the far corner. I sat down on a bench across from the lake with the turtles, overlooking the Delacorte Theater and Belvedere Castle on the hill above it. Tyler and I used to spend the evenings cooking, eating, drinking wine, and talking. Since I was on my own, I'd lost all desire to cook, so I either prepared something fast and easy, like pasta, or ordered in. I ate while watching a film or reading a book, my iPad propped up next to my placemat. Tonight, between Katya's disappearance and my upsetting conversation with Tyler, I was particularly loath to walk into the empty apartment. The pregnancy hormones surely magnified my emotions, but knowing that didn't make me feel any better.

I called Angie. "Heard anything new?"

"You saw the *Post* article, right?" Angie's beat was art and entertainment. She was following this story because of me.

"Nothing I didn't know," I said. My eyes followed a toddler running ahead of his mother. "I think I better go to the police."

"And tell them what?"

"About my outing with Katya that Saturday night. What if that rooftop Jacuzzi guy has done something to her?" A shiver ran through my body just speaking the thought out loud. "The cops can look through the club's security tapes and talk to the staff. Katya is not a girl who goes unnoticed."

"True. But who are you going to say you are? Katya's . . . what? Baby mama? Surrogate? Beneficiary of her egg donation? Or are you going to introduce yourself as her stalker? *Officer, I saw her on the subway and followed her.*"

"Very funny." I got off the bench and started walking. "What's wrong with simply saying that I'm a new friend of hers? She fell on the street. I rushed to help her and we clicked. The Bulgarian connection . . ."

"Ah, friendship at first sight," Angie said. "And it just so happened that you're pregnant with her eggs. But that's just a minor detail."

I took my time in the park. I even walked up the stairs to the castle, stopping on the way to admire the tulips and lilac bushes in Shakespeare Garden. At the top, I leaned against the stone wall and stood there looking over the lake. The chatter of the birds in the trees grew louder as the sun dipped lower behind the rooftops to the west.

It was past eight p.m. when I finally made it home. I was so engrossed in my thoughts that when I heard Tyler call my name from the living room, I nearly shouted back, "Hey, baby!" Then I caught myself. Mouth open, hand still holding the door ajar, I could only stare as Tyler came into the corridor with Plato purring in his arms.

"Sorry," he said, smiling, his hand brushing Plato's back. "I hope I didn't give you a fright."

17.
KATYA

Damian was a bit hot-blooded, but I liked that about him. It kept me on my toes. Like, the other night we went to the Beekman—that posh hotel in the financial district. It was a mild fall night. I didn't even need a jacket over my dress. A red vintage dress I'd scored at the flea market last weekend. The bars and clubs downtown were bursting with people. From the moment we walked in, I felt like I was starring in a film set in the 1800s. The soaring atrium, the lacelike ironwork of the balustrades, the Persian rugs, leather club chairs, bookshelves and oil paintings, everything exuded old New York. The crowd was older, swankier than in most of the places I hung out.

I followed Damian to one of the lounge tables and sank into the soft armchair. While he examined the bar menu, I snuck in a few snaps on my Insta story. Damian wasn't that old, but social media wasn't his thing. My posting "all the time" amused him at first but lately he'd been complaining about it. Looking at the cocktails, he decided that it would only be appropriate to order the Moscow Mule. You know, because I was Bulgarian. I didn't bother explaining that Bulgaria was actually in the EU and had nothing to do with Russia. Communism and the Cold War were over before I was even born. But whatever. I'm not a vodka fan and certainly couldn't imagine mixing it with ginger beer plus honey, lime, and rosemary. I love tequila and asked the waiter for an El Diablo instead.

Damian had a fit of laughter. Started teasing me that El Diablo was a more fitting description for me anyway. "My sexy she-devil," he called me. It was cute the first time, but by the second round of drinks, it really got old, not to mention annoying. Maybe because it resonated with my fears about myself. I started playing with the lamp that stuck to the table like a magnet while Damian looked through the menu, debating what snacks to order. I wasn't hungry, but he insisted. "My she-devil needs some fattening."

That did it. I would show him my true evil side since he was such a smart-ass. I excused myself to go to the bathroom and sauntered through the place with just the right swing in my hips, making sure the eyes of every man in the room were on me. I knew I looked hot in my red dress and strappy black stilettos.

The young guy at the end of the bar—more or less my age by the looks of it—followed me with his gaze. He'd been staring at me across the room ever since I'd walked in. I liked him. He had that dashing Mediterranean look I adored.

I smiled as I passed, then lowered my eyes before looking up again.

On my way back from the ladies' room, I stopped in front of one of the paintings on the wall right next to the bar. It looked like someone had taken yellow and blue watercolors and blotted out large sections of a perfectly good portrait of an old man. I didn't have to wait long.

Over my shoulder, I heard a friendly baritone say, "Beautiful."

I turned, smiling. He was even more handsome up close. I started saying something about not knowing who the artist was, but he interrupted me. "I don't mean the painting."

It sounded like a line he'd heard in a film and had been using ever since. But I didn't care. It was all going according to plan and I was just thinking, *I hope Damian is watching*, when I heard his voice right behind me. "Hey, pal," he said, and wedged himself between the two of us. "Can I help you?"

The young guy stepped back. "Sorry, man, I didn't realize she was your daughter."

Another movie line? That guy was bold. From behind, I saw Damian's ears go red. He leaned forward. "What did you just say?"

"I believe I called you an old bastard preying on beautiful young—"

Damian punched him. Just like that, a hook right in the face. I gasped as the guy's head spun back. He lost his footing, stumbled a few steps backward before regaining his balance. Like in a movie, was all I could think as I stood there in shock.

Next thing I knew, one of the security guards had Damian in his grip. Damian didn't fight him, thank God, but his face was crimson, nostrils flaring, eyes shining like a beast's. I shuddered, at once frightened and high on adrenaline.

Luckily, he hadn't broken the guy's nose or anything, and we got thrown out of there without the police getting involved. I should have gone home at that point. That much I knew. But when I told Damian I had a paper to write (which was actually true), he said, "I don't give a fuck," and stuffed me into the taxi he'd just hailed. During the ride he didn't say a word, but I could tell he was fuming. He might have punched the cocky young guy, but it was me he was really angry with. And for good reason. I didn't know what had possessed me. Why I'd tried to provoke him, flirting with someone else.

When we made it to his loft, he poured himself a Scotch—didn't ask me if I wanted any—gulped the whole thing down, then poured himself another. Only then did he look at me, and with burning eyes he said, "Don't you *ever* do that again."

"You should have seen him the next day," I told Josh. "He sent a huge bouquet of flowers to my dorm. It was quite embarrassing, actually—like some nineties rom-com. At dinner, he was sweet and apologetic. Told me he'd been 'a tad overprotective' because he was so 'smitten' with me. Promised to be gentle and docile like a puppy from now on. We had the best sex ever that night."

Josh raised an eyebrow. "So you plan to continue seeing him?"

"But of course. What girl doesn't want a man willing to fight for her?"

Josh rolled his eyes.

"Okay, okay," I said, and laughed. "I'm exaggerating. But there is some truth in it. Plus, it was all my fault. I had no business flirting with that guy. I'd wanted to piss Damian off and I'd succeeded. Spectacularly, you may say." I grinned and went on. "And he learned his lesson: there are guys galore out there, so he better be careful."

"His explosive streak doesn't bother you?" Josh said. "The fact that he treated you as his property?"

"Seriously? C'mon, Josh. You jealous or something?" I said, and stood up. "I believe we're out of time."

At the door, I turned and smiled. "I love it when you worry about me."

18.

LANA

"What the hell are you doing here?" I asked, still holding the door open.

"I was worried about you," Tyler said, and took a few steps forward. Plato stirred in his hands. "You sounded really distraught on the phone. I wanted to make sure you were okay."

"Tyler, you have no right to let yourself in and—"

"I'm sorry. I waited for you downstairs but I didn't expect you to be so late and . . ." He shrugged, pulling his lips back in that self-mocking I'm-only-human expression. "I really needed to use the bathroom. So I thought I might as well wait for you inside." He stroked Plato's fur. "And I wanted to see this guy."

I let the door close behind me and walked into the kitchen. He followed. I dropped my purse and the mail on the counter and sat down at the breakfast table, sandwiched tightly in the corner. Tyler let Plato down, pulled out the other chair, and turned it to the side so that he could face me.

"You know that's not okay," I finally said, trying to control my voice. "You don't live here anymore. And what if I'd come home with a guy?"

He flushed; a wounded expression settled on his face. "Are you seeing someone?"

"That's not the point, Tyler."

"You're right. I'm sorry." He relaxed back in his seat. "The thing is, I worry about you. You were so upset—"

"A little too late for that, don't you think?"

He bit his lower lip as if to keep himself from fighting the point, pressed his hands on the table, and, looking me in the eyes, said, "I know why you're so distraught about this girl going missing."

"You do?" My stomach tightened.

"You were so set on doing that donor egg cycle," he said in a gentle, almost loving way. "But that's exactly why I had to leave. We needed a break from all the fertility treatments to collect ourselves and heal after the last miscarriage." His eyes narrowed and his tone turned clipped as he continued, "But you wouldn't hear of it. You had stopped hearing me, period."

"Tyler, I'm not interested in—"

"Hear me out, goddammit." He shoved the chair back and began pacing the length of the kitchen. I'd never seen Tyler so angry. Not even close to it. Had I really been blind to his feelings? When he'd pushed for a vacation last fall, I'd dismissed it, thinking he was worried about *me* and how I was going to cope with yet another loss. It hadn't occurred to me that *he* might have needed the break.

Tyler stopped pacing and leaned against the door frame. "I know you're worried about this girl because you fear that you won't find another Bulgarian donor. I know it's a big deal for you because of your mother. I understand. But there are so many other good donors, even if they're not from that part of the world."

My shoulders relaxed. I had no idea where he was going with this, but at least it sounded like he had no clue about my pregnancy.

"We got on the baby-making treadmill," he continued, "eight fucking years ago and we never even stopped to catch our breath. To do something fun. To pack our bags and go hiking out west. Or even drive up to Bear Mountain for the day. Go for a walk together, or a bike ride. See friends for dinner. Hell, we barely even had sex unless you were ovulating." He paused and looked at me. "What happened to the free-spirited girl I met on Kilimanjaro?"

"What do you think happened, Tyler?" I snapped, clenching my fists. "Life happened. *Infertility* happened."

"But that's exactly what I mean. We let the infertility take over our lives. We didn't stop to reconsider our priorities as our circumstances changed and we moved from one treatment to the next. We didn't re-evaluate the risks we were taking. And we lost something vital in the process. We lost *us*. We were no longer a couple making decisions to-gether. You were making decisions for us. On the few occasions I dared to disagree, you guilted me into doing as you wished because you were the one undergoing the surgeries, injecting the hormones, lying nau-seous on the sofa only to be shattered by another miscarriage. But I was grieving, too." He sighed, peered into my eyes before continuing. "It really pains me that you think I replaced you with another woman."

"C'mon, Tyler. How stupid do you think I am? For years you refuse to bother with texts, then suddenly you're texting at all hours of the day? You're distracted and irritable. Then, out of nowhere, you decide to forgo the donor egg cycle we'd spent our last savings on. What am I supposed to think?"

He stared at his shoes. A muscle in his cheek was quivering. "You're right," he said finally and looked up. "But while there was someone else—let me finish—that is not why I left. You and I had come to a dead end, a stalemate, and we couldn't push past it. I couldn't reach you anymore."

I sat there with my mouth open, gripping the sides of my chair. I felt like I couldn't breathe, my mind stuck on "someone else," stumbling over it like a broken record. While I'd suspected it all along, hearing it from Tyler was a fresh blow. "Wow," I finally said. "That's a lot to take in." I met his eyes. "What do you expect me to say?"

"You don't have to say anything. I just needed you to listen." He smiled. "For a change." But I didn't find it funny. I watched him stand-ing there, leaning against the door frame, at once so familiar and for-eign. How many times had I seen him in that exact spot, wearing that very same blue shirt and pair of jeans? He continued, shifting gears. "I just wanted you to know how I felt. Because we can't move forward, we can't heal the relationship if—"

"Wait. What?" I sat up with a jolt. "What relationship? You said you were done, remember?"

"I said I was done living like this. That we needed a fresh start and I didn't see any other way."

"You've gotta be kidding me."

"I never wanted us to split up. I love you, Lana."

I covered my ears. "I can't listen to this. It's crazy. You turned my entire world upside down and now you want back in? It doesn't work like that. You can't patch a broken vase."

"I don't want to do any patching up. That's why I thought we should start from scratch, put the baby quest aside and focus on us. Because the endless heartbreak, the grueling march forward without even knowing—"

"Enough." I stood up. My head was spinning. "Whatever you meant or wanted is beside the point now. That ship has sailed. I've begun building my life again and it doesn't include you."

He straightened up, a hurt look on his face. "I know I rocked the boat, but I had no choice." He took a step toward me. "All I ask is that we keep talking. That you don't shut me out—"

"Well, you just got your wish. We talked. Now I need to eat dinner and go to bed. It's been a long day." I walked into the corridor, making it clear it was time for him to leave.

Tyler followed me. At the door, he stopped and turned. "I know this is a very hard time for you. And the Bulgarian donor going missing must have hit too close to home."

If he only knew.

"That's why I wanted to come and comfort you." He leaned forward and smiled. "I asked around a bit and the word on campus is that the cops aren't concerned. They've found no signs of foul play."

I exhaled with relief. After Tyler's sharp reaction over the phone, I hadn't expected him to look into it. At least his visit had brought me some comfort about Katya.

❖

At night, I lay in bed, wide awake, my mind going in circles. One minute I felt guilty for having alienated Tyler, the next I was angry he hadn't stuck it out through the donor cycle. If it hadn't worked out, then we could have talked as much as he wanted or gone on vacation or whatever he wished to do. He'd been unwilling to take the risk of one more disappointment and had pulled out of the game. I got that. But by doing so, he'd made the same mistake he'd accused me of—making a choice for both of us. Luckily, I'd decided to go it alone. But that had meant bending the rules and going ahead with the cycle behind his back. I had done something unethical and maybe even illegal.

I didn't regret it. If I hadn't, I wouldn't have my little miracle growing inside me. I pressed my palms gently to my belly as I did every time I thought of my baby. I was seven weeks and one day pregnant today; two more days until my next ultrasound—

I sat up in bed, seized by panic. I'd forgotten the progesterone shot.

Dr. Williams had me on hormonal support until the twelfth week of pregnancy when—he had assured me—the placenta would take over the hormonal production. Until then, I was to take two estrogen pills daily, affix four estrogen patches to my belly every other day, and give myself progesterone injections every night. I had no problem administering the small injections in my belly. But learning to jam the enormous needle into my buttock—while standing in front of the mirror with my pants down—had been quite a challenge. Tyler had always done that one for me.

His visit tonight had rattled me so much that I'd forgotten all about it. I looked at the clock on my bedside table. It was ten before midnight. Technically, it was still Monday, I thought, and got up. I pulled my supplies—I had an entire drawer full of syringes, different types of medications, pads, and alcohol wipes. Hopefully, doing the shot a few hours later than usual wouldn't make much of a difference. I was still spotting on and off, a constant reminder of the hematoma and the fact that things could take a turn for the worse at any point even without me screwing up my meds.

I returned to bed even more livid with Tyler and his intrusion. How dare he ambush me like that, telling me it was all my fault we were no longer together? After admitting there had been another woman? The mere thought of it turned my insides. He'd said it so matter-of-factly, a trifling detail. How could he possibly think that it was okay as long as he hadn't left me for her? I should have told him that was enough of a reason for me to have left him. But he'd caught me by surprise. Finding him in the apartment had given me quite a start, and his I-love-you bullshit had nearly undone me. I was upset with myself, too, because, for a moment there, I'd actually loved hearing him say it.

I shivered and pulled the blanket tighter around me. At least I knew the police hadn't found anything worrisome about Katya's disappearance. But as I turned and tossed, the old fears crept in. What if the cops didn't know about her boyfriend's temper? What if he'd learned about Jacuzzi Guy and flipped? Did the police even know about either of them? I pushed the covers back and sat up for a second time tonight. I had to find out when exactly she'd disappeared. The missing-student alert hadn't been posted until a week after she and I were at the club. Maybe I was driving myself crazy for no reason. I turned on the light and grabbed my phone from the nightstand. How could I not have thought about it until now?

My back propped against the wall with my pillow, I opened Facebook and searched for Katya Dimitrova. I scrolled through the long list, scrutinizing each photo. It was a rather common Bulgarian name. There were also accounts in Russia and Ukraine. I kept scrolling down with my thumb but couldn't recognize Katya on any of the profile photos. I gave up before reaching the end. Maybe I'd have better luck on Instagram.

Katya was fifth on the list of users with her name. Her profile photo was a stunning close-up of her in a coffee shop, although a quarter of her face was out of the frame and the background was slanted at a sharp angle. She hadn't exactly aspired to originality with her user name, @BGgirl, where BG of course stood for Bulgaria. I clicked on her feed and the screen populated with a patchwork of square images. She'd been a regular, posting a few times a day. But—as I'd feared—her last one was from Saturday night, more than a week ago.

I stared at the photo of the two of us on the swing in Mehanata. Our faces a bit distorted from the close-up and the lack of light. But our eyes were alive with laughter. Katya's free hand was lifted in greeting and the more I looked at it, the more I felt like she was beckoning me, imploring me to do something.

I put the phone down and before turning off the light, I reset my alarm for an hour earlier. If I skipped breakfast, I would have just enough time to stop by the police station on my way to work.

19.

KATYA

"I don't get Halloween," I told Josh. "Everyone dresses like a favorite character, right? Little boys want to be superheroes, little girls—princesses. And college girls want to be what? Cats? Sex objects? The other night, on campus, I ran into girls dressed as sexy M&M's, sexy beer cans, and at least a dozen cats—any excuse to bare legs and boobs. At least college guys go with funny or stupid or I'm-above-it-all hipster costumes."

There was a suggestion of a smirk on Josh's face as he asked, "What were you?"

"A Freudian slip," I said proudly, and told him how I'd found a white lace slip in a vintage shop and had worn it over black tights and a black long-sleeve T-shirt. "I wrote on it with a sharpie: *Ego, Id, Super Ego, Oedipal Complex.*"

Josh laughed and I wanted to hug him. "It's funny, right? Most of my classmates didn't get it. Damian wasn't impressed, either. But at least I wasn't half naked, freezing my ass off. And I didn't see another person who wore a costume even close to it."

"I bet," Josh said with a smile. "Maybe I should borrow it next year."

"Shall I save you the heels, too?"

"Hm, that might be hard on my phobia of heights."

We were both laughing now. I loved making Josh laugh. He would chuckle here and there when I said something funny, but he had never outright laughed like this or gone back and forth with me like we were a team. Like I was more than just one of his many patients.

Like I was special.

When you spend most of your life fearing that you're this horrible, unlovable person, feeling special—even for a fleeting moment—is in-toxicating. It was the drug I craved. Maybe that was why I liked older guys. They knew how to make me feel loved, adored. Like my father had when I was a kid. Every evening when he'd return from work, he'd pick me up and twirl me around the room and tell me that I was his "one and only Daddy's girl."

Tears filled my eyes at the memory and I tilted my head back to keep them from spilling. When I turned to Josh again, he was looking at me with a soft expression. "Have you been sleeping any better?" he asked. He said it like he cared, and that touched me.

I shook my head. I didn't dare speak or I might start crying. There was something special in the room today, an intense warmth that was making me all gooey.

"You feel like talking about it?"

I shrugged. Truth be told, I felt like I would burst if I didn't. But I no longer knew if I should do what I felt like doing.

"It might help," he said.

I was gnawing on my lip, looking at the floor. Thankfully he didn't claim to know that it *would* help. I hated it when people told me what I should do to feel better as if they knew shit about what I was going through. All these platitudes on social media. *Time heals all wounds.* Bullshit. Have you experienced all wounds to know? Or *Life is a gift.* Really? So why does it so often feel like torture?

"The nightmares you told me about. When did they begin?"

"I was eight," I said, and lifted my gaze. "And I know why I have them, if that's what you're trying to get at."

"You want to tell me?"

Again, he was giving me a choice. I appreciated the lack of pressure. The freedom to leave it for next time. And I was definitely tempted. Every fiber in my body was screaming *run*.

"Sure," I said finally.

He smiled tenderly, encouragingly, like a poet beckoning his muse.

I looked up to the ceiling as if hoping for reassurance from my

Roman friend. But the surface seemed white and empty today, ready to swallow me if I stared for too long. I turned back to Josh, and his gaze anchored me.

"I told you I had a brother, right? What I didn't tell you is how much I hated him."

I'd never told anyone about it. I'd never thought I would. But once I started talking, I couldn't stop.

When my father died, I began, my sense of security was shattered and I clung to my mother, terrified that something might happen to her, too. But she couldn't care less. Before I knew it, she'd brought her lover into our house. Ivan took Daddy's chair at the table and his place in her bed. Worst of all, he took my mother. Seemingly overnight, she became sick, throwing up all the time. I was sure she was dying, that Ivan had poisoned her. I was five. My imagination was running wild. It got so bad that I wouldn't let her leave the room without me. I would wrap my arms around her leg, and she had to walk, dragging me.

Finally, she figured it out and to reassure me, she told me the good news: I was going to have a baby brother or sister. The baby was growing inside her belly. That was why she wasn't feeling well. Was it any surprise that I would hate whatever was making my mother sick? I was hysterical with fear when she went to the hospital to give birth.

She returned with the baby in her arms. "Come see your little brother," she told me. "Isn't he cute?" I felt like plucking the bundle from her hands and throwing it out the window. When she came to kiss me good night that evening, I scratched her face.

"I don't remember that part actually," I told Josh. "My mother told me about it. But I vividly remember seeing the baby for the first time. His name was Alexander. Alex for short."

I swallowed. Looked at my feet.

My mother showed him off all the time. "Isn't he the cutest baby you've ever seen?" she'd say to neighbors and friends and even strangers on the street. I thought things would get better when Alex got older, but they didn't. He went from being "the cutest baby" to "the smartest kid ever." The more my mother loved him, the more she seemed to hate me. She was upset with me because I wouldn't let him touch my toys or because I wouldn't play with him. I lay in bed at night wishing Alex would go away. Once and for all.

I looked at Josh, held his gaze. "I didn't wish Alex dead exactly. I just wanted someone to come and take him away."

When Alex was three and I was eight, we went to a beach resort on the Black Sea. I loved swimming back then, maybe because my dad had taught me. I felt at peace in the water, my body relaxed as if I were back in his arms. One hot afternoon—I can still feel the burning sand under my feet—I was bored and said that I was going to the water. Alex started crying. He always wanted to do whatever I did. My mother looked up from her book and told me, as she often did, that I couldn't go unless I took Alex with me.

"But he can't swim," I said.

"Of course he can't swim. He's three. You couldn't swim when you were that age, either. Just take him to the edge and play with him."

"But I want to swim."

She told me that I could go again later and so I sighed and headed down, with Alex running behind me, a big victorious smile on his face. I tried to build him a sand castle but he kept stepping into it or kicking it. Soon, I was sick of playing that game. I knelt in front of him in the sand. "Do you want to build a really big fort?"

He nodded. His cheeks were crusted with dry tears. His curly blond hair was caked with sand and so was his blue swimsuit.

"Here, I'll show you." I started digging, piling the sand in front of me, smoothing it at the top. He joined me, his little hands, like a doll's, striking hard but barely making a dent in the hole.

I got up. "Keep digging, I'll be right back."

"Where you going?"

I hesitated. "I'll go look for seashells in the deep. For our fort. You keep digging."

"I want to go."

"You can't swim."

"I can." He kicked sand in my direction.

"No, you can't."

We went back and forth like that; you know how kids are. Finally, I got tired of it. I stood up and went to the water, splashing my feet in the shallow part. He ran after me, crying, but I refused to turn. I knew he couldn't swim, no matter what he said, so it wasn't like I had to worry that he would follow me in. There were so many people around. Kids with inflatable tubes, bobbing in the waves, adults standing there talking or floating aimlessly. I jumped in, the cool refreshing water closing around me like a liquid embrace. I swam breaststroke toward the buoys like I used to with my dad but didn't dare go all the way on my own and turned halfway, trying out my crawl on the way back.

I barely heard the screams through the splashing of my arms and legs. I switched to breaststroke again, keeping my head above water. That's when I noticed the commotion. People had gathered on the beach. They were shouting. I saw my mother running.

I will never forget her face, the howling sounds coming out of her.

I rushed out of the water and made my way through the ring of people, my hair dripping, my arms prickled with goose bumps. I saw the guard first, on his hands and knees in the sand. The little boy he was trying to revive had on a blue swimsuit like Alex's, the same yellow hair. Slowly, as if through a thick fog, it dawned on me—that little boy was Alex.

It wasn't the first time my brother had been hurt. He would fall and scrape his knee and my mother would yell at me, "You see what you did! How many times did I tell you not to push him?" Or not to lift him. Or whatever it was that she thought I'd done to him. But as I stood there, watching the guard pushing down on Alex's chest, I realized this time was different. Because this time Alex wasn't crying. There were no pitiful tears, no sobs begging for our mom's attention. And when the ambulance came and took Alex away—the way they'd taken Daddy—I knew that was really it.

My mother didn't say a word to me. I would have rather had her scream at me that I'd killed her little boy than seen her stare into space, mute. There is no worse punishment than a mother's silence. I don't think she spoke to me for the rest of the year. She might not have spoken to Alex's father, either, because Ivan left soon after the accident.

Eventually, she began talking again. She would hug me and tell me that it was just the two of us left.

"Every time she said it," I told Josh, "it felt like a reproach. Like it was my fault. Which is what I already believed anyway."

Tears were streaming down my face, and Josh handed me the tissue box.

"I'm so sorry," he said when I'd finally quieted down.

"I know I didn't kill my brother," I said, looking at my hands in my lap. "That my mother shouldn't have left a three-year-old kid with an eight-year-old. I understand all that. Of course. But you can't argue with feelings. Every night I go to sleep with the same thought: if only I hadn't gone into the water or hadn't teased Alex that he couldn't swim, he would still be alive and well."

I blew my nose. Wrapped my arms around myself and stared at my shoes.

"Maybe if I had meant for him to drown, if I had taken him by the hand and dragged him into the water, maybe then I could have eventually forgiven myself, realizing that I'd been too young. That I hadn't and couldn't have known better. I would still have to live with the guilt, but it would be guilt over *one bad decision*. Which is not as horrible as living with the thought that you're a *bad person*, period, and everything you touch turns to ashes whether you mean it or not. That's absolutely terrifying because you have no power to change it."

I looked at Josh.

"How can you atone for something you never meant in the first place?"

20.
LANA

Detective Robertson was the stereotypical clean-cut police officer: short, neatly combed hair, white shirt freshly pressed, brown jacket, and blue tie. He sat with his back erect and his chest thrust forward like someone who spent his time off pumping iron. His desk was in the back of a large cluttered room with about a half-dozen desks and twice as many file cabinets. Plainclothes officers were staring at computer screens, speaking on their phones, or leafing through folders. Nothing here resembled the high-tech ambience portrayed on *CSI* episodes.

The uniformed cop downstairs had already taken a preliminary report before sending me up. Robertson scanned it, fished out a yellow legal pad from under the piles of paper on his desk, and fixed his eyes on me. "Did your friend mention that she was going to take any trips?"

I shook my head. I was sitting on the edge of my chair, ready to bolt. Why the hell had I come? Angie was right. There was no way to explain my relationship with Katya without getting myself in trouble.

"How about that she no longer cared about school? Or that she was struggling under the pressure of classes?"

"She never really talked about school with me." Of the three times total I'd spoken to her. But I wasn't going to volunteer that information.

"Was she scared of someone?"

"She did mention that the guy she was seeing had a temper," I said, and recounted my conversation with Katya.

Robertson took notes as I spoke, barely looking at his pad. "Do you know his name?" he asked. "From what we gathered she'd been seeing *a bunch* of guys." He flipped his gaze upward as if to say, *If you know what I mean.*

"All I know is that he's in his late thirties and looks like Tom Cruise."

He jotted something down, then looked back to me. "Do you think she has a reason to want to disappear?"

"I can't imagine. Why?"

He looked at the report again. "So you last saw Katya on the night before Mother's Day. Is that right?"

"That's correct."

"Where exactly was that?"

I told him about Mehanata. How I'd left Katya there dancing with a stranger.

"And you haven't heard from her since that Saturday?"

"She sent me a photo and a couple of texts after we parted. It was past midnight, so I guess . . . technically, it was Sunday."

"Do you still have them?" he asked, and I nodded. "Let me see." He extended his hand.

I pulled my phone out of my purse and opened the thread with Katya's texts, then handed it to him. I watched him as he read, my gaze lingering on the wide shoulders and bulging chest under his shirt. What was wrong with me? I was lusting after every man I came into contact with—first, the guy at the nightclub and now, the police detective. It must be all the hormones coursing through my body. Between the estrogen pills, the patches, and the progesterone shots, I was a walking chemical experiment.

He handed back my phone with a smirk on his face. For all I knew, while I was picturing him kissing me, he was imagining Katya in that rooftop Jacuzzi.

"Thank you. We'll check all this out, of course, but so far all the evidence points toward voluntary disappearance."

"What does that even mean?"

"Adults have the right to disappear if they wish," he said, leaning back in his chair. "And they often do. Three years ago I worked the case of another Columbia student gone missing."

I told him I'd heard about it.

"Right. So that girl turned up in Brooklyn. She'd rented a room, closed her social media accounts, and changed her phone number and bank account without a word to her family, her friends, or the school administration."

"Why would anyone do that?"

He shrugged. "Cowardice, usually. I had another case—the wife reported her husband missing. Five years later, the guy resurfaced in Florida. Guess what? He had a new family there."

"What a surprise," I blurted. Between my mother's experience with men and Tyler's betrayal, I'd turned into quite the cynic. Robertson gave me a knowing look and I felt my neck flush with embarrassment. I rushed to change the topic. "So you think Katya might have pulled off something like that other Columbia student?"

He straightened his back. "There are many similarities here. Your friend has been missing classes. She didn't show up for a couple of her finals." I nodded. She'd been Rollerblading in the park and spending an afternoon at the Met when she should have been studying. "She has nearly emptied out her dorm room," Richardson continued. "And, just a few days before the two of you went dancing, she withdrew most of what she had in her bank account."

I stared at him. And I had been worried about her. Losing sleep over it.

"It was a substantial sum," he added, wrinkling his brow. "She didn't pay off her student debts with it, I can tell you that much."

Of course. The money from the donor cycle. The money I had paid her. It could last her for a long time if she lived cheaply enough.

"What makes this case even more interesting," Robertson went on, "is that she's an international student and has to leave the country when her student visa expires. She could get a year's extension if she secures the right job, but she hasn't."

I remembered how adamant Katya had been that she wasn't going back home after graduation. At the time, I'd thought about my own experience, how I hadn't wanted to go back to Chicago after college.

But it hadn't occurred to me that Katya couldn't just choose to stay in New York the way I had.

"But why not get her degree and then vanish?" I asked.

He shrugged. "That I can't tell you. But if she's planning on changing her identity, she'll have no use for a diploma under the wrong name."

It made sense; still, I had a hard time accepting it. "So you're saying that she doesn't want to be found—"

"I'm not saying anything. It's a working theory in the absence of any signs of foul play." He closed the pad and put his pen in his shirt pocket. "There are so many undocumented immigrants in this city using fake social security cards. Just walk into any restaurant. It's not that hard to disappear in New York, let me tell you."

"Do you think you'll find her?"

He pursed his lips in a dismissive frown. "If the missing person doesn't turn up within a few weeks, the precinct will hand the case off to Missing Persons. But I must say, unless there is evidence pointing to an involuntary disappearance we just file paperwork."

"So that's it?" I said, more to myself than to him.

"Look, individuals over the age of eighteen legally do not have to return home. If your friend wishes to quit college, take all her money, and start a new life away from friends and family, she has the right to do so. It's a different story if and when she overstays her visa—she has a sixty-day grace period after graduation—but then she won't be my problem. As I'm sure you know, there is a government agency that deals with illegal immigrants." He got up and extended his hand. "Thank you for your help. We'll be in touch if we have more questions."

I walked out of the station and hurried to the subway. It was a beautiful spring morning—blue skies, sparrows chirping in the bushes, kids laughing on their way to school—not that I was in the mood to enjoy it. I'd been upset that Katya hadn't called me back. But to stage her own disappearance was like not returning my calls times a thousand. I couldn't believe I'd been worried about her. That I was going to be late for work because of her. I felt so stupid to have fallen for it. Duped.

Maybe that was why she'd insisted I go dancing with her. I'd thought it weird at the time that none of her friends were around to go with her. Turned out, she hadn't wanted any friends around. A stranger wouldn't spoil her plans. A stranger wouldn't report her missing.

But she was not my concern anymore. My ultrasound was tomorrow and I needed to relax, take care of myself and my baby. Focus my attention where it mattered.

21.

KATYA

My nightmares intensified as December rolled around and the end of the term approached. Most people dream of being chased by killers. In my dreams, I *am* the killer. In my latest, I was killing a woman. I didn't know who she was or why I was doing it. I'd never seen her in real life. But in my dream, I was at once explosively angry and bone-chillingly terrified. It was like I was watching myself from the ceiling as I was cutting her in half with a dull kitchen knife. Not horizontally at the waist. Oh, no, that would have been too quick and easy. I was going vertically, the long way, right down the middle of her face and chest. I woke up screaming in a pool of sweat. Luckily, I had a single room this year.

It was obvious. I didn't need Josh to interpret it for me. I might not have known the woman, but I knew the anger. And I knew the fear. The woman might have represented my mother or myself. It didn't matter. The point was I was about to start my last semester at Columbia and was petrified of having to return to Bulgaria, where my demons awaited me. To stay in the States, I would have to find an employer willing to sponsor me for a work visa.

Josh was right, I thought as I paced up and down the dorm's corridors at four in the morning trying to calm down after my nightmare. I should have been sending out résumés and focusing on my classes. But I felt paralyzed. Like I was having stage fright, just that the stage in this instance was my own life. Instead, I went out. Every night at first, and then I added afternoons when I didn't have classes. Before I knew it, I'd started skipping lectures, too, spending my days at bars and lounges.

Damian and I had been hooking up for close to two months, which was as steady as I'd ever gone with anyone. We weren't exclusive or anything. Damian might be the jealous type, but he certainly wasn't the settling-down type. He'd made sure to tell me so right off the bat. God forbid I got the wrong idea. That, of course, worked out brilliantly for me. We saw each other a couple of times a week and he never insisted that I stay after we'd had sex. I couldn't have asked for a better deal.

On my "evenings off," I hung out in Coogan's, an Irish place in Washington Heights. I liked the bartender there, Nick. He was a cool guy with gorgeous tattoos all over his arms and upper chest who wasn't trying to be anything special—a great relief from my classmates' anxieties and ambitions to conquer the world. Come to think of it, he was the exact opposite of Damian—young and easygoing, not a sharp edge about him.

We'd been friends with benefits for a while before it occurred to me that I was now steadily hooking up with not one but two guys.

The other night, I was at Coogan's when Damian texted. He'd gone on a business trip to London earlier that week and I had no idea he was back in the city. He wanted me to go over to his place, to which I texted back: *Fat chance.* In response, he phoned. It was two in the morning and he sounded drunk. Clearly, a booty call. I told him that I was hanging out with friends in a bar in Washington Heights and there was no way I would go downtown at this hour. He was pissed.

"What's so good about that fucking place that you can't leave?"

I explained, again, that I was here with my friends, that he and I didn't have a date so I'd made other plans.

"What's the name of that bar?" he asked, and I told him.

"It's a simple Irish pub," I added. "Not your kind of joint."

He must have taken that as a challenge because in a little more than half an hour he walked in through the door in his Hugo Boss black wool coat. His hair was dusted with snow and when I looked out the window, I saw big fat snowflakes swirling in the golden light of the streetlamp.

It was just past three on a weekday and the place was nearly empty. I was sitting at the bar, chatting with Nick and a med student, Chris, who, like me, was a regular. The TV screens were on mute, tuned to a soccer game somewhere in Europe. Beyoncé's *Lemonade* album was playing over the speakers. Chris and I were both nursing Coronas.

"Hi, babe," Damian said with a big drunken smile. He took my face in his hands and kissed me, staking his claim just in case anyone had any wrong ideas. Nick knew about Damian, obviously, but Damian didn't know about Nick.

"So these are your friends?" Damian said, and took off his coat. He had that crisp winter smell to him even though he must have just run up to the door from the taxi. I brushed the snow off his hair and introduced him to Nick and Chris. He barely nodded in acknowledgment.

"Hey, man," he said to Nick as he draped his coat over the back of the stool, "give us two raspberry Stolis."

I looked at him. "I don't like vodka, remember?"

"Oh, sorry, babe, I forgot." He turned to Nick again. "And give the lady another . . . *beer*," he said, scoffing at my Corona bottle.

I tried to get a conversation going, involving Nick and Chris, but Damian turned his back on them and after taking a sip of his Stoli, he interrupted me. "Come here," he said, and leaned over and started kissing me, his hands digging under my shirt. I could smell the vodka on his breath.

He'd barely been there for fifteen minutes when he whispered in my ear, "Let's take this party to my place."

I pushed him away and told him I was going home tonight. I had a class tomorrow morning, which was true. I should have been in bed long ago.

"Oh, c'mon, babe, you can't do that to me. I've come all the way here to whisk you away from this dump."

"I didn't ask you to, did I?" He was really starting to piss me off.

He kissed me on the neck in response and wrapped his arm around me. The two of us and Chris were the only customers left at this point.

"Seriously, babe," he said, slurring his words. He'd already downed the first of the Stolis and was working on the second. "You'd rather sit here with these boneheads when you can come home with me and have the sex of your life?"

I pulled away from him. "Damian, which part of *no* don't you get? I'm going home, end of story," I said, and got off the barstool.

That was when he snapped. "You fucking bitch!" he yelled, and grabbed me by the arm. "I came all the way to fucking Washington Heights for you and you're telling me that you're going home?"

I was so startled and embarrassed that I didn't see Nick come out from behind the bar. He looked almost scrawny next to Damian's buff chest and shoulders, but at six two, Nick towered over him.

"Get your hands off her," Nick said as he grabbed Damian's free arm and twisted it behind him.

Damian cried out and let go of me. His face went red, nearly purple with anger.

"You motherfucker!" he said, and tried to pull himself free, but he was too drunk to figure out a way to stand on his feet, let alone fight back.

Still holding Damian's arm twisted behind him, Nick grabbed his coat with his free hand and walked him to the door. "Time to go home," he said as he pushed him out. "And don't come back."

The red neon *BAR* sign on the window flickered. Snow fell steadily, quietly outside. *Kiss up and rub up and feel up*, Beyoncé sang. Like a scene in a movie, I thought as Nick locked up and flipped the *Closed* sign.

"So now I have two guys willing to fight for me," I told Josh at my next session.

Josh, being Josh, frowned back at me. "So you're going to continue seeing Damian?"

"He might act like a pig sometimes, but sex with him is steaming hot," I said, and winked at Josh.

How could I explain that Damian made me feel wanted, desired, like nobody before? There was a certain intensity about him, passion that felt primal. Something in me responded to it. It made me feel alive. Or maybe it was because I was in such a bad place at the moment and I needed all the distraction I could get. Anything to keep me away from the nightmares.

22.

LANA

Dr. Williams walked in with a smile. "How are you feeling today, Lana?"

He was a tall man with thick black eyebrows and gray hair. His bedside manner was impeccable. I'd chosen my first reproductive endocrinologist solely based on gender. If I was going to have someone poking and prodding inside me, my legs spread and propped up on metal holders, it had better be a woman. By my third in vitro cycle, I couldn't care less who was doing it. All I wanted was a baby, and Dr. Williams was rumored to be one of the best in the country. Couples traveled across the globe to do a cycle with him.

Dr. Williams looked at my record on the computer screen. "I see Dr. Bouchard found a subchorionic hematoma last week," he said, and spun on his chair to face me. "Have you had any more bleeding?"

"Just some spotting. On and off."

"Okay, let's see what's going on."

I gripped the sides of the table and began praying as he inserted the magic wand. I had many reasons to be worried, not least the fact that I hadn't kept my promise to tell Katya the truth about who I was.

"Here it is," Dr. Williams said. I held my breath as I stared at the black kidney bean on the screen that kept changing shape as he moved the stick inside me. He finally chose a frame and zoomed in.

"You see this flicker?" he said, pointing with his finger at the screen. "That's the heartbeat."

I exhaled, my legs weak from the postrush of adrenaline.

"I'll start the sound for you," he added.

Tears flooded my eyes as my baby's heartbeat filled the room.

"Good strong beat," Dr. Williams said. "One hundred fifty-three bpm."

He did a few more measurements while I wiped my tears with the back of my sleeve and tried to compose myself.

"Now, here is the hematoma," he said, indicating a small dark mass next to the gestational sac.

He pursed his lips, nodding to himself as he measured it. Finally, he looked at me. My heart sank as I saw his concerned expression. "I'm sure Dr. Bouchard has already explained to you that most clots resolve on their own by twenty weeks of pregnancy. What causes me concern here is that it's measuring bigger than last week. And what we want is for it to be getting smaller."

I clenched my fists. "So what do we do?"

"Look, I'm not going to lie to you. With a clot this size, it can go either way. There is nothing to be done but wait and see. Hopefully, it stops growing and eventually it either bleeds itself out or your body absorbs it." Dr. Bouchard had said the same.

"But is there anything I can do? Should I try to stay off my feet?"

He shook his head. "Later on, we might need to put you on bed rest but let's see how it goes. We'll monitor you weekly."

I nodded, blinking my tears back.

"And don't panic if you get a heavy bleed. The baby could still be okay even if you have a hemorrhage."

With his full head of gray hair, rosy cheeks, and friendly face, Dr. Williams had the aura of a grandfather. Everything about him—his low voice, his mild energy, the way he looked you in the eye—inspired confidence. His presence alone usually helped me relax, knowing he'd take good care of me. But not this time. He could perform miracles in the lab, but there was nothing he could do about my blood clot except monitor it and hope for the best.

At the door, he stopped and turned. "Try not to read the horror stories online. Focus on the positive ones."

◈

I took my time walking the ten or so blocks to the Met, hoping the cool morning breeze would freshen my face and help erase the signs of crying. But the tears kept coming, my eyes growing puffier with each step. All my previous problems had resulted from chromosomal issues in the embryo due to my aging ovaries. Finally, I was pregnant with a healthy baby from the egg of a young woman and a damn blood clot was threatening to destroy it.

I stopped at a small coffee shop a few blocks from the clinic. Tyler and I had made a habit of getting a treat there after our appointments. I ordered a decaf latte and a croissant and took a seat at a table facing the window. Maybe because I was conscious of my red eyes, I had the feeling someone was watching me. I kept turning and looking around to make sure nobody I knew was here. I shouldn't have stopped in a place so close to the museum. Or maybe it was because this was part of my routine with Tyler and it felt weird to be here alone now, to be facing the uncertainties of the future without Tyler holding my hand, telling me that it would be okay. I considered texting Angie, but I knew she'd call me right away and I wasn't ready to talk about it without breaking into sobs. Calling my mother was out of the question. I hadn't even told her I was pregnant.

If only Katya were still around.

I could see why she might want to go "missing." I understood she was an adult and could choose to disappear if she so desired. But she'd stormed into my life, laughing, dancing, swirling me along with her, only to then vanish just as suddenly. I could hear Angie's voice in my head pointing out that maybe if I hadn't stalked her, I wouldn't have a reason to complain now. True. It was all my damn fault. And I was okay with that. If only I hadn't made that foolish promise to tell Katya the truth in exchange for the welfare of my baby. How was I going to keep my end of the bargain now?

Dr. Williams, of course, would think I was crazy to even entertain the thought that my pregnancy could depend on telling someone something. But I'd rather be superstitious than powerless. Because there is nothing worse than being at the mercy of chance. The belief that there is something you can do—if only I prayed hard enough, if only I eliminated sugar from my diet—can help regain a sense of control. My pregnancy might be in God's hands—or random chance or whatever one believes in—but coming clean to Katya about it was something *I* could do even if I had to search door-to-door to find her.

There had to be a way to track her down. Maybe I could unearth a clue on her Instagram. But if she didn't want to be found, did I have the right to search for her?

I'd crossed so many lines already, one more wouldn't make a difference, I thought as I left the coffee shop.

When I finally made it to my office, I had five new e-mails from my boss, the latest one just three minutes ago, asking if I was coming in late *again*. It was 9:28 a.m. Not really "late" by most standards. In the other Met departments, people trickled in between nine and nine thirty, even ten. But my boss, senior art curator and head of the Drawings and Prints Department, Mr. Alistair Bramley—fancy British accent, kerchief in the pocket—was a stickler for rules and punctuality.

To hell with him, I thought, and replied that I was here already if he needed me. Then I opened my Internet browser and pulled up Katya's Instagram account.

23.
KATYA

I was leaving the cafeteria when I caught a glimpse of the pink sheet of paper pinned to the bulletin board. It was a gray day in January nearing the end of the break. The city was in a panic, bracing for a blizzard, but the campus was quiet with only a few of us having stayed during the holidays. I'd hardly seen my country mentioned anywhere so I had to stop, find out what the notice was all about. I couldn't believe it. A couple was looking for an egg donor from Bulgaria, of all places. Little tiny Bulgaria, barely seven million people. I called right away. I didn't know if that would be something I'd want to do but I had to at least find out about the Bulgarian connection. The guy on the other end sounded nice, excited to hear from me. We arranged to meet the next day. I was a bit apprehensive at first—what if he was some weirdo?—but he turned out to be pretty cool. A professor at the university. Teaches philosophy, of all things. I started laughing when he told me. I mean, I'd guessed him to be an ex–basketball player or maybe a tennis player. Anything but an academic with his nose buried in books all day.

It was one of those still winter mornings that followed a snowstorm. There were hardly any cars on the streets, and I was excited to have a reason to go out and brave the cold before the white blanket covering the sidewalks had turned into gray slush. We met at the Hungarian Pastry Shop on Amsterdam, across from the cathedral. He said it was a Columbia classic. Students and professors have been going there for decades. It looked a little shabby to me—old wooden chairs and tables, framed book covers hanging on the walls, an AC unit by the window—but it had a certain charm. Like a worn-out sweater that's cozy for the memories, not so much for its look. Anyway, it was warm inside and the coffee was good, so I wasn't going to complain.

His name was Tyler. Tyler Jones. I liked it. I hadn't met any Tylers before.

"My partner and I really want a baby," he said, and gave me a brief overview of their struggles to conceive. His eyes were deep blue and sad like the ocean on a clear winter day. At first, I thought he was gay. I mean, what would you think when a guy talks about his partner? Either he's referring to his boyfriend or someone he has business with. And I told him so. He laughed. Some men roar like predators, hyenas on the prowl (though I'm sure they're picturing themselves as lions). But Tyler's laugh was soft, boyish somehow, even though he was a tall, big man.

"Sorry," he said. "I should have made it clear. We're not married but we've been living together for eight years and have been trying for a baby for nearly as long. So *girlfriend/boyfriend* just doesn't do it justice. The relationship, that is."

"Why haven't you gotten married, then?" I asked. A fair question, right?

He rubbed his chin. "It's complicated."

"Why? You come from feuding families? Like Romeo and Juliet?"

That got him laughing again. I cracked up, too. Just watching the serious philosophy professor laugh was hilarious. His whole face lit up, like a kid.

"She's a feminist," he explained, "and doesn't like the patriarchal connotations of 'wife' as a husband's property. 'Partner' implies equality."

I liked her already, that partner of his. Tyler told me she wanted her baby to have the genes of her people. I was stunned. I'd never been the patriotic type but admired those who were. I would have gone for a pretty girl, myself, if I were looking for a donor. Pretty and smart. Ideally, a girl who looked somewhat like me. So that it wouldn't be obvious, you know, that the child wasn't mine. Who cared where the genes came from? It wasn't like you could put it on your job application: *BA,*

Harvard College, summa cum laude, Bulgarian genes. Or on your Tinder account, for that matter. Guys don't favor particular genes the way they dig big tits and blond hair.

I asked Tyler why she hadn't joined us. I was curious about the woman who didn't want to be called a wife and who so cherished her lineage.

Tyler leaned closer and told me in a hushed voice, as if divulging top national secrets, that she didn't know he had put up a flyer.

"Oh," I said. "It's a surprise?"

He shook his head. He seemed sad, hurt by it somehow. "Actually, I don't plan on telling her."

Which made no sense to me—how could they use my eggs without her knowing about it? Until he explained that I needed to register with the donor agency they were using. That way they could "select" me from the inventory of donors. The problem, he told me, was that his partner wanted to do an anonymous cycle. "You see," he said, lowering his voice again, "she's scared of complications in the future. You know, that the donor might come back and claim the baby."

I had to laugh. Not because it was a ridiculous fear. I got it. I'd seen a movie where a couple had adopted a child but the mother who had given it up at birth came looking for it years later. No, I laughed because I didn't want to have children. And I told him so.

"Anyway, it's much easier to use the agency," he said. "The staff will handle all the formalities." Apparently, there were tons of legal documents to sign, medical exams and consultations to deal with. "Let me tell you a bit about the process," he said, and gave me a brief overview.

I'd already done some research online. It wasn't like donating a kidney or anything that we have a limited number of. I wouldn't have fewer eggs myself to use in the future if I gave some away. Each month a woman loses a bunch of her eggs. Only one of them matures and can be fertilized. More rarely two—which is how fraternal twins are conceived. Doctors use hormones to stimulate a lot more eggs from that monthly set into maturity in order to collect them. It seemed to me it was really a lot more like donating your old coats instead of dumping them into the garbage, or in this case flushing them down the toilet.

"You won't believe this," I told Josh first thing as I walked into his office two days later, my gloves and hat still on.

He smiled. "I'm all ears."

I pulled out the pink sheet of paper from my coat pocket and handed it to him. "How lucky is that?" I said, and as he unfolded the paper and read it, I took my gloves and hat off and sat down on the couch. "If this doesn't help me turn my life around, I don't know what will."

He gave me back the flyer. "Why do you think so?"

"Don't you see? This is my chance for redemption."

He furrowed his brow. "How so?"

"I can't bring Alex back. Obviously. But I can give what I took—a life. I can give the gift of a baby to a hopeless couple."

Josh did a string of slow nods, like he was finally starting to get what I was talking about. "And it's not like I got pregnant and will have a baby I'd like to get rid of. No. It will be quite an ordeal injecting myself with hormones and undergoing procedures, including a minor surgery to retrieve the eggs. It will be painful, as a proper penance should be. But in the end, I will have made one unlucky couple happy and helped bring a new life to this world." I looked at Josh. "It will be my atonement for Alex."

Josh's eyes softened. The radiator was blasting in his office and I was starting to sweat. I remembered I still had my coat on and took it off.

"The kicker is I'd get paid ten thousand dollars." We'd already talked about how even if I started a job the day after commencement, it would take time to get my first paycheck. With the money from the donation, I'd be able to pay first month's rent and a security deposit, buy office clothes and all that. Now I only needed to find a job that would give me a work visa.

"How about Damian?" Josh asked. "What does he think about you becoming an egg donor?"

"Seriously?" I looked at Josh with my eyebrows hiked up on my forehead. "You can't possibly be suggesting that I need to talk to Damian about it? This has nothing to do with him. It's not like I'll be taking a job as a *hooker*."

Josh laughed. "But I imagine it might affect your 'hooking up' with him—or anyone else for that matter—during that month. Something to think about if you plan on keeping that relationship."

"Relationship?" I rolled my eyes just in case stressing the word wasn't enough. "Please." But Josh had a point. "I guess I do need to figure out a way to keep him at bay for a few weeks. Though I imagine I'll be hooking up with somebody else by then. From what I read online, it takes months to get it all going. All the tests and paperwork and then the medications to prep both women for it. Either way, I'm not worried. I'll think of something when the time comes."

Josh didn't even ask what was wrong with just telling the guy—whoever he was—the truth. He'd learned by now when to push me and when to let it go.

"Anyway. Doing this . . ." I pointed to the flyer. "This will finally set me free!"

24.

LANA

NOW

Katya's Instagram feed was composed of moody shots of coffee cups, candy and chocolate bars, fire hydrants, buildings leaning to the side, hands holding drinks, and selfies in different but mostly unrecognizable locations. She hadn't bothered to tag people and places. I stared at the quilt of colorful images on my screen, my hand on the mouse, ready to click to a different window should Alistair walk into my office.

Some of Katya's selfies featured other people, like the one she'd taken with me at the club. Strangely, as I scrolled through, I couldn't find a single photo with—or of—anyone who even remotely resembled Tom Cruise. In fact, the only guy who appeared repeatedly in her feed was the heavily tattooed bartender who'd gotten us the table outside at the Irish pub in Washington Heights.

Then it hit me. Hadn't she told me she lived around there? That she'd found a cheap room to rent in a friend's apartment instead of moving in with her possessive boyfriend? Robertson said she'd emptied out her dorm room. Her new place, then, the place where she was living her new life under a new identity, must be in Washington Heights. I was willing to bet that the bartender knew something about it.

I told Alistair I wasn't feeling well and left the office early. He was clearly unhappy about it and pointedly asked about my presentation for the Visiting Committee meeting on Monday. It was already Wednesday and I'd barely completed the outline. Still, I reassured him that it was coming along well and promised to have it done by end of day Friday. That gave me two full days to finish it.

I reached Coogan's shortly before five p.m. For all I knew, Katya's friend wasn't even working today, but I had to take my chances. It was a cold spring day, the threat of rain lingering in the air since morning, and the outdoor café was closed. Inside, the sour smell of beer turned my stomach. A sure sign of pregnancy that I found comforting. As I'd hoped, the place was still pretty empty except for a few guys at the bar. An old Sinéad O'Connor song played softly over the sound system. I couldn't remember the title but the voice was unmistakable.

Katya's friend stood at the back end of the bar, slouched over his phone. Or at least I thought it was him because of the shaved head and tattooed biceps showing under his black T-shirt. I walked straight there and slid onto a stool in front of him.

He looked up—yes, it was him—his expression loud and clear: *What the fuck did you sit all the way over here for?* He was younger than I'd thought, twenty-five at most. I wondered if *he* was the friend she'd moved in with.

"Hi," I said before he'd had a chance to make his escape, leaving the other bartender to deal with me. "You remember me?"

He squinted at me questioningly.

"I was here with Katya a couple of weeks ago."

At the mention of Katya he seemed to flinch. Or was I imagining it? He squinted at me as if trying to place me. "Oh yeah," he said, but I could tell he had no clue.

I leaned in. "How is she?"

"Fuck if I know." He clicked his phone off and put it in his back pocket. "Can I get you something?"

I asked for club soda. He arched an eyebrow but poured me a glass and put it in front of me without a comment. I said, bluffing, "I thought you guys lived together."

"Why would you think that?"

"Katya told me." I lowered my voice.

"Ha. And did she tell you that she stood me up yesterday?"

"Yesterday?"

"Yup." He leaned on the bar. A wolf's face poked through the dense vines on his forearm. "If you see her, tell her that Nick's fucking pissed. All right? She's not answering her phone."

"Do you have her new number?"

He pulled back. "She changed her number?"

Either this guy was a great actor or he had no clue about Katya starting a new life.

"When was the last time you saw her?"

"A week ago." He rubbed his chin. "No, wait. More than that. Maybe two weeks. Why did she change her number?" Another Sinéad O'Connor song came on. This one I remembered well: "Nothing Compares 2 U." I wondered if this guy was even born when that album came out.

"When did you schedule yesterday's date?" I asked.

"That's been in the works for some time. She even made me set up a reminder on my phone with an alarm. Then *she* fucking doesn't show up."

"So she doesn't live with you?"

He rested his elbows on the bar and locked me in his gaze. "She was supposed to move in yesterday," he finally said. "Officially, anyway. She'd already brought all her shit."

I felt a tightening in my stomach. "She did? When?"

"Why are you asking me all this?"

I sighed. "You don't know, do you?"

"Know what?"

"Katya's missing."

He blinked at me, seemingly confused. I took my phone out and opened the *Columbia Daily Spectator* article before handing it to him.

"Fuck me!" he said, and let go of the phone. He poured himself a shot of tequila and downed it before turning back. "I had no fucking idea. Haven't opened Facebook in ages."

"The police think she meant to disappear," I said. "Because she emptied out her dorm room. But you're saying . . ."

"We were supposed to . . . shit. You think she's okay?"

"I was hoping that you'd know. But if you haven't seen her . . ." I bit my lip.

He looked at his empty shot glass, then back at me. "We were supposed to get married yesterday," he said, and went to the other end of the bar.

I stared after him as Sinéad O'Connor cried from the speakers: *Nothing compares to you.*

❖

"Nick, you have to go to the police," I said slowly, trying not to sound panicked.

"Like fuck I will." He took a gulp of his whiskey. He'd poured us each a glass. Mine sat untouched; his had two fingers left when he put it back down.

I looked up to the ceiling as I always did when I felt exasperated. It was too much to process. Katya was planning to marry this guy? What happened to the Tom-Cruise-look-alike banker? Wouldn't she have told me she couldn't move in with him because she was getting married to this other guy? Instead of this whole thing about how she didn't want to be "tied up" or however she'd put it. Meanwhile she'd transported her things from the dorm to this guy's apartment? It made no sense. But why would he lie about it?

The important thing was that he had her stuff. Marriage or no marriage, she'd planned to live with him and that meant she hadn't intended to "disappear."

"Don't you get it?" I said, raising my voice. "The cops need to start searching for her."

He swirled the whiskey in his glass, looking at it intensely, as if along with the ice cubes he could rearrange his thoughts.

I shrugged and stood up. "You're leaving me no choice but to go and tell them myself. I'm sure they'd love to know how come you hadn't reported—"

"Fine," Nick said, and gulped the last of his whiskey. "I'll go to the station when the other bartender shows up at six. Now if you'll excuse me, I've got work to do." And with that he walked to the other end of the bar and started pulling glasses out of the dishwasher.

"I hope you don't mind me asking," I said, following him, "but how long have you two dated?"

Without looking up, his attention on the glasses he was lining up on the counter, he muttered, "Lady, that's none of your business."

Something about the way he said it, under his breath and pausing after each word, made it sound more like a threat than frustration.

What had Katya gotten herself into? I thought as I walked out.

25.
KATYA

"Do you know anyone who might want to go in on a green card marriage with me?"

Nick rested his elbows on the bar and stared at me. It was nearly two in the morning and there were only three other customers left. I'd spent the past week researching it. The going rate was between eight and thirty thousand dollars. What better use for the ten grand I'd make for my donation? I'd be guilt-free *and* legal. I would no longer have to worry about finding an employer willing to sponsor me for a visa. I couldn't have asked for more.

I'd come to Nick for obvious reasons. He knew a ton of people who came to the bar. He lived in the neighborhood. He was my best bet.

"How much?"

"Ten grand."

He whistled, then locked me in his gaze. "Yeah, me."

"I'm serious."

"So am I. Why pay some motherfucker you don't know?"

"Nick, this is no joke. You can get in real trouble if we get caught. They interview you separately, asking you shit like which side of the bed I sleep on, what color toothbrush I use, and then they compare our answers. We have to prove we live together; we need a joint bank account, utility bills, shit like that."

"Again, why trust a stranger?"

I thought about it. "True. You and I already have a story. No need to make up shit about how we met and when we first hooked up. I have shots on social media at the bar that date back months. A couple even with you and we can easily add more before we sign the papers."

He raised the right corner of his lip. That counted for a smile with Nick.

"You know this is at least a two-year commitment, right? We'll continue our own separate lives, sure. But what if you meet a girl you want to marry for real?"

He stared at me as if to say, *Who, me?*

"We really have to be careful." I went on. "Your roommate will be a problem. He can testify that we're not living . . . Wait. Can you get rid of him? I'll need to find a room after graduation anyway. Why pay rent to some stranger when I can be your roommate?"

He poured us both a shot of tequila and lifted his in a silent *Cheers*. I followed suit.

"Roommates with benefits. I like it," he said, and drank it down. "I like it a lot."

"Now we're talking." I laughed and set my empty glass on the bar. "I'm thinking we can do it on the day of graduation. I'll wear a white summer dress and we can show them the party photos as our 'wedding' shots."

"That's like four months from now, no?"

"We need that time to prepare. It can't look like we got married the day I have to leave. That will be suspicious. We'll get the marriage license like a month in advance to show we've planned it long before."

I thought about it as he drank.

"You're right, the best part is that I can trust you. I will give you the money before we do the deed in city hall. This way it won't look suspicious. You know what I mean?"

He shook his head.

"Like we get married and the next day you deposit ten grand into your bank account. Duh. Instead, I'll write you a check a few weeks *before* we become 'husband and wife.' So nobody can put two and two together. No, wait. I better give it to you in cash. We don't want to leave a paper trail of money changing hands."

We clinked glasses and drank to seal the deal.

26.

LANA

"Lana, can you come in, please?" Alistair called out the next day as I walked by his office with two folio volumes from the Watson Library downstairs under my arm. "I'd like to have a chat."

Here it comes, I thought, but smiled and said, "Sure."

His office was as constipated as his appearance. There was not a book on his desk, not a sheet of paper, not a loose pen. If he had stacks of documents, to-do lists, correspondence, he kept it all out of sight in drawers and cabinets. His art books and catalogs were lined up on the bookshelf and organized by region and period, not piled on the desk or strewn all over the floor like mine. Everything in Alistair's life seemed to be arranged just so, down to the kerchief in his pocket. Today it was a burgundy red (to match the tie) with a pink trim, folded in such a way that one of the two corners that showed was bigger and taller than the other, creating the silhouette of a mountain. At other times, he would have three corners poking out spread like a flower, or just one solid triangle. Sometimes, the part showing would be simply parallel to the line of the pocket. I'd always wanted to ask him how he determined which shape was suited for each day.

"I know you're undergoing medical treatments," he began, "but this is getting out of hand. You come in late. You leave early."

I nodded patiently. I apologized. I promised my work hadn't suffered. What was I supposed to say? *See, Alistair, sometimes life gets in the way of art?*

"I don't understand what's happened to you," he continued. "You used to be a responsible, dedicated researcher."

My hands curled into fists. I wanted to tell him to shove his kerchief up his ass. I was sick of his questioning the quality of my work just because of my schedule.

"Now, listen to me," he began in his typical patronizing manner, and went on to tell me he'd just gotten off the phone with a prominent European dealer who'd informed him that a private collector was planning on selling a drawing by Charles de La Fosse that we'd long hoped to add to our collection. Alistair was going to have to fly to Paris tomorrow, which meant he would have to miss the Visiting Committee meeting on Monday. "It will be up to you," he continued, "to present the Parmigianino show."

"Of course," I said, thrilled for the opportunity.

He leaned forward. "I'm counting on you to dazzle them," he said, but by the way he was looking at me, his head tilted, his eyes narrowed, I knew what he really meant was: *I don't trust you, but I have no choice.*

"You have nothing to worry about." I got up to leave.

"And Lana," he said, still squinting at me. "I'll need your presentation by Saturday, Sunday at the latest, so that I can review it and send you notes by Monday morning."

I sighed with relief because it didn't look like I'd be able to finish it by end of day tomorrow as I'd promised.

Back in my office, I dropped the folios on my desk and pulled up my chair. Before starting on the presentation, I went online to check the news about Katya. Nothing. It was already two p.m. Assuming Nick had gone to the police station yesterday—as he'd said he would—there should have been some media update by now. I tried to imagine the order of things: interview Nick, go look at Katya's stuff in his place, take her computer in case there were some clues in there, check out Mehanata's footage of that night, and try to identify Jacuzzi Guy. I was basing this, of course, on what I'd seen in movies. Maybe in real life things moved at a slower pace.

Or maybe Nick hadn't gone to the police at all.

At four, I checked the Internet again. Still no news on Katya. It had been eleven days already. Was there still a chance for a good ending? I googled *missing woman* and browsed through the entries, reading articles and notices about girls gone missing all over the country. Along with the stories that were happily resolved, I found just as many cases that had ended in tragedy. The exercise reminded me of the search I'd done for *hematoma*. Things could turn out well or badly, and nobody could tell you on which side of the divide you'd land.

We just have to wait and see, Dr. Williams had told me.

I felt like I would burst if I did any more sitting and waiting. Two lives were hanging in the balance—and, strangely enough, they had the same genes.

One thing I'd learned from my quick read on the Internet: when a woman goes missing, the first person the police look into is "a spouse or a partner, or a spurned lover," as one detective was quoted. There were at least three men—that I knew of—in Katya's life: her Tom-Cruise-look-alike "boyfriend"; her fiancé, Nick, presuming he hadn't lied about that; and Jacuzzi Guy, with whom she'd gone home that night.

On my way home through the park, I had the nagging feeling that someone was following me. I turned to look over my shoulder not once but three times. Of course there was nobody. I was on heightened alert simply because of all the horrible stories I'd just read. Nick had given me the creeps yesterday, too. I had to know if he'd gone to the cops or not. Every minute counted.

I pulled out my phone and called Coogan's. A woman answered and I asked for Nick. She didn't say anything but it didn't seem like she'd hung up because I could hear music and voices in the background.

"Yeah?" he said into the receiver.

"This is Lana, Katya's friend. Just wondering if you went to the police."

Nick blew the air out of his lungs loudly. "They kept me there all night. Thank you very much."

"Oh." I felt bad for him. But it had been a small price to pay for finally getting the cops' attention. "But they let you go in the end—"

"With a warning not to go anywhere until my stories check out. And just so you know, they weren't impressed a bit that I'd gone to talk to them myself. Apparently, killers like to meddle with investigations and are known to lurk around."

"Killers? Are they worried she was killed?"

"Aren't you?" And with that he hung up.

I sped up my steps, anxious to get out of the park.

27.

KATYA

It was happening. I was going to be an egg donor. In my excitement, I even told my mother about it. We connected on Skype every now and then. She called me all the time, actually, but I hardly ever answered. What was there to talk about? Since I never really called *her*, when I finally did last week, she nearly had a heart attack.

"Katya, are you okay? Is everything okay?" She started fretting before I'd even said "Hello." She looked tired, deep dark circles under her eyes.

"Good news," I said to preempt any further worrying. She lit a cigarette and stared at the computer screen as if she hadn't seen me in years. She kept her old Dell laptop in the kitchen on a shelf under the TV. Her entire life was in that small dark kitchen. She got home from work, turned on the television, and spent the rest of the evening smoking and watching reality shows, Turkish and Indian soaps, and, of course, the news. Her neighbor across the hall—a divorced woman about my mother's age whose son was in high school—often came over in the evenings. The two would have a glass of *rakia* and some meze, clouds of cigarette smoke floating over their heads, especially in the winter when the windows were closed.

Anyway, she freaked out when I told her about the egg donation. She didn't exactly know what it was. She'd only heard about it on television. But once I explained the process, she got it.

"As long as it's not dangerous," she said, "and you'll still have eggs left for the future, for your own baby."

I refrained from mentioning I wasn't planning on having any babies of my own. One shock at a time. But I did tell her that I was doing it for Alex. We hadn't spoken of him all these years. Not a word. She went to the cemetery all the time—All Souls' Day, the anniversary of Alex's death, you name it—but we never talked *about* him, only about his grave (the stone needs cleaning; the weeds need weeding). So it was a big deal bringing it up. Just mentioning his name made her cry. And it wasn't like I talked about what had happened. I only said, "I'm doing it in memory of Alex. A payback of sorts."

She lit a new cigarette, fumbling with the lighter in an attempt to hide her tears.

"I don't know what I'd expected she'd say," I told Josh. "It wasn't like I was looking for approval or a pat on the back. I just wanted her to know, I guess."

Josh did one of his bobbing nods, jotted something in his notebook.

"Anyway, I'm super excited. I'm officially one of the agency's donors. You should see my profile. I look really good on paper. Tyler told me to say that I'd already graduated so as not to alarm his partner." I smiled. "I need to stop thinking of him as Tyler. I signed up for one of his classes, actually, and starting tomorrow, he will be Professor Jones."

Josh sat up. "You're taking a philosophy class?"

"Why not? Damian asked me the same thing. I haven't told him—obviously—about becoming a donor. But is it so absurd to want to learn a bit about Socrates, Plato, and Aristotle? People keep quoting them. The mighty ancient Greek philosophers."

Josh blinked at me. "You don't think it would be awkward to have Tyler Jones as your professor?"

"Why? It would be great. I'd get to know him better."

I'd checked out his profile on the philosophy department's website: *Prof. Jones specializes in logic, philosophy of mind, and epistemology. . . . He has a particular interest in modal logic, topological and probabilistic semantics, and philosophical theories of chance, coincidence, and luck.* I didn't understand many of the terms, but the last bit about chance and luck seemed quite interesting. Like, if I'd gone back to Bulgaria for the winter break, I wouldn't have seen the donor egg flyer.

I'd always been intrigued by the fact that our lives often hung on the smallest, most trivial decisions. Go for a drive at the wrong time, or for a swim, in my case. It's almost like it's not the action that's *good* or *bad* but what happens afterward that colors it and gives it meaning. Who hasn't answered their phone while driving, right? We can't even remember each time we've done it because there is nothing inherently wrong in the action. It's not like stealing or cheating. Until that one time when a child happens to run across the street and you don't see it because for a fraction of a second, you've looked away to pick up your phone.

"And he doesn't mind that you'll be his student?" Josh asked, pulling me away from my thoughts.

I shrugged. "I'm sure he won't. I mean, we've already met. His partner is the one who wants it all anonymous. But Tyler's okay."

"Professor Jones," Josh said.

"Oops. Yeah. *Professor Jones.*" It rolled easily off my tongue. I could almost taste it. Sweet and smooth, like chocolate. *Professor Tyler Jones.*

28.

LANA

On Friday morning, I turned on the local news and stared at a freeze frame from a security camera of Katya and Jacuzzi Guy walking out of the Bulgarian club, his hand behind her back. The banner read: *Police seeking man in photograph in connection with missing Columbia student's case.*

Finally.

By lunchtime, Jacuzzi Guy, whose name apparently was Mark Patterson, "had been detained by police for questioning," according to *Gothamist*—a neighborhood news site that Angie had told me about.

Part relieved, part scared, I kept checking for news of Katya's whereabouts the rest of the day. By the time five o'clock rolled around, I'd barely made any progress on the damn presentation for the visiting committee. Since Alistair wasn't in the office today, I packed up and left, thinking that the trip home would reenergize me and then, after an early dinner, I could work all evening.

Before going to bed, I made the mistake of turning on the eleven o'clock news. The police had apparently let Jacuzzi Guy go. Mark Patterson was not a suspect, the anchor read, and the police were pursuing other leads.

I turned off the TV and went to bed. An hour later, I was still too agitated to sleep. I was furious. They'd kept Mark Patterson, an investment banker at Goldman Sachs, for only a few hours while Nick, a bartender in Washington Heights, had spent the night at the police station, even though he hadn't even been with Katya on the night she'd disappeared. Unless . . . Could she have gone "home" to his place that night?

I gave up trying to sleep and sat up in the dark to surf the Internet, hoping to distract myself. I had my laptop propped on top of a pillow instead of directly on my belly. Maybe the whole thing about computers emitting harmful waves wasn't true, but why add yet another unknown variable to the equation? After I'd exhausted my tolerance for other people's vacations, meals, and baby photos on Facebook, I signed on to the Fertile Thoughts forum. I didn't post any updates. I didn't even search for posts about hematomas. I just scanned through the messages, responding to those I could, trying to be helpful and encouraging to other women doing a donor egg cycle.

I answered a question about the process of selecting a donor, then another one about donors' medical histories and how to spot potential red flags. It had never occurred to me before but I wondered what donors talked about in their section of the forum. You have to request to join each group if you want to post, answer questions, or interact with other members, but the threads are public and can be read by anyone on the Internet.

I scanned the posts quickly at first, feeling like I was trespassing. Donors seemed to be mostly concerned with the retrieval surgery (*Was it painful? For how long are you out?*) and with the injections (*How do you administer them? Do you go crazy because of the hormones?* And so on). As I scrawled through the exchanges, a user name jumped out at me: *BGgirl.* My pulse sped up. Katya's Instagram ID was @BGgirl. Could it be?

I clicked on *BGgirl* and started reading through her posts. Her last one read: *Don't worry, ladies, the surgery is no big deal. Loving the high from the anesthesia ;)*

I checked the date: one day before Good Friday, the day of Katya's retrieval.

I kept reading. The usual concerns about the hormones and the different steps of the process. More exchanges about the effects of the drugs, the cramps and . . . the cute doctor at the clinic. What? That was not a discussion I'd ever seen on my side of the forum. Of course, it was very different on the donors' end—they were going through all of it while living their lives as single women.

I barely had time to consider which of the doctors at my clinic Katya might have found attractive when I read:

BGgirl: *OMG, have you ever had a crush on the guy??? You know, THE guy who would be the father!*

My heart racing, I picked up the phone and dialed Tyler's number.

29.

KATYA

Professor Jones was a passionate lecturer. He liked to push and provoke us. At his first lecture, he walked in and stood at the lectern, tall and imposing, scanning the rows of faces in front of him. Seeing me he paused, a look of surprise flitting across his face, before he took in the rest of the auditorium. Finally he spoke.

"Albert Camus famously said: 'There is but one truly serious philosophical question, and that is suicide. Judging whether life is or is not worth living amounts to answering the fundamental question of philosophy.'" Tyler gave us time to absorb his words before continuing, "If the answer to that question seems obvious to you, you're lucky—you're not a philosopher."

The hall erupted with laughing.

"For the rest of you," Tyler said, raising his right arm, "don't expect that you'll find the answer in this class. Or any other class for that matter."

More laughter.

"I imagine by now you're wondering what, then, you're going to learn here. I'll tell you what. You'll learn to question things, to wonder, to be curious." He then suggested that those of us who weren't interested were free to leave. Nobody did. The hall was so quiet, I didn't dare breathe. At the next lecture, the number of students had nearly doubled.

We were now halfway through the semester. Winter had given way to spring, the weather turning warm and sunny, the daffodils poking their heads all over campus. Tyler's Intro to Philosophy class had become my favorite of all time. I hadn't realized I talked about it nonstop until Damian declared he was sick of hearing about that "damn philos-ophy professor of yours." He was jealous, obviously.

I wasn't alone in my enthusiasm for Tyler's lectures. We all sat there watching him, spellbound, as he spoke in his velvety voice, gesticulating, asking us questions back and forth, like a tennis match, even laughing with us. It felt less like a lecture and more like a joint enterprise. Like together we were figuring out the meaning of beauty, knowledge, hap-piness. We were discussing Plato's *Symposium* today. It was a particu-larly raucous debate—we were all such experts on love, of course—but I didn't participate. I was looking at Tyler. The way he leaned against the wall and crossed his arms while listening to my classmates ex-press their opinions, the way he smiled, the way he held on to his chin as he thought.

There were stars in my eyes, I'm not going to lie.

But it wasn't sexual or anything. It was more like being in church. As I sat there, listening to Tyler in sheer awe, it suddenly hit me: I was going to have a baby with him. At the thought, I swelled with pride. I looked around the class—everyone staring at him with their mouths open—and thought, *I will have our professor's baby. It's just that another woman will carry it.*

Josh freaked out when I told him about it during our session two days later. "This sounds fucked-up," he said.

"Which part?" I asked, taken aback. He'd never used such language before.

"Sorry. Just slipped out of my mouth." Josh paused. "Does Professor Jones know any of this?"

"Of what?"

"How you feel about him and your donation?"

I hadn't yet started the hormone injections but all the documents were signed and we were ready to go in a few weeks. "Of course he doesn't," I said. "How would he?" Josh was starting to piss me off. "We don't talk about matters outside of the class material."

Tyler had called me up to his office after our first class and explained that we had an ethical problem. A conflict of interest. "People might think that I would be more lenient with you because you're our donor." But I'd reassured him that I didn't expect that and trusted that he wouldn't allow himself to be swayed. "Also," I said, "how would anyone know? I wouldn't mention it and, in fact, this would be the last time the two of us would speak about it." He smiled at that, thought a little more, then said, "Okay, if you have any questions about the material, stop by during office hours." And that was that.

I was doing great in his class anyway. The topics blew me away. I read not only the required but also the suggested readings. I ate it all up. No surprise then that I aced the midterm and got an A+ on my first paper. Next to the grade, he'd scribbled that my grasp of the issues was outstanding. "Not bad, huh?" I said to Josh.

He did one of his "impressed" nods—eyes wide open, head slightly tilted—but didn't say anything.

I went on. "If I'd taken that class in freshman year, I might've ended up a philosophy major. I find it really fascinating, pondering all that stuff. And it comes easy to me. I'm good at arguing a point. Of making a case for any position I choose. Playing the devil's advocate."

Josh pursed his lips in a smirk as if to say, *Don't I know it.*

30.

LANA

"Is everything okay?" Tyler asked, his voice groggy with sleep. The alarm clock on my nightstand showed 1:33 a.m. but I didn't care.

"What's her name?" I asked.

"Whose name?"

"The woman you're fucking."

"Lana, I'm not fucking—"

"We're no longer together, Tyler," I said, stressing each word. "It's okay. I just want to know her name."

"Lana, it's the middle of the night. Do you really want to—"

"*You told me* there had been someone else," I said, my stomach clenched like a fist. "What's her name?"

"That's over and I never said that she and I slept together—"

"Christ, Tyler, spare me the details. Just give me the damn name."

I heard the rustling of covers, the sound of bedsprings. He must have gotten up, started pacing. "Look, she's one of my students," he said.

My ears began ringing. I felt dizzy and leaned back against the headboard.

"It's all my fault," Tyler was saying, "but I can explain."

"Her name?" I managed to say, and held my breath, terrified of the answer.

He sighed. "Lana, why are you doing this to yourself?"

"Just say it, damn it!"

"Fine. Her name's Elaine. Are you happy now?"

"Thrilled," I said, and hung up.

Fucking hell, I thought, and tossed the phone on the bed. I got up and went to the kitchen. There was an old half pint of frozen strawberry yogurt in the freezer and I pulled it out.

Back in the bedroom, I took my phone and texted Angie. *Are you awake?* I saw the typing icon flash and exhaled. I'd already pressed Call by the time her *yep* arrived. As usual, she was on a deadline and working late.

"Can you believe it? One of his TAs?" I said once I'd given her the highlights.

"Such a cliché," she said. In my mind I could see her shaking her head.

"And please don't tell me it's love," I went on. "Love takes time. It can't happen without allowing it to. You know what I mean? The flame of love can't burn if you don't stoke the fire."

Angie laughed. "You're turning into quite the poet, my dear. Having your heart broken might be the key to your literary success."

"I think I'm going to stick to art, but thanks." I sighed, suddenly feeling very tired. "At least it wasn't Katya. I really freaked myself out there for a moment."

"C'mon," Angie said. "*You* were the one who stalked *her*, remember? She doesn't even know Tyler."

"It's just mind-boggling to me why she would write that."

"Who knows? Maybe she was considering a cycle with another couple and was referring to another guy. Or maybe she was making shit up just for the fun of it. Didn't you two come up with fake names and jobs that night at the club?" I could hear Angie's mouse clicking, her fingers tapping on the keyboard. "Either way, my friend," she went on, "you're becoming paranoid . . ." Her voice trailed off. I was about to bid her good night and let her finish her assignment when she gasped: "Oh, my God!"

"What?"

"I'm so sorry," she said, barely audible. Then: "Just sent you the link."

I knew it. In the pit of my stomach I knew it even before the page had loaded. The headline read: *Female body found in the Hudson Friday morning believed to be missing Columbia student.*

PART 3

I LOVE IT WHEN YOU WORRY ABOUT ME

31.

LANA

I sat at the piano, staring into space, my hands resting in my lap, my fingers burning with pain. I had played like mad all afternoon in a desperate attempt to silence my thoughts. Sunlight streamed into the room in thick shafts. Plato was sprawled on the floor in a sun patch by my feet, one of his legs sticking out straight from under him, looking like a chicken thigh. Sparrows chirped in the lone tree outside with grating exuberance, but I didn't have it in me to get up to close the window. I'd tried to go for a walk earlier but had barely made it to the entrance of the park before turning back. Wherever I'd looked, I'd seen baby strollers, kids pushing scooters or pedaling tiny bikes.

Meanwhile, Katya lay dead in the morgue.

There was a brief mention of her in the morning news and the local papers. *Mystery thickens*, the *Post*'s caption stated, *as the body of the missing Columbia student is found in the Hudson*. I read the article three times, taking in each word: *The body of Columbia student Katya Dimitrova, who was last seen leaving a nightclub on the Lower East Side on the night before Mother's Day, has been found, NYPD officials said. Her body was recovered in the Hudson River near Hoboken and positively identified through dental records. The Hoboken Police Department and NYPD Detective John Robertson, who has been working the missing student's case, did not immediately reply to requests for comment. The medical examiner's office will determine the cause of death.*

Katya's animated face flashed in front of my eyes wherever I turned, whatever I did. I saw her as clearly as if she were right there, joking about being a gold digger, laughing, dancing. So young. So beautiful.

I should have never left her in the club. What was I thinking? I should have been a better friend and stayed with her or insisted that we leave together. Instead, I'd been so selfish, worrying about my pregnancy, which was in essence Katya's gift to me.

I was sure it was just a coincidence. Yet I found it hard to ignore the fact that I'd started bleeding right around the time she must have died.

I felt sick and rushed to the bathroom. I no longer knew if it was regular morning sickness or the thought of Katya's body floating in the Hudson.

Back in the living room, I sank onto the couch. It occurred to me that the only thing left of her was the baby—her flesh and blood—growing inside me.

Katya's death only elevated the stakes for me to carry the pregnancy to term. No longer just for my sake, but for hers.

I was thinking about this, my hand caressing my belly, when the doorbell rang. The *ding* reverberated between the walls, loud, obnoxious. I sat up, startled. Another ring. I headed for the door, running my fingers through my hair at an attempt to comb it, expecting a deliveryman who'd gotten the wrong apartment number.

I looked through the peephole. Tyler. My hands clenched.

I'd left him a frantic voice mail this morning about Katya's body floating in the Hudson. But I hadn't asked him to come over. And he could have called to warn me. I flung the door open ready for a fight.

He didn't say a word. Just stood there, shaking his head, lips pursed, eyes moist. The man I'd been yelling at on the phone last night. The man who'd left me for a woman named Elaine. But I felt broken and seeing him in person was all it took. He opened his arms and I rushed into his embrace. Muscle memory. My body just went for it.

His hand stroked my hair and even after my sobs had quieted, I didn't want to move. I wanted to remain there with my eyes closed, taking in his familiar scent, his touch, the way his body fit against mine, and pretend that the past month had never happened.

"I still can't believe it," I said when I finally pulled back and we walked inside.

He shook his head again and sat on the couch. "I came as soon as I got your message."

I flopped on the armchair across from him. Now that I was no longer in his arms, I felt awkward around him. Plato didn't seem to share my problem and pranced over and started nuzzling at Tyler's ankles. He picked him up and plopped him on his lap. The damn cat began purring before he'd even stroked his fur.

"Even Plato's been missing you," I said.

Tyler turned to me with a glint in his eye. "Does that mean you have?"

My instinct was to lie. *Never show vulnerability,* my mother whispered in my ear. But Katya's death had undone me. "Why would I call you if I didn't?" I said instead. "Of course I've missed you." I paused. "I hate you and miss you at the same time."

There was a grave ring to his laughter, an aching overtone. "I'm sorry," he said.

"Katya's death . . . it puts things into perspective, doesn't it?"

He nodded. "Don't let it get to you so much. I know it seems big just because we knew her . . . knew *of* her. It's that connection that makes it seem more significant than if she were a stranger."

But I did know her, I wanted to scream. *Worse, a part of her is growing inside me . . . Along with a part of you.*

I filled my lungs with air, exhaled slowly. "What do you suppose happened?"

"She got herself into trouble." He looked at Plato, stroked him slowly.

If I could only tell him I'd been with her that night and it had all seemed normal. As normal as any other night out in New York City. But I couldn't. So much had changed since he and I were a couple. I could pretend as much as I wanted, but the fact was he'd left me.

Katya's death didn't change that.

It was time I weaned myself from leaning on him. "Thanks for coming," I said, and stood up. "I have a report to finish before the end of the day."

"On Saturday?" He nudged Plato off his lap and onto the couch, stroke him one last time, before getting up. "You work too hard."

Not even close, I thought. But I wasn't going to go into it with him.

At the door, he turned, peered into my eyes. "You've got nothing to prove. You're a brilliant woman whether your mother sees it or not."

"Gee, thanks! I could use some patronizing right now," I said wryly. I knew he meant well, but deep down I was furious. He had no business telling me what to do. Hell, he had no business coming here to comfort me. Not after walking away on me, leaving me stranded at the worst possible time.

32.

LANA

It had been a slow news weekend, without any major events at home or abroad, and Katya's story had been picked up by the network news. By Monday morning, everyone was talking about the beautiful Columbia student from Bulgaria and her tragic end in the Hudson just shy of graduation. I could barely focus on work and I couldn't afford not to because tonight was the Visiting Committee. I'd finally managed to finish the presentation over the weekend after Tyler had left. Anger was a powerful motivator. This morning, I'd woken up to Alistair's notes in my inbox. I didn't need to open the e-mail to know that he'd have a lot of "suggestions." By lunchtime, I'd finished the revision and sent it to Caitlin to look over and print out a clean copy. On my way back from the cafeteria, she handed me the pages.

"It's fabulous," she said, smiling her big dimpled smile. "You're going to wow them." I was glad she was coming to the event tonight. Ordinarily, it would be Alistair and me, but since he was away, I'd asked Caitlin to join me. She might not be the most brilliant of scholars but she was a fantastic networker. Upbeat and vibrant, she worked the room at department functions without a sign of hesitation, as if our patrons— often more than twice her age—were her college pals. Nor did she seem intimidated by scholars, collectors, or private dealers with as many years of experience as she was old.

First thing I did back in my office was check the news. According to the latest *Gothamist* article, an NYPD spokesman stated that Katya's case was "an active investigation and the cause of death is pending." They were still waiting on the autopsy report. More tests needed to be performed, including a toxicology report.

I'd barely closed the screen when my phone rang. I didn't recognize the number but decided to answer it. I could use a distraction even if it was just a marketing call.

"Lana?" a female voice said.

"Yes?"

"I'm calling from the Bulgarian consulate," said the woman on the other end. She introduced herself as Anna Konstantinova and explained that Detective Robertson had given her my contact information. She told me that Katya's mother had flown in from Bulgaria and was with her at the consulate at the moment. How crushed this poor woman must be, I thought. Her only child found dead in a foreign land. "She speaks no English," Anna continued, "but she'd like to meet with some of Katya's friends. Detective Robertson told us that you are also Bulgarian—"

I stiffened. "Actually, my mother is Bulgarian. I don't really speak the language. I understand a bit but can't—"

"No worries," Anna said. "I'll come with her. You work at the Met, right?"

"Yes, but I am . . ." I hesitated. Could I really tell a mother who'd just lost her only child that I was too busy at the moment to see her? "Sure, no problem," I said. We agreed to meet at the Starbucks on Madison in twenty minutes.

I had plenty of time but the air in the office felt stale all of a sudden. I grabbed my purse and left. A short walk around the block would help me calm down. I was already outside when I realized I should have brought along my jacket. What had started as a sunny day had turned gray and breezy. I walked briskly to keep warm. My mind was racing. What could I tell Katya's mother? *I didn't really know your daughter? I actually stalked and befriended her just a few days before her death?* Or worse: *I left her in a club with a stranger. Oh, and by the way, I'm pregnant with her eggs.*

I halted midstep as it dawned on me that, genetically speaking, I was carrying this poor woman's grandchild.

Penka Dimitrova may have been a beautiful woman at one point, but when I met her in the afternoon at Starbucks, she looked old and shriveled in her outsize black T-shirt and worn-out jeans, a ghost of a person. The black scarf around her neck only accentuated her pallid complexion. In reality, she couldn't have been that much older than me. Having experienced the grief of miscarriage, I couldn't even begin to contemplate what it must be like to lose a child. Your only child.

Katya's mother didn't speak a word of English. Anna, the young woman I'd talked to on the phone, explained that Penka hadn't traveled much outside Bulgaria and wouldn't be able to manage on her own. She couldn't navigate the subway or even take a taxi, let alone deal with the police, the morgue, and all the necessary arrangements for the funeral. "Poor woman," Anna told me in a hushed voice. "She can't afford to fly the body back to Bulgaria. It costs a fortune."

I wondered about the fee Katya had collected for her egg donation. She must have been paid right after the retrieval. Where had all that money gone?

Anna went on to explain that Penka was hoping I could tell her a bit about Katya and her life in New York.

I rested my elbows on the table, entwined my fingers, and looked at Penka. "Your daughter was a wonderful young woman," I said. While Anna translated, I nodded, recognizing most of the words.

I went on to tell them how smart and mature Katya had been for her age. How much fun. I explained how we'd met—omitting *when*—and how excited Katya had been to learn about my Bulgarian mother. Penka stared at me as I spoke, as if trying to decipher the meaning of the English words from my face, impatient to wait for the translation. Her eyes—already red and puffy—teared up and she took time blowing her nose to calm herself. A couple of times she reached into her purse but her hand came out empty. I knew what she was looking for. I could smell the cigarettes on her from across the table.

As we parted, she hugged me and thanked me for being Katya's friend and for looking after her. I felt like such a fraud. I only hoped I'd at least given Penka some peace of mind that her daughter had been loved and had had a good life in America.

"Feel free to call me if there is anything I can do," I said, and handed Penka my card while Anna translated. *"Dovizhdane,"* I added, mangling the pronunciation for sure, but Penka took my hand and squeezed it.

"Dovizhdane," she said, not letting go of my hand.

That was when I knew I had to tell her. After she'd had some time to grieve and I'd passed the dreaded three months, I would have to tell her about my baby. Her grandchild.

They headed east on 86th Street toward the subway station. I stood in front of the coffee shop, watching them. Penka was a thin woman and from the back, in her jeans and T-shirt, she could pass for a twenty-year-old. But her steps were heavy, labored; her shoulders slack, weighted with grief. The thin black scarf she wore around her neck flapped behind her. The wind had picked up. There was a rainstorm in the forecast for tonight. I sighed and walked back to the Met with a lump in my throat.

I had no idea how I would make it through the Visiting Committee meeting tonight. Having just met Katya's mother, I had a hard time summoning the excitement needed to "dazzle" the trustees with our upcoming Parmigianino exhibit. I didn't dread the presentation as much as having to make small talk during the cocktail hour, laughing at people's stupid jokes, or, worse, trying to sweet-talk them into giving us more money. Luckily, Caitlin would be there with me, I thought as I started up the front steps of the Met.

"Lana," a familiar voice called out behind me. I turned. Detective Robertson and a woman I hadn't seen before stood in front of me. My muscles clenched, my heart sped up.

"This is my partner, Detective Sanchez." Robertson motioned to the woman. She was about my age, no makeup, dark hair pulled back into a tight ponytail.

I nodded, then glanced over my shoulder to make sure none of my colleagues were around. There were fewer people hanging out on the steps today, maybe because of the strong wind blowing along Fifth Avenue. Even the pigeons seemed to have gone. I felt exposed, standing there with two NYPD detectives, as if on a stage for everyone to see.

"Would you mind coming with us to the precinct?" Robertson said before I could get my bearings. "We have a few follow-up questions for you."

"Now?" My mouth went dry. "It's really not a good time. I have a presentation—"

"We could come up to your office," Sanchez said, with a tight little smile. "But I don't think you'd want that."

The smell of hot dogs wafting from the cart vendor was nauseating. "You haven't been to my office already, have you?"

She took her time before finally shaking her head.

I let out a sigh and looked at my watch. A few minutes to four. I had three hours until the presentation. Beads of sweat ran down my back as I started to panic. Would I have enough time to stop home after the police station, shower, and change, before heading to the event? But what choice did I have? The cops must have found out who Katya was to me. Dear God, how was I going to explain our chance meeting? The fact that I'd followed her?

Luckily, I'd already laid out my outfit: a classic black cocktail dress, green strappy heels, and a clutch to go with my silk medieval millefleur scarf from the Met store that was the perfect conversation starter at events like this. With light makeup, I could be done in thirty minutes if I had to.

33.

TYLER

I sat in my office in the dark, my head propped in my hands, staring out the window at the solid gray sky. It was only four in the afternoon but my office faced north, and on cloudy days like today, it felt as if it were already dusk.

Goddamn Katya! I pulled up her last text: *U motherfucker, don't think you can get out of it so easy. U fuck with me—I fuck with you.*

The phone rang in my hand. Lana's mother. I thought of letting it go to voice mail but reconsidered. She would keep calling until I spoke to her. I might as well get it over with.

"Tyler, honey, what's going on between you and Lana?" she said when I picked up. Natalia Kuzmanova was not one to bother with small talk.

I ran my hand through my hair. "We just need some time to work things out. That's all."

"Can't you work things out while you're together?"

It was hard enough trying to explain it to my sister. Talking to Lana's mother about it made me feel like a first-class jerk. Maybe that was precisely why she'd called. I was surprised it had taken her this long.

"It's complicated," I said. Natalia let out a deep sigh and I rushed to comfort her. "I promise, it will be all right. Just give us some time."

Natalia was the kind of woman who made you want to please her, to impress her, to take care of her. Lana thought that, like all men, I'd fallen under her spell, but I had yet to meet anyone—man or woman— who said no to her. Lana kicked and screamed but even she, in the end, did what her mother wanted. Except, of course, marrying me.

"So where are you living now?" Natalia asked.

I hesitated. "I found a cheap sublet not too far from the university."

"But Tyler—"

"Just for a couple of months," I said, realizing it had been the wrong answer. What she'd wanted to hear was that I was crashing on a friend's couch. "Please, don't worry," I said, but she snorted in response, made me promise we'd talk again soon, and hung up.

In the dark, the phone screen glowed in my hand with Katya's text. I could hear her voice in my head as if she were shouting at me from the morgue—*U motherfucker*. A shiver ran through me. I shook my head and deleted the message. Took a deep breath before I got up and turned on the light. I stuffed my papers into my bag and left. I needed a drink.

34.
LANA

Detective Robertson leaned across the table and locked me in his stare. "So tell us again how you know Katya Dimitrova?"

His partner, Detective Alicia Sanchez, sat quietly, nodding here and there as I went over my story: Katya's fall, rushing to help her and then clicking over our Bulgarian roots. I didn't linger on details. I had no time. Before walking in, I'd set my phone alarm for six, an hour before the start of the Visiting Committee. It was the latest I could leave. If I skipped going home, I could still make it to the Met in time. My mother would be appalled to know I was contemplating showing up for an event of that scale in a skirt and a blouse, but it was better than being late. And hopefully I would be out of here long before six.

"From what we've gathered," Robertson said, his cold eyes piercing through me, "Katya wasn't particularly well liked. Many might have wished to see her gone." He paused. Leaned even closer. "But you have the most to gain from her death."

"What?" I snapped back in my chair. "What are you talking about?"

The small "interview" room where Robertson and Sanchez had suggested we go "to find some quiet" seemed to close in on me. Bare brick walls painted over in gray, cement floor, a metal chain-link panel over the window to my right and what I could only assume was a one-way mirror across from me. I didn't need to look at the ceiling to know that there would be a camera. What the hell?

Sanchez stood and, with a couple of slow graceful movements, came around and sat on the table next to me, blocking the window. She was a tough-looking woman with a hard smile and calm, intelligent energy.

In different circumstances, I might have liked her. I admired women working in male-dominated fields.

"Without Katya, the baby is yours," she said, looking at me with exaggerated compassion from her perch on the table. "Isn't that right, Lana?"

"But it *is* mine," I shouted, and stood up, pushing back the chair. Startled by my own outburst, I breathed in slowly, breathed out, looked at Sanchez, then Robertson, and finally sat down. "I'm pregnant from a donor egg cycle," I said. "The baby is mine. This is not like with adoption where—"

"And you forgot to mention to us that Katya is your donor?" Robertson asked.

"It was a weird coincidence. Katya didn't even know who I was and I didn't see how that would help you find her."

Sanchez, who seemed to be playing the "good cop," smiled. "Okay, let's backtrack for a moment." She walked around the table and slid into her seat. "How exactly did you two become friends? Because according to the agency, you did an anonymous cycle, right?"

I looked down at the metal table, ran my thumb over the sharp edge. "I was curious," I said. "It was stupid, I admit. But it's true. She wasn't just a stranger I helped on the street. I knew she was my donor."

"You did?"

"I recognized her on the subway and . . ." I hesitated. "And I followed her."

"Interesting. And why would you do that?" Robertson asked.

"I wanted to get to know her. To learn more about my baby's genes."

"Of course," Sanchez said. Then turning to Robertson, she continued, "I'd like that, too, if I were in her shoes." She paused, looked back at me. "But then, Katya was not an easy person. She had no filter. She said and did infuriating things. And your pregnancy and the baby, well, it's a painful topic. Things got heated." She bit her lip. "Of course, you didn't mean to . . ."

I gaped at her. "You can't possibly think . . . This is madness." I shook my head and pushed my chair back again. I'd watched enough crime shows to know that I'd come here voluntarily and could leave at any point. I didn't need to talk to them unless they arrested me and read me my Miranda rights. At which point, I'd need a lawyer. But really? Were they at such a loss that they were suggesting I had anything to do with it? I stood up.

Sanchez followed suit. She was a couple of inches shorter than me but could still stare me down. "Okay. Let's say we believe you," she said, and, pressing her palms on the table, leaned forward. "Who, then, would want to get rid of her?"

I shrugged. "I don't know. I worried maybe that guy—"

"How about your ex?" Robertson interrupted.

"Tyler? He doesn't even know that I'm pregnant."

"Ah, but you see, his reasons have nothing to do with your pregnancy."

"No?" I sat back in the chair. "Then why?"

Sanchez returned to her seat, shuffled the papers in front of her. Finally, she said, "Two days before Katya disappeared, she went to the Ombuds office."

"She wanted to know how to file a complaint against Professor Tyler Jones," Robertson added.

I looked at him, then Sanchez. My head felt heavy, loud with static as I tried to make sense of what they were saying.

"She'd tried to end the affair," Robertson continued with a smirk, "but lover boy wouldn't have it. He'd been waiting for her in front of the dorms, threatening her."

I shook my head. "You've got it all wrong. Tyler doesn't even know Katya."

"It's hard not to know one of your students, don't you think?"

I felt like I'd been punched. Gripped the chair. Took a string of fast breaths.

Robertson glared at me. "Let's cut the bullshit. As you can see, we've done our homework."

I wanted to defend myself, to explain that I had no idea about any of it, but the static in my mind had only grown louder.

"Good," he continued, taking my silence as an agreement. "So we come to the second reason why you'd want to get rid of her." His eyes burrowed into me. "The young and beautiful girl whose baby you're carrying is sleeping with the father of said baby. Who had just left you."

Sanchez cocked her head and asked, "How did you find out? Did you see them together?" She said it with pity, a woman-to-woman kind of thing. An empathic *Aren't men such pigs?* expression on her face.

I ran my hands through my hair, pulling it back at my temples as reality finally sank in. *Tyler and Katya were having an affair.* The stale air in the room was making me dizzy. I took a sip of the water they'd brought me in a plastic cup.

"Did you worry that they would take their baby from you? Leave you alone and empty-handed?" Robertson asked.

"Of course she'd worry about that," Sanchez said, screwing her face into that concerned expression again. "I would be terrified. After all that hard work to get pregnant."

"So you stalk and befriend her and then, when she trusts you, you take her down." Robertson looked at me, eyebrows up as if to say, *Am I not right?*

Continuing his thought, Sanchez added, "You reclaim your motherhood on Mother's Day."

I just sat there, staring at them, my ears ringing, the room swirling in front of my eyes.

My phone started beeping, the jarring sound echoing off the walls of the empty room. The thought of the Visiting Committee floated into my brain and I felt the prick of tears at the realization that I was most likely not going to make it. I turned the alarm off and slumped into the chair, blinking hard to prevent the tears from spilling. A beautiful young girl lay dead in the morgue, my ex-partner had been having an affair with her, and the cops were insinuating that I was somehow implicated in her death. Against that backdrop, persuading a bunch of rich folks to give money to the museum seemed trivial at best. But I couldn't afford to lose my job. Not with a baby on the way.

I inhaled, exhaled slowly, and quickly typed up a text to Caitlin to take over the presentation for me.

35.
LANA

"What the hell's going on?" Angie said when she released me from her hug. Then, before I'd had a chance to open my mouth: "Never mind, we'll talk in the taxi. Come."

She took my arm and together we walked down the precinct steps.

It was drizzling outside. The sidewalks shone wet in the glow of the streetlamps. I paused and looked up and down the street, took a few moist breaths. I'd spent four hours inside the police station, but it had felt like days. I would have preferred to walk and stretch my legs after being cooped up in that suffocating room, but the rain seemed to be picking up so I let Angie steer me to the taxi waiting for us. It was stuffy inside, smelling of sweat and cheap perfume, one of those awful air fresheners that New York cabbies are fond of. I cracked the window on my side, preferring to get wet rather than nauseated. Angie gave my address to the driver and turned to me as the car started down the street.

"Thank God they didn't keep you overnight."

"They have nothing on me other than motive. And apparently lots of people had a motive. Tyler included." I rubbed my temples. "She was his student, Angie," I said, shaking my head. "And his lover."

"What?" Angie stared at me, her eyes blazing with the streaked glow of streetlights.

"I'm still in shock."

She pressed her hand against my arm. "I'm so sorry, hon. I guess her posts online were no joke."

"Yeah, but a crush . . . a crush sounds so innocent now. Quaint even," I said, anger clutching at my throat. If he had to be the cliché professor sleeping with a student, why did he have to do it with our donor of all people? I turned to Angie. "Katya told an Ombuds officer that when she'd tried to break it off, he'd lost it. He'd started pressuring her, stalking her even." I sucked in my lips. This was way too big for me to begin to comprehend. "I just don't see Tyler forcing anyone to . . ." I let the sentence hang, the thought too upsetting to complete.

Angie's eyes had gone big. "Could he have done something to her?"

"God, no!" I shouted. "He couldn't hurt a mouse," I added, lowering my voice.

"You didn't think he knew Katya, let alone that he was sleeping with her, and yet . . ." Angie shuddered. "Eww, just the thought of it."

"He told me the name of the other woman was Elaine," I said, and pulled out my phone. "And that she was one of his TAs. Let's see if we can find her."

I ignored a slew of frantic texts from Caitlin. There was nothing I could do now. The event was already over. Luckily, it was the middle of the night in Paris. I wouldn't have to deal with Alistair's wrath until tomorrow. I texted Caitlin back, *Please let me know how it went*, before switching to the Safari app. I went to the Columbia Philosophy Department page and clicked on the Graduate Students tab. I should have done it back then, but the news of Katya's body floating in the river had pushed it out of my head. Angie and I huddled together in the back of the taxi, staring at the screen, as I scrolled down the list. Out of seventy-five MA and PhD candidates, only fifteen were women. None of them was named Elaine. There wasn't an Elena or an Ellen or even an Emma.

I put the phone away and looked out the window. The rain was coming down hard, the taxi's windshield wipers swinging back and forth fast and with urgency. Like a ticking bomb.

"It makes no sense," I said, turning back to Angie. "If Katya *were* Tyler's mistress, wouldn't she have known I was his partner? Okay, maybe I'm not the only Lana in town, but how many of us also have a Bulgarian mother? You'd have to be a moron not to put two and two together and realize I was Tyler's partner."

"You're assuming he told her anything about you. For all we know, Katya thought he was single. No band on his ring finger, nothing to suggest that the cute professor she was hooking up with was coupled."

I sat up and stared at her.

"But then," Angie went on, "she found out he was in a serious relationship and told him to go to hell."

I shook my head. "She wrote in her post that she had a crush on *the guy* who was going to be *the father* of the baby. She'd known who Tyler was and that he had a partner."

"But she could have been writing about someone else, as we thought at first."

"That seemed plausible back when the thought of Katya and Tyler was inconceivable. With all that we know now, it would be too much of a coincidence," I said as the taxi pulled in front of the building. I looked at Angie. "You wanna come up?"

"You can't possibly think I'll leave you alone tonight," she said.

I paid and followed Angie out of the car. She ran up the three steps to the building's entrance, holding her purse over her head. I let the rain wet my hair, drip down my face and shoulders, as I slowly climbed the stairs. I unlocked the door and as we walked in, I looked up at the security camera in the entry hall. The footage from the night Katya went missing would confirm that I hadn't left my apartment until the next morning when I'd gone to the clinic.

In the elevator, Angie said: "Okay, so then she must have known Tyler had a partner but didn't know anything about her."

I nodded. "That's the only thing that makes sense."

We ordered Chinese takeout and ate dinner in silence. I didn't have much appetite but forced myself to finish my kung pao chicken. My baby needed the calories. Afterward, we made chamomile tea and moved to the living room with our cups. I dimmed the lights and lit a couple of candles in an attempt—however futile—at unwinding. We sat on either end of the couch, Angie with her legs folded underneath her while I stretched mine out on the coffee table. Plato jumped on the pillow between us, sprawled on his belly, his front right leg sticking out straight, and started purring. This could have been a blissful moment: two friends who'd met in an infertility support group, both finally pregnant, relaxing together on a quiet rainy evening.

"So here is what we know," I said, and picked up a pen and a pad from the coffee table to jot down a list. "The agency sent us Katya's profile in early January and we booked her right away. Two weeks later, when the semester started, Tyler must have discovered that our donor-to-be was in his class. He didn't tell me about it, probably because he knew I'd freak out. But he must have told her who he was . . ." I paused. "Before or after they'd started sleeping together."

"But he never mentioned your name," Angie said. "Or that your mother was Bulgarian."

"Right."

"Then, he decided he wanted to be with her, panicked that once you got pregnant he'd be stuck and decided to bail while he could. He left you for her but—surprise—Katya wasn't looking for a relationship and told him to go to hell." I nodded and Angie went on. "He got upset. Of course he did. 'I left my partner for you, bitch.'" She imitated his voice.

I felt the blood drain from my face. "Oh, my God," I said, and stood up.

"What?"

"Could he be the possessive boyfriend Katya was talking about? Who'd seemed pretty chill at first? Sure, because he was living with me. Tyler isn't a Tom Cruise look-alike but he has blue eyes and brown hair. Who knows what Katya saw? And he is in his late thirties."

Angie opened her mouth, then closed it. "Oh, my God," she finally said. "So he pressured her to move in with him after graduation. She got worried and went to the Ombuds office." Angie looked at me. "Didn't *you* urge her to talk to someone about it?"

"I did." I got off the couch and went to the window. The wind outside had picked up and rain pelted the glass. I pushed my forehead against it and stood like that, looking at the drops running down the panel like giant tears.

"Then, at the Ombuds office," Angie continued behind me, "Katya inquired how to file a complaint against him."

I turned. "But she never did."

"He stopped her," Angie said, and covered her mouth with her hands.

The night sky lit up with bolts of lightning. I stood at the window, my legs weak, my breathing fast, waiting for the thunder, as if that could bring some relief and make things right again.

36.

TYLER

The interrogation room was small. Brightly lit with a fluorescent tube on the ceiling that made a low buzzing sound. You could smell the fear of those who'd been here before you, sweating on that same folding chair. Made of metal, with a rigid back, it was not designed for comfort. A loud crack of thunder sounded outside and the window shuddered. A car alarm began wailing. I nearly laughed at how appropriate it all seemed. Detectives John Robertson and Alicia Sanchez sat across the table from me. He looked the part—barrel chest, thick neck. She was harder to pin. Could have been a teacher or an office manager—hard face, dark hair pulled into a ponytail. She seemed bored, staring somewhere to the left of me while Robertson asked the questions.

"Why don't you tell us about your relationship with Katya Dimitrova?" he said. We'd already covered what I did at the university, how long I'd worked there, and if I got along with my students.

"Katya's one of my undergraduates," I said. "Was. She was in my intro class this past semester." I paused. Looked down, unsure how much I should tell them. I'd seen Robertson walk Lana out earlier, while I was going over my contact information with a uniformed officer in the main room. I was furious they'd dragged her into this. Clearly, it was a setup. They'd meant for me to see her. She'd looked crushed, shell-shocked. I was glad she hadn't seen me. I couldn't imagine what I would have said to her.

I looked back at the detectives across the table. "Katya was also our egg donor," I said. "My partner and I . . . We're currently apart but we were planning on doing a fertility treatment using a donor egg."

Sanchez got up and started pacing the room, seemingly uninterested. Robertson stared at me like an asshole. I couldn't stand guys like him, pumping iron all day and acting like they were hot shit. "That's it?" he asked, eyebrows up.

"That's it."

Sanchez stood in front of me and, leaning down, her face right in mine, said, "Was Katya perhaps the reason for your *separation*, Professor Jones?"

I pulled back. "What do you mean by that?"

"Maybe your *partner* found out about your relationship with Katya," Robertson said.

Sanchez straightened up. "I wouldn't have liked that if I were—"

"I had no relationship with Katya," I said, interrupting her. They were really starting to piss me off.

"C'mon, man." Robertson laughed. "Don't tell me that a stunning girl like Katya comes into your life and you don't take advantage of it. It's not like you were married or anything."

"I said, I didn't have—"

"Interesting," Sanchez said, and walked toward the mirror window as if talking to those behind it. She took her time before she turned back, leaned against the wall, and crossed her arms over her chest. "Because Katya told an Ombuds officer that she'd been having an affair with you."

I felt the blood rushing to my face. My hands clamped into fists. "That's a lie. She made it up."

Sanchez arranged her lips in an exaggerated smile. "And why would she do that?"

"How am I supposed to know? Because she's crazy?"

"Of course." Sanchez laughed as she came back to the table. She pressed her palms on top and leaned forward again, her face stony. "You didn't mind her being crazy when you had sex with her, did you?"

"I never touched her. Ever. I haven't so much as shaken her hand, for fuck's sake." I slammed my fist on the table. My ears and neck were burning. I clenched my jaw and tried to calm my breathing. The siren of a fire truck sounded outside, the Klaxon noise growing louder and more piercing as it neared, then receding until it was gone.

"Hm." Robertson took his jacket off and rolled up his shirtsleeves. "Why don't you tell us when you last saw her?"

"Saturday night, two weeks ago."

"The night she went missing?" Sanchez asked. Her smug attitude was grating at me. I would take Robertson's bullying over her insolence anytime.

"The night she went missing," I repeated, trying to keep my voice down.

"And what time was that?"

"I'm not sure," I said. "Around four a.m."

The two of them exchanged looks. She raised a mocking eyebrow. "I don't remember there being classes on Saturdays at four in the morning." That venom in her voice again. "You mind telling us where exactly that meeting took place?"

I sighed, shifted on my seat. The silence was thick and sticky. The buzzing of the fluorescent light seemed to have grown louder.

"My apartment," I finally said.

37.

LANA

I woke up to a voice mail from Alistair but couldn't bring myself to listen to it. I didn't even bother looking at my e-mails. I knew what I'd find. At least Caitlin had texted last night that it had gone well. *Everyone seemed excited*, she'd written. Whatever had happened or was to happen, I would deal with it when I made it to the office, I thought, and got out of bed.

It was barely seven a.m. but Angie was already up, sitting on the couch with her MacBook Pro on her lap and Plato at her feet. I'd left her there last night, curled up on the narrow cushions like a child.

"I just can't believe it," I said in lieu of *good morning*. "Tyler was the possessive guy Katya was telling me about?"

Angie closed her laptop. "Maybe not. Sounds like she'd been making the rounds: Tyler, the bartender, Jacuzzi Guy. Who knows how many more there were."

I pulled Plato into my arms and joined her on the couch.

"She told the Ombuds officer about Tyler, though," I said, running my hand through Plato's fur with too much force. He squirmed, clearly unhappy, and I let him down. "But there is no way he did something to her. He might be a cheater but he certainly isn't a killer. He couldn't be."

I looked at Angie for reassurance but she only shrugged, then patted my arm. "Did you get enough sleep?"

I shook my head. "I can't imagine you got much, either, on the couch," I said, then added, pointing to her laptop: "Are you on a deadline?"

"Don't worry. I'll get it done."

Angie was her own boss and had the flexibility of working whenever she wanted. Often, she worked all night, then slept during the day.

"You were right," Angie added with a head tilt to the framed photographs on the piano. "Katya does look a bit like your mother." She walked over to take a closer look at my mother's portrait.

"You're starting to show," I said, staring at her baby bump.

She smiled. "I know." Now that she'd passed the dreaded first three months and the NT scan, she was careful not to talk about her pregnancy around me. "Oh, you have some new ones," she said, and picked up a photo of my mother in a handstand, her legs spread nearly 180. "Did she ever teach you how to do that?"

"She tried, believe me," I said, and joined Angie at the piano. "Gymnastics, ballet, dance—I was hopeless. Hence, the piano." I took the frame from her and studied my mother's strong, taut little body.

"Holy cow, when did you run a marathon?" Angie asked, pointing to a photo of me wrapped in a silver emergency blanket and looking rather haggard. Tyler had snapped it without warning, and my eyes were trained on something to the left of the camera. I wasn't even holding my medal to show it off. But my smile said it all. I'd done it.

"Ah, the good old days," I said, which in our world meant pre-infertility. I'd put up a bunch of new photos to replace the shots I'd had with Tyler. It hadn't occurred to me that they all dated to the good old days.

"Where is that?" Angie gestured to a photo of me crouched on a rooftop, wielding a hammer. My friend Jen was next to me, nail puller in hand, both of us laughing.

"I haven't told you about New Orleans?"

Angie shook her head.

"After Katrina. A friend and I went down with Habitat for Humanity."

"And this?" Angie asked about another "working" photo of me, this time holding a hoe over my head.

"Kenya, just before Tyler and I met."

"Dear God, woman!" Angie shrieked. "What else have you been hiding in your closet?"

"It's not what it looks like," I said, feeling self-conscious about the photos. "I just needed a boost. You know. To remind myself that I'm—"

"Superwoman?"

"I was going for strong . . . Ah, forget it." I waved my hand.

Angie gave me a long look, a slow smile.

The crunching sound of Plato chewing pellets of dry food came from the kitchen. I looked at my watch. "I have to be in the office in an hour," I said. "Come, let's have some breakfast." I didn't bother explaining about the missed presentation last night. I couldn't even think about it. If I did, I'd have to face the fact that my career at the Met was most likely over.

Plato barely glanced at us as he continued eating. He wasn't particularly skittish and Angie wasn't a stranger in the house.

"I've only got milk, cereal, and some berries," I warned her, surveying the empty shelves in the fridge.

Angie laughed. "It's more than I have."

I washed some strawberries and blueberries to add to our flakes and set the kettle on for tea. "Let's see if there's anything new," I said, and turned on the TV in the living room. I couldn't see it from the kitchen but I often had it on in the morning, listening to the news, as I got ready for work. Tyler used to tease me that I would be better off listening to the radio.

I flipped to NY1, which repeated the local news every ten to fifteen minutes. A commercial about a constipation drug came on and I muted the volume.

"Wait," Angie said. "We might need that."

I shot her a look over my shoulder. "I was hoping that once I stop the progesterone at twelve weeks . . ."

"Keep dreaming," she said, standing at the doorway, watching the TV. "I'm fifteen weeks with no relief in sight."

"I hit eight yesterday," I said, setting out the bowls with our breakfast on the table. "All that drama with Tyler and Katya . . . it's almost taking my mind off the—"

"Speaking of . . ." Angie said, and grabbed the remote from the table and increased the volume. I joined her in the living room just as Tyler's photo filled the top left corner of the screen. The anchor, a pretty woman in a pink dress, was speaking in a fake concerned voice: "Columbia professor Tyler Jones has been detained for questioning by NYPD investigators in connection with the case of missing Columbia University senior Katya Dimitrova, whose body was recovered in the Hudson River last Friday."

I looked at Angie, shaking my head.

"An NYPD representative told the press they are interviewing a number of persons of interest." The frame switched to footage of the 26th Precinct, where I'd spent four hours yesterday. Detective Robertson spoke over his shoulder as he walked, flanked by reporters: "We're still waiting on the autopsy report to determine cause of death," he said. There was a muffled question, to which he responded, "I can confirm that there were no visible signs of foul play, yes. But we're not ruling out anything at this stage."

The news switched to a story about a fire in Queens and I turned the television off, relieved that they hadn't mentioned anything about me. "What's that mean?" I said. "No *visible* signs."

Angie shrugged. "I guess the body was intact. She wasn't shot—or worse—before being dumped into the river." I shuddered as Angie continued, "But that doesn't mean she wasn't pushed or drugged or—"

My stomach turned, its contents rising in my throat, and I ran to the bathroom.

"Morning sickness?" Angie shouted after me.

❖

I'd just walked into the office when Sam called. I nodded to Caitlin, who was already out of her chair, clearly anxious to brief me about last night. I motioned to her that I needed a minute, before closing the door behind me. This was not a conversation I could risk my colleagues overhearing.

"Lana, thank goodness I got you! I'm totally freaked out. You know about Tyler, right?"

"What about him?" I snapped. The last thing I needed right now was to talk about Tyler with his sister.

"Did you not watch the news this morning? He's been detained for questioning about that Columbia student."

"You mean the one he was having an affair with? The one who split us up?" I said, my voice higher than I'd intended. I was suddenly livid with Katya. It wasn't like she'd had a shortage of guys. Did she have to go after those who were taken? Destroy families? I couldn't believe I had actually liked her. That I'd even considered having her as my baby's auntie. And now she was dead. I couldn't even get angry at her without feeling horribly selfish.

"I'm sorry," Sam said. "I didn't know anything about that. I just saw the news." She paused. "He couldn't possibly have done something to her. You know that, right?"

I sighed. "I do."

I'd barely hung up with Sam when my mother called. "Have you seen the news?" she asked, her voice strained, tentative. I could hear the muffled sound of her television in the background.

"I'm afraid so," I said, pushing around the piles of papers and books on my desk.

"You don't think Tyler could be involved—"

"Of course he's not," I said a bit too sharply, trying to convince myself along with her.

"But why are the cops questioning him, then?"

"They can make anyone look guilty. Believe me. They interviewed me yesterday, too."

"They *did*?" she gasped. "Why? You don't work at the university. What do you have to do with that student?"

Right. "That's what I mean," I said as I typed the password to my computer. "I'm sure they'll let him go soon, if they haven't already."

It was ten to nine. I had to speak to Caitlin, respond to Alistair, and figure out how to deal with the repercussions of last night, before it got any later than it already was.

"I knew nothing about a missing student," my mother was saying. "You haven't told me anything. The police have questioned my daughter and she hasn't told me—"

"Mom, I need to go. I'll call you tonight. Okay?" I said, and hung up.

Luckily, she didn't know the half of it.

❖

It took me an hour to compose an e-mail to Alistair, apologizing for having failed him so miserably. What could I say? *I spent the evening at the police station being interrogated in a murder case?* Certainly not something you want to share with your boss. And what do you follow it with? *But not to worry, they let me go? I'm not even a person of interest. Unlike my ex-partner.*

In the end, I settled for a short note apologizing for not being able to attend without going into details. *I will explain when I see you*, I wrote, then apologized again and promised to make up for it. How? I had no idea.

He wouldn't be back until tomorrow, so I had time to figure something out on both counts.

I was being delusional—I knew as much—but I had to keep going, moving through the motions. At least I'd had the presence of mind to text Caitlin. I'd run into Jonathan, my colleague from European Paintings, this morning at the museum's entrance, and he'd filled me in on the excitement Caitlin had generated with *her* presentation. I didn't tell him I'd written it. It didn't matter. Caitlin had done a great job delivering it. Far better than I would have had I been able to make it, I was sure of that. "She was passionate and convincing and *very charming*," Jonathan said. "The patrons loved her."

I was so relieved to hear it, not that I'd doubted Caitlin's abilities. I should have been angry to have missed my chance. Mortified to have let down Alistair. Distraught that I would most likely lose my job over it. Instead, I simply felt numb.

38.

LANA

My stomach had been queasy since morning and by four, I'd made three runs to the bathroom. I'd been avoiding talking to my colleagues all day. I had no idea who might have seen the news and recognized Tyler as my partner, the guy they'd chatted with at the office Christmas party. I'd gotten a few funny glances, but it might have all been in my head. Outside, the sun was bright, the storm of last night a distant memory. The drone of traffic down Fifth Avenue drifted through the open window, punctuated by the horn of an impatient driver every now and then. The world went on as if nothing had happened.

I tried to focus on work. There were the usual loan requests, including one from the British Museum for Michelangelo's Sibyl studies, which I had to respond to ASAP since we were borrowing a bunch of Parmigianino drawings from them. I also needed to answer a colleague from the Getty, asking for my insights pertaining to a drawing attributed to Guido Reni. I'd just clicked Reply when my phone rang.

Tyler's name flashed on my screen. *Fucking bastard*, I thought, but deep down, I exhaled. The cops must have let him go. That was all I needed to know. If they didn't think there was a reason to hold him, then I had nothing to fear. But I sure as hell didn't want to speak with him. I simultaneously worried and hoped that Robertson had told him about my pregnancy. Anger is a funny thing. It can make us ignore our own interests in favor of hurting someone else. My mother loved to quote an old Bulgarian proverb: *I don't care if I'm okay, as long as the neighbor isn't.*

My actions, while not exactly ethical, were in no way a betrayal of him. Whereas he'd had an affair with our supposedly anonymous egg donor. That was more than I could deal with even without her turning up dead in the Hudson.

❖

It was nearly seven by the time I decided to wrap it up and go home. There was nothing I could do to make up for missing the presentation last night, but at least I'd kept myself busy. I dreaded going back to the apartment. If only I could sleep for days—no, months—until it was time to give birth. Then I could wake up and deal with the world.

I signed out of my computer and tidied my desk, stacking into a neat pile all the books I'd brought from the library in the past couple of weeks and left lying around open, merely a few pages in. On my way out, I glanced at Alistair's dark office. I had to figure out what I would tell him tomorrow. He hadn't responded to my e-mail, which I assumed meant he'd rather yell at me in person. To make things worse, I had my ultrasound appointment in the morning. I could possibly call and re-schedule, but there was no way I would voluntarily wait an extra day. What if the hematoma had gotten worse? All this stress couldn't be good for a normal pregnancy, let alone for a complicated situation like mine. My baby trumped everything. I could find another job, maybe even another partner, but this was my last chance at motherhood.

Most everyone had gone home. With Alistair out of town, there was no reason to show off working late. The front office, with worktables and desks for the fellows and assistants, was deserted, taking on that quiet library feel. Caitlin was the only one left, scribbling something on a yellow sticky note, her computer screen already dark. "Good night, Caitlin," I said without pausing.

"Ah, Lana!" she said behind me in her perpetually cheerful voice. "Wait, I'm leaving, too."

I pretended not to hear her, but she caught up with me at the door. Walking the empty halls of the museum used to be my favorite part of the job. I never could get enough of it even though I'd seen some of the pieces hundreds of times. But this evening, I had no eyes for the art on the walls.

"How's the procedure going?" Caitlin asked in a hushed voice. People at work knew about my infertility treatments. There was no way around it. You can hide one, maybe two IVFs, but not years of endless doctor visits and surgical procedures. I'd only told Caitlin that I'd had an emergency situation last night. She must have thought it had to do with my latest cycle.

"So far so good." Until the pregnancy was far enough along and the baby out of danger, I wouldn't tell anybody.

"Fingers crossed," Caitlin said as if we were talking about a fellowship application. But I was thankful that she didn't pry.

Outside, tourists lingered on the steps enjoying the magic hour, some standing, chatting in different languages or taking selfies; others sitting around, leaning against backpacks, legs stretched, staring at the façades across Fifth Avenue bathed in golden light or people-watching as New Yorkers went by, jogging in and out of the park, strolling with their dogs, baby carriages, or both. There was something about warm late-spring nights; they acted like opioids on our psyches, regardless of nationality, gender, or age. The dogs seemed happier, too. Hell, even the pigeons seemed to be bobbing their heads more cheerfully than they would on a frigid day in February.

I paused, letting the stress drain out of me. If it weren't for Caitlin, I might have even considered sitting down myself. Maybe I could still do so on one of the nearby benches. I was just about to tell her I was going to walk across the park and bid her good night when she leaned closer and whispered, "By the way, I saw Tyler on the news this morning."

I'd expected it all day and yet, when Caitlin looked at me, her face contorted into a fake expression of concern, I found myself unable to respond. What do you say to something like that? *Oh, yeah, he looks great in that photo, doesn't he?* I knew she was fishing for information but I had no intention of giving her any. So I just shrugged and started down the stairs.

Caitlin followed after me. "Some of the others were speculating that you guys might have broken up," she said. "You know, he hasn't been calling you at the office. His photo is gone from your desk . . ." She shot me a side look and patted my arm. "You're better off without him."

As if on cue, I heard Tyler's voice calling my name. My throat tightened. I turned and saw him rushing down toward us. He must have been waiting at the top of the stairs, hidden by all the people milling around. I looked back at Caitlin and forced a smile.

"Sorry. I need to go," I said, and walked toward Tyler before he'd caught up with us and the awkwardness level reached cosmic proportions.

Fucking Tyler. He'd been calling and leaving me messages all afternoon.

"What are you doing here?" I said, trying to keep my voice down.

"You won't pick up the phone and you were pissed last time when I came to the apartment—"

"Tyler, if I wanted to talk to you, I would have called you back," I said, and started walking toward the bus stop so we wouldn't have this conversation on the front steps. I'd lost all desire for the park. "You can't force me to engage with you," I continued. "You've made a fool of yourself—best-case scenario—and it's all over the news for everyone to see."

"But that's exactly why I'm here," he said, keeping up with my fast pace. "I don't care what other people say but I want you to know that none of this is true."

"How stupid do you think I am?"

"Lana, please." He took my hand and stopped. His hair was disheveled. There were bags under his eyes. "You need to believe me. I had nothing to do with Katya's death. I never had a relationship with her. You know me. I would never—"

"I *thought* I knew you. You've proven me wrong." I pulled my hand out of his. "This is a very difficult time for me and I need you to leave me alone. Okay?" I turned and walked away before he had a chance to fight it.

One thing was clear, I thought as I boarded the bus: Tyler still didn't know I was pregnant.

❖

After a quiet evening watching reruns of *Friends*, I made the mistake of going online and checking the news before I went to bed. There were no updates on the progress of the investigation. But in the absence of news from the police, the media had uncovered that "Columbia Professor Tyler Jones, who had been questioned in connection with Katya Dimitrova's mysterious death, had been involved with another student. Rachel Grant, a PhD candidate in philosophy, did not respond to requests for comment, but other students reported having seen them together."

My hands clenched into fists. How many women had there been? One could be dismissed as a mistake. But two, two screamed a pattern. Had our relationship been a total sham? How had I been so blind to the real Tyler?

I shut the computer and picked up Plato from his favorite napping spot on the armchair.

"Bedtime," I said, and dropped him on top of the covers next to my pillow.

39.

TYLER

I was on my second beer when I got the text from Rachel. I hadn't even bothered to look at the name of the bar. I'd just walked into the first joint I found after Lana had given me the boot on the museum steps. It wasn't my kind of place—sleek, shiny ambience; young privileged crowd. Guys in suits and ties, straight from the office. Bottle-blond girls with perfect manicures and fancy clothes. Even if they wore jeans and a tank top, it looked like the outfit had been snatched off a mannequin at Saks. That was the Upper East Side for you—sharp-edged and stiffly starched. I'd have preferred a good ol' Irish pub. But I was desperate. I couldn't bear going back to the depressing studio I was renting in Washington Heights, my duffle bag still half unpacked on the floor, blocking the way to the bathroom.

Rachel's text read: *Did you see this?* followed by a link. I clicked on it and my sorry face came up next to the headline: "Learning with Benefits: Columbia professor questioned in connection with international student's mysterious death over Mother's Day weekend had been involved with yet another student." I read long enough to see that Rachel was mentioned by name. Those motherfuckers. I'd hoped they wouldn't drag her into this. I'd even given Lana a made-up name, to protect Rachel's privacy.

I am so sorry, I texted her back, and downed my beer. Decided to switch to bourbon and asked for Maker's Mark on the rocks. I held the glass in my hand and gave it a jiggle, swirling the ice before taking a sip. I'd forgotten how much I liked bourbon. I'd been drinking wine these past few years and only with dinner. Alcohol supposedly reduced the production of normally formed sperm. Ha. Some men watched their cholesterol, others their blood pressure, and I—my sperm count. No more.

The vagaries of life and love. Less than two months ago, Lana and I had been conversing over dinner about sperm shape and motility. Now I had to stalk her at work for a chance to speak to her.

It was all my fault. I'd invested my energy into taking care of Lana and along the way I'd neglected my own feelings. Worse, I'd felt like I had no right to grieve because I wasn't experiencing half of what she was going through. The hormones, the injections, the morning sickness followed by miscarriages. The surgeries. Every time Lana had a surgical procedure, however minimal, she took a risk. She'd done it so many times, she barely noticed. After her last miscarriage, she'd even joked that she couldn't wait to have the D&C because she'd wake up with the numbing effect of the anesthetic. The same drug that Michael Jackson had supposedly overdosed on.

But every time she was wheeled into the operating theater, I was left behind in the waiting room, surrounded by strangers, terrified. What if she didn't wake up? What if she was one of the unlucky seven in a million who didn't?

I couldn't share any of my anxieties with Lana. I was her support. I was the one to comfort and encourage her when she fretted over every blood test result, every ultrasound, every IVF cycle. There was no space for my fears. Still, I should have told Lana how I felt instead of opening up to Rachel.

My phone lit up with another text.

Can we meet? Rachel wrote. *I need to talk to you.*

Not a good idea right now, I texted back.

My burger arrived. I took a fry, pushed the plate aside. I hadn't had much appetite to begin with. After seeing the latest news report, I'd lost it entirely.

"Not hungry?" asked a girl who'd just climbed on the barstool to my left.

I turned to face her and smiled, but not because I meant to. It was a reflex. She was beautiful, if not my type—a bit too generic, Barbie-like—but still, a stunner. She crossed one long leg over the other, slow and determined, making sure I was watching. She couldn't have been more than twenty-six or twenty-seven. Rachel's age.

"You mind if I have it?" she said, tilting her chin to my plate, and then she laughed, arching her long neck.

The music was blasting so loud I wasn't sure I'd heard her right. It didn't matter. What she'd said was beside the point. It was all in the smile, the tongue tracing her lips as she leaned closer to me. She was gorgeous and she knew it. Why couldn't I have gotten that attention in high school? College? Girls never noticed me back then.

I stared at her. The full glossy lips, the silky skin, the perky breasts pushing against her lacy top.

"It's all yours," I said, and nudged the plate toward her, with a stupid grin on my face. I gulped down my bourbon. Let the heat settle in my stomach.

Two hours later, I stumbled out of her apartment on Second Avenue, drunk and disoriented. Rachel had sent another text: *Please. Tomorrow. Same place same time.*

40.

LANA

NOW

The clinic was busy this morning. Nearly every seat in the waiting room was taken, which meant the wait would be longer than usual. Of course it would be, on the day I was desperate for news of my baby and couldn't afford to be late to work. I claimed an armchair in the back near the elevators and surveyed the crowd. There were professional women, dressed for the office, working their phones and impatiently glancing at the nurse's desk. I suspected the women in designer jeans who were leafing through magazines or scrolling through their Facebook feeds were stay-at-home wives. A couple of them held on to purses that cost perhaps as much as an IVF cycle. The woman next to me—early thirties and extremely anxious—told me it was her first and last time. Her insurance paid for only one cycle. "You're lucky," I said. "That's more than mine ever did." She looked at me, her forehead furrowed, and I bit my lip. *Lucky* was not a meaningful word when dealing with infertility. I smiled and added, "All it takes is one successful cycle."

I had just wished her good luck when I heard the *ding* of the elevator behind us, the doors opening and closing. A mother walked in with a stumbling toddler holding on to the empty stroller. The energy in the room changed instantly. The boy was beautiful and rowdy, his laughter echoing in the bare waiting room. I caught the eye of a few of the women sitting near me. The one I'd been talking to seemed on the verge of tears. It wasn't fair to bring a child here. It was particularly hard on those of us whose cycles weren't progressing normally or those who were about to hear bad news.

When the mother and child reached the reception desk, a woman

across from me leaned in and said under her breath, "If you can pay for
IVF, surely you can afford a babysitter for two hours while you run to
the clinic."

I shrugged. "Maybe the babysitter canceled last minute." It was hard
to know what any of us was dealing with in addition to the misfortune
of infertility. Life didn't grind to a halt just because of it. Katya's death
had had a sobering effect on me.

When my turn finally came, Dr. Williams reassured me that everything looked good. I'd never experienced anything more intoxicating
than the sound of my baby's heartbeat. It's a treat for any mother-to-be,
but especially for those of us who've experienced a miscarriage and
worry all the time if the baby is okay. Because we know it isn't a sure
thing. That it can end at any point. The only time you could be sure was
during those few minutes in the doctor's office when you could hear the
heart beating.

I could sit there listening to that golden sound for hours, days,
weeks. My stress about getting to the office faded instantly. But I knew
that the high would last me only an hour or so after the appointment,
when the doubts and worries would start anew.

Dr. Williams couldn't tell if the hematoma was getting smaller, but,
"As long as it's not getting any bigger," he said, "I'm not worried."

I walked out of the clinic feeling "cautiously optimistic"—a term I'd
picked up on the infertility forums.

So far so good, I texted Angie.

One day at a time, she texted back, followed by hearts. *One day at a
time*, I repeated in my mind as I headed to work.

It was ten a.m. by the time I made it to the museum. Caitlin informed
me that Alistair wanted to see me. What a surprise. But I was prepared.
I'd decided to tell him the truth. I didn't have to go into detail. I could
just say that I was a friend of the Columbia student whose body was
found in the Hudson (hopefully he'd heard about it) and was called in

by the police to help with the investigation. I'd even thought of a joke I could make: You can't tell the cops, *Sorry, I'm going to be late for a cocktail party.*

His office door was open, so I gave it a courtesy knock to alert him and walked in. He was leaning over some sheets of paper, writing with a flourish, his bald spot shining in the light.

"I came as quickly as I could," I said before he'd had a chance to berate me for being late.

He pointed to the chair for me to have a seat. There was a lime kerchief in his pocket, a matching expression on his face.

"I'm terribly sorry about the Visiting Committee meeting," I said, launching straight into it. "Believe it or not, I was detained by the—"

"It's irrelevant *why* you didn't make it," he interrupted with a dismissive wave of his hand. "The fact of the matter is you weren't there. I know you're going through a difficult time—and I'm very sorry about it—but it's affecting your performance. Your work has been consistently sloppy in the past year, short on details and depth of descriptive research, sometimes missing research altogether." I nodded, biting the inside of my mouth as he continued. "I agreed to give you a chance when we had our chat about it a few months ago. Clearly, I made a mistake. And I definitely made a mistake entrusting you with the presentation on Monday."

"I understand, of course, and I was thinking that to make up for it I could organize—"

"Lana, what I'm saying is . . ." He cleared his throat. "I'm going to have to let you go."

The hum of the air conditioning seemed to grow louder. I heard the door to the department opening and closing. A muffled conversation somewhere in the front. The scraping of Caitlin's pumps as she walked by on her way to her desk. Had she known about it yesterday?

I swallowed. Stared at him. The sour expression on his face had given way to impatience mixed with annoyance. I wanted to defend myself, to explain how much this job meant to me. That I couldn't leave before seeing the project I'd been working on for over a year come to fruition. But I knew none of it mattered. There were hundreds, maybe even thousands, of others out there who loved art just as much as I did and were just as qualified to do the work, if not more. I wasn't special.

Tears stung my eyes but I wasn't going to give him that satisfaction. I clenched my fists and looked at him. "Effective when?"

"Effective immediately. You can arrange for the transition with Caitlin, who'll take over the Parmigianino."

I gritted my teeth. "Sorry I let you down," I said, and stood up.

He extended his hand. "Best of luck."

I stood by the open window with an empty tub of ice cream in my hand, the spoon licked clean. The trees below had the fresh light-green color of early summer. Children's voices drifted in from somewhere down the street. Then the grating melody of an ice cream truck. As if I needed any more of it. Plato was on top of the piano next to me, craning his neck, mesmerized by the world outside. As a kitten, he'd tried scratching out the screen. He'd learned to leave it alone.

I was at home at three in the afternoon on a Wednesday and I had no idea what to do with myself. I'd tried reading a book, watching television, but had no desire for anything. It had taken me nearly twenty years to build my career. Alistair might be a pompous ass but he was right, I'd neglected my responsibilities. Forget about the presentation— that was the last straw. My head hadn't been in it for more than a year. Maybe two. Since my first chemical pregnancy; or was it before that? Regardless. My dream job had been within reach and I had lost it. Everything I'd ever worked for, gone. I tried not to despair, but getting fired from one of the most prestigious museums in the world could be fatal. Alistair would give me a token reference, sure, but in the super competitive art world, anything short of a glowing reference was no reference at all.

I was to be a single mother without a job, barely any support network and no savings, scarred by the knowledge that my baby's genetic parents had actually had an affair and one of them was a suspect in the death of the other.

And that was the best-case scenario, assuming I was lucky and the pregnancy stuck.

41.

LANA

Katya's memorial service was held at 2:30 p.m. in St. Paul's Chapel on campus. It was a miserable day, dark and spitting rain. Students rushed between buildings in jackets and hoodies pulled low over their foreheads. There was the occasional umbrella. I resisted the urge to think that Mother Nature was crying for Katya. Still, it was a welcome change from the bright, chirpy summer weather we'd had in the past couple of days. The redbrick and limestone façade of St. Paul's blended in with the rest of the buildings on Morningside Campus. Ironically, it was right next to the Philosophy Department's building. As I walked by it, I wondered if Tyler was in his office and whether he would come to the service.

The church was cool and surprisingly airy inside. I loved the pink tiles of the interior, the blue stained glass that let in muted light, the central dome ringed with windows. There was nothing fake, exaggerated, overdone. Anna Konstantinova was speaking to the priest in the back while Penka stood to the side, staring up at the dome. Standing there in the middle of the empty church, she looked even more frail than when I'd first seen her. As if the pain of the last week had shrunk her in all directions. Anna had called me yesterday, asking for my help. "It would be great if you could come early and just hang out with Penka," she'd said. "You know, so that she has someone to lean on when I'm needed to take care of the logistics."

I was torn. Since I was still reeling from Katya's affair with Tyler, the last thing I wanted to do was go to her memorial. But I felt sorry for her poor mother, who was dealing with the death of her child in a foreign country with no family and friends to support her. As I headed toward Penka, I realized I was grateful for the opportunity to invest my energy into something. To get out of my apartment. To avoid facing the fact that I'd been fired.

My steps echoed as I walked across the marble floor. I nodded to Anna and the priest and went straight to Penka. I hugged her, said, *"Mnogo sazhalijavam,"* then shrugged helplessly. The occasion called for a more sophisticated exchange than "I'm so sorry," but that was all I could manage with my rusty Bulgarian.

The place quickly filled with students and faculty. There were a few reporters, too—you could spot them approaching people, jotting notes on their phones or tiny notebooks—but thankfully no TV crews.

After the ceremony, I stood next to Penka, holding her arm as people stopped to express their condolences. Only a few turned out to have been friends with Katya and could say a word or two about her to Penka. Most seemed to have been drawn to the service by the tragedy that had made headlines rather than by their personal relationship to the deceased.

I was speaking to a guy from the medical school who knew Katya when, in my peripheral vision, I noticed Tyler making his way from the back row of seats. I stiffened. I couldn't believe he had the balls to come over and talk to Katya's mother. He nodded but I just stared through him as he moved toward Penka. I thought she would take his eyes out, but she shook his hand and said, "Thank you," the only words she seemed to speak in English. Could she not know that he had slept with her daughter? Or, maybe in the larger scheme of things, that was beside the point.

Tyler was followed by a young athletic-looking guy in khakis and a blue striped shirt. He gave Penka a long hug and told her what a wonderful person Katya had been. How smart and beautiful and accomplished. It was clear it meant a lot to Penka. Her face didn't exactly brighten, but there was a lightness to her expression that hadn't been there before. Her nods were more vigorous, her thank-yous more passionate. I wondered if he, too, had been one of Katya's beaus. I kept looking around for Nick but didn't see him. Of all people, shouldn't he have been here? If they were indeed planning to get married, shouldn't he be at her memorial?

When it was all over, I offered to take Penka home. Anna was thrilled to have that responsibility off her full plate. The consulate, she told me, had put Penka up in one of their apartments that was not in use at the moment so that she didn't have to spend money for a hotel. "It's on the Upper East Side. A safe and easy neighborhood to navigate," Anna said. "Penka can make a meal for herself there instead of having to eat out all the time."

The rain had stopped by the time the three of us left the church. The clouds had cleared, leaving a stark blue sky. The grass patches seemed that much greener, glistening wet in the sun. The buildings that much more stately and majestic. We walked through campus slowly, allowing Penka more time to take in the place where her daughter had spent the last four years of her life. She lit a cigarette and I discreetly moved to her other side, making sure the smoke blew away from me. That was when I saw him. Standing at the corner, behind Low Library, watching us as we walked down the steps.

I'd noticed him earlier lurking in the back of the church. Around my age, handsome, wearing an expensive sports jacket over a black T-shirt and jeans. But only now, in the light, did I see how much he resembled Tom Cruise. The blue stare, Katya had said. Or was it blue steel? I was at once relieved and apprehensive. So Tyler wasn't the guy Katya had told me about after all. But if this man was her boyfriend, then why hadn't he come to speak to Penka after the service? Why was he standing there, watching us? He saw me looking at him but didn't avert his gaze. "I forgot something," I said to Anna. "I'll catch up with you at the gates." I turned and walked toward him. He waited for me to get closer before giving a nod of acknowledgment. He was startling from up close, his eyes pulling you in, demanding attention.

"Hi, I'm Lana," I said tentatively. "Katya's friend. I believe I know who you are."

"Damian." His voice was low, measured. "I need to talk to you."

Good, I thought, *because I want to talk to you.*

"It's about Katya," he added.

"I figured." I glanced back but Penka and Anna had already disappeared behind the building. "I don't really have time now. Can we meet later today?"

He thought for a moment. "How about six at the Soldiers' and Sailors' Monument? You know it? At 89th Street and Riverside Drive?" I nodded and he continued. "There are a bunch of benches there. It should be quiet at that hour."

Penka and I said good-bye to Anna and hailed one of the green taxis that dominated Upper Manhattan. We rode down Broadway and across the park in silence. I stared out the window, wondering why Damian wanted to talk to me. If he knew something, he should be going to the police. *Should have gone* a long time ago. Was it smart of me to get involved? But I had to figure out what had happened to Katya. I owed it, if not to her, then to the baby growing inside me. Besides, I owed it to myself. I'd lost my job over it, for Chrissake.

When we reached Penka's building at the corner of York and 83rd, she turned to me and said, *"Kafe?"*

I nodded. *"Chai?"* I said, and she smiled.

"Govorish li Bulgarski?"

"Razbiram no ne govoria mnogo," I said, explaining that I used to speak it as a child but was out of practice. I didn't mention that I'd stopped because I'd grown tired of my mother correcting me all the time. By the time I was twelve, we'd established a routine where she spoke to me in Bulgarian and I answered her in English. So I understood everything but found it hard to string together the words into sentences.

Penka squeezed my hand reassuringly, saying that my Bulgarian was pretty good if she could understand me.

The five-story building was a renovated redbrick with an elaborate green cornice and a fire escape zigzagging down the façade. Next to it on York Avenue was a shiny new high-rise; across the street was a construction site, surely another residential tower. The apartment was a small but light one-bedroom with high ceilings and beautiful moldings. There was a faint smell of Bulgarian spices—paprika, summer savory, and spearmint—that I remembered from my childhood when my mother cooked Bulgarian dishes exclusively: stuffed peppers, grape leaves, or cabbage; moussaka; grilled lamb, pork, and chicken; or my favorite *kofte*, made of ground pork and lamb. At any other time, I would have enjoyed the familiarity of it, but today my stomach was so unsettled that the slightest aroma could unleash a bout of nausea.

Penka led me to the kitchen. She set the kettle for tea and, to my great relief, cracked the window open, letting in some air. While we waited for the water to boil, she made herself Turkish coffee. I was surprised there was one of those old copper *jesve* pots in the apartment. My mother used to have one, too, back when I was a kid. Penka must have read my mind because she pointed to a coffeemaker in the corner and said, shaking her head with a displeased expression on her face: *"Ne go haresvam."*

I smiled. *"I az,"* I said. "Me too." I'd always preferred espresso to drip coffee. But I liked it with milk, ideally a latte, though I could settle for a cappuccino, especially a wet one. Penka's coffee would have been too strong for me even with milk. As it began boiling, it created a dense creamlike bubbling layer that threatened to overflow, but she pulled it off the stove just in time. The thick aroma alone was enough to give me a caffeine boost.

Penka had a box of different teas and I selected peppermint, hoping it would help settle my stomach. We brought our cups to the small kitchen table and sat, smiling awkwardly at each other.

"Znaesh li? Do you know?" I began struggling to find the right words. With the help of hand gestures where I lacked vocabulary, I managed to ask if she knew about Katya's egg donation.

"Da," Penka said, pointing to her stomach. *"Donatsia."*

"Za men," I said, and held my belly with both hands to indicate I was pregnant.

She stared at me. Her eyes were red and watery, the circles under them as dark as bruises.

"Bebe?" Penka finally asked.

"Da, bebe," I said, and looked down at my hands still resting on my belly. "Katya *bebe.*"

Penka just sat there staring at me. The *rat-a-tat* of jackhammers came in from the construction site across the street. The shouts of the crew, the growl of heavy equipment. Had I made a mistake telling her?

"Bebe," I said again, and motioned toward her. *"Baba.* Grandmother."

A tear rolled down her cheek, leaving a moist trail. *"Bozhe moi, bebe,"* she said, sniffling. She leaned over and hugged me. *"Na Katya, bebe."*

I held her tight, my own tears mixing with hers. *"Bozhe moi,"* I repeated after her. "My God."

I walked out of Penka's apartment feeling lighter. But it was more than just unloading a huge burden. We'd bonded over our shared grief and our hopes for the future of the baby growing inside me. I was surprised how much Bulgarian I remembered. And the more we talked, the more it was coming back to me.

I'd spent nearly two hours there, consuming copious amounts of tea and cookies while Penka told me stories about Katya's childhood. Part of me found it painful to hear about the woman Tyler had had an affair with. But as a mother-to-be, I was eager to know more about the woman whose genes my baby would inherit. Penka lit up, talking about her daughter. Katya had been a very bright child. Always excelling in school, always far ahead of her classmates. She'd scored through the roof on the SATs and received a few scholarships that had made studying in the United States possible.

"She always took care of herself," Penka said, her face glowing with a mother's pride. "We were poor. I was working two jobs. There was no time to make her breakfast or help her with homework. And certainly no money to pay for school."

Katya had been competitive and determined since she was very young. If she lost a board game, she had to play again and again until she won. "Until she got you back," Penka said with the faintest of smiles, but a smile nonetheless. It was good to see her put her grief aside for a moment and remember the good times when her daughter was a stubborn little girl.

"She was feisty, too," Penka added. "Never a crybaby."

She told me how when Katya was in first grade, some boy pulled on her braid during roll call in the courtyard. Instead of crying out in pain, Katya clenched her teeth and waited. When the teacher let them go, she leaned over, grabbed a rock, and hit the boy on the head. He had to be rushed to the hospital to get stitched up. "It was the first time I was called to the principal's office," Penka said, the edges of her mouth curling up. "Over the years, I would become a regular."

But Katya hadn't just defended herself, Penka told me. If any of the other kids were bullied or wronged in any way, Katya jumped to help them, even if that meant getting herself hurt or in trouble. "The only reason they didn't expel her," Penka said, "was that she was their smartest student."

I listened, nodding and smiling. Luckily, Penka didn't ask about the baby's father. She also didn't mention anything about Katya's untimely and mysterious death and I wasn't going to ask her. This afternoon was about celebrating Katya's life, not mourning her demise.

42.

TYLER

The moment I walked in, I knew it was a mistake to meet Rachel at the Hungarian Pastry Shop. I'd expected it to be empty on a Thursday afternoon, a week after commencement. It was the quietest time on campus, a short respite before summer classes started next week. Contrary to my expectations, the place was teeming with people. The day had turned sticky after the rain this morning but it was nice and cool inside, the AC unit above the door blasting cold air. Rachel was already there, sitting in the back at what seemed to be her favorite table.

"I'm sorry I couldn't meet yesterday," I said when I joined her with a plate of baklava and a cup of coffee. "Are you okay?"

"I'm totally freaked out. I can't believe they're writing all these things about you." Her voice was low, strained.

I frowned. "Don't worry about it."

"I just want you to know that I didn't say anything," she said, staring at her cup. "I have no idea who spread the rumor about us, but it wasn't me."

"I didn't think it was you."

"I should have denied it." She looked up. "But I was caught off guard. I thought that no matter what I said they could twist my words, make them mean anything out of context, so I thought it better not to comment."

She seemed so nervous, scared like a little bird. "You have nothing to apologize—"

"You've done so much for me," she continued, ignoring my words, "and this is how I repay you." Her eyes were moist with tears. I wanted to reach over and take her hand and comfort her. But I knew better.

She must have sensed my thoughts because she sighed and, picking at her chipped nail polish, she said, "Most of all I want to apologize for that time."

I shook my head. "It was entirely my fault. You were barely coherent with grief."

Rachel had lost her mother just after the winter break. She was particularly devastated about not making it home in time. That her mother had died without her by her side. By the time Easter rolled around, between the stress of her thesis, her responsibilities as a TA, and the guilt around her mother's death, she'd unraveled. We'd been sitting right here, in the Hungarian Pastry Shop, talking about her thesis when she'd folded over her notebook and started crying midsentence. I'd wrapped my arm around her and walked her out. The streets were empty, everyone gone for the Easter weekend. We'd wandered for a bit in the park by the river. It was an unseasonably cold Good Friday but she'd said the wind felt refreshing, it cleared her head. Eventually, we'd sat on a bench and I'd taken her hand and told her that everything would be okay. We'd stayed like that listening to the birds chirping in the trees, the light vanishing around us. And then she'd looked up and kissed me.

I chased the memory away and took a bite of baklava, then pushed the plate toward her, but she shook her head.

"I didn't know what I was doing," she said.

"It was only human. We both needed it." It had taken me some time to disengage. It'd felt good. Different. Intoxicating. *Lana and I don't kiss like that anymore*, I'd thought on the way home that night.

Rachel took a sip of her coffee and looked at me, biting her lips.

"It was a special moment," I said, and smiled, hoping to reassure her. I couldn't let her feel guilty.

She nodded. Thought about it. "I'm sorry about you and Lana. I hope I didn't facilitate your—"

"Of course you didn't. It was just a kiss." I stared at her, hoping to cement the point. Not that Lana would have been thrilled to hear about it but, to our credit, we'd stopped there. Still, I'd felt so guilty about the intimacy I'd allowed to develop between the two of us that, like an idiot, I'd told Lana there had been someone else. She of course took it to mean a full-blown affair. But in many ways, such intimacy was a worse betrayal than a booze-fueled one-night stand. I should know after the other day with that girl. I barely even remembered what she'd looked like.

"Infertility is hard on couples," I told Rachel. "Research shows that those who are unsuccessful break up at three times the rate of those who succeed."

She studied me uncertainly.

"The irony is," I continued, "if Lana and I had known when we met that for whatever reason we couldn't have kids, it wouldn't have destroyed us. We would have gone straight to donor egg or surrogacy or adoption. What killed us were the grueling years of 'trying for a baby.' Lana kept her eyes on the prize. She didn't know how to stop and take a break. I used to love that about her. Ever since we'd first met." I smiled at the memory. "It's hard to believe that it ended up being the very thing that got in the way of our relationship."

Rachel was listening, lips parted, hands folded in her lap. Her coffee stood abandoned to the side. "How did you guys meet?"

I told her about Kilimanjaro.

"Seriously?" Rachel leaned closer over the table. "That's so romantic."

"Lana had just finished her PhD at Columbia," I said, "and I was about to start teaching there in the fall." I shrugged as if that somehow explained it all. In our eyes it had. It was meant to be, we'd thought. The hubris of youth.

Rachel was nodding. I didn't share that last bit with her. She had plenty of time to enjoy being young and foolish. I'd done enough damage as it was.

We reconfirmed our agreement to keep our distance. She would have to find a new adviser in the fall. In the meantime, she was teaching a philosophy intro course in the summer session. I recognized some of the titles I'd recommended in the pile of books by her mug. I wished her good luck with the course and a good summer and left without as much as a hug. We'd looked at each other awkwardly. Hesitated. There were too many students around, too many familiar faces, too many glances in our direction. It was better for both of us, I'd decided, opting for a pat on the shoulder.

I felt like such a schmuck.

And as one does in times like that, I walked straight into a bar, an old favorite dive of mine on Amsterdam.

◆

It must have been past midnight. I was quite smashed. Not a bad feeling. The scratchy voice of Tom Waits came over the sound system. A moody Celtic-flavored ballad. It was the perfect soundtrack for the scene: dark, damp, and deserted. There were three other guys there, slouched over their drinks. The buff, middle-aged guy behind the bar was talking to one of them at the other end. The booths behind us were empty. It stank of fermented beer. The two TV screens were old and bulky, both showing different soccer games.

The music reverted to a mishmash of accordion, stomping feet and Tom Waits shouting in Russian *raz, dva, tri, cheturie.*

Ironically, the very reasons that had made Lana and me grow apart—the endless infertility struggle—had brought Rachel and me together. I took a sip. Tom Waits was singing "I'll shoot the moon," accompanied by what sounded like the plucking of a saw, a horn, and who knows what else.

They say intimacy is built on baring your soul. On making yourself vulnerable. That was where I went wrong. That was my original sin.

I should have come clean to Lana. Instead, I'd gotten deeper into it.

My tongue felt thick and heavy. I took another sip. Listened to the brooding, melancholic song. Something about November. I had a feeling we'd already heard that one. Great. *The Black Rider* album on a continuous loop. My head was already fucked-up.

Go away you rainsnout, Tom Waits sang, *Go away, blow your brains out.*

The room swiveled. Drinking is like falling for someone—you don't realize you've gone too far until it's too late to do anything about it. And you find yourself smooching on a bench like a horny teenager, wrecking your life and the lives of those around you.

❖

I woke up curled up in the back of a cab, the driver knocking on the plastic partition: "Sir, we're here," he shouted in a strong Pakistani accent. "Sir?"

I sat up, feeling woozy, my head heavy. I glanced at the fare, pulled out my wallet, and handed him a $20. "Keep the change," I said, and squeezed out of the car.

I took a step, then another. Paused to collect myself before tackling the stairs to the building's entrance. I pulled out my keys and, after some juggling trying to find the right one, I managed to open the door. I got into the elevator and was about to press the fifth-floor button when I realized this was my old building. Lana's building.

I'd given the cabbie the wrong address. I hesitated, my finger hovering over the button. I pictured Lana curled up on the right side of the bed—her side—the covers bunched around her waist, the silky pajama camisole hugging her skin. What if I simply let myself in and slipped under the covers next to her?

The very thought sobered me. I turned and walked out. I was in enough trouble as it was.

43.

LANA

Damian was sitting on a bench next to one of the cannons, facing the monument. As he'd predicted, there was nobody around. That had sounded like an advantage earlier but as I approached Riverside Drive, I started to feel uneasy. The sun wouldn't set for another two hours but on this gray muggy early evening, the park looked dark and desolate. He stood up as he saw me and, following our awkward hellos, waited for me to sit down before joining me. He pulled a flask from his pocket, unscrewed the cap, and offered it to me.

I shook my head. "I'm good, thanks." I wondered how much he knew about me.

He took a sip and said, "I think I know what happened to Katya."

"You do?" My heart sped up. I leaned toward him. "Have you told the cops?"

He screwed the cap back on and put the flask away. "I can't," he said, staring at his feet. His brown leather shoes seemed expensive. "They don't know about me and Katya." He looked at me. "I used a burner phone."

I cocked my head, confused, but before I could ask why he would do that, he flipped his palms up defensively and said, "I have a wife and kids in the suburbs. I don't want any trouble."

So he was one of those guys. An apartment and a girl in the city for "late nights at the office." Still, a burner phone? He was a pro.

"The point is," he continued, "I know Katya paid ten grand to some dude for a green card marriage."

I sat up. "She did?" Nick hadn't mentioned it was a green card marriage. That made more sense. And it explained what she'd done with the money.

Damian bit his lower lip. "I told her it was a bad idea to give him the money in advance. In cash, at that. But she wouldn't listen to me. She thought I was being jealous. That I wanted her for myself." He kicked the ground with his heel. "I've been following the news but haven't seen anything about that guy."

"You think he—"

"I think he got rid of her once he got the money. He works at an Irish pub in Washington Heights. Just a few blocks from the river. Katya used to hang out there until the wee hours. It wouldn't be that hard."

An image of Nick's heavily tattooed arm clasped around her neck flashed in front of my eyes and I shuddered. My hands were cold and clammy and I tucked them under my thighs. "Why cash?"

"She was worried about leaving a trail and the government figuring it out."

I sighed. "Why tell me?"

"Who else? You have an interest in finding the guy. Unless of course it's your ex-boyfriend, the professor. But if I was going to bet I'd go with the bartender."

I nodded, unsure if I should feel grateful that he didn't think Tyler could have done something to her, or pissed at him for bringing up Tyler.

"How do you know all that?" Tyler had been on the news, of course, but there had been no mention of me except for a fleeting reference as his ex-partner in a *Post* article.

"Katya told me she was going dancing that Saturday with her new friend, Lana. She was so excited to have met another Bulgarian, she wouldn't quit talking about you." He took a sip from his flask. "I didn't know what to think when I found out she was missing. I did a bit of digging. Followed you a couple of times, hoping you'd lead me to her." He paused, looked at me. "I knew you worked at the museum."

I nodded, remembering the uneasy feeling of someone watching me on my way home through the park. I hadn't imagined it after all.

"What I didn't know," he continued, "was that she'd been screwing your boyfriend."

Makes two of us, I thought, suddenly impatient. "So, what exactly do you expect me to do with this information?"

"Tell the cops so that they can get the motherfucker."

"What is it to you? Sounds like you can toss away the affair along with your burner phone."

He knocked his heels against each other, looked up at me. There was hurt behind the steel of his gray-blue eyes. "Believe it or not, I was thinking of leaving my family for her."

Katya seemed to have had that kind of effect on men. I felt the sting of Tyler's betrayal with renewed force.

Before I left, I asked, "How can I reach you?"

"You can't."

I squinted at him, surprised.

He shrugged. "I told you. I don't want any trouble."

I stood up to go, then hesitated. "Did she know you had a family?"

"No. But she knew I was hoping we would move in together. Why?"

"Just wondering," I said, and bid him good-bye.

At least she hadn't knowingly wedged herself in between yet another couple, I thought as I walked away. I still couldn't believe the irony of her telling me to punish my partner for leaving me, while all along she'd been sleeping with him. Sure, she hadn't known I was Tyler's significant other, but she'd known he had one. That they were trying for a baby, for Chrissake.

On the way home, I wondered if I could trust Damian. I had no clue who he really was. I had no contact information for him. No last name. How did I know he wasn't steering attention away from himself? What if he was the scorned lover who, in the heat of rage and jealousy, had killed Katya and now wanted to get rid of Nick, the guy who'd fucked it all up for him?

I was in way over my head. This was the kind of information I should be going to the cops with but after being interrogated, I wasn't sure that was such a good idea. What if they didn't believe me? Worse, what if I somehow implicated myself even more?

I had to talk to Nick. I couldn't imagine he'd admit to it—if Katya had indeed given him the money—but I had to at least get a sense of what was going on before I even considered calling Robertson. I just had to make sure not to scare Nick. Ask him only about the green card marriage without mentioning the money.

I called Coogan's as I headed toward the subway. A woman's voice answered. "Yeah?"

"Can I speak to Nick, please?"

"There is no Nick here."

I halted. "The bartender," I said, confused. "Nick, the bartender with the tattoos."

"Sorry," she said, and hung up.

I stared at my phone and pressed redial. "Yeah?" The same woman again. She was clearly not in the habit of mentioning the bar's name or asking how she could help.

"Hi, I'm sorry but this is Coogan's, right?" I asked.

"Yeah."

"I was there last week and spoke to the bartender. Nick. Tall, skinny, shaved head, tattoos all over his arms."

"He no longer works here."

I felt a jolt. "Do you know where—"

"Nope." Click.

I'll be damned.

That bastard. It had all been one big performance, hadn't it? *Oh, I didn't even know she'd gone missing. Oh, she stood me up. I'm so heartbroken.* He must have waited for the cops to look elsewhere, and then he'd quit his job and split. Even if he hadn't done anything to Katya, the little weasel wanted to pocket her money. Assuming he hadn't put it in the bank—which seemed to have been the plan—the cops had no way of tracing it to him. Unless, of course, they had a reason to request a search warrant and found it stashed in his apartment. I dialed

Robertson's number before I chickened out. He picked up on the second ring, no greeting, just a cold, snappy "I'm listening."

I hesitated. "You might still think that I had something to do with Katya's death," I began, "and maybe I'm stupid to be calling you, but this is really important." I told him what I'd learned about Nick and the fact that he had conveniently disappeared.

"And how did you come to know this?" Robertson asked.

I recounted my meeting with Damian, painfully aware of how suspicious the whole story sounded. "I don't expect you to believe me," I said at the end. "I don't even know if his real name is Damian. But I thought I should tell you about the money."

"Thanks. We'll look into it," Robertson said, and I was about to exhale when he added: "We might need you to come to the station again. If any follow-up questions come up."

My hand clenched around the phone. "Sure. Let me know," I said and hung up.

Hungry and depleted, I hurried toward the subway on 96th Street. At the corner, just before the entrance, I spotted a Mexican food truck and slowed down, my mouth watering at the pictures of handmade corn tortillas piled with beef, onions, sour cream, and tomatoes. The last thing I wanted to do when I got home was to cook. I might as well get a burrito and a couple of tacos and call it a night.

Back home, I prepared to binge on Netflix, resolved to put Katya, Tyler's betrayal, and the loss of my job out of my mind. They were all linked to Katya in one way or another but I refused to think about it. The Mexican food wasn't sitting well in my stomach and I curled up on the couch, going through the new releases. I'd just settled on a Showtime comedy series when the doorbell rang. "Are you kidding me?" I said out loud as I got up.

I opened the door to find Sam standing there, smiling awkwardly, hesitantly. She had leggings and running shoes on. Her thick brown hair was pulled into a loose ponytail.

"Is everything okay?" I asked. "Come on in."

"Sorry for not calling first," she said, and followed me inside. "Our phone conversation was a bit awkward the other day . . ." She let her voice trail off as she eased herself into the armchair. "Anyway, Mark's home with the girls. I was going to go to the gym but thought I better stop by and see how you're doing."

I was touched. Sam was a good friend. I shouldn't have been so short with her over the phone. Her brother's mistakes weren't her responsibility. "I'm sorry about the other day," I began, "but I'd just learned about—"

She waved me off. "Don't mention it," she said, her eyes on the empty ice cream tub I'd polished off last night that was still sitting on the table, the smears left by the spoon on the carton crusted hard. My shoes were at the foot of the couch, where I'd kicked them off as I'd come in half an hour earlier.

"Sorry about the mess," I said. "I've been feeling pretty lousy today." I picked up the Ben & Jerry's container to take it to the kitchen. "It's late for coffee but maybe a glass of wine? I'm afraid I don't have anything else."

She said she was fine, didn't need anything, so I got us both water bottles from the fridge and a couple of glasses. If she thought our last conversation was awkward, this was proving to be worse.

"I heard about your job," she said, and put her hand on my arm. "You must be devastated."

"Who told you?"

Sam pursed her lips into an apologetic frown before she said, "Tyler."

I sat up straight. "How the hell does *he* know?"

"I think your mother told him," Sam said, her voice rising at the end as if she were asking a question.

My mother, of course. I should have never told her, but she'd called me yesterday afternoon when I was at my lowest, too crushed to bother coming up with an excuse for why I was at home so early. I wanted to scream. Just when you thought it couldn't possibly get any worse. I filled my cheeks with air and let it out through puckered lips.

"I just . . ." Sam began, paused. "I know things are really strained between you and Tyler—"

"Strained?" I blurted. "You know he left me, right? In the middle of our donor egg cycle? For *the donor*, who turned out to be his student. Or was it for the grad student the papers reported on?" I was breathless. The nausea had become really bad and I felt the blood draining from my face and hands. I closed my eyes, hoping for relief.

"Oh, honey. I'm so sorry. But Tyler swears—"

"I'm sorry." I got up and rushed to the bathroom. I barely had time to shut the door before I hugged the toilet. I wished I'd turned on the sink to drown the noise, but there wasn't time.

"You okay?" Sam asked when I returned.

"Sorry, I had some tacos earlier." I sank into the couch. "I guess the spices didn't agree with my stomach."

"Can I get you something?"

"I'll be okay. Just give me a few minutes."

Sam looked at me. Her eyes lingered on my swollen breasts. I could see the recognition light up her face. "Are you . . . ?" she began. "Could you be . . . pregnant?"

I couldn't imagine lying to Sam. Not when she asked outright. She'd been there for me, every step of the way, and now she'd come to check in on me. Penka had taken the news so well, I thought, surely Sam would, too.

I slowly nodded.

"Oh, my God," Sam shrieked, and came to hug me. "But wait. When?" she asked as she pulled back and settled on the couch next to me.

That was the hard part. Admitting to what I'd done. It wouldn't have been an issue had I just gotten pregnant naturally. "You know Tyler left just three days before the transfer, right? The embryos were ready, everything was set to go." I looked down at my hands. "I didn't have it in me to cancel."

She stared at me, her mouth agape. "It was my last chance, Sam. I had to take it."

"I'm glad you did," she said, and looking at me tenderly, she smiled.

I sighed, relieved. "But please, you can't tell Tyler."

"What?" She pulled back. Her smile faded. "You mean he doesn't know?"

"He left me, Sam. He did some horrible—"

"No, I'm sorry," she said, shaking her head. "My brother is finally going to be a father and you expect me to—"

"But he didn't want the baby. And the whole business with our donor . . ."

"Look, I can't speak for Tyler. In all honesty, I've no clue what's going on with him. But this . . . I'm sorry, Lana. He might be a jerk—and I understand how pissed you are—but you can't keep something like this from him."

I stared at her. She couldn't be serious. "Sam, it was his choice. He walked out. This baby is all I have—"

"I don't care what he did." She stood up. "He ought to know he's going to be a father."

"Sam, please! I'm not even past the danger zone—"

She grabbed her purse and headed out. I followed, my stomach in a knot, a metallic taste in my mouth.

At the door, she turned. Her expression was pained, disappointed. She held my gaze before she said, "Lana, this is not okay."

"I know," I said quietly. "Please give me a chance to tell him myself."

"Tomorrow. You have until tomorrow evening." She turned and walked away.

I let the door slam behind her, feeling let down, angry, terrified. But deep down I knew she was right.

44.

LANA

NOW

At ten the next morning, Tyler was waiting for me at the entrance to Riverside Park's Cherry Walk at 125th Street. I'd considered having him come over to the apartment, but I wanted the freedom to leave if and when I needed to. A coffee shop or a café was out of the question. He wasn't the type to raise his voice in public and make a scene. But what did I know? I could no longer trust who he was and what he was capable of. Sitting on a bench would have been awkward; I would be fidgeting, uncertain what to do with my arms, crossing and uncrossing my legs, worrying that I was too close to him or too far. Better to talk while walking down a set path. It would be good low-impact exercise for me, too, I reasoned, as I laced my running shoes. The cherry blossoms would be long over by now so there shouldn't be many people.

Only once I reached the underpass of the Henry Hudson Parkway and glimpsed the water, glittering in the sun, did it occur to me that we would be walking along the river. My stomach twitched at the thought of Katya washing ashore on the other bank. Then again, it might not be such a bad idea to have our conversation tinged with the memory of her at each step.

"Thanks for agreeing to see me," Tyler said after we'd exchanged self-conscious greetings and headed down the path, the river on our right, hidden by a thicket of bushes, lush with spring.

I looked at him. "I called you." My eyes lingered on his face. I'd forgotten how much I liked his cheekbones, the line of his jaw. His hair had grown long, beyond his usual short-crop cut, but I'd always preferred it that way. It gave him a boyish air.

"I know. But I've been asking you for so long and . . . what I mean is, thanks for talking to me one way or another." He sounded confused, broken. "I need you to know that I didn't—"

"I don't give a damn, Tyler. Whatever you did, it's your problem."

"But I want to—"

"I listened to you last time. I let you tell me at length what a horrible partner I'd been—"

"I didn't say *horrible*. I just pointed out some issues."

"And you were right. I *had* lost track of reality, of the point of it all. I was working too hard. Not to excuse my behavior—but as a way of explanation, it helped having something to pour my energy into during the grueling infertility treatments." I paused to take in the view. The river stretching ahead of us, lower Manhattan's skyline in the distance. "The thing is," I continued, as we resumed our walk, "after each failure, I put all my energy into the next cycle, hoping that it would be the one to finally solve the problem. Once we had a baby, I thought, then we could start building our life. But that time kept getting pushed further into the future."

I stopped to zip up my sweatshirt. The wind had picked up after we'd left the buffer of bushes behind. We were now walking along the bank, just a small pile of boulders away from the water. Apart from the occasional bicyclist and a couple of joggers, we were the only ones around. It was late morning on a weekday.

"Along the way I lost the spark, the curiosity, the sense of adventure," I continued. "I lost myself. And I guess I lost 'us.' In retrospect, it was largely because I knew the infertility was my fault—well, my body's anyway—and I didn't know how to deal with it. I just wanted to solve it."

I felt him turn to me but I was looking at the ground, the large cracks in the cement snaking across the path.

"I tried to—" he began, but I raised my hand to stop him.

"You tried to reassure me. I know." I looked at him. "I actually called you to discuss something else. But before I launch into it I just wanted to acknowledge that I heard you the other day and I see what you meant. We're past it now." I took a deep breath. "There is something else I need to tell you."

We'd reached a section with linden trees, their sweet fragrance thick in the air. At a different time, I would have stopped and pulled on a branch, smelled the blossoms, maybe plucked a few.

"What?" Tyler said, and looked at me with such alarm that I thought of bailing out.

Years ago, when we'd first started trying for a baby, I'd pictured the moment I would tell him that I was pregnant. In my fantasy, he wraps his arms around me and lifts me off the ground and swirls me like a kid, before setting me back down and kissing me. Even later, after the initial and less invasive fertility treatments, when I'd still been using pee sticks, I'd held on to the hope of experiencing that moment. With the IVF cycles, the news came via a phone call. It had been nerve-racking, waiting for the damn phone to ring, for hours on end. I'd taken the first call at work. A negative. After that, I'd started taking sick days for the occasion. Tyler would stand next to me and hold my hand as I picked up the receiver.

The three times we'd gotten positive results, our joy was tinged with fear. Was it going to stick?

I looked at Tyler and clenched my fists. "Okay, here goes," I said, but couldn't continue. What if he got really upset and pursued some legal action against me?

We'd stopped in the middle of the pathway. A barge powered up-river silently. I could smell the water, splashing brown against the boulders. A hint of ocean salt in the air. Tyler was staring at me. The expression of dread on his face had given way to fear. "You aren't sick, are you?" he asked.

"God, no. Why would you think that?"

He exhaled, visibly relieved. "I don't know. You've been looking pale the last few times I've seen you. Your mother said you'd lost your job but, for all I know, you'd quit. And you have something to tell me but you have trouble saying it. . . ."

"I'm pregnant," I blurted out. "There, I said it. You're going to be a father, Tyler Jones." I let out a long breath, relieved to finally have it out there.

He tilted his head, furrowed his brow as if he had trouble hearing. "Is this some kind of a joke?"

I told him how I'd gone through with the transfer as scheduled.

"You did what?" he said with a sharp intake of breath.

"I went against your wishes, I know, but I promise not to ask you for any support. You don't even have to acknowledge paternity—"

"Is it for sure? How far along?"

"Almost nine weeks."

"My God, Lana." He stared at me, his forehead crunched, his eyes cloudy before, finally, a smile began to make its way onto his face. He hugged me and held me tight. His familiar scent, his arms wrapped around me just so, it all felt right, comforting, like returning home from a long hard trip. We stood like that, the river flowing beside us, birds twittering in the trees. It was a quiet moment—two broken souls finding a reprieve in the middle of a storm. In the end, I had to wiggle out of his embrace for some air.

"I hope that means you're okay with it?" I said with a tentative smile. "You aren't mad at me?"

"Are you kidding?" He hugged me again, then let go and just stood there staring at me as if trying to glean the baby growing inside me.

"Let's keep walking," I said. "It's a bit chilly." My T-shirt was soaked under the thin sweatshirt that was no barrier for the wind.

"What does Dr. Williams say?" Tyler asked. "Are we out of the woods at this point?"

I sighed. "There are some complications."

He halted. "What complications?"

I told him about the hematoma.

"Fucking hell. That's one issue we haven't had yet," he said. "There's always something, isn't there? But he says not to worry, right?"

"So far, so good." We resumed walking. The path in this section was squeezed between the river and the parkway. Cars whizzed by at high speed. Just as life had passed us by during those eight years of trying. "I'll keep you posted."

"What do you mean, you'll keep me posted? I want to be there, at the next appointment."

It was my turn to pause and stare at him. "Tyler, we're no longer a couple."

"But it's my child."

"You are the father, yes, and once the baby is born we can talk about a visitation schedule and all that."

"Visitation schedule?" He took my hand. "Lana, you can't do that." He looked straight into my eyes as if by sheer will he could convince me.

I shook my head, pulled my hand away. "You walked out on me, Tyler. On us. You got involved—"

"I screwed up big. I know. I messed it all up. But nothing that was reported in the media is true."

"I believe you had nothing to do with Katya's death." Just the thought of her made my heart race. "But your relationship with her makes any reconciliation between us—"

"I had no relationship with Katya outside of the classroom."

"Right. That's why you didn't tell me she was your student. Good-bye, Tyler." I spun on my heel, started walking away.

"I didn't know she would turn out to be crazy," he said as he caught up with me.

"Of course. It's always the woman's fault. She either turns out to be crazy or a bitch."

"I only wanted to find a Bulgarian—"

"And how about your TA?" I snapped. "Elaine? How stupid do you think I am?"

"I'm sorry. I wasn't thinking straight. I wanted to protect Rachel."

"Rachel? How about protecting me?"

"I know. There is no excuse. I was a moron."

"I don't need your apologies," I said, and picked up my pace.

"Please let me explain."

"Don't make me run to get away from you!" I shouted, feeling out of breath, claustrophobic almost, with him shadowing me like that. "You know exertion could be harmful to the baby."

He grabbed me by the arm. "Lana, you can't keep me away."

"Sorry, but you forfeited your rights when you left."

He shook his head. A look of desperation crossed his face. When he spoke, his voice was grave, halting. "This baby is more mine than yours. And I will fight you on it if I have to."

I pulled out of his grip and strode off, my ears buzzing.

A few steps farther as the path ended, splitting into a maze of trails, I looked back. Tyler was standing at the exact spot where I'd left him, staring at the river. A couple of cyclists swooshed by but he didn't seem to notice them. His words echoed in my mind: *This baby is more mine than yours.*

I sped up, feeling faint with fear.

PART 4

PLAYING GOD

45.

KATYA

The topic of Tyler's lecture today was Plato's theory of forms. As usual, there was not a sound, not a single movement in the auditorium full of captivated undergraduates. "While the forms are timeless and unchanging," he was saying, "physical things are in constant flux. While the forms are unqualified perfection, physical things are qualified and conditioned."

I nodded along, thinking that maybe that was why Tyler could see past my looks. He lived in the world of ideas whereas my body was—at best—just a shadow of the form of Beauty, like the shadows in Plato's allegory of the cave. I loved that about him. I loved everything about him.

"All the girls in class have crushes on Tyler," I told Josh at our next session. "With anyone else, that kind of mass infatuation would have actually made me dislike him. But Professor Jones. Oh. My. God."

Josh raised his eyebrows.

"I know," I said. "I sound like a starry-eyed teenage girl going gaga over her favorite pop star."

"Is that how you feel?" he asked, his eyes boring into me.

"God, no. Such a relationship would actually kill the buzz for me. You know what I mean? The thing about idols is that they are unattainable. Mortal girls don't mingle with the gods. There are a bunch of exceptions, of course, both in Greek and Hollywood mythology."

Josh smiled. Noted something in his notebook.

"I'm not saying he isn't sexy," I went on. "He's hot as hell." I paused, picturing him. The boyish hair, the lopsided smile. The blue stare that warmed you up and made you feel like you mattered. "I would have totally gone for him," I said, "if it weren't for the fact that I'm going to be his egg donor.'"

Josh nodded. Waited for me to say more. But I was done.

Finally, he asked. "So why do you think you like him so much?"

"You mean other than being so hot and all?" Sometimes I really wished I had a girlfriend to talk to. Josh was a poor substitute. You couldn't even crack a joke with him.

The thing was I was feeling particularly horny these days. Maybe it was the hormones. I'd started the injections two days ago. Around the day of the spring equinox, actually, which I took as a good sign. I'd always liked spring, a time of hope and excitement, when flowers bloom and trees blossom and the birds sing to no end. There weren't any song-birds in New York, really. I'd heard the screech of a blue jay a couple of times and even spotted a cardinal in the park once. But mostly, it was the sorrowful *Hoo-ah-hoo . . . Hooo . . . Hoooo . . . Hoooooooo* of mourn-ing doves I woke up to in the mornings, which was still something.

Anyway, the injections. What an ordeal. I did it after dinner when most people went back to studying. Thank God for my single room this year or I don't know how I would have explained it. All these syringes. If anyone walked in on me, they would think I'd become a druggie.

"They can't know in advance when exactly my eggs will be ready," I told Josh at the end of the session. "Women respond differently to the hormones. But the doctor said my retrieval would be at some point late next week. Easter week." I clasped my hands and smiled. "Imagine if it happened on Good Friday."

Josh tilted his head.

"Think about it," I said, leaning forward, too excited to sit still. "I'm going to have Tyler's baby without us having had sex. I won't even carry the baby. Talk about immaculate conception."

46.

LANA

I was sitting on the couch, with my laptop propped open, researching reproductive rights lawyers when Penka called. Her voice quivered, like she'd been crying. I couldn't understand much other than the cops had been there earlier and that she really wanted me to come over. *"Idvam,"* I told her as I grabbed my purse, slipped into a pair of flats, and rushed out without bothering to change out of the black leggings and ratty T-shirt that I only wore around the house.

It was an overcast Saturday afternoon, warm and humid, and I was already sweating by the time I descended into the sauna that was the subway platform. I shouldn't have walked so fast but I couldn't help it. My first thought was that the cops had made a breakthrough in the case. That they'd found Nick and he'd confessed. But there was nothing in the news about Katya. I kept checking my phone while on the train and then the crosstown bus, the suspense driving me mad until I finally rang Penka's doorbell.

She felt so thin, so frail when I gave her a hug. Her face was red from crying but there was a spark in her eyes as she led me to the kitchen. *"Dobra novina,"* she said, and I held my breath as she proceeded to tell me that the cops had recovered Katya's money.

I exhaled. So they had found Nick.

"I can bring her home now," Penka said, eyes welling up. Her Bulgarian sounded different from my mother's, her vowels softer, the sentences more melodic. "I will be able to visit her," she continued. "Together with my son." A tear rolled down her cheek and she wiped it away.

Her son? I stared at her, my heart aching at the realization that Penka had lost two children.

"Predi mnogo godini," she said, explaining that he'd been only three when he'd drowned many years ago. I squeezed her arm, blinking hard to stall my own tears.

Penka poured two glasses of lemonade and put a plate of cookies on the table. When we sat down, I took a deep breath and asked, "Did they tell you where they finally located Katya's money?" I was already getting better at finding the right words in Bulgarian. At least, Penka seemed to understand me.

"Her friend," she said. "Nick, I think was the name."

"So is he in custody? Do they think he . . . ?" I let the question hang, unable to say it out loud.

Penka shook her head. "They said he'd tried to steal the money but he hadn't done anything to her. He'd been with another girl that night."

My shoulders went slack with disappointment. Craving closure, I'd convinced myself that Nick was responsible for Katya's death and it was only a matter of time before the cops found him and brought him to justice. Still, I was relieved that Robertson had followed up on my tip and recovered the money so that Penka could take her daughter back home.

When she finished her lemonade, Penka pushed her glass to the side, blew her nose, then pointed to the bedroom, her eyes glassy with tears. "I'm having a hard time going through Katya's stuff. I thought maybe you can help me sort it out."

❖

The bedroom was light and airy, with beautiful moldings and high ceilings, like the rest of the apartment. Two cardboard boxes sat between the bed and a small desk tucked in the corner.

With a heavy heart, I started sorting through Katya's clothes, while Penka worked on the box filled with notebooks, toiletries, and makeup. My fingers ached at the touch of Katya's sweaters, T-shirts, and jeans. No wonder Penka had called me to help her. I nearly gasped as I pulled out the pink dress I'd met her in. It was that dress that had first attracted my attention. Had she worn something less bright, I might never have noticed the girl standing just a few feet away from me. I might never have looked up to her face and recognized her. I put the dress in the pile to keep and paused to collect myself.

I was having a hard time navigating my feelings for Katya. There were moments when I was furious, the thought of her sleeping with Tyler unbearable. But more often than not, I was overcome with sadness at her tragic, untimely death. If there was anyone to be angry at, it was Tyler. He was her professor, for God's sake.

"Wait, is that her laptop?" I pointed to the MacBook Air on the desk, the cord folded loosely on top of it.

Penka nodded. "The cops just dropped it off."

A flutter of excitement ran through my body at the thought of having access to Katya's calendar, contacts, texts, e-mails, and social media. I turned back to the pile of clothes but couldn't focus. I kept stealing glances at the laptop, anxious to open it. Not that I knew what to look for. I was simply seized by the urge to check, to see what might be there. *Stop it!* I chastised myself. *It's your damn curiosity that brought you to this point.*

"Do you think she kept a diary?" I asked, trying to sound nonchalant.

Penka wore one of my mother's signature expressions—corners of the lips down, eyebrows up—that meant *I've got no clue.*

And what if she had? It would be wrong to read another person's diary. I knew that much. Just as it would be wrong to browse through someone else's e-mail and social media accounts. But what if the person was dead? I looked at Penka, bent over her daughter's stuff. Would she mind?

"Maybe there is . . . you know, something on her computer," I said in my fumbling Bulgarian and stood, unable to restrain myself any longer. "A *clue*," I added, remembering the word, "to what might have gone wrong that night."

"The cops would have seen it, no?" Penka said without looking up.

I went to the desk and plugged in the computer. "Not if it's in Bulgarian."

"True," she said, and, to my relief, came to join me.

I drummed my fingers on the desk as we waited for the laptop to power up only to come face to face with the lock screen.

I looked at Penka. "Could you guess her password?" It was stupid, I knew. What were the chances? But you never know. It wasn't like it was the password to her bank account or even her e-mail. She would have had to type it every time she opened the computer, so it had to be easy.

Penka furrowed her forehead. "I wouldn't know."

"If you were to guess . . ."

"Maybe her father's name?" she said. "Katya loved him dearly. After he died, she'd write his name over and over, pages of it, in her notebooks."

"Okay," I said, unable to contain my impatience. "What was his name?"

"Petar." She sighed. "Petar Bogdanov Dimitrov."

Something about it rang a bell but I was too anxious about cracking the password to think about it and typed quickly, my fingers punching hard on the keyboard. I held my breath as I hit Enter. The wiggle of the dots. Wrong. Damn.

I tried again without a space in between the names. I tried all small letters. I tried all capital letters. I tried combinations of name and family name or name and middle name. Nothing. Maybe I needed to add numbers. "What year was he born?" I asked Penka, who had gone back to her sorting. "What year did he die?" Again, nothing. "I give up," I said finally, and went to the bathroom. It had a window—a real luxury in Manhattan—that looked at the brick wall of the building next door. I lifted it and stood there for a moment, letting the breeze hit my face, taking in slow deep breaths. I returned to the bedroom resolved to help Penka sort out Katya's belongings without getting distracted.

But I'd barely picked up a pair of shoes when I had a new idea. "Last try," I said, and opened the laptop again. I typed Katya's year of birth followed by her father's first name followed by his year of death. I pressed Enter and stared, stunned, as the desktop opened to a photo of a tropical beach.

"I got it!" I shouted. "We're in!"

I brought the laptop to the living room couch and Penka and I huddled over it, going through every document in every folder.

York Avenue was quiet, less hurried on Saturday afternoon. A woman walking her poodle, a young couple pushing a stroller. Barely any cars waiting at the traffic light. Even the construction site across the street seemed dead. It was that leisurely time between brunch and dinner, when people were in the park or napping back home. I stepped out of Penka's building, my disappointment feeling that much heavier against the relaxed weekend vibe. After two hours of sorting through Katya's documents, we hadn't found anything. No journal, no notes, no texts, no e-mails that pointed to what might have happened to her that night.

The humidity outside felt oppressive. The sidewalk stank of urine. It wasn't even Memorial Day yet but summer seemed to have started already.

On the subway, I sat down and closed my eyes, feeling spent. The high of getting into Katya's computer had only made the crash back to reality that much harder. My mind drifted from one topic to another. Suddenly, my eyes popped open. I sat up. Peter Bogdin—my so-called *secret admirer*. Katya's father's name was Petar Bogdanov.

With shaking hands, I pulled my phone out of my purse and tried to open my Instagram account. There was no connection. I got off at the next station without even paying attention to where I was. Leaning against the cold tiled wall, I scrolled to a post on my wall just a few days before Katya and I went to the Bulgarian club. I pressed on the two dozen "likes" I'd gotten and pulled up the list. Sure enough. Peter

Bogdin was one of them. *He* had also acknowledged the photo I'd posted the next day. The shot I'd snapped of the bone marrow plate at dinner that evening was the last image he'd liked.

Peter Bogdin had vanished along with Katya.

❖

"Katya was my secret admirer!" I shouted into the phone as soon as Angie picked up. I was walking up and down the subway platform, oblivious to the oppressive heat, the beads of sweat running down my back.

"Who?" It sounded like Angie was in a store. I could hear voices in the background. "Sorry, let me get out of here," she said.

"Katya knew," I said when it was finally quiet at Angie's end. "All along, she knew who I was."

"Wait. What?"

"Remember the guy I told you about who was watching all my stories on Instagram? You gave me shit about it?"

"Yeah?"

"There was no guy. That was Katya."

"But didn't you tell me about your secret admirer *before* you met her?"

I tried to remember. We'd been sitting on a bench in the park the day I'd found out I was pregnant. "You're right," I said, and felt goose bumps prickle my arms despite the heat. An express train barreled through the station and I pressed my palm against the other ear.

"Between your stories and photos," Angie said, "she knew where you worked, where you bought your coffee, where you took your lunches. She knew—"

"Where to find me, if she wanted to," I said, finishing her sentence. "Dear God!" Had it all been a charade? Could she have staged what I'd thought to be a chance meeting?

"Turns out the stalked *was* the stalker."

"But why?" I asked. "It makes no sense."

"Nothing about her makes sense."

A train approached the station and came to a stop with a groan. The doors opened, people walked out, others pushed in. I stood there as the doors closed and the train disappeared into the tunnel, the number 1 glowing in a red circle on its back. A rat scuttled across the tracks and I watched it zigzagging until it vanished out of sight.

47.
KATYA

"I'll be giving the gift of a baby to a wonderful couple," I told Josh. "The best, really. What a perfect match—a philosophy professor and an art curator. How glamorous. She's beautiful, too."

Josh cocked his head questioningly, in the adorable way dogs do. Behind him the sun shone brightly. I could see a patch of blue sky.

"I looked her up online," I explained. "It was easy. How many curators are there at the Met with the name Lana?" Tyler had told me her name and what she did back when I first met him at the Hungarian Pastry Shop. It seemed so long ago. I couldn't believe there had been a time when I wasn't his student.

I got up and started pacing the room, too excited to stay still. Josh wasn't happy about it. "Katya, please sit down."

"Pretty name, right?" I said, and paused by the window. The tree branches below were starting to bud. "It's really Svetlana but who can pronounce that in America?" I said before returning to the couch.

"You should see her," I continued. "So elegant—cocktail dresses, skirts and blouses, scarves and high heels. Always high heels. I found photos of her at all these art benefits and functions. She did her undergrad at Princeton and her PhD at Columbia. Not bad, huh? And the whole *partnership* thing. I just love it. That's my kind of woman: elegant, intelligent, and independent. EII. I want to be like her when I grow up."

Josh chuckled. He and I had fallen into an easy stride these days. I'd come in, sit down, and start talking. I didn't need much prompting or handholding. Josh's occasional nod or laughter were enough for me to know he was listening.

"Of course, you can't tell from the photos if she is nice," I went on, "but I can't imagine Tyler going for someone less than wonderful."

Josh had a frown on his face now, like he didn't get it or something.

"He's the most awesome professor I've had," I continued, ignoring Josh. "You can tell he *loves* teaching. That it really matters to him if we're learning. I've never had so much fun in a class." I paused, then unfolded and refolded my hands before I went on. "Tyler doesn't seem to care that he's in a dying field. He's one of those absentminded professors who have their heads in the clouds. He'll head home from campus, walking down Broadway but he'll pass 112th Street, where his apartment is, and not notice until he has hit the traffic lights at 110th. Sometimes not even until the split to West End Avenue at 108th."

"How do you know that?" Josh said, his firm voice betraying his rebuke.

"I saw him on campus the other day. I waved at him, but he was so absorbed in his thoughts, he passed me like a lamppost."

Josh was looking at me with narrowed eyes, his head tilted, like he was judging me. I didn't like that. I didn't like it at all.

"I only followed him to make sure he was okay," I lied. "That's all. I'd looked him up online, so I knew his address. I found it under Lana's name actually. She seems to have been there for over fifteen years. I try to picture her as a young girl—more or less my age—arriving in New York. She's from Chicago, a Midwesterner."

The shadow of reproach on Josh's face grew thicker. "Did the agency tell you all this?"

"Oh, c'mon. What's the big deal? I'm not stupid. I did my research. I suppose if I were doing this donor thing only for the money, I wouldn't care. But this is my chance at redemption. I couldn't—wouldn't—just give my baby to anyone."

Josh opened his mouth to say something, but I lifted my hand to stop him.

"I know, it's not really *my* baby. Fine, the baby conceived with my eggs. Anyway, this baby is my way of paying back for Alex. I want to make sure that it has a stable home where it can grow up happy, surrounded by love. Not like Alex and me. Is that so wrong? To want to make sure that I'm not condemning that child to a neglectful mother? I mean, given my experience. Can you blame me?" I stared into his eyes, willing him to understand. "I'm okay with a brilliant, if preoccupied, father. But the mother, the mother has to be perfect. I would have liked to meet Lana, but I totally respect that she wants it to be anonymous. I *love* the fact that she's already so protective of her child. Before it's even conceived, she's anticipating potential dangers. This is not a woman who would send her three-year-old son with her eight-year-old daughter to play in the sea alone."

Josh nodded, scribbled something in his notebook. Outside, traffic droned on Broadway. A distant honking. The rumble of a truck.

"I can't even begin to imagine how hard it must be on her. Luckily, she has a place to vent. She goes to an infertility support group. Every other Friday at the YMCA."

"You've been following her, too?"

I couldn't help it and grinned proudly. "She never bothers glancing back. A woman on a mission."

Josh gave me that stern, judgmental look again. "You realize what you're doing, right?"

I rolled my eyes. "I'm not stupid. It is the very thing Lana is afraid of. *I know.* And believe me, the last thing I want is to mess with the child's mind. But before it has been created, I have to make sure its parents are going to be good."

"You know that stalking is illegal and punishable by—"

"But I'm not *stalking* anyone. Check the dictionary. The legal definition of stalking is: *Criminal activity consisting of the repeated following and harassing of another person.* I'm not *harassing* them, am I? I'm simply gathering information. People do it all the time before signing all sorts of deals. It's just that they usually hire private detectives to dig up the dirt if there is anything to be dug. I don't know of any private eye going to jail because he's doing his job. Nor the housewife who hired him to spy on her husband."

Josh took his time. Finally, he nodded, a bit stronger than his usual *I'm listening* nod. More like: *Okay, fair point.* But I still didn't feel like he approved.

"I can't fuck this up," I said. "Don't you get it? This baby is my one chance at getting myself on track. I know it won't bring Alex back but, in my mind, it'll provide a counterbalance."

I leaned forward, peering into Josh's eyes. "So you see. I've got to do it right." Only then would I be free.

I wasn't scared of needles or blood, but injecting myself—and in the stomach on top of it—made me sweat like a pig. I'd gone to a training session at the clinic to learn how to do it. They told us to experiment on a grapefruit but no matter how much I practiced, the moment I looked at my own flesh, I panicked. I sat at my desk with my shirt lifted for like ten minutes, trying to summon the courage. One hand pinching my belly to get a layer of fat, the other hand holding the syringe poised to strike, alcohol wipe and a pad at the ready, next to me. There was something very counterintuitive about jabbing yourself with a needle in the softest of spots. I would get used to it, I was sure. The girls online who had done it a bunch of times said it got easier with practice. One wrote that she'd even done it standing in the bathroom of a plane.

I couldn't believe Lana had gone through this nightmare eight times. And I was doing just one half of the process. The more I learned about her, the more I liked her. I had a total girl-crush on her at this point. She was everything my mother wasn't and more—strong, protective, successful.

Every time I went to the clinic, I looked for her, hoping to see her sitting in one of the chairs, leafing through a magazine. It's not like I would have gone over to talk to her—she would have recognized me right away—but just sneaking peeks at her, observing her in the flesh would have been cool. There was something so exciting about seeing in person someone you knew so much about and admired from afar. Like seeing a famous person on the street or in a restaurant. You don't talk to them or anything but just their presence in the same location is rewarding. Like their awesomeness rubs off on you or something. I'd once spotted Hilary Duff in SoHo and for the rest of the day I'd felt excited, as if I were somehow special.

So far, I hadn't seen Lana in the waiting room, but maybe she came in the mornings while we donors were called in the afternoons. I'd thought she wouldn't start her part of the cycle until they'd retrieved my eggs. But according to my online research, she already must be taking hormones to prepare her uterus for the embryo. She should be coming in for monitoring as frequently as I was, so that they could tweak the hormones if things were not developing right. Such a complicated game. Everything had to be just so and there were so many components to worry about.

I guess playing God was no joke.

48.

LANA

The ringing of the phone woke me. Sunlight streamed in through the window; I'd forgotten to pull the shades down when I'd finally crawled into bed last night. The clock showed 8:35 a.m. Who was calling me so early on Sunday morning?

I stretched, rubbed my eyes, and got up to look for the phone. By the time I dug it out from under the pillows on the sofa, the call had gone to voice mail. It was my mother. Of course. I decided to talk to her after breakfast and headed to the bathroom. I'd barely splashed cold water on my face when I heard it ringing again. I rushed to the living room to pick it up, the towel still in my hands.

"Mom, what's so important that it can't wait—"

"My own daughter is pregnant and she didn't even bother telling me," she said, her voice high and quavering, her accent thicker than usual. "How could you, Lana?"

I filled up my cheeks with air and blew it out hard as I sank into the sofa. This was going to be a long conversation.

"That I should find out from Tyler and not you," she went on. "That is . . ." Her voice seemed to catch. "That's insulting."

What a bastard. I couldn't believe he told on me to my mother. My knee-jerk reaction was to avert the crisis, to reassure her, make her feel better. Which only made me angrier. I was done taking care of her. My problems were far too great at this point to worry about her fragile ego. It was time I focused on myself. The baby growing inside me needed me.

"This is precisely *why* I didn't tell you," I snapped into the phone instead. "Because *you* make such a big deal out of everything. I'm sorry but I have other, more pressing problems to deal with right now than my mother's hurt feelings. The world—believe it or not—doesn't revolve around you."

"Lana, this is not a way to speak to—"

"And that's another thing: I'm sick of your admonishments, your prescriptions for how I should live my life."

"I'm just worried about you, honey. Tyler told me you won't let him go to the doctor with you. He's really excited about the baby—"

"Mom, he left me."

"If you'd only listened to me and married him."

"Yeah, because getting married sure stopped Dad from leaving you, and then it sure kept Jack—"

"Relationships are hard. I'm not saying they aren't." She paused. "But a commitment like marriage makes you work at it. Otherwise, at the first sign of hardship, you pack your bags and go. That's all I'm saying." She sighed. "But, no, you were too good for marriage with all your feminist ideas."

"Has it occurred to you," I interrupted her, "that maybe I was too scared to get married?"

"Why would you be scared?"

"Because I didn't want to end up like you. That's why."

I heard her swallow. "Like *me*? What's wrong with me?"

"You forget I took care of you when Dad left and you fell to pieces, refusing to eat, crying yourself to sleep. Then again with Jack, then Paul."

"So you thought that as long as you didn't get married—"

"I wouldn't be setting myself up for disappointment. That I wouldn't be making myself vulnerable. Yep. That's exactly what I thought." I'd never before articulated it to myself—or to Tyler for that matter—but in retrospect it seemed obvious.

"Oh, honey," she said, almost gasped. "I hate to tell you this, but when a man leaves you, it hurts just as much no matter what you've been calling him: boyfriend, husband, or *partner*."

"Well, I learned my lesson, didn't I?" I said, and started laughing. To my surprise, she joined in and the more we laughed, the funnier it became.

"We should do this more often," I said after I'd calmed down.

"What? Fight?"

"I meant *laugh*, but, yeah, if we have to fight to get there, sure."

Before we hung up, she said, "I just don't see what's so wrong with having Tyler there with you. It's his baby, too, you know?"

Oh, I do know, I thought, and hung up. *His and his student's.*

My baby would be the embodiment of Tyler's betrayal. Literally.

❖

As the day dragged on, I only got myself more worked up about it. Finally, I couldn't help myself and typed up a text to Tyler: *Did you know your mistress had been stalking me?*

But remembering the newspaper report about his involvement with yet another student, I changed *your mistress* to *Katya* before sending it.

His reply came an hour later. I was on the sofa, scrolling aimlessly through the TV channels and making my way through a bag of Cheez-Its. I'd developed a craving for salty snacks. They also seemed to settle my stomach, so I had a good excuse. Plato was next to me, licking one of his hind legs intently.

Tyler's message said: *I told you she was crazy.*

"Not crazy enough to stop you from fucking her!" I said out loud, and tossed the phone onto the empty end of the couch, startling Plato.

I heard it buzz again but refused to get it. When I finally did—on my way to the bathroom twenty minutes later—I found another text from Tyler: *I hope you'll reconsider and let me join you at the next doc's appointment. If not, I'm sorry, but I'm prepared to fight it in court.*

Feeling nauseous, my head buzzing with anxious thoughts, I curled up on the couch, hoping to find some peace. But it wasn't meant to be. The neighbors' Yorkie was yelping like he hadn't been fed for days. How could such a tiny thing—he was smaller than Plato, for Chrissake—produce so much noise? I pressed one of my ears against the cushions and covered the other with one of the throw pillows. I could still hear it.

◆

Dusk was settling into the room when I awoke. I went to the window and looked out. The gloaming could be beautiful in the city, the building façades dark and crisp against the deep blue of the sky to the west; the streetlights already on, glowing yellow with the promise of a night on the town. Music sounded faintly, probably from one of the bars around the corner. People, alone, in couples or groups, walked purposefully, rushing to get places. The pit in my stomach grew heavy. The day had come and gone. The evening ahead seemed long and empty. I had no plans, no place to go to, no loved ones to see.

My eyes rested on the photos on top of the piano. I took the one from Kilimanjaro and held it toward the fading light, scrutinizing my red cheeks, my smile, my fist pumped high above my head. As much as I hated to admit it, Tyler was right. Where had that daring, fun-loving girl gone? My world had shrunk. I'd let the infertility take over my life and, in the process, I'd lost so much of myself. I'd stopped going hiking, volunteering; I'd dropped out of the book club I'd started. I'd even neglected my work—the career I'd hustled so hard to build. One by one, I'd lost my friends—except for Angie, who was my infertility buddy, so it almost didn't count—and then I'd lost my partner and now my job.

I put the photo down and returned to the couch.

I'd thought of myself as a strong woman. But it was only a mask I'd been hiding behind. I'd fooled everyone: my mother, Tyler, even myself.

I'd thought I was standing up for myself when I went to the clinic to have the embryo transfer despite Tyler bailing. Bullshit. That was the coward's way. I'd gone through the back door, behind his back, hoping I wouldn't be found out. What I should have done was call him on his behavior, tell him that walking out on me at that time was not okay. That if he wanted to go off with some other woman, it was his choice, but I was going to do this donor egg cycle—with or without him.

Instead, I had dug myself into a hole and there was no getting out of it. I could even lose my baby over it.

I tried to shake off the self-pity and opened my laptop, hoping some quick research would help me figure out my options. What I learned was that laws varied between states and that the contracts signed at donor agencies might not hold up in court. But I couldn't find anything about parental rights in situations like ours. It would have been a different story if we'd already had the baby and been named as legal parents. But as it was, Tyler was undisputedly the father while I had no genetic connection to the baby and could be seen as nothing more than a gestational carrier. It didn't help my case that Tyler and I weren't married and that I'd proceeded with the cycle without his knowledge, let alone agreement.

Some might say I'd stolen myself a baby, only I'd done it before it was born. The fact that the "genetic parents" had been willing to give it to me just a few days earlier wasn't the best defense. Even mothers who give up their newborns for adoption have the right to change their minds during a certain period after that.

It was time I sought legal advice. I jotted down the numbers of three reproductive rights lawyers on a piece of scrap paper and stared at it before scrunching it into a ball and tossing it on the floor.

Who was I kidding? I had no money to fight Tyler on this. Not without a job and with a baby on the way.

I clenched my fists. The very idea of having Tyler with me at the doctor's office, knowing all I knew about him and Katya, cut like a knife. But losing the baby was not an option.

49.

KATYA

They came out of the Hungarian Pastry Shop, turned on 110th, and headed to the park. I'd been waiting across the street behind the Peace Fountain, fuming. What the hell was Tyler doing with that mousy grad student? They met here at least twice a week, but I'd also seen them at Tea Magic a few times. I followed them at a distance. Not that there was any danger they would see me. I could tell she was crying, judging by how many times she stopped to blow her nose.

At Riverside Park, they turned south and kept going, past the soccer field, the Dinosaur Playground and the Hippo Playground. Finally they halted at the 91st Street Garden but instead of turning around, they sat on a bench and stared at the flowers. Red, yellow, and purple tulips, daffodils and a bush of white lilac. A green plastic watering can lay on its side in the middle of the pathway.

It was just starting to get dark. A cold spring evening, too cold for Good Friday if you ask me. Bone-chilling. Miserable. But a decent reflection of the way I felt.

I watched as if in slow motion as she raised her face to him, whispered something, their eyes locked on each other, and he leaned over, pushed the hair away from her face, timidly, gently as if handling a precious butterfly, before their lips met and they began to kiss.

I felt a sharp pain below my sternum. Like my insides were being twisted into a tight knot.

I wanted to scream. To run fast and far away until I was gasping, breathless, and finally woke up—like I did from my nightmares.

I averted my gaze. Focused hard on the watering can, feeling just as discarded, emptied.

How could he do that to Lana? To me? To our baby?

I clenched my fists. Not the baby. I couldn't let him do that.

Somehow I found the strength to turn and snap a few shots of them, smooching, before I bolted the hell out of there.

◆

"I can't fucking believe it!" I cried out when Josh finally picked up. I didn't have his phone number. He wouldn't give it to me and I hadn't found a way to get it. Yet. But I had his Skype. We'd done a couple of online sessions during the winter break, while he was briefly out of town. It had worked remarkably well. Nothing like talking on the phone. I would have hated that. There was something to be said about seeing the person you were divulging your most intimate secrets to. I fed off people's reactions. I couldn't talk without knowing what effect my words were having.

But this time Josh didn't turn on his camera. I heard noises. Distant chatter, people laughing, music. For a moment, I worried he might be visiting his family for the Easter weekend. But by the sound of it, he was in a bar. Fine. I turned my camera off, too.

"Katya, what the hell, it's past midnight," Josh said. "Are you okay?"

"No, I am not. That fucking asshole—"

"Has Damian hurt you?"

"God, no!" I should have never told him about Damian's temper. "No. This has nothing to do with him."

"Katya, you know the rules. Unless you're in imminent danger, please come to the office at the usual time and we can talk—"

"You don't understand!" My voice cracked. I paused to gather myself before I went on. "Tyler fucked it all up. Everything's ruined."

"I'm sorry to hear that," Josh said, and, for a moment, I thought I'd got him. But then he went, "I look forward to seeing you next week," and hung up. He actually hung up on me. I was about to call him again when his icon went dark. He had signed off, the asshole.

But of course. What did I expect? That time in the fall, when I'd asked him to go grab a drink with me, explaining how desperate I felt, even hinting at suicide, what had he done? He'd pulled out his phone to call the hospital. He would rather commit me to the loony bin than spend an hour with me, chatting over a pint of beer.

◈

"So what's going on?" Josh asked at our next session without a trace of remorse for leaving me hanging the other day.

I hadn't said a word since I'd walked in. I was just sitting there, like a dark cloud hovering over his couch. Meanwhile the damn April sun was blasting outside. The chatter of students came in through the open window. An ambulance wailed in the distance and I listened as it grew louder, then tapered off. A shiver ran through me.

"Are you cold?" Josh asked, and got up to close the window. Back in his chair, he said, "You want to tell me what Professor Jones did?"

I let the silence grow. It wasn't so much that I wanted to punish Josh for Friday night as much as I was worried that, if I opened my mouth, I'd start sobbing.

"You didn't sleep with him, did you?"

"Are you crazy?" I waited for Josh to cringe but he seemed to have given up on his stupid rule about the word *crazy*. "That's sick," I continued. "Like doing it with my father or something." I crossed my arms, started rocking slightly in my seat before I went on. "He has a mistress, Josh. I saw them kissing." My heart sped up. I felt out of breath just talking about it.

"What about it upsets you?" Josh asked.

"You're kidding, right? This was supposed to be my way of making amends for Alex. The whole point was that I would give a baby to a happy couple so that it would grow up in a healthy environment. Unlike Alex and me. And there goes Tyler, sneaking out with another woman, while Lana is at her infertility support group, very likely upset about how few eggs they got off me."

Josh raised an eyebrow.

"I can't even go there," I said. "I mean, imagine. I'm supposed to be the egg donor and I barely produce nine eggs? The doctor assured me that all we needed was one good one and since I was young, we had eight more than we needed. Not to worry. But still, all these other girls online had numbers in the twenties and thirties, and one girl even had fifty-six eggs. I can't possibly imagine how bloated she must have felt. I was in so much pain with only nine. So here I am, all worried if my eggs will be good enough to give them a child when I see Tyler kissing *another woman*."

Tears filled my eyes and I reached for the box of tissues on the side table. Blew my nose and tried to collect myself. The damn hormones were making me particularly emotional. It had been only a few days since my retrieval. But hormones or no hormones, I still would have been furious.

"On Good Friday, no less," I continued. "You should see her. A little thing with ratty blond hair, thin lips, and pathetic slutty outfits. None of the beauty and class of Lana."

"Is it possible that you're jealous?" Josh asked.

"I'm not jealous. I'm enraged. What a bitch."

Josh did cringe at this word but I couldn't care less. "I'm finding it interesting," he said, reverting to that shrink voice of his, "that you seem to be blaming the woman for the guy's transgressions."

"Oh, please. You Americans have to turn everything into a political issue. If some asshole had slept with Lana, I would have been just as incensed with him. But believe me, the person I'm most furious with is Tyler. What kind of monster has an affair while his significant other is undergoing invasive infertility treatments so that *they* can have a baby?"

"Maybe it was a one-time thing," Josh said.

"Oh, yeah, that would make it better. *Not to worry, sweetheart, we had sex only once.*" I let out a forced chuckle. "And anyway, there is no such thing as one time. You're either capable of it or you're not. My father would never have done something like that to my mother although she sure deserved it." I paused to catch my breath. "I'm sure you think Tyler's infidelity is not my problem. But it is. I can't have my baby—" Josh opened his mouth to object but I stopped him. "Fine, the baby from my eggs. I can't have that baby grow up in a dysfunctional family. With a father who cheats. Like my mother. No way. I can't take the risk that my gift will turn into poison."

"So what are you going to do?" he asked. He'd long abandoned the "tell me more" routine.

"I called it all off. I had no other choice."

"You did?" Josh's eyes opened wide. "I didn't think you could do that so late in the game. Didn't you tell me they already transferred the money to you? After the retrieval? Didn't you sign papers about it?"

Poor naïve Josh. I laughed. "Don't worry. I haven't broken the terms of the contract. Though I would if I had to. This has never been about the money and you know that."

Josh nodded, and I told him how I'd surprised Tyler in front of his building after I'd seen him kissing his TA.

It was dark by then. I was freezing, having waited for nearly half an hour. Tyler was startled to see me there. "What a coincidence," he said. "Are you waiting for someone in the building?"

"Yup," I told him. "You."

His jaw began twitching as he realized this was not an innocent, joyful happenstance. I let him stew in it before I finally told him that I'd just seen him with that slut. "Don't think you're going to get away with it," I said.

He took a step back. "Let's move a bit," he said. "Maybe walk around the block and talk?"

"Why? You don't want to take me to the park?"

He looked hurt. Imagine. As if I'd unfairly accused him of a crime he was incapable of. I did follow him away from the entrance and together we walked across the street and circled the block.

I told him this was a deal breaker for me. I couldn't have the baby conceived with my eggs grow up with a cheating father. I told him I was going to tell Lana about his affair if that was what it would take to stop the transfer. "I know what she looks like," I said. "And I clearly know where you guys live."

He got all freaked out. "Please, don't do that," he said. "I don't want to hurt her. She's been through a lot."

Duh. Why didn't you think about that before you got yourself a mistress?

"Call it off, then," I said.

"What?" He paused, looked at me, before resuming walking. "I can't do that. We're in the middle of the cycle. We have a contract. The money has been transferred."

"And so have my eggs. The retrieval procedure wasn't particularly pleasant and neither were the hormone injections. But I did it all, just as we'd agreed." I paused, let him take it all in, then switched gears. "You have twenty-four hours before I send this to Lana." I showed him the photo I'd snapped of them kissing on the bench. Even in the muted light of the streetlamp, I could see his face lose color. "Instagram message. Easy as a click," I said, and switched to Instagram. "Ah, here she is—*Lana Stone, Art Curator. Visual notes to my life*—"

"Katya, c'mon. I'm not having an affair. It was just a kiss."

"*Just* a kiss?" I was outraged. "Let's ask Lana how she feels about that 'just a kiss' of yours."

"It was a mistake. It will never happen again."

"Do you expect me to believe you?"

"It's the truth."

"Yeah, right. I've seen you around campus. The two of you. Inseparable."

He looked down at the sidewalk, ran his hand through his hair. "Rachel and I are friends."

"Sure, I've got a friend like that, too. You can call it whatever you want but I don't want my baby growing up in such an environment."

He stared at me like I was crazy. "You understand it will not be *your* baby, right?"

I halted. A hot lump swelled at the base of my throat. Was *he* lecturing *me*? After what I'd just caught him doing? "You know what," I said, and turned to go back. "Why don't I just go to Lana and—"

He stood in front of me, blocking my way. "Stay away from her. I'll take care of it myself. There . . . there won't be a baby. I promise."

I stood there watching him as he walked across the street and into his building, his shoulders slouched, his step uneasy, weighted.

I stared at the closed door long after he'd disappeared. I didn't know what to do with myself. I couldn't just turn around and go home and study. What was the point anymore? I walked the streets aimlessly for hours. Damian texted, asking to get together, but I couldn't even think about hooking up. I was scared to go home, where the nightmares would be waiting for me. So I went into a bar and then another one but the liquor only made me feel worse.

"That's when I Skyped you," I told Josh.

He shook his head. Went on again to explain that it was unacceptable to be calling him every time I felt let down by someone. "This is only for emergencies."

"It was an emergency. My entire future had just been shattered."

"How?" Josh said, flipping his hands palms up. "So your professor's a scumbag. Who cares? You got your money for the donation, didn't you?"

"Have you been listening to me? Sure, I got my money and that's great. But I lost the baby."

"You're young," Josh said, and proceeded to count on his hand, "healthy, smart, beautiful, and about to graduate from an Ivy League school. You're getting married to an American and that marriage—fake or not—will allow you to stay in the country, get a job, make as many babies as you want. By most people's standards, your future looks pretty damn good. In fact, many would kill to—"

"That baby was supposed to be my redemption!" I shouted, and stood up. "It was meant to make things good again. It was my ticket to a guilt-free future, to sleeping without nightmares, to a normal life. That's all I'm asking for. A normal life." I narrowed my eyes at him. "You don't understand my craving for it because *you've already got it*. I don't want the extras. Beauty, degree, marriage, citizenship—none of that matters if you don't have the basics. You can only give a damn about those things if you're whole. And I'm not. I thought you knew that, Josh."

I shook my head and stomped out of his office.

50.

LANA

NOW

Monday morning hit me hard. Not going to work on Thursday and Friday had felt like a long weekend. Albeit a miserable one. Between Katya's memorial; telling Penka, Sam, and then Tyler about my pregnancy; his threat to take my baby; and the final blow—the realization that Katya had been stalking me—I'd barely been able to pause and catch my breath. But settling on the couch after breakfast this morning instead of heading to the museum gutted me.

It was now ten thirty and I was still on the couch, my legs propped up, a cup of mint tea getting cold on the coffee table next to me, when a new e-mail from Caitlin popped up. At seeing her name in my inbox, I felt a jab of regret in my stomach. It had yet to sink in that I was no longer a curator at the Met.

So sorry to hear you won't be with us anymore, Caitlin wrote. *When might be a convenient time to transfer your files to me? I'll be taking on the role as you might have heard.*

I knew she deserved it. But it hurt just the same.

I sent her a quick note back, congratulating her and arranging for the transfer on Friday afternoon. I needed time to process and grieve before I returned to the office. I also knew Alistair left early on Fridays and hoped to avoid seeing him.

A text from Angie flashed on my phone: *Turn on NY1.*

I grabbed the remote, my fingers nearly numb with anxiety. After numerous punches on the power button I finally got it to work and navigated to the right channel. As I'd expected, Katya's face flashed on the screen. I increased the volume to max:

". . . the death of Columbia student Katya Dimitrova has been ruled a suicide," the female anchor was saying. "She is believed to have jumped off the George Washington Bridge in the early hours of Mother's Day." I stood there, remote in my hand, staring at the screen. The picture changed to a black-and-white freeze frame of a young girl I could only assume was Katya. The photo was heavily pixelated and taken from above so you couldn't see her face that well, but I recognized the jeans and spaghetti strap top she'd had on that night.

"Footage from surveillance cameras on the bridge shows her entering the pedestrian ramp at five oh eight a.m.," the anchor continued. "According to records at the university's Counseling and Psychological Services Center, she'd been battling depression on and off over the past year. It is unclear if she had been on any medication."

I shook my head in disbelief. The picture switched to footage of Columbia's campus. The athletic-looking man from the memorial came into focus, entering one of the buildings, waving away reporters. "Her therapist at the counseling center, Josh Wozniak," the anchor continued, "declined to comment." So that was who he was. It made sense he'd known so much about Katya, that he'd come to comfort her mother.

I turned off the TV and slumped on the couch. Plato jumped up next to me, making a little squeak with the effort, and began purring. Soon he quieted down and fell asleep. The Yorkie in the apartment below was yapping. Recurring rhythmic thuds came from the next-door neighbors' apartment—their kids playing ball, I suspected. The distant wail of a police car outside.

I was still sitting there, remote in hand, when Angie called a few minutes later.

"I don't get it," I said. "A *suicide*?"

"The medical examiner's report says she died of . . ." Angie paused for a moment before continuing, clearly reading from somewhere, " 'of multiple blunt-force injuries, due to an elevated fall such as from a bridge or overpass into the Hudson River.' "

"But why? Why would she do it? I saw her just hours before. She didn't seem upset at all. If it weren't for the footage of her entering the bridge, I'd think it was bullshit." I sighed. "Still, how do they know nobody pushed her?"

"Video from the CCTV cameras, maybe?"

"The reports didn't say anything about it. Only video of her *entering* the bridge. Plus, wouldn't the cops have seen it earlier? What, they interrogated a bunch of us just for the fun of it?"

Angie chuckled.

"On top of it," I continued, "she had a history of depression? Seriously? There was nothing to even remotely suggest a mental illness in her application. She actually told me—imagine!—that she would never go to a shrink. Turns out she'd been in therapy for a year." I slowed to catch my breath. "Either she's a liar or the cops have it all wrong."

"Or both."

"Or both," I repeated.

The police station was bustling with activity as usual. "At least the media crews left," the officer at the entrance told me. Upstairs, uniformed and plainclothes cops walked in and out. Some of the detectives were looking through files or staring at their computer screens; others were talking on the phone—like Sanchez in the corner—or with each other. Robertson seemed rushed but smiled curtly and showed me to his desk. I was spared the "interview" room this time. Of course, the case was closed. Still, it felt weird to be back, my heart rate picking up the moment I'd entered the building.

"Let me guess," he said as we sat down. "You're here to ask me if we are sure she committed suicide." I gave him a blank stare, uncertain how to feel about him having read me so easily.

"I know you're busy and I'm not exactly family," I said, "but can you please help me understand? Because it just makes no sense."

"Suicide is hard to accept," he said. "People tell me all the time—even when there's a suicide note—that their loved one couldn't have done something like that. It's hard to believe and hard to deal with because there is no one to blame. No one to point a finger at and ask for justice."

"I get that," I said. "But you didn't answer my question. Are you sure it was suicide?"

"As sure as we can be in a case like this." He furrowed his forehead. "When a person dies as a result of a fall from a height—whether it's a bridge or a cliff—it's often very difficult to determine whether the fall resulted from an accident or whether it was a suicide or homicide, especially if there were no witnesses and no note."

"So you don't have footage on the security cameras of her actually jumping? The media reported that she was seen—"

"The CCTV cameras don't cover every inch of the bridge. She must have been in one of the blind spots."

I folded my hands, thought about it. "How do we know then that nobody pushed her?"

"We pursued all leads of possible foul play . . ." The corner of his lip curled. "Including your involvement. But found nothing."

"And you're sure about Nick? He works and lives right there—"

"Nick went home that night with another woman."

"But what if . . . I mean, whoever that woman is, they might have been in it together." Robertson was looking at me with his head cocked. "For the money," I added, feeling self-conscious. "They could split it . . ."

"I should hire you to work for me." He chuckled. "But, yes, their story checks out."

I nodded reluctantly. "And how about that guy from the club?"

Robertson smiled, seemingly more amused than impatient with my line of inquiry. "The building's security cameras show that he didn't leave his apartment until the next morning at eleven, when he joined friends for brunch."

I hesitated, the very thought unimaginable. "And Tyler?"

"He was tough to eliminate," Robertson said, and paused as if meaning to torture me. "No security camera in his building, no woman in his bed to prove that he wasn't on the bridge at the same time as

Katya. Luckily for him, he has a peeping Tom for a neighbor and after Katya left he—"

"Wait, after Katya left where?"

"Tyler's apartment."

"She was at his apartment that night?" I clasped the sides of the chair as I leaned forward.

Robertson nodded and went on. "The guy's in his seventies, an early riser. He has his eye glued to the peephole at the slightest sound. According to him, Katya left at four thirty a.m. The next time Tyler's door creaked open again was at eight fifteen a.m., nearly four hours after she'd left. It all checks out with the story Tyler told us." Robertson paused, looked at me. "So there you have it."

I sighed, my stomach in knots. I didn't know how to feel. I was relieved Tyler had been cleared of suspicion but the whole business with Katya wasn't sitting well with me. She'd gone to his apartment after being with Jacuzzi Guy? Then she'd walked onto the bridge and jumped?

Robertson glanced at his phone, finally growing impatient with me. I was surprised he'd told me as much as he had. Maybe he felt guilty for having been so hard on me the other day. Or maybe he just happened to be in a good mood.

"How about Damian? The guy who told me about the green card marriage?"

Robertson shrugged. "We came across the burner phone in her records. She had no communication with him that day. No texts, no calls, nothing unusual or outside of their routine. We've followed her every step that night and have exhausted all the options."

I sat there, thinking. "And nobody else was on the bridge at the time?" I asked. "No stranger, no crazy person who could have pushed her—"

"It's a popular bridge. On weekends, joggers and cyclists start arriving at dawn. She wasn't the first person to enter the ramp that morning and a few came on not long after her. Which is why we had to make sure that none of you who had a motive to get rid of her were one of those people."

"You can't tell?"

"A helmet on, bent over the wheel . . ." He mimicked leaning over a bike. "No, you can't make out the person."

I made a skeptical face and he handed me a thin folder. Inside, I found three fuzzy black-and-white images—two bicyclists and a runner. Robertson was right. I looked at the first photo, stamped 5:03, five minutes before Katya had entered. The way it was shot from above and with the person leaning over the wheel, all I could see was the helmet. The shadows cast by it rendered featureless the bottom part of the face that was visible. You couldn't even make out the nose. Judging by the arms and thighs, it was most likely a man in the typical cyclist garb: tight shorts and a short-sleeve top with a zipper in the middle, gloves, and a regular road-type helmet with vents. He was riding a road bike, curved handlebars and thin tires. Same with the next photo, stamped 5:23, fifteen minutes after Katya. Again, my guess was it was a male. Another road bike and helmet, this one patterned with two lighter stripes on both sides. The guy was wearing a T-shirt and shorts, no discernible gloves.

The third photo, taken at 5:43, was of a male runner, ripped and with a decent-size bald spot. Maybe one could make out the runner, but not the cyclists. If Tyler was one of them, even I wouldn't recognize him. I certainly wouldn't make out Damian or Nick. I gave the folder back to Robertson.

"Could it have been an accident? Could she have fallen without meaning to?" One of the articles I'd read on my phone while waiting for him to see me stated, *The only barrier between people wishing to commit suicide and the Hudson River, 25 stories below, is a chest-high metal handrail.*

Robertson made a sweeping motion with his eyes. "You have to ask yourself: what was she doing there at that time? She wasn't jogging, biking . . . Unless she was meeting someone, the idea that she'd go onto the bridge just for a stroll at that hour and somehow happened to slip or a stranger gave her a shove is a bit far-fetched. She was on that bridge for a reason." He glanced at his phone again before continuing. "There are many indicators we look at in such cases: previous suicide attempts, a history of depression or other mental disorders, leaving possessions on the bridge. None of these factors can necessarily be proof of suicide but taken together, they might lead us to conclude that suicide was the most likely explanation in the circumstances."

"Did Katya leave anything on the bridge?"

He shook his head.

"But she had a history of depression?" I still refused to believe the reports about it.

"She had no diagnosis of clinical depression or any other mental health illness, for that matter." I stared at him, confused. "But," he continued, the university's psychological services center confirmed that she'd been seeing a counselor for much of the past year. The records show she was suffering from mood swings, insomnia, and bouts of depression. Nothing serious enough to raise red flags or require medication. Still, it's clear she was having a hard time."

She was hiding it well, I thought. The Katya I'd known had been laughing and dancing and joking, seemingly not a care in her life, just a few hours before.

"But why?" I said, lifting my arms in exasperation. "Why that night?"

He shrugged. "You do my job long enough and you'll witness plenty of senseless behavior. People are capable of stranger things."

I nodded but part of me still couldn't believe it. Something wasn't right. That much I knew.

On my way home, I couldn't stop thinking about the fact that Katya had been in Tyler's apartment that night. After she'd gone dancing with me just a few hours earlier and even sent me a text, calling me "sis."

What fucked-up game had she been playing?

51.

KATYA

THEN

I woke up screaming, drenched in sweat. My heart pounding, I waited for the nightmare to leave my body. It always took its time, the bastard, tiptoeing out with a smile and a promise to be back. My victim this time was a baby. It was giggling—a loud, ringing sound—as I sliced its throat, inch by bloody inch. I could still hear it, echoing off the walls of my brain. I clasped my hands against my ears even though I knew it wouldn't help. Anger was my only weapon. It could silence the demons, burn through the fog of my fear. I set my thoughts on Tyler and his betrayal. When my breathing had finally calmed, I pushed back the covers and got up.

It was 3:13. I'd slept for two hours at most. I donned an old T-shirt and a pair of jeans and walked out. The corridors were dead. We were nearing finals and nobody was partying. I walked back and forth, my bare feet feeling cool and light on the linoleum floor. The baby was Alex. Of course it was. I killed him over and over again in my dreams. At five thirty, I went back to bed. I was at once desperate and terrified to fall asleep.

Outside, a garbage truck screeched to a stop. The grinding, clanking sound of bottles crashing into the pit. The engine revving before moving on and the cycle of noises repeating farther down the street. People in the country wake up to the songs of birds; in Manhattan, we wake to the sounds of garbage trucks.

It was noon when I finally got up. I'd slept through a test but I couldn't give a damn. I went out to get coffee and something to eat at a bagel place on Broadway. I'd just put my credit card back in my wallet when the asshole behind me went, "Are you going to smile?" I spun back and said, "Excuse me?" He repeated, "Smile," as if it was the most innocuous thing. I went bananas. "Why? You don't like frowning women?" I said loud enough for everyone in the line to hear. "I'm spoiling your sick fantasy, is that it? Fucking misogynist pig."

The lady behind the counter laughed loud and deep; a middle-aged woman waiting for her sandwich clapped. The moron paid for his coffee and skulked away.

"I don't get it," I told Josh during our session in the afternoon. "Why do men insist that we smile for them? Wives, girlfriends, coworkers, politicians, and even strangers walking down the street. We're all expected to be pretty and sweet, smiling dolls. Because we're made out of their rib and here for no other reason than to serve and please them?"

Josh knew enough not to laugh. Or worse—to try to defend his sex. He just sat there with a grave expression. Nodding. Watching me. Waiting. God knows for what. Most likely for the fifty minutes to be over so he could be rid of me.

"As if I needed another reason to be pissed at men," I said, shaking my head.

I'd barely left my room this past week except for going to get something to eat on the rare occasions when I felt hungry. I'd told Damian I was sick, which in a way I was. He was starting to get suspicious but I didn't care. I wouldn't be surprised if he showed up waiting for me in front of the dorm.

"I thought about doing another donor cycle," I told Josh. "With a nice couple this time. But how do you ever know, right? How can you ever trust again?" I gathered up my legs, wrapped my arms around my knees and started rocking slightly on the couch. "Everyone I've ever trusted has abandoned or betrayed me. Starting with my father." The more I thought about it, as I rocked there on Josh's couch, the more I felt sorry for myself and the more unbearable the heavy rock in my chest became.

I looked at Josh. He was the only one who was still sticking by me.

I felt a sudden craving for him. For his hands on my breasts, his lips on mine. I needed that physical connection, the reassurance—even if for a fleeting moment—that he wanted me. That I was worthy of love after all. Only he could give me that. Because only he truly knew me. In all my shapes and forms and ugly permutations.

I got up and took a step toward him.

He shot out of his chair. "Katya, we've talked about this. Remember?" But I kept going. I smiled and told him I needed him.

He moved to the side, stood between the window and his desk. "I can't have sex with clients. You know that."

"Oh, c'mon. Therapy with benefits. It doesn't get better than that." I sat on the desk in front of him, let my skirt hike up, exposing my bare thigh.

He looked away as if it burned his eyes.

"These are exceptional circumstances, no?" I pushed on.

"Katya, don't make me call security."

I curled a strand of hair around my finger. "What if I stop being your patient?" I asked, even though I knew I could never do that. He was the only person I could talk to. The only one who knew the real me. The ugly me.

"It makes no difference," he said.

I crossed my legs, exposing even more of my thigh. "Why?"

"Because it's not ethical," he said raising his voice. "Because I'll get my ass fired. That a good enough reason for you?"

Was he fucking kidding me? I offered to stop seeing him—the one thing I had left—and still he was turning me down? I bit the inside of my cheek until I felt the metallic taste of blood. I hated him so much at that moment, I felt like I'd burst.

"Fine," I said, squinting at him, "Then I'll start bragging that I've been hooking up with my therapist. How long do you think it'll take before word gets to your boss?"

He stared at me, his jaw quivering.

"Your word against mine," I said.

"Why would you do that?"

I cocked an eyebrow. "If you're going to lose your job for having sex with me, might as well enjoy it, no? Just saying."

He was looking at me like I was the devil. Good. It was time he figured out who he was dealing with. I got off his desk. "Your choice," I said, and walked out, slamming the door behind me.

◆

By the time I made it back to my room, the anger had given way to hatred. God, I hated myself. It was pointless. Trying to start anew had proven to be a joke. Who had I been kidding? I was a fucking bitch; there was no way around it. Poor Josh. I'd taken it all out on him for turning me down. When all he was doing was looking out for me. I should have known that. He'd only done what a nice guy would do—he hadn't taken advantage of me. How could I have been so mean to him of all people? I owed him an apology for my stupid threats.

And anyway, what was I thinking? I needed him to want me, to crave me, not to be blackmailed into having sex with me.

So I went back to his office. I was prepared to wait for him to finish for the day but the receptionist smiled and told me that I was lucky because his next slot had just canceled. And she buzzed him, announcing me.

◆

"I'm so sorry," I said at the door, unsure if he'd let me in. He smiled, the skin crinkling around his puppy eyes, and closed the door behind me and stood there, just inches away, as I launched into my apology. "I didn't mean to be such a bitch," I said, breathless, eager to get it out before I lost my courage. "It's just that I felt . . . I felt so . . . wretched, so unwanted." I hid my face in my hands. "So alone," I said.

"Katya, you're not alone." In my mind, he reached over and peeled my hands off my face and stared into my eyes. In reality, he was still standing there, arms wrapped around his chest. Defensive gesture, I thought. We'd studied that in Psych 101. Was he scared of me? Or of himself?

"I'm feeling woozy," I said in a weak voice, realizing I still had a chance. "It's all black . . ." I let my voice trail off and collapsed onto him.

He grabbed my shoulders. "Are you okay? Can you hear me?" I stayed limp in his arms for a couple of seconds before opening my eyes and blinking as if disoriented. His face was close to mine as he peered into me, this time for real. There was a fresh scent on him, something minty and sweet. I inhaled deeply, let him think I was short of breath, and pressed myself against him while trying to regain my footing. "Are you okay?" he repeated. "Let me take you to the couch." I held on to his upper arms. He was buffer than I'd realized. I ran my hand down his back, felt him shiver. So he wanted me, too. Just too much of a coward to break the stupid rules.

"I'm better now," I said, and pushed against him, began moving my hips, almost imperceptibly at first.

"Katya, please!" he said, and let go of me. But I could hear the weakness in his voice.

"Let it happen," I said, and reached down for his crotch. He pulled away. I pushed back on him, my hand pressing firmly, warm and gentle. I felt him get hard. There was nothing more intoxicating than feeling a guy's erection in my hand.

"Katya, I'm desperately trying to . . ." His voice trailed off as I pulled down his zipper and worked my hand inside. He tensed up for a moment before sighing in resignation. The room seemed to spin—this time for real—as he leaned closer and hooked a finger around a strand of my hair and, pushing it off my face, he kissed me. I arched my back, leaning against the wall. He rummaged under my skirt, pushed my lace thong to the side, and slid a finger inside me. Later, he scooped me up and carried me to the couch where we finally fucked while I bit on one of the pillows to muffle my moans.

52.

LANA

I didn't wake up until after nine on Tuesday morning. The good news was I didn't have to go to work. The bad news was I didn't have to go to work.

Over breakfast, I read every article about Katya's alleged suicide I could find online. I was stunned to learn that *every 3.5 days someone attempts suicide off the George Washington Bridge.* Further down in the same article, the author quoted an expert from the rescue teams saying, *"There are whirlpool currents under that bridge, going in opposite directions, hence it's hard to find a body."* I shut down my laptop.

The media had so quickly wrapped up Katya's case as just another suicide from the bridge. But I didn't buy it. I'd seen her dancing happily just hours before. Could she really have been in so much pain that she'd wanted to end it all? More importantly, could she have hidden it so expertly?

There was only one person who could answer these questions. I called Columbia's mental-health center, but Josh Wozniak was with a patient. That was what they'd told me yesterday when I'd tried to reach him. Again, I left my name and number and asked that he call me back.

What now? I thought as I put the phone down. Too wired to sit around waiting, I decided to go see Penka. If I was so rattled by the news, I could only imagine how she was feeling.

❖

Like me, Penka had a hard time accepting that her daughter had committed suicide.

"Katya was always a moody kid," she told me as we sat at her kitchen table, a cup of tea for me, coffee for her. "Her father's death, when she was so young, devastated her and then Alex . . . it was too much for a little girl. She had trouble sleeping, was terrified to be left alone in a room. But then she outgrew it."

Penka took a sip of her coffee and stared at her cup. The refrigerator hummed. From the outside came the high-pitched yap of a pooch followed by the deep single woof of a big dog.

"Did you know she was seeing a therapist?"

"Katya didn't share much," Penka said, shaking her head. "I made a lot of mistakes with her. I was young, barely twenty when I had her. And then when Alex drowned . . . I didn't know how to deal with it. I withdrew in grief, neglecting her for years. By the time I was back on my feet, she'd sealed her heart from me." Penka's voice quivered. She ran her hand through her hair before continuing. "We talked on Skype. But you know, she was always busy, always rushing. Except for the time she called to tell me that she was doing the egg donation. She was so excited. I've never seen her like that." Penka smiled at the memory.

A warm feeling nestled in my chest at hearing that. I pressed my hands against my belly and held them there for a moment. I'd been doing a lot of that lately. As a form of communication with my baby, a way of reassurance. As if to say, *I'm here, my little one. Everything will be okay.*

"I was excited for her," Penka went on. "She hadn't been a particularly generous child, never sharing her toys or candy, so it was good to see her happy to be doing something for others." Penka sighed. "But it was short-lived. By the next time we talked, she seemed low on energy, morose. I asked if she was okay but she dismissed my concerns. Something had happened." Penka paused, clenched her jaw. "But I can't imagine her taking her own life. If anything, Katya's response to pain was anger. You hurt her, you paid for it."

❖

I walked hesitantly through the campus gates at 116th Street. It was 12:15 p.m. on a beautiful early-summer day. A pale blue sky, a light breeze swaying the branches of the trees along the pathway. Students hurried to get lunch between classes, passing me in both directions. I could almost see myself fifteen years earlier, going to a lecture, my steps light and buoyant with the promise of things to come—a career, love, family. How had it all gone so wrong so quickly?

When I reached the steps in front of Low Library, I called the counseling center. "Is Josh Wozniak back from lunch?" I asked.

"He hasn't gone out yet," the receptionist said. "He's with a patient until one p.m."

I thanked her and hung up. I had thirty minutes to get tea and stoke up my courage. He'd never bothered to return my calls, so I'd decided to come in person.

Shortly before one, I stood in front of the doors of Lerner Hall, where the center was located, according to their website. I didn't have to wait long. The fit young man I'd seen at Katya's memorial walked out hurriedly and headed toward the sandwich shop at Furnald Hall next door, where I'd just purchased my cup of tea. I couldn't miss him; he stood out among the students in his baby-blue buttoned-down shirt and brown slacks.

I followed him inside and once he'd picked a sandwich and joined the line, I stepped behind him and tapped him on the shoulder. "Josh," I said. "I'm Lana, I left you a couple of messages."

He blinked at me and looked around before saying in a hushed but stern voice, "I'm not in a position to speak to you." I wondered if he'd already gotten in trouble with his superiors for talking to the police.

"Of course." I smiled. "I was just hoping you could help ease my fears," I said, then added: "And her mother's."

He shook his head slowly, exaggeratedly to stress the point, then turned his back on me before stepping up to the cashier.

I waited for him outside, a couple of feet from the door, hidden behind a group of students standing with their cups of coffee, chatting. Wozniak came out, looking around and over his shoulder. Seeing me, he veered in the opposite direction. With a few quick steps, I caught up with him. "You don't have to tell me anything that you feel uncomfortable—"

He stopped and stared at me like I was a moron. "You don't under-stand," he said. "I cannot discuss patients with you. Or anyone else, for that matter."

"I know. But in this case . . ." He was already turning to walk away. "It's not like she would mind," I said, raising my voice. But he only picked up his pace. "Fucking coward!" I yelled after him.

Passersby turned their heads; a guy behind me whistled in amuse-ment or maybe approval. I blushed, embarrassed, and rushed out of there.

I was going down the steps to the subway, when my phone rang. Surprised to see Penka's name come up on the screen, having just seen her, I felt my heart begin pounding before I'd even answered.

"Izviniavai che te bezpokoia," she said. "I'm sorry to bother you." She paused. "But I found something I think you should see."

53.

KATYA

I was on my way to the cafeteria across campus to get something to eat when the lady from the donor agency called. It was midafternoon, about to start pouring rain. One of those quick spring showers that come out of nowhere. I was looking forward to it. The smell of wet soil, the trees heavy, dripping—a respite from the cheerful sunshine. Hooking up with Josh last week had lifted my spirits. But the high hadn't lasted. As usual. If I could only bottle up the feeling and take a gulp of it every time the demons hit, like a cough syrup or something.

I'd continued to miss classes and skip assignments. At least I'd managed to move forward with my postgraduation plans, even if without much enthusiasm. I'd already transferred most of my stuff to Nick's place. We'd hung out last night but again I hadn't slept, not even after the second time we'd had sex.

It was starting to drizzle when my phone rang, so I stepped into the library's lobby to answer the call. I would have let it go to voice mail but I recognized the agency's number and was curious why the hell they were calling me. I'd already been paid and all.

"I've got good news," said Evelyn, one of the two ladies I'd been working with there.

"Yes?" I said, confused.

"You're now a proven donor."

"Huh?"

"The couple you donated to," Evelyn said cheerfully, "they're pregnant."

I swallowed. Leaned against the wall. "Are you sure? You're not mistaking me for someone else?"

She laughed. "No, Katya. I'm not mistaking you for anyone else. Your donation has resulted in pregnancy. Which is great. Should you decide to do it again, as a proven donor, you could get more money. Now, let's see if we get a live birth."

I stood there with my back pressed against the wall, stunned, long after she'd hung up. *Don't worry*, Tyler had reassured me. *There won't be a baby, I promise.*

"How could I have been so stupid to believe him?" I asked Josh when I saw him two days later.

He was sitting in his chair, his pad on his lap, his head slightly cocked to the side as usual. He'd become colder, more detached since our little tryst two weeks ago—overcompensating, clearly—but I hoped he'd get over it soon. In our next session, he'd given me that whole spiel again about counselor-patient relationships, how we'd severed the trust and it was in my best interest to find another shrink. Bullshit. I didn't want to work with anyone else and I'd told him so. "You aren't going to get rid of me so easily," I'd told him. He might have taken it as a threat though, because he'd let it go after that.

"Tyler thinks he has fooled me," I went on. "But I'm smarter than he thinks."

Josh raised an eyebrow and I continued.

"I can't stop the pregnancy—obviously—but I can tell Lana that Tyler is cheating on her."

"And you would do that because . . . ?"

"Because I can't let my baby grow up in a toxic environment."

Josh was staring at me like I was possessed or something.

"What?" I said.

"I'm just wondering if you shouldn't perhaps let them sort out their own problems and focus on yourself. Graduation is right around the corner and you've missed—"

"I thought you weren't here to *advise* me what to do."

"Katya, I'm worried about you." I rolled my eyes but he ignored me and went on. "I see how this might be helping you feel better about yourself—like you're that baby's savior—but it hasn't even been born yet and for all we know Tyler has ended the affair and will prove to be a great father."

"Right. Just like my mother." I glanced at the clock. "Looks like we're out of time," I said, and got up to go. Before I opened the door, I turned and blew him a kiss. He could pretend as much as he wanted, play professional and all that, but I could see the desire burning in his eyes.

◆

I left Josh's office more convinced than ever that I had to tell Lana. People don't change no matter how hard they try. Nobody knew that better than me. Which was why I wasn't going to sit around hoping that Tyler would get his shit together and make things right. He'd already fooled me once with false promises. It was the right thing to do. The problem was I couldn't just walk up to Lana. I knew she feared her donor crashing her life and I worried that seeing me approach her would be enough for her to run away and not hear me out. Or worse, call the police on me for stalking her.

I thought about it all night and finally came up with a solution just as dawn was starting to break. The trick was to run into Lana "by chance" and strike up a conversation with her. Pretend I didn't know who she was. One of the last lectures of Tyler's I'd gone to, he'd talked about probability theory and coincidence. *A coincidence is an event which can be divided into components separately produced by independent causal factors.*

My plan was to get her to show me a photo of her husband—partner, boyfriend, whatever she called him—and then I'd say, "Oh, that's Professor Jones. I'm taking a class with him, actually. But wait, I thought he was dating one of the grad students. I've seen them kissing." Then, I would put my hand in front of my mouth as I "realized" the implication of what I'd just said. Oops. But, by then, the truth would be out and in the open.

Lana could figure out the rest for herself. My job would be done. I just had to find a way to "run into her" that didn't look suspicious. Going to her local coffee shop would be like showing up at her doorstep. I couldn't crash her infertility support group or her yoga for pregnant women class. Obviously. I wished she took a language or knitting class or anything that would seem plausible for me to join. I kept thinking about what the two of us had in common. And then it hit me. She must be as curious about me as I've been about her all this time. She would want to learn as much about me as possible, given the fact that the baby would have my genes. Girls on the online forum who'd done an open egg donation complained about all the questions prospective parents asked them—health, habits, interests, tastes, you name it. I was sure Lana had to be just as desperate to know all that but had chosen the safety of anonymity over the comfort of knowledge.

The coincidence example Tyler had discussed in class was about meeting a long-lost friend at the train station. Both of them had their own independent reasons to be there. Which gave me the idea to create my own "chance meeting" on the subway. I gambled that if Lana were to see me, she'd follow me, the way I'd been following her for weeks. It was a long shot, but I had to take it. And so, the next day, an exceptionally warm day for May, I put on a bright pink dress—one that would attract attention—and went to wait for her at the subway platform two stops after hers. I knew what time she returned from work. I also knew that she always boarded the first car on the train so that she could exit right in front of the steps at her station.

"It was a piece of cake," I told Josh when I saw him next. "You should have seen her, running across the street to my rescue after I pretended to fall. She was so sweet and nervous."

Josh was shaking his head in disbelief but I ignored him.

"It was all going according to plan until I brought up the question of her boyfriend. I was getting ready to ask for his photo when she announced she was single. How's that for a twist, eh?"

Josh frowned.

"It turned out Tyler had left her for that stupid TA I'd seen him with. Left her pregnant on top of it. Lana, of course, didn't know who the woman was or anything. But I did. And I was bursting with anger while Lana went on and on, blaming herself. Can you imagine?" I said, and Josh nodded, scribbled something in his notebook. "So right then and there, I decided: if she wasn't going to make him pay for what he'd done, I would be happy to do it for her."

Josh looked up. "What are you planning to do?"

I smiled, took my time before I said, "I went to the Ombuds office earlier today and told this very sweet woman that I've been hooking up with my philosophy professor."

"You did what?" Josh jolted back in his seat. I was prepared for his disapproval. But maybe it was plain old fear that had drained the color from his face. Josh Wozniak was worried that I would tell about our little dalliance.

I ignored him. "I told her that after I ended the affair, he kind of lost it. So I asked her where I could file a complaint against him because he's been creeping me out, waiting for me outside the dorms, showing up at my favorite coffee shop."

Josh was staring at me aghast. "Why would you do that?" he asked finally. "He could lose his job over something that never happened."

"Bullshit. They'll just have a talk with him. Give him a warning and tell him to stay away from me."

"You don't know that."

"Oh, c'mon. It's not like I said he'd raped me or something."

Josh winced. "You are claiming he's stalking you, which is punishable by law."

"Well, I haven't filed a complaint yet, have I?" I said, angry with him for putting me in a position where I had to defend myself. "I'm thinking about it, though. Because, you know, someone has to make Tyler pay. For Lana and for our baby's sake."

"*Our* baby?"

"Well, yes. Now that Tyler is out of the picture and Lana and I are becoming friends . . ." I shrugged before I went on. "She's carrying the baby, sure. But it came out of my egg. It has my genes. Plus, she's choosing to hang out with me."

Josh squinted at me like he didn't believe me.

"We're actually going to a club on Saturday. Celebrating Mother's Day together. Can you believe it?"

"Katya, you can't do that. Any of it. It's crazy."

I stared at him with my eyebrows cocked.

He clasped his hand to his mouth. "Sorry." His neck was crimson. "I'm having a very hard time—"

I waved him away and with a victorious smile continued, "She must be feeling it, too. That special bond. I mean, we have this baby in common, whether we like it or not. It's a thread that runs through both of our bodies. Think about it. A part of me is growing inside her. And I'm not talking about a kidney. I'm talking about an actual human being."

Josh was nodding but it was the I-hear-you nod. Not the I-agree nod. Fuck him. I didn't care if he liked it or not. These were the facts.

"Anyway, given that Tyler has abdicated his responsibilities," I went on, "Lana might need some help raising the baby. Not to mention company. That's all I'm saying."

54.

LANA

"Here it is," Penka said, and turned Katya's laptop toward me. We were sitting at the kitchen table. She'd had the tea ready when I arrived and a plate with shortbread cookies. Her two big suitcases stood packed by the bedroom door.

I looked at the screen. Katya stared back at me from what looked like the George Washington Bridge. She was smiling big for the camera, leaning back against the railing, which came up barely to her chest. The river stretched behind her, glistening silvery-gray in the sun like a snake's skin. Katya was wearing shorts and a sports bra. Her face was flushed, her arms and legs sweaty. From the look of it, she'd gone out for a run. I checked the date; it was taken a year ago.

"Clearly, she'd been on the bridge before," I said. "She'd known what to expect that night when she headed there." I no longer struggled finding the Bulgarian words. It all just flowed maybe because I was no longer self-conscious about it. I was sure I messed up the grammar and the word order but unlike my mother, Penka never corrected me.

"Who do you think took the photo?" Penka asked.

I shrugged. "She could have asked any passerby." There were no other people in the series of images she'd taken that day of the bridge and the Manhattan skyline. I felt disappointed. My fantasy—as I'd rushed to Penka's apartment—had been that she'd found an important clue, something that would solve the puzzle of Katya's death. Seeing her standing on the bridge was poignant but didn't tell us anything.

We drank our tea and ate the cookies in silence. From outside came the banging of hammers and the high-pitched hiss of construction equipment.

"I want to make sure that we stay in touch," Penka said. "Katya and I spoke on Skype. Maybe we can do the same?" She looked at me expectantly, her eyes puffy from days of crying.

"That would be great." I smiled and ran my hand over my belly. "I want you to see the little one grow." Penka was the only person biologically linked to my baby with whom I had no misgivings about a future relationship.

Penka's computer back home was very old and she was planning on replacing it with Katya's laptop. But it didn't have Skype on it.

"Katya had the app on her phone," Penka said, "but I'm too old for that. It's easier on the big screen."

While she went to smoke out the bathroom window, I downloaded Skype for her. As I waited for her to return and log in, I decided to check out Katya's account. I typed *BGgirl* as her ID and same password as her computer. Sure enough, I got in. The thrill of success mixed with the buzz of stealing a peek behind the curtain of someone's life.

The last call in Katya's history was with her shrink. I stared at the date and time.

"Oh, my God!" I exclaimed out loud. Katya had been on Skype with Josh Wozniak at 5:17, nine minutes after the security camera had her entering the bridge. The conversation had lasted only three minutes. But the previous call just half an hour earlier, also with Wozniak, had gone on for ten minutes. Robertson hadn't said anything about her talking to her shrink before jumping. I felt a shiver run through me. That's because Robertson didn't know, did he?

Katya's phone records would only show her calls and texts. Skype calls wouldn't register except as data usage, which could be anything, even background updates. Her phone, along with the Skype app and her history, was at the bottom of the river. When the cops had looked through her laptop there had been no Skype.

Why had Josh Wozniak kept his conversation with Katya from the cops? He was the last person to have spoken to her. He owed it to Penka to explain what her daughter had said and felt in her last moments.

To hell with his stupid therapist code of ethics. I had to get him to talk to me.

55.
KATYA

The evening started out great. The weather was warm, the sky pale blue with wispy clouds that stretched across it like stripes on a sailor's shirt. The setting sun was shining under the lowest one, bathing the buildings with golden light. The Lower East Side was alive with music and laughter, spilling from sidewalk cafés and bars. A perfect Mother's Day weekend. Lana and I went to dinner before going to Mehanata. Lana was having a blast, I could tell. It was clear she, too, felt we shared a special connection. I could see it in the way she was talking and laughing, the way she was listening to me like she couldn't get enough. I'd never had a good relationship with a woman, not with my mother and certainly not with the girls in school. I'd never really had a role model. A woman I admired. Even the female professors looked at me with suspicion, as if they didn't trust me, as if I were a threat. But Lana, Lana was different.

I snapped a selfie of the two of us on the swing at Mehanata, smiling and hugging like sisters. These guys we met there earlier actually asked if we were sisters. I told them, "Yes, of course." It wasn't really a lie. I was beginning to feel a sisterly love toward her. The older sister I could look up to.

Believe it or not, for a moment there, I even thought I would make a great aunt. Auntie Katya. I could babysit when Lana was busy, pick up the kid from school while she was at work. We would go together for walks in the park with the stroller. At the playground, we would chat while the baby played in the sandbox. I would love that child to death. And spoil it. Boy, would I spoil it. Our baby would be the happiest baby on earth.

All that wouldn't erase the big fat fact that I'd gotten Alex killed—I knew as much—but maybe the good would equalize the bad, hide it like a slipcover draped over an old ugly sofa. Maybe then I could be happy.

Lana left early and it all went downhill from there. I know she's pregnant and all, but she could have stayed a little longer. I mean it was only eleven. It wasn't like she'd turn into a pumpkin at the stroke of midnight just because she had a fetus inside her. Still, I was grateful she'd come at all and hoped she wasn't mad at me for trying to get her to stay longer. Just in case, I texted her our selfie on the swing. It came out really good.

I'd been coming to Mehanata on my own for the past two years but tonight, after Lana left, I felt weirdly, unbearably alone. Discarded, like an old stuffed animal the kids have long since outgrown.

The hollow feeling inside me swelled and I clung harder to the handsome guy I'd been dancing with. He was cool. None of that smooth-talk bullshit I couldn't stand. Got straight to the point: "My place?"

And quite the place he had—an entire brownstone in Tribeca. Everything was automated, from the curtains to the music and the lights. The control panel by the entrance was the size of an iPad and the menu of options looked as complicated as a spreadsheet. The best part was the rooftop terrace with a view of the Freedom Tower. And, surprise, an actual Jacuzzi bubbling away outside, under the night sky and the lights of Manhattan. I'd seen some glamorous apartments in the four years I'd been studying in New York, but this was too much.

He popped open a bottle of Dom Pérignon and we got into the hot tub. I was a bit nervous at first, but the damn thing was pretty shallow, the water barely up to my waist. It was perfect, romantic even—and I'm not one to fall for romance.

There was nothing unusual until we went back to his bedroom and it became apparent this guy liked it rough. "You dirty little bitch," he said as he smacked my ass with his hand. One cheek, then the other. I stiffened. I wasn't above a few ass-slaps here and there, but I sure as hell didn't like him calling me a bitch. I told him to stop. "Shh," he said, and pushed my face into the pillows, pinning me down with his thighs and hands. "I know you like it."

It wasn't the pain as much as the feeling of helplessness that made me scream and struggle to get out of his hold. Until I realized he actually liked me fighting him, so I stopped. Shut my eyes and gritted my teeth to wait it out. If only I could get to the Mace in my clutch. I could see it clearly in my mind—a simple black envelope clutch—lying on the floor next to the pile of clothes at the foot of the bed. Out of reach. Useless.

I clenched my jaw harder. The hum of the central AC. His breath warm and clammy on my neck. The rich fruity scent of his cologne turning rancid with sweat. And then, finally, his ugly grunts. But not before one last whisper in my ear, "You dirty little bitch. You know you deserve it."

Did I? I wondered as I scrambled to put my jeans back on. For having sex with a man I didn't know, trusting that he wouldn't hurt me? For telling the Ombuds officer that Tyler had been stalking me? For crossing the line with Josh? Or was this the punishment for all my sins, going back to the original one? Back to Alex?

I fought those thoughts away, desperately clinging to the idea that the baby growing in Lana's womb would finally erase Alex's death from my slate.

When I was dressed and ready to flee, I came around the bed and forced myself to look at him. He lay on his back, limbs spread, eyes closed, his breath still heavy, triumphant. I glanced at the gaping bedroom door just a couple of feet behind me and opened my clutch. "Hey, asshole!" I shouted. He sat up, startled. His eyes went big at the sight of the Mace in my hand before his face vanished in a cloud of spray and I bolted, slamming the door behind me.

"Fuck!" His screams followed me down the stairs. "Motherfucker!"

I stormed out of the building and ran. I ran like mad through the dark empty streets until I was out of breath and barely coherent.

But the guy's words kept playing in my head: "You deserve it, bitch. You know you do."

◈

The New York subway turns into a freak show after midnight. Young people on their way to or from parties and clubs, folks working the graveyard shift, the homeless and all sorts of crazy people talking to themselves or reciting the Bible. I took the number 1 train uptown and sat in a nearly empty car. My flesh burned against the plastic orange seat. My mind was bruised, swollen with anger, throbbing with pain and humiliation.

I stared at the ads overhead—some zit doctor and a bunch of other medical services—as we went, stop by stop, through the Village, Midtown, and the Upper West Side.

At 79th Street, I was left alone with a young red-haired guy in dirty jeans and a T-shirt, sitting across from me, his legs spread like he owned the train. Rap sounded from his earbuds, loud enough to echo in the empty car. He looked at me, his eyes squinting appraisingly, and I felt my chest constrict. My breaths turned shallow and quick. I couldn't get enough air into my lungs. The rap music blasted, the lyrics unrecognizable but the beat clear enough.

I wanted to run but there was no place to go. I considered moving into another car, but the thought of sliding the door open and the noise of the train barreling through the dark dingy tunnel had me paralyzed in my seat, sweating in my jeans.

A heavyset older woman got on at the next stop and sat at the other end on my side of the train. I couldn't see her, unless I turned and stared, but I felt her presence. Warm and soothing. Finally, I was able to take a good breath in, then another.

I felt alone and empty. Empty like this train. Every now and then someone came along for the ride but nobody rode *with* me. I had no man by my side, no friends, no family. *But that's how you've always wanted it, isn't it?* I heard Josh's voice in my head. *That's beside the point,*

I thought as a way of an answer. The point was there was nobody I could call in the middle of the night, nobody to take me in and hug me and reassure me that everything would be all right.

Damian was never around on weekends. Not that I could run to him and tell him what had happened. He'd either go smash the face of that guy or throw me out for having been with someone else. Most likely both. And, honestly, the last thing I wanted at that moment was to see Damian.

Lana? I'd only just met her, even if I'd known her from afar for months. I couldn't go knocking on her door at this hour. I wasn't supposed to even know where she lived. And anyway, I didn't want her to see me like this. To know how fucked-up I truly was.

That left Nick. Friends-with-benefits Nick, soon-to-be-husband Nick. He had to still be at Coogan's. The bar didn't close until four a.m.

◆

There were only about a half-dozen patrons left when I got there. The hard-core alcoholics and the occasional having-a-bad-night drinkers. I didn't see Nick at first and had to make a second sweep of the place before I spotted him at the end of the bar, making out with a girl, his face hidden behind a curtain of blond hair. It felt like a slap in the face. The one time I needed him. I stumbled to a stool and sat down, my heart pumping fast, making a gushing sound in my ears. The other bartender tonight, Alice, took one look at me from under her bangs and said, "You okay?"

She was a few years older than me, with thick hair and freckles all over her nose. I liked her all right but I'd never bothered talking to her much. I wasn't going to pop open the whole jar of worms now. Tell her that my insides felt like the sweaters my mother washed in the winter and hung to dry on the balcony's clothesline only to find them frozen solid in the morning. Not that she would care to listen. Bartenders get that shit all the time. People dump their stories on them, talking for hours on end, before finally getting up and leaving a meager ten-buck tip.

I told Alice I was fine and asked for a glass of water that I drank down in a few big gulps. When I felt a bit better, I asked for a tequila. I took a sip, savoring its sharpness. Maybe the fire it left in its wake would help melt the chunk of ice stuck in my throat. But halfway into the glass, the damn thing was still there weighing me down. Maybe it wasn't ice after all but a pile of rocks. The cobblestones that had paved the trail of disappointment and rejection going back to my father's death. It was the same pain I'd experienced back then—that suffocating feeling that strangles you from the inside.

Nick finally disengaged from the girl's lips and came over to say hi. He asked if I was staying at his place. "'Cause I'm, you know, thinking of taking Kim home," he said with an eye tilt toward the blond girl. I forced a grin, told him that I'd come just for a drink, and wished him a good time. Then I downed my glass and was about to get the hell out of there when my phone buzzed with a text from Lana: *I woke up bleeding. I'm afraid I've miscarried.*

Fucking hell! A few people at the bar looked at me and I realized I'd cried it out loud. I blew the air out of my cheeks through puckered lips. "Fucking hell," I said again, and walked out.

I'd lost it all. This time for real.

56.

LANA

I waited for him, hiding by the entrance of the building next door. I'd called the counseling center to make sure he was still there. It was shortly past five thirty p.m. According to their website, the center didn't close until six. The day had turned gray and humid and I was beginning to sweat. But my hands were cold and clammy with anxiety. The thirty-minute wait felt like hours. The university had a relaxed vibe during the summer sessions. The stream of students flowing in all directions during the fall and spring semesters had dribbled to a few here and there, strolling across campus or hanging out in front of the buildings after classes. The pace with which they walked seemed slower, too, their steps less purposeful, their faces more relaxed.

When he finally walked out, I didn't accost him. I'd learned my lesson. Instead, I followed him. I was becoming good at it, feeling much more relaxed about it compared to my first time with Katya. Or maybe it was the anger that gave me confidence and kept me coolheaded.

Wozniak took the subway uptown. It was rush hour and the train was packed. No danger of him seeing me at the opposite end of the car. I had a sense of déjà vu when he exited at 168th Street, just as Katya had. Broadway was busy at that hour and so were the sidewalks. I had to navigate around mothers with strollers, a kid or two walking in tow; a rowdy group of teenage boys, jostling around; guys hanging out in front of small bodegas. When Wozniak passed Coogan's without entering, I sighed with relief. Who knew how long I would have had to wait if he'd gone in for a drink. He turned on 174th Street and entered a white-brick building on the right halfway down the block. Across from it was a school with a large glass stairwell. A group of students lingered outside. I slowed down, pretending to be checking my phone. To orient myself, I opened the map app and stared at the screen. The cross street ahead of me was Fort Washington Avenue. I hadn't realized how close I was to the Henry Hudson Parkway and I-95. Only six blocks to the George Washington Bridge's entrance. Five minutes max on a bike. I halted.

Could he have been one of the cyclists on the CCTV photos?

I charged forward, propelled by a rush of adrenaline and anger. At his building's entrance, I scanned the apartment panel. Wozniak 3B. I rang a few bells at random, saying, "Delivery," until someone finally buzzed me in.

I should have called Robertson but I was too worked up to think straight. My plan began and ended with confronting Wozniak.

The entrance hall was dark and dingy. There was a narrow staircase on the left. Luckily, I only had to go up two flights. Still, I started out too fast and arrived winded. There were four apartments on the landing and I took my time catching my breath before I pressed the bell. Nothing. I pressed again and again, holding my finger on it.

He flung the door open after the fifth ring. He'd changed into shorts and a T-shirt. "What the hell—"

"Hi," I said. He started closing the door but I was prepared and slipped my foot in to stop it. "I know what happened that night," I said.

Bluffing had worked with the bartender; hopefully the shrink would fall for it, too.

"Then you don't need to talk to me."

"Oh, but I do. Some of the details are a bit murky. Like, was she looking at you when you pushed her off the bridge or did she have her back to you?"

"What are you talking about? That's absurd. I was in bed, deep asleep."

"Hm." I cocked my head exaggeratedly. "Her Skype history shows you were very much awake." His eyes widened. "I suspect you'd rather tell me about it inside," I said. "You never know if one of your neighbors has his ear pressed to the door. It saved Professor Jones's ass, I'm told, but you might not be so lucky."

Wozniak blinked at me. His face had lost color. For a moment, I thought he would pass out but then he opened the door and, without a word, disappeared inside. I followed him. At the thud of the door shutting behind me, I had the fleeting thought that I should have told Angie what I was up to. Texted her the address at least. So that she'd know where to look for me. Should I go missing, too.

57.

KATYA

The streets were dark, empty, dead. Not even rats scurrying away from the trash at the sound of my steps. Tyler's new place was a four-story walk-up a few blocks south of Coogan's. I'd followed him there the other day, after Lana told me he'd moved out. The building was a far cry from his previous abode. But the neighborhood was full of Columbia students and employees thanks to the affordable rents and proximity to the university. Tyler's apartment was on the fourth floor, his kitchen window overlooking the street. I didn't know what I was going to say to him. Or even why I was going there. I wasn't exactly thinking. All I knew was that the tight heavy wall I'd carefully built over the last few months to keep my demons at bay had suddenly and mercilessly collapsed on me.

I blamed Tyler for it. Because, really, who else was there? God? Myself? I'd blamed myself for everything since Alex. It was the very thing I'd been hoping to finally escape. And anyway, it was obvious—the stress of the breakup must have provoked Lana's miscarriage. I could tell how wretched she felt knowing Tyler had met another woman. It was all his fault. He'd started this ball rolling whichever way you looked at it. He'd posted a flyer looking for an egg donor for his partner while cheating on her. Then he'd gone ahead and left her. Pregnant.

Tyler opened the door, furious. "Katya, what the hell?"

"Aren't you going to invite me in?"

"What are you doing here?"

I hardly knew myself. For a moment, I stood there staring at him, confused. He looked like shit in his white T-shirt and gray trunks. His hair was stuck to one side. Nothing like the striking figure he cut in the lecture hall. I almost felt sorry for him.

"You're a cheating bastard," I said finally. His eyes grew darker, narrower. "And you're going to pay for all the pain you've caused."

"Please leave."

I'd expected anger. Hoped that a fight would cool the burning ache inside me. But the desperation, the revulsion behind those two simple words cut like a knife.

"I went to the Ombuds office yesterday," I said.

"What? What are you talking about?"

"I'm going to file a complaint against you."

He didn't blink. He didn't say a word. He simply closed the door on me midsentence. Like I was a rat to be shooed away with a broom.

I stood there, my chest tightening again. There wasn't enough air in the small windowless landing. The strong smell of curry. The sound of my heart beating. The walls seemed to close in on me.

The words of the guy from the club sounded in my head: *You dirty little bitch. You know you deserve it.*

I ran down the three flights of stairs and burst onto the street.

❖

"For fuck's sake, Katya! It's five in the morning." Josh was pissed. Boy, was he pissed. "You know the rules. You cannot be calling me in the middle of the night. You cannot be calling me period."

So what if I'd woken him? I needed him. "I'm shaking," I said, and leaned against a building to steady myself. I had the phone in my hand, camera on, buds in my ears. "I don't know if I can speak."

"Then go to bed, damn it. I'll see you in the office—"

"Don't hang up on me, Josh. You will regret it, I'm warning you."

"So you can speak, apparently." He sounded cold, angry. Like he was fed up with me.

"I got raped tonight," I said, hoping that would get his attention.

"Of course you did. Let me guess, Tyler? Or another professor you have a grudge against?"

"Josh, this is for real."

He skipped a beat before saying, "Go to the police then. Why are you calling *me*?"

"Because . . ." I couldn't find the strength to say it out loud. "Because, it's gone, Josh," I finally said, my voice quivering. "My baby is gone. The miracle that was going to save me is no more."

"Miracle? Are you crazy? Nothing can save you!"

His words landed with a thud. He'd given up on me. My legs felt weak and I slumped to the ground, my back propped against the building. I rested my head on the wall and looked up at the sky. Towering over the rooftops at the end of the street, I saw the George Washington Bridge. A glimmer of light in the night sky. Josh was saying something about me losing it but I could barely hear him.

"Josh, I'm going to jump off the bridge."

He laughed. "Like that time you wanted me to go for a drink with you?"

"This is different."

"Katya, enough! I'm going back to sleep."

"I'm telling you, Josh, I'm going to jump off the George Washington Bridge."

"Go ahead," he said. "Jump!" And hung up. The fucking bastard hung up on me. He didn't think I would do it. Or maybe he just didn't give a damn.

I'd show him.

❖

The barrier barely came to my chest. But I knew that already. I'd come up here a couple of times on my runs along the river. Still, I was shocked how low and easy the railing was to scale. I rested my hands on the bar and stared into the darkness below. Cars zoomed behind me. I wasn't worried drivers would see me. I'd picked a dark spot where the walkway wrapped around the stanchion, creating two little nooks at the corners away from the road. I'd seen night photos of the bridge with the towers glowing white, illuminating the intricate lace of steel. But both of the towers were dark today except for the blinking red lights at the top. Maybe they only lit the rest for special occasions.

There was a tall fence around the stanchion—maybe ten, twelve feet high—with outward spikes at the top to prevent you from climbing it. But to discourage you from jumping off the bridge over the breast-high railing, the authorities had chosen suicide prevention signs. *You're not alone*, read a sign next to me. Seriously? And how the hell did they know? They didn't even know I was here. The only camera I could see was pointing up at the tower. *Suicide is never the answer*, another sign read. I hated platitudes in my best of moods, swiping through Instagram photos or Facebook posts. But seeing them here made me want to jump for real.

I looked down. From the little balcony that jutted out along the tower, I could see the cars on the lower level. I gripped the railing harder and gazed into the void below. The cool air felt good on my skin. The wind blew my hair.

It was time to Skype Josh again.

58.

LANA

NOW

The first thing I noticed was the road bike propped against the wall. The black helmet hanging off it had two gray stripes on the sides, just like the one on the CCTV photo. My legs felt weak. I paused to examine it, not really looking for anything but more so to calm my breathing. There must be many helmets like this one, I told myself. For all I knew, the one in the black-and-white photo had white or yellow stripes. The rest of the room was nearly empty but for an open futon with the sheets bunched up in a ball, a dresser, a couple of chairs, clothes draped over both of them, and a fruit crate that doubled as a coffee table, judging by the mug on top of an old issue of *Men's Health*. The place would have been lighter if it weren't for the trees in front of the two windows and the fire escape cutting diagonally across one of them. There was a tiny kitchen off to the side.

Wozniak emptied a chair for me and sat on the bed. He was older than I'd thought, furrow lines already creasing his forehead.

"So why don't you tell me how it all happened?" I said, breaking the silence. I'd long ago learned to take charge as a way to mask my fear.

He stared into space, seemingly unaware of my presence. The hum of the refrigerator coming from the kitchen filled the room.

"I should have known better," Wozniak said finally. He was looking somewhere to the right of me as if at my reflection in an invisible mirror. "She was a master manipulator and went to great lengths to punish those who had hurt her." He paused and I thought of how astounded she'd been that I wasn't planning on making Tyler pay for leaving me. "She made elaborate plans," Wozniak continued. "She stalked you and then tricked you into meeting her."

I nodded. It still hurt to think that her excitement about meeting me had been fake.

"She'd been manipulating me for months," Wozniak said. "I had to stop going to my local bar because she showed up there one night last semester, not long after she'd first hit on me. I thought it was a coincidence. After all, Coogan's is around the corner from the Columbia medical school. I thought she'd come with some of the med students. Only later, when she started stalking you and Tyler, did it hit me that she'd planned it." He looked up to the ceiling, shook his head. "I should have deleted her from my Skype contacts. But I was scared of upsetting her. She was unraveling as it was and I knew she was capable of anything. She'd reported Tyler to the Ombuds office, for fuck's sake. And he hadn't even slept with her. I was terrified I'd lose my job—"

"Wait, are you saying that she and Tyler weren't involved?" My stomach swooped at the thought.

Wozniak snorted. "No way. She put him on a pedestal. She was able to restrict her feelings and stay away from him because, in her mind, he wasn't capable of doing anything wrong. Then she saw him kissing another woman and went nuts. It was a double offense for her. First, he'd disillusioned her, proving he was just another mortal capable of cheating, and second, he'd fallen from grace with a woman who wasn't her."

So Tyler was telling the truth? I filled my lungs with air, exhaled slowly.

"Katya was desperate that night," Wozniak went on. "She even claimed she'd been raped. I knew better than to fall for it, of course. After all the lies about Tyler and her threats to me . . ."

Jacuzzi Guy. The thought, cold and poisonous, coiled at the bottom of my belly. The bastard had raped her. Even Katya wouldn't lie about something like that. I made a mental note to make sure he wouldn't get away with it.

"When I refused to play her game," Wozniak was saying when I turned my attention back to him, "she snapped. And I fell right into her trap." He wiped away the sweat from his forehead. His voice was strained, his breathing fast as he continued. "It wasn't the first time she was calling me in the middle of the night. It wasn't the first time she'd threatened to kill herself. So when she said she was going to jump off the bridge, I told her, 'Go ahead, jump!' I fucking said that, then hung up. I turned Skype off and pulled the blanket over my head. But I couldn't go back to sleep. The bitch was messing with my head. I took my phone and turned Skype back on. Sure enough, thirty minutes after the first call, she rang me again. It was dark and I could barely make out her face but I could see the red blinking light on top of the bridge tower above her. She was on the goddamn bridge. I sat up in bed like I'd smelled fire."

His voice cracked and he bit his lower lip before continuing. "I told her to stay where she was. That I was getting on my bike and would be there in five minutes. She said it had been fun knowing me, blew me a kiss, and hung up. She actually blew me a kiss."

Josh shook his head, looked at his feet. Outside, a car drove by with the music blasting. A Latin tune that lingered long after the car had passed.

"I rode there like mad," he continued after a while. His voice was now steady, like he was narrating a movie playing in his head. "My building is only six blocks away but it seemed to take an eternity. My fear had turned into rage by the time I got to the bike ramp. She couldn't just go and jump. She had to drag me into it. Finally, I approached the tower. Katya must have been standing somewhere in front of it when she called me because I could see the light above her, but she wasn't there now. So I pedaled even faster. I was terrified that she could have jumped ten times by then." He paused. "I wish she had," he said, and took his head in his hands.

I stared at him, cold sweat running down my back. Something told me I didn't want to hear what he was going to say next.

59.

KATYA

THEN

A sense of victory washed over me as I saw him coming. Dawn was starting to break over the rooftops behind him. I lifted my leg and straddled the railing. There were barely any cars on the bridge at five a.m. on a Sunday but just in case, I'd picked a dark spot shielded from the road by the enormous cable.

"Katya!" he yelled, and screeched to a stop a couple of feet from me.

"What the hell are you doing here?" I was barely able to keep the triumph out of my voice.

"Get the fuck down from there," he said, and dropped the bike.

I started laughing. Poor old Josh was truly scared, but he put on such a show of being angry. I wanted to hug him. "You didn't think I'd do it, did you?"

"Why don't you come here and we'll talk?" he said, and inched a step forward.

It felt good to see his concern, a small chip at the ice in my chest. But I wasn't ready to let him off the hook yet. "I'm thrilled you'll be here to see me go," I said, and holding on to the railing, I swung my other leg over and planted my feet on the concrete edge on the outside. It didn't even occur to me to be scared. I was high on adrenaline.

"Fucking hell, Katya!" he cried, his eyes twice as big.

"It's the perfect way for me to go, if you think about it. To drown, like Alex. There is a certain symmetry to it. A closure."

"Katya, please! Don't be stupid. You can still turn things around if you want to. Please."

I locked him in my stare. Had I misjudged him? What if he truly cared? "And how would I do that?" I asked.

He took another step forward.

"You're a proven donor now. You'll be in high demand. You can choose the couple yourself next time. Make sure they are right. You told me this yourself."

"What do you care?" I asked and held my breath. *Just say it once, Josh*, I thought, desperation taking over me. *Just this time and I'll stop the game.*

I peered into his eyes with anticipation, but instead of love all I saw was terror, and before he'd even spoken, my pathetic stupid hope had turned to stone.

"Of course, I care," he said. "I'm your therapist." The blow of his words shook me so hard, I instinctively gripped the railing. Josh wasn't here because he cared for me. He was here because it was his job. I would never be anything more than a patient to him. A patient he could fuck, but that was it. Anger constricted my throat. He'd fooled me there for a moment, the bastard. And he would pay for it.

He was still talking, saying something in his deceptive therapist voice, but I was no longer listening.

"My hands!" I screamed. "They're slipping." He lunged forward and grabbed me by the shoulders, clutching me so hard I nearly cried out in pain. His face was inches from mine, sweat dripping at his temples. I couldn't hold it any longer and began laughing. "I got you!"

He stared at me. His hands relaxed their grip on my shoulders as it slowly dawned on him that I was fucking with him. His face went from white to red in a flash. His eyes glowed like a wild animal's. There was something primal, intoxicating in his anger, and I inhaled its scent greedily.

The momentary surprise when I felt his hands strike my chest gave way to an immense relief. This was what I'd wanted all along, I realized as the railing slipped from my hands and I fell backward. Ever since Alex's death, I'd been inching toward this moment, hoping someone would free me from myself.

My lips parted to say *Thank you* but it was too late.

60.

LANA

I stared at the man slumped on the futon in front of me, merely a silhouette in the dim light of the streetlamp streaming through the windows behind him. It had been nearly two hours since I rang his doorbell and dusk had settled over the city. Josh Wozniak seemed to have forgotten me and was talking as if to himself. "I was starting to calm down, you know, thinking that I had her attention. That she would climb back onto the bike path and everything would be fine. Then suddenly she cried that her hands were slipping. I threw myself at her and grabbed her by the shoulders. My heart was racing. Sweat was running down my forehead as I held her."

Wozniak looked at me and I felt my skin prickling as he continued. "Next thing I knew she was laughing. Hysterical, surreal. 'I got you!' she said, nearly spat it at me." His face contorted in pain. I held my breath as I waited for him to go on. "My brain short-circuited," he said finally. "The adrenaline, the shock. It was a knee-jerk reaction. I barely felt her weight against my hands before I realized what I'd done."

His jaw began quivering and he stared at his feet. I couldn't see his tears in the faint light, only his hand brushing them away. Soon, his entire body began to shake with convulsions, scary sounds coming out of his chest.

"I killed her," he sobbed. "I pushed her to her death."

I sat there in shock. My heart ached for Katya. Such a tragic, pointless way to go.

"I really cared for her," he said in a coarse voice as if the words were being torn from somewhere deep inside him. "Any other patient, I would have dropped at the first red flag. But Katya . . . I got caught in her spell. I didn't know how to deal with it. I wouldn't admit it even to myself."

With a whimper, he crumpled on the bed. A broken man.

I got up and made my way to the kitchen, where I flipped on the light and filled a glass with water and drank. When I returned, Josh had slumped to the floor and curled into a ball, pressing his palms against his ears. His sobs had subsided.

"You know I have to call the police, right?" I said.

He nodded. Closed his eyes. "I keep seeing her," he said. "Standing there on the other side of the railing, her hair blowing in the wind. Her laughter rings in my ears. 'I got you!'"

61.

LANA

"I'm so relieved you're okay," Tyler said, and stood up abruptly, rattling the silverware and glasses on the table. "I can't believe you went to that guy's apartment alone."

I shrugged and sat down, ignoring Tyler's outstretched arms. Was I making a mistake meeting with him? I'd been looking forward to my appointment with the lawyer this afternoon. I'd decided I should at least have a consultation, figure out what my options were. But my experience with Josh last night had muddied my mind and I'd awoken this morning thinking that I should sort things out with Tyler face-to-face before I spent money I didn't have for legal advice. While still in bed, I'd called him, asking if we could talk in person. "There is nothing I'd like more," he'd replied.

And so here we were, awkwardly sitting across from each other at Henry's—our favorite weekend brunch place on Broadway, just a few blocks from the apartment. Thankfully, the sidewalk section was nearly empty at noon on a Wednesday even though it was a perfect day for outdoor dining: dry and breezy, the temperature only in the midseventies.

Tyler was wearing the faded blue T-shirt I liked so much on him because it made his eyes stand out. The idea that he'd put some thought into dressing for our lunch was touching. Or maybe it was just a coincidence. I had on a black wrap dress with a white jacket and sandals only because I was planning to go straight to the lawyer's office from here and wanted to look professional. I should have skipped the lipstick, though. Hopefully, it wouldn't give Tyler the wrong idea.

I'd told him briefly over the phone about my encounter with Josh last night, but that wasn't what I wanted to talk about. As soon as the waitress walked away with our orders, I leaned forward and fixed Tyler in my gaze. "I need to know the truth," I said. "About Katya, about your teaching assistant—"

"I've been trying to explain, but you wouldn't hear it."

Here we go again, I thought, with that damn defensiveness. But I wasn't here to fight him.

"Yes, that's entirely my fault," I said, forcing a lighter tone to my voice. "Please, can we accept that we both made mistakes and move on from there? This is not a competition. There are no medals awarded for the one who's least guilty."

"No?" He looked at me with a playful glint in his eye. "Damn."

"No medals for making me laugh, either," I said, chuckling despite myself.

He grinned back, relaxing his shoulders.

"And no penalties," I continued, "so please just tell me everything. What the hell has been going on?"

He sighed. "It's actually quite simple. I made one big mistake and then I made more mistakes trying to cover it up."

"Spoken like a true philosopher," I said, and looked at him pointedly. "But I need the details. About your relationship with Katya, with your—"

"First of all, you have to know I've had no relationship with Katya," he said, his neck turning red with anger. "None. I haven't touched her. I haven't so much as accidentally brushed her shoulder. Whatever she told the Ombuds officer was a lie."

Josh had already told me as much, but it felt good to hear it from Tyler. I exhaled and leaned back in my chair, a warm wave of relief spreading through my body like the herbal tea with honey and lemon my mother made me drink as a kid.

"Katya was just another one of my students," Tyler went on.

Only you neglected to mention that detail to me, I thought, and had to bite my tongue before I said it out loud. If I wanted him to open up and be honest with me, I had to play nice, pretend I didn't care.

But as he launched into the story of how he'd bonded with his TA, Rachel, after our miscarriage last fall—last fall, for Chrissake!—I found it hard to keep my composure. To avoid tearing up, I trained my eyes on the white picket fence behind him that separated the café area from the sidewalk. Not the kind of thing you'd expect to see on a busy New York City street. We'd been coming here for years but I'd never paid it much attention.

Tyler's voice trailed off and I turned to see the waitress coming with our orders—kale salad with grilled shrimp for me and a chicken club sandwich for Tyler. I'd lost all appetite, but Tyler dug in as if he hadn't eaten for days. I'd always envied his ability to compartmentalize.

Between bites he proceeded to explain that his relationship with Rachel hadn't been sexual. "I wasn't looking for an affair. I promise you that was the last thing on my mind." He paused to swallow. "But it was a mistake anyway, opening up to Rachel. I should have talked to you, made it clear how sick and tired I was of all the fertility treatments. I never should have introduced a third person into the equation."

Damn right, I thought.

I pushed the kale around my plate as he continued. "We'd become confidants of sorts and when her mother died, Rachel broke down. She was so distraught and I was trying to comfort her and before I knew it, we were kissing. I won't lie, it felt good—"

"Christ, Tyler! Spare me the details."

"Sorry, I thought you said you wanted details." He brushed his hand through his hair, seemingly more confused than accusatory. He could be so smart about abstract ideas and so dense when it came to feelings and emotions.

I had to smile. "Not how-it-felt details."

"Sorry," he repeated. "What I mean is—nothing more happened. That was it. We'd crossed a line and we both knew it. We agreed she'd switch to a different adviser. It was to be the end. But . . ."

I leaned forward, my stomach clenched in anticipation. "But?"

"It turned out, Katya had followed us and snapped a photo. She threatened to show it to you if I didn't cancel the cycle."

I stared at him. "That was it? Katya had you for a kiss?"

"I know." Tyler shook his head as if he, too, couldn't believe it. "I should have just told you. But it wasn't the kiss I worried about as much as Katya. I would have had to come clean about the whole damn thing."

"You mean that she was your student?"

"I mean about the flyer," he said, his hands crumpling the white paper over the tablecloth like the folds of an accordion. "I knew you'd go ballistic if I told you about it. And rightfully so. The way Katya was acting . . . It confirmed your fears. You had been right and I didn't want to hear you say it." He let go of the paper and looked at me, his eyes red and moist. "I'm sorry," he said yet again, and pursed his lips.

I was looking at him, my brain incapable of computing his words.

"What flyer?" I asked finally. "You didn't put—?"

"I did," he said, and looked down.

I rubbed my temples, trying to make sense of it all. "So it wasn't just a coincidence that she happened to be a student at Columbia?"

He reached for my hand on the table and squeezed it. "I'm afraid not."

The static in my ears grew louder than the Broadway traffic.

"I knew it had been a mistake," he continued, "as soon as Katya showed up in my intro class. But even then I convinced myself that it wasn't a big deal. That meeting me had simply stirred her curiosity about philosophy. I couldn't have imagined how much worse it would get. When I found out that she'd been following me, I panicked. I mean she was talking about *her* baby. I realized—no matter what *she* wanted—*we* couldn't continue with the cycle and have a baby with her eggs. Because she wasn't just going to go away." He swallowed before continuing. "I thought taking a break might actually be a good thing for you and me, an opportunity for us to start our life together from scratch in a month or two. And"—he looked down at his empty plate— "it stopped us from going ahead with the cycle without me having to fess up to my sins."

I nodded, incapable of speaking. What was there to say? His intentions had been good. He'd meant to spare me pain, and that touched me. I stared at my salad, wilting in the sun. I had pushed all the shrimp to the side. "As hard as this is," I said, "I wish we'd had this conversation back when she'd threatened you."

"I know. I fucked up." He took my hand in both of his and, looking into my eyes, said, "Will you ever forgive me?"

I held his gaze. Would I? It was hard to even think of it right now. Finally, I shrugged. His face seemed to fold; his hands relaxed their grip on mine.

"But if you still want to come to the doctor's appointment with me," I said, "I'll be okay with it."

He smiled and I realized then that I would forgive him. Of course I would. But would I ever be able to trust him again?

62.

LANA

The sky hung low and gray over the buildings. Gusts of wind swept through the streets and whipped the tree branches outside the window. It was starting to sleet. But the apartment was warm and cozy even if I had to turn on the lights at three in the afternoon.

Angie and I were on the couch, holding our babies and staring at my laptop on the coffee table in front of us. Her son was asleep but my daughter was getting fussy and I started rocking her. Penka had joined us on Skype from her kitchen in Sofia, where it was ten in the evening. I'd called to invite her to the christening in a month, hoping she would be able to spend a few days with us in New York.

"Angie will be her godmother," I said, tilting my chin toward Angie. "Her son is only two months older than our girl." My Bulgarian had gotten better as a result of my Skype calls with Penka. But I was finding it harder today, having to go back and forth, translating for Angie.

Penka had aged over the past nine months, the grief etched permanently on her face. And while she brightened up when she saw the baby during our video conversations, there was always a moment or two when a cloud of sadness would cross her face and she'd go quiet. I imagined it reminded her of Katya. Or of her son who had drowned so many years ago. How hard, how tortured Katya's life must have been having carried the guilt of her brother's death from such an early age with no one to support and comfort her. No wonder she'd unraveled in the end, overstepping all boundaries by stalking us and meddling in our lives. How could I blame her? It takes a mother to understand her desire to protect the life she'd helped conceive, her flesh and blood, at any cost.

Two weeks after the birth of my daughter, I'd gone to the George Washington Bridge with a long-stemmed rose to pay my respects and thank Katya for her gift. To my shock, a tall chain-link fence had been erected in front of the old barrier and connected to a netting that hung like a canopy over the pathway. A quick search on my phone confirmed what my eyes refused to believe. The Port Authority had installed a temporary fence last September, four months after Katya's death, in an attempt to prevent suicides. There was no mention of murder in the article. A permanent fence was to follow.

I stood there, a cold lump swelling in my throat, as bicyclists rode by me in both directions. Only four short months earlier and Katya could still be alive, I thought as I pushed the rose through one of the links in the fence. I hadn't told Penka about it and didn't plan to.

The baby made a gurgling sound and Penka smiled and cooed to her from the screen. Her smile was big and warm, even if tinged with sorrow. But it was her eyes I kept staring at, the green almond-shaped eyes with which my daughter looked at me. Katya's eyes.

They were of course very much my mother's eyes, too, if not in color, then definitely in shape. I was quite apprehensive about my mother meeting Penka at the christening. The two women were so different. It was hard to picture them side by side. My imposing mother all made up—hair, makeup, silk scarf neatly wrapped around her neck—her chin jutting forward, shoulders pulled back, standing tall next to Penka, always casual in dress and demeanor, slumped over and weighted with grief. My mother could be so judgmental, so forward with her opinions whereas Penka was shy and demure. But they were born and raised on the same soil and spoke the same language and now shared a grandchild.

I made a mental note to speak to my mother and ask her for once to let go of her competitive streak and show Penka a little grace.

After the call, Angie and I sipped coffee while our babies slept. Outside, the wind seemed to have intensified, the sleet giving way to snow. A car alarm screeched somewhere down the street.

"So I see Tyler's back on the piano," Angie said, nodding toward the framed photo of the two of us on top of Kilimanjaro, our young faces flushed with the high of new love. "Are you guys getting back together?"

"We're talking about it. It won't be easy to move beyond the betrayals and the ghosts of the past. I do miss him, though, so we'll see." I kissed my little angel on her forehead before continuing. "But if we do, we'll get married this time."

She shot me a look, eyebrows up. "I thought you didn't believe in that *patriarchal* shit."

I shrugged. "I might have confused my fear of abandonment for feminism."

When Angie left, I finished breastfeeding the baby, and as I headed for the bedroom to put her in her crib, I paused at the piano.

I'd arranged my photos in two sections—present and past. Front row center was a portrait of my daughter, one month old, flanked, on one side, by a shot of Angie and me pushing our strollers in Central Park and on the other, by a photo of me in the hospital, my newborn on my chest. Behind them, I had my mother on the beam at the Montreal Olympics, Tyler and me atop Kilimanjaro, and Katya and me on the swing at Mehanata. I could trace the beginnings of my baby from Montreal through Kilimanjaro and, finally, to a Bulgarian nightclub in New York. But those threads would not have come together without the flyer Tyler had posted on campus—even if behind my back and against my wishes.

So much in our lives hinges on random and not-so-random, big and small, happy and tragic events. Had Tyler not made the flyer, the two of us might have still been together. Katya might still have been alive. But how could I wish the past away if it meant the little girl I was cradling in my arms wouldn't have existed?

I picked up the last frame on the piano and stared at the pink sheet of paper, the large black letters spelling the beginnings of my daughter: *Loving couple seeking egg donor from Bulgaria.* I pictured Katya reading it, full of hope and excitement for a future she would never see.

But her gift lives on—*our* miracle baby. Alex.

Acknowledgments

This book is dedicated to my grandparents, who weren't able to go to high school, let alone college, but worked two jobs and saved every penny so that I could. I owe everything to you.

I would like to thank my agent, Lisa Grubka, who believed in this story when it was nothing more than an interesting premise. I'm deeply grateful for your guidance and continued support. My editor at Putnam, Margo Lipschultz, whose insightful comments and questions helped me make this book as good as it could possibly be. Thank you, Margo, and everyone at Putnam who assisted with this project, including Monica Cordova, who is responsible for this beautiful cover.

I'm indebted to my friend and critique partner, Kyra Robinov, who has read every iteration of this story. Many thanks to all my early readers, many of whom are dear friends: Phil Roosevelt, Svetlana Tsoneva, Fe Kagahastian, Gigi Griffis, Jessica Lewis, Amanda Skelton, Lynda Montgomery, Kristin Vukovic, Melissa Witcher de Jesus, and Andrew Skelton. This book wouldn't have been possible without your feedback and encouragement.

Huge thanks to Detective Daniel Churla (NYPD) for his extraordinary patience with my questions and hypothetical situations. Also Jeff Guerrier, who helped me with the art citations and the daily tasks and duties of an art curator.

Thank you to all my writing teachers over the years: Leslie Sharp, Curtis Sittenfeld, Anthony Doerr, Susan Shapiro, and Taylor Larsen.

I've been blessed with a great support network of family and friends. Special thanks to my mother, who has always been my biggest cheerleader. I'm especially lucky and grateful to have my partner, Willy Burkhardt, who has read numerous versions of the novel, has endured endless dinner conversations about Katya, Lana, and Tyler, and has had to put up with me working at all hours of the day and night, during holidays and vacations. You're my inspiration, my partner in crime.